Leecher Chronicles

Book 1
Moonlit Blood

Words Matter Publishing
P.O. Box 531
Salem, Il 62881
www.wordsmatterpublishing.com

ISBN 13: 978-1-947072-81-7
ISBN 10: 1-947072-81-1

Library of Congress Catalog Card Number: 2018947785

DEDICATION

I dedicate this novel to my parents, Jane and John Barton, who made this happen with their support that has always been there.

In loving memory of my sister, Catherine Barton.

ACKNOWLEDGMENTS

Without the support of my family, this book wouldn't exist right now. I thank my parents who gave me the chance to take this first step to live my dream. To my friends who took the time to read earlier drafts and critique my attempts. To my amazing girlfriend, Sarah Huxley, who has to put up with my long periods of silence and random questions. For always telling me never to give up and often ordering me to get some writing done when I'm procrastinating. For my son Logan who keeps me feeling young and gives me the inspiration to work hard. For understanding that when I'm on my laptop, I'm not watching videos or playing games.

To Tammy Koelling for answering so many questions I had and being very supportive of me. To the editor for making my book perfect and the cover designer for giving it an eye-catching look. And finally thanks to Words Matter Publishing for taking the chance on me and giving me the chance to get my book out there on the shelves.

CHAPTER 1

The night sky loomed over me, stars twinkling like lights on a blanket of darkness. As I slowly trudged along the road, I tried to think of what had happened last night. What happened before the last memory of walking along this road?

I lifted my fingertips up and rubbed my eyes, before opening them to see a sign coming up on the right. It told me I was just walking into Branswell which meant five more minutes and I would be at home. Which was almost as bad as not remembering the night I had just endured. This wasn't the first night I had a blackout, and it wouldn't be the first time my parents had shouted at me for it.

By the time I had gotten home my legs were aching. I had no idea what had happened last night, but they were feeling the pain from it. Moving through the garden, I saw my parents chatting in the lounge. They didn't seem at all worried that I hadn't come back home yet.

I forced my feet forwards towards the front door. My hand grabbed the handle, but my luck was still non-existent since it was locked. I reluctantly knocked on the glass window allowing me to see into the kitchen. The light popped on revealing my father walking towards me. He did not look happy. He was wearing his usual after-work attire: the black trousers from his suit and the light blue shirt he had been wearing all day. This fact was enforced by the creases all over them and a coffee stain on his sleeve.

He walked across the tiled floor with a disappointed look on his face. I looked everywhere else but his eyes until he had unlocked the door. Before his hand could land on the handle, I quickly pushed it open and blew right past him. He shouted something at me, but I ignored it. I was aiming to get to my room and shut the world out, but I was stopped. My short mother was suddenly standing in the kitchen doorway. Her arms were crossed over her chest which allowed her to fill the space. There was no room for me to slide past. I stopped and mimicked her stance, breathing in and out heavily.

"Where the hell have you been?!" she shouted.

"Out." That was all I could answer because I honestly didn't know. "It's no big deal."

"We're not going to take this for much longer. You know what that means?"

"You'll threaten to send me off somewhere? Just get out of my way." I practically pushed past her to turn left down the hallway. I didn't bother switching the light on because it didn't seem that dark. Instead of going into my bedroom I took another left and went into the bathroom. Switching the light on flooded the room with light. I walked past the toilet on my right and the bath on the left. The mirror attached to the wall above the sink was my target straight ahead.

I looked down at the sink until I was directly in front of the reflective glass. Flicking my head up I prepared to see the damage that was always there after a blackout. This time was no different. There was a thick red line of blood traced from the edge of my forehead all the way down to my chin. The weird thing was, that was the only damage I could see. There was no cut or gaping wound to be seen.

I pulled a towel off the railing to my right and dampened it with some water, I then cleared away the leaked liquid revealing a small red line. It wasn't a cut or a scar, just simply a difference in skin tone. My fingertips touched that spot, and I got a flash of memory. Nothing that made sense, just the sound of glass cracking, and pain in my head.

I shouldn't have been so surprised that it was completely healed. This wasn't the first time it had happened. A few times I've woken up with cuts from a blackout then they've magically disappeared. It was just another weird thing I can put at the back of my mind and try to forget. No doubt it would come up in my nightmares like everything else had been for years.

Swallowing I blew out a long breath and took a step back. That's when I noticed the clothing I wore wasn't anything I owned. It didn't even seem to be female attire. Looking down I quickly unbuttoned the baggy shirt and chucked it to the floor. Shaking my hips, the over-sized jeans slipped off easily. I wasn't even wearing any underwear this time. Again, not the first time this has happened.

Climbing into the shower, I hit the power button and smiled as the water hitting my body soaked away any immediate thoughts. Just reveling in the pressure, giving me something else to think about for a moment. Leaning my palms on the glass, I opened my eyes and saw the pile of clothes that weren't mine.

My brow creased together as a memory of those clothes sitting on the floor came to me. It ran through my mind as I remember the two people having sex on a blanket in the forest. I also remembered the cheering of a bunch of drunken teenagers nearby. They must have been the male's jeans and shirt because he was a bigger fellow.

Flashes of the night were coming back to me slowly, but I was positive, large chunks of the night would still be shrouded in mystery. Too many times this had happened for me to hold out hope for full recovery.

Running my hands over my body with the water I felt dirt dropping from my skin. This didn't surprise me since I had to steal clothes. I must have woken up naked again. My parents never understood how I could go through so many outfits.

Looking down I noticed dry blood being carried down the drain with the dirt. I quickly scanned my body with my eyes and my touch but couldn't find any wounds. Nothing that would explain the presence of blood. The only mark I had on me was the slight redness on my forehead. I scrunched up my face feeling the slight ache pulse through my skull.

I stared at the reflection in the glass, staring back at me asking what the hell happened last night. Leaning forward my skin touched the cool glass, and the flash of hitting my head came again with the feeling of flying. I shut my eyes and held onto that thought as I tried to rewind my thoughts. Moving back through the past as I found myself walking along a road.

Wearing the jeans and baggy shirt as a truck came driving up behind me, slowing down with the window down. An old man grinned at me from the driver's side. I wanted to tell myself not to get in the vehicle, but I did when he offered the lift.

I braced my hands on the shower door as I remembered the truck driving off. I could feel the man's stare moving over my body. It had me cringing as we drove, him asking me various questions that made me feel even more uncomfortable in his presence. Asking me where my friends were and what I was doing out here all alone.

I was just hoping a village or a town would come up soon so I could jump out and get away from him. Just as a sign came up into view, I felt his touch on my leg. It was firm and controlling as his fingers grabbed my thigh and squeezed.

My hand shot out without me having to think, and I grabbed his middle finger. Twisting it sharply the bone snapped in two places making the man scream out. His other hand left the steering wheel as he clutched his injured finger.

My eyes shot open as the truck hit the verge and was sent spinning through the air. My head cracked into the truck window before we crashed into the ground. Quick flashes of climbing out and walking off came before I was looking back at myself again.

There were no memories of how the truck driver was, but I couldn't imagine he would be driving anytime soon. The metal mess I had walked away from had me surprised I managed to survive. I rubbed my eyes and fought back the tears, taking a few deep breaths. And I repeated the mantra I had used so many times before.

"It wasn't you. You are not responsible for the things that happened. You blacked out. It wasn't you." I demanded my mind to believe what I was saying.

A sudden knock came at the door. My dad shouted something through the wood, but I couldn't hear it over the water, so I ignored him. After five more minutes, I climbed out of the shower and wrapped myself up in a towel. I shoved the stolen clothes into the washing basket. I would have just thrown them away, but that would mean venturing out to where my parents were. And right now, I just wanted to get some sleep.

Cracking open the door, my eyes searched for my parents. They weren't there waiting for me, but I only got two metres into the hallway when my mother showed up suddenly. She had her arms crossed in her usual angry stance.

"Did you hear your father?" I shook my head. "It's been done. This is the last time. You're not our problem anymore."

She didn't wait for me to respond and turned around and walked back to the living room. No doubt to continue drinking her bottle of wine. I put her words down to an empty threat just like the hundred times before. Just another thing I wanted to forget right now.

Getting into my safe haven, I slipped into a pair of shorts and a tank top. It wasn't exactly warm outside, but my body heat was above normal at the moment, and I couldn't handle my usual bedclothes like this. I perched myself on the edge of my double bed and placed my face into my hands.

Shutting my eyes, I sucked in a long breath before letting my mind move back in time. I quickly went back from the walk, through Branswell, to the crash. Then back to stealing the clothes. I was finally back to waking up naked in the forest, and it stopped. That was the last thing I remembered before getting to drinks with my class from the university. That had been Friday night. I looked over at my alarm clock. It was 12:48 Saturday morning. It was still the same night, but I was missing a lot of hours.

The memories wouldn't come back just yet, and I wouldn't get all of them back anyway. It was a simple thing of forgetting about it because it was my only option. Another night where I just got drunk and passed out, hopefully. That's what my parents were thinking anyway so why shouldn't I? I knew it was denial, but it was a way of coping with something I couldn't understand.

Thinking about waking up in the middle of nowhere again I felt something shining across my skin. It was a touch of light from above, and when I looked, I noticed the moon glowing in the night sky like a headlight.

I couldn't remember seeing it like that before. It was so bright and yet I didn't have to shield my eyes from it. If anything, I was drawn to it. Like it had some kind of power over me. Looking over my shoulder in my room I looked out the window. The mood was still there, shining in the dark only it didn't seem so bright this time. It was just a normal moon that I had no interest in.

With that last thought, I fell back onto my bed and climbed under the quilt. I drifted off to sleep playing over in my mind the last forty minutes of my night. Trying to forget about it but unable to block it away until I drifted into a deep sleep.

CHAPTER 2

I hadn't believed my mother when she gave me that threat. It wasn't until my cousin came to pick me up in the morning and take me far away that it sunk in. My parents had really gotten sick of me and wanted me out of the house. They had decided to ship me off somewhere. I'll lose the only friend I had. I would have to start all over. A new university with new lecturers. I found it hard enough to make friends at the best of times. This wasn't going to be easy.

My parents had packed my bags when I took a shower. It was nine o'clock in the morning when he came. I had only met him a couple of times when I was younger so I couldn't remember anything about him. When he knocked on the door, I got my first good look. If I remember correctly, he is only eight years older than me, but right now he looked much older. His bald head and the full beard he was sporting made him look forty.

He greeted me with a nice smile and a big hug. It felt weird, but he seemed happy to see me. My parents didn't even see me off. They pushed me out the door and went back to their own lives like I had never existed in the first place. Their new lives without a rebel for a daughter. They must be so happy at the moment. Looking forward to their new-found freedom so they can sit inside the house drinking without any disturbances or worries. It made me wonder if they cared about me in the first place.

My cousin and I walked over the green outside of my old home. He was talking non-stop, "My name is Keith which I'm sure you remember. Bethany, right?" He didn't wait for verification. "We haven't seen each other since that holiday in Ireland. That must be twelve years ago now. I remember you being quite the rebel." Great, he was already thinking that without giving me a chance. "I remember you sneaking out in the middle of the night and not coming home till morning. I tried following you one night to see where you went, but you seemed to just disappear into the night. It was really weird. One second you were there on the path ahead of me, then you were gone. I put it down to being tired and just went back to bed. So how's your university work coming along? Don't worry about your new uni. I've already talked to the lecturers that teach your courses, and they're willing to treat you like everyone else. You might need to catch up on a few things, but everything will be fine. Your parents have explained how you're still sneaking out at night and coming home in all kinds of states. They said last night you had hit your head?" So, they had noticed. Didn't seem too bothered by it at the time. "Can I see?" He leant forward to look for the wound.

"It was nothing. I think they are creating stories to scare you." I let out a little fake laugh.

He gave up his search for the cut and laughed as well, "You'll be living in my spare room since I couldn't get you into one of the university dorms at such short notice."

"Don't worry, my parents were too late at the start of the year to get me into some here. I'm used to it."

"Excellent and don't worry, my place doesn't have many rules. You're free to come and go as you please."

"That'll be a nice change." The conversation took a pause as we arrived at his car. I stared at it in disbelief. It looked like it couldn't get around the corner, let alone all the way to… I paused my thoughts. I didn't actually know where Keith lived. "Where are we going?" I asked.

"Didn't your parents tell you?"

"We don't really talk unless they're telling me off for something."

"At least I won't have to worry about any long phone calls then." He laughed a little too hard at his own joke. Maybe living with him wouldn't be too bad. Hell, I didn't have to spend all my spare time with him. "I live in Ingleford. It's much bigger than Branswell but not as big as a city. There's lots for you to do there though. Plenty of bars for you to sneak off to." He gave me a playful punch on the arm and walked around to his side of the car. I was quickly starting to like him. I didn't want to sound too optimistic, but maybe I could end up actually liking a member of my family.

He looked at me over the roof of the lump of junk on wheels, "I have some manners, but you'll be waiting a long time if you expect me to open your door for you." He darted into the car like I was going to return with a barbed comment or run around and hit him. Instead, I laughed a little inside. How can my parents be related to this guy? He seems to have the ability to have fun. Very much the opposite of them.

I pulled opened the passenger door expecting it to fall to the floor. Instead, it opened smoothly with only a little squeak. I climbed onto the leather-clad seat. My first attempt landed my butt on a sharp spring. I jumped up quickly letting out a little yelp of pain. Re-positioning my rump, I found a nice soft spot. I closed the door and pulled the seatbelt over me. "Sorry, the car is a little old. I've had it for a long time though. I've become a little attached."

"Gets you from A to B without breaking down, hopefully?"

"Sometimes." He said in a happy voice. He pulled a quick smile and turned the key in the ignition. The first two times it just turned over, shaking the car. He tried for the third time, and the engine roared into action. The car didn't look like much, but the engine sounded powerful. Sounded like the car could move fast enough to out-run the cops. I thought about Keith being a getaway driver for a bank robbery. Then it hit me. I didn't actually know anything about him. For all I knew, he could be a getaway driver. The state of the car ruled out a doctor, but maybe he was a male nurse. I imagined Keith in a nurse's uniform. I imagined he had hairy legs which looked extremely funny. The pink lines on the collar seemed to draw attention to his beard. His green eyes glowed like he enjoyed his attire. I laughed inside my head.

Maybe he would have a girlfriend or a wife I could hang out with. Maybe he would have kids. I hoped not because I wasn't a natural with children. I don't think I would be a particularly good role model for them either.

I jolted in my seat as he reversed out of the parking space. He revved the engine a couple of times before speeding off towards my new home. Keith was surprisingly quiet for most of the journey. It may have something to do with my short replies and the lack of conversation at the start of the journey. Although it wasn't awkward, just silent.

As we passed a sign saying Ingleford, he suddenly sprang back into talking mode. He started talking about all the houses around us. The estates to stay clear of and the nice neighborhoods. We left the houses behind and drove past a couple fields of sheep before being back in civilization again. We passed two car dealerships and a pub before the road was bordered by more houses. We traveled for five more minutes before crossing over two roundabouts. We then came to a crossroads, governed by traffic lights. He pointed out of his open window down the road to our right. "The university is pretty close, only about two hundred metres down there."

"Where do you live?"

The light turned amber, then green, "Just down here."

We took the road to the left. We past shops like an arts and crafts place and one selling motorbikes. Keith stopped at a small roundabout near the bus station. We crossed over, passing a video rental shop and a baby store. We slowed down, so we didn't hit any of the stupid people walking on the road and turned left. He quickly pointed at a gap in the buildings. "That is the town centre over there. They opened a new shopping complex not too far over that way." He pointed again as we carried on with our car journey. As I looked at the surrounding buildings, Keith pulled into an alleyway just wide enough for the car.

We past in-between a fancy dress shop and a tattoo place. I took a quick glance in the window of the tattoo shop. The designs looked cool, and I had always wanted one. My parents had always said they would chuck me out if I got a tattoo. They had just done it, so there was nothing stopping me now.

Except for the pain. I hated getting my ears pierced and ended up just getting my right ear done. Never wore an earring in it though because it just looked weird. Now there was just a little dip where it had closed up.

The alleyway walls stopped, and they moved out into a small car park. There were barely any of the parking spaces taken. We moved straight forwards and got the closest one to the exit. Keith turned to me and smiled, "We're here." He quickly exited the car. I looked out my window at the back of his apartment. It looked run down and cheap just like his car. There was a small balcony with stairs leading up to the door. I didn't want to use them because I could see my death at the bottom of them, lying underneath the rotting wood.

One of the windows had a plastic sheet over it, and the other two didn't look very clean. I felt the boot of the car slam shut. The vibrations rocked the car making me want to get out just in case it did fall apart. I shut the door and walked round to see only two suitcases sitting by his feet. My clothes alone would have filled at least four of them. "Is that all they packed for me?"

"Well they packed everything, but as you can see, the boot of my car isn't very big. They're going to be sending the rest of your stuff up later sometime."

"I'm betting they won't rush." I picked one of the bags up with frustration. As I went for the other Keith beat me to it, giving me a friendly smile. He locked the car and started walking. We got closer to the stairs which didn't look any better close up. He walked up them making them creak. I hesitated at the bottom for a few seconds before nervously climbing up to the door. Keith was already unlocking it with his keys. They were pocketed, and I watched him punch in a number code on a keypad.

He pulled the door outwards revealing another one. He put in a different code and then pushed that one inwards. A sudden smell of lavender blew out towards me. It didn't smell like a guy's place. The sudden thought of Keith being gay made me smile. Could be the reason I was able to stand him.

He walked in first, placing my bag down just inside the door. I copied him and followed his footsteps. I shut the door and walked past the coat hooks. The inside of the apartment didn't match the outside at all. At first, I couldn't understand why he had two doors and three locks. Now it was obvious.

Every inch of the floor of the open planned apartment was hardwood. It shined underneath the fancy lights sticking out of the ceiling. The left wall had a long painting of a city landscape at sundown. The water along the bottom reflected the sun just disappearing behind the skyscraper horizon. Below the painting was a very large television. I hadn't even seen one this big before. It was sitting on top of a cabinet with many doors. It was safe to say Keith had all kind of electronics hidden in those cabinets. A corner sofa sat in front of the screen covered in black leather.

There was a clear space from where I stood to the opposite wall. It was broken into two parts by a hallway. I could see a few brown doors down in the dim light. My eyes moved right landing in the kitchen. It lined the back wall with black cabinets. I could see a toaster, microwave and the most expensive looking oven I'd ever seen. It was black and matched the black tiles lining the wall and the black marble countertops. Between me and the kitchen was a long light brown table. It had six chairs surrounding it with black velvet cushions on them. There was a black lampshade hanging from a long wire above it.

I followed it up to the high ceiling. It was painted black but was high enough for the apartment not to look small. I moved further into the apartment and found a stereo system standing to my right. It was sitting on top of a long, dark brown display cabinet. CD's lined the inside of it. There were so many of them Keith could have opened up a record store. A quick glance revealed tastes in heavy metal and pop amongst many others.

Keith appeared from down the hallway. "Bring your bags, and you can unpack." He went back through the door he had walked through. I quickly grabbed my suitcases, wanting to see how flash the bedroom was going to be. My trainers slid across the wooden floor as I rushed a little in excitement. I moved down the hallway and through the open door to my left.

My bedroom was huge. If his bedroom were bigger, it would be almost as big as the main room. The left side of the wall was lined with a built-in wardrobe. Two of the sliding doors were open with Keith standing in front of them. "I believe there will be plenty of hanging space for all of your clothes when they get here." I couldn't think of anyone who could have filled that whole thing.

He moved past the foot of the bed and over to the dresser that sat against the right wall. "You have these four drawers for your delicates and other things. You have a mirror behind you there." His arm extended past me. I followed his pointed finger to the floor to ceiling mirror. The frame was dark brown matching the wardrobe doors and the set of drawers. Either side of the mirror were glass shelves. They were all empty apart from the one at eye level. On it was a single picture frame. The photo inside was of a happy family. They were all standing out the front of a large house perched next to a lake. I didn't recognise the house, but I definitely recognised the little girl at the front. I remembered my aunt braiding my hair that morning in that side plait.

Amongst the other children was a little boy with spiky brown hair. I remembered playing with him a lot that holiday. I imagined that was Keith. I couldn't remember exactly, but that would explain the easiness I was feeling around him. The cool apartment may have something to do with that as well though. Keith stood in the doorway casually leaning against the door frame with a soft smile on his lips. "The bathroom is opposite you as you come out of your room and my bedroom is down the end. Plus, so you don't lose sleep thinking about it. My bedroom is much bigger." A huge smile wrinkled his skin.

"How did you know I was thinking that?"

"All the girls want to know how big the bedroom is." I joined his sudden laughter. "Unpack, and you can either explore the town by yourself, or I can show you around. Your choice."

"Thanks." He smiled and shut the door behind him. I was actually given a choice. Something my parents very rarely gave me. I dropped down onto the edge of the bed and took another look around the bedroom. The contents of this apartment probably cost more than the house my parents lived in. The size and space weren't much different either.

I lifted my suitcases onto the bed and unzipped both of them. The clothes were in bundles, clearly tossed in without a care in the world. They would need ironing which would be easy if I knew how.

It only took twenty minutes for me to empty the bags and fill a small fraction of the wardrobe. My delicates went into the top drawer of the dresser, and my socks went into the one below it. Once all the clothes were gone, I dived through the small pockets of the suitcases. I was wondering what extra bits my parents decided to chuck in there. Most of the pockets were empty which didn't surprise me. I did find a few necklaces in one of the pockets and a ring in another.

It was an ordinary ring, nothing special. It wasn't pricey either. It had large sentimental value though. I hadn't been given it by a boyfriend. Mainly because I couldn't hold onto one long enough to get a gift out of them. They didn't seem to like having a girlfriend who disappeared during the night.

My last boyfriend dumped me as soon as the rumours of me walking around naked were spread around school. They weren't false though since I had been spotted after one of my blackouts, but he didn't even talk to me about it. Just dumped me and moved onto the next female he could grab hold of.

It was after that that I was given this ring. Frank was my best friend. Most likely my only friend. I had got really drunk one night and hit on him. I blacked out for the night but when I woke he was there. He was cradling me with his arms wrapped around me. I wasn't naked like last time, but I was hurt. He didn't ask any questions about what had happened. Even though he no doubt knew more than me. He just held me. We didn't move until the sun started poking up behind the horizon.

From that night onward he was always there for me. Now I was far away from him. The long distance didn't feel good now that he came into my thoughts. I didn't love him, but I did need him in my life. He was the biggest normal thing I had. Most people had relationships with their parents and siblings. I just had him. I didn't even get to say goodbye to him before I was shipped off this morning.

I placed the silver ring on the shelf beside the photo frame. Two parts of my history side by side. The green gem winked at me underneath the light. I smiled at the ring before placing the suitcases inside the wardrobe. As I turned back around I caught a look at myself in the mirror.

Looking at my clothes, I decided to change into something a little warmer. So I changed my trousers for some thick, black jeans and my vest top for a long sleeved one. Black just like my bottoms. Chucking my last outfit into the washing basket in the corner, my eyes rested on the bed. I wasn't tired, but it looked so comfy I could imagine hibernating for the next few months wrapped up in that cover. I ran my hand across the top of the quilt before moving back out into the rest of the apartment.

Keith's bedroom door was open, so I walked out into the larger room. He had his head stuck in the fridge. From the look of the door, it was one of those fridges that looked like an ordinary cupboard. He heard my footsteps and stood upright. He had a bit of chicken hanging out of his mouth. It wasn't an attractive look, and I told him so. He laughed not making the look any better. He shut the fridge allowing it to blend back into the rest of the kitchen. "You going out?"

"Yeah. Figured I'd take a look around."

"Cool. I'm ordering take-out at five. If you're not back by then, you'll have to sort out food for yourself." He sucked the piece of chicken into his mouth as I felt happy that I was finally being treated like an adult.

I looked at the cooker's clock. It was only half-two. "Cool. I'll be back by then." I gave the clock another glance. I had two and a half hours. I doubt I would be that long. "I'll see you then."

"Oh, before I forget." He turned around to the counter and pulled out a pad from a mail basket and got a pen from the small pot sitting next to it. I watched him scribble something down before he replaced both objects. He held out the ripped off piece of paper for me to take. I did so and looked down at some numbers, both were four digits long. "The codes to the doors. Here's your key as well." I took the gold key from his grasp. "Try and memorise the codes and throw the paper away when you do."

"Easily done." I didn't have a photographic memory, but I was very good at remembering things. That was until it came to blackout memories. I read the two numbers three times before returning them to Keith. He opened the cupboard sitting below the sink and chuck the paper into the bin. I wiggled the key in my fingers. "Thanks. I'll be back for the food."

"Okay. Enjoy yourself." He went back to the fridge looking for more food. Weird since he was planning on ordering take-out in less than three hours. I walked over to the front door. As I moved, I slipped the golden key onto the ring holding my others. One to the front door of my parents' house. Plus the one to the garage where I used to sneak in and get drunk late at night. I don't think my parents even knew I had one for the garage.

I popped the keys into my jeans pocket and exited the apartment. My knees felt a little weak as I moved down the creaking stairs out the back. Looking over my shoulder, I took in the run-down look of the place again. But I wasn't going to judge Keith until I knew more about him and how he could afford an apartment like that. I will ask some questions at tea time.

Now it was time to explore the place my parents had shipped me off to. I looked over at the rust bucket Keith called a car. It in no way matched the price tag of the contents in his apartment. Maybe it had sentimental value. I left it behind as I walked through the dark alleyway to get to the road. Within seconds of being on the pavement, I saw five cars all better looking than Keith's. I looked down the hill to my right finding nothing of interest, so I decided to head up to the town centre to my left.

As I turned to start walking, I noticed a group of guys hanging out on the other side of the street. They were sitting out in front of a little café shop. One of them lifted his head up from his newspaper as I walked off. I ignored him as he looked back at his news' articles.

It didn't take long to get to the town. The first shops I found were mainly clothes ones. The guy's ones didn't interest me obviously, but neither did the girl's clothes. The mannequins looked ridiculous in the shop windows. I wouldn't have been caught dead in those kinds of clothes. Walking around the town didn't take very long. I ventured into a couple of the shops and looked around. Nothing really jumped out at me, and I was starting to get bored. Even the guys walking past didn't perk my interests. They were mostly boys dressed as skaters and way too young for me.

I walked some more until I found the new shopping complex my cousin had mentioned. It looked completely different than the town. There they had old looking buildings and boring shops. Here it felt like walking into a different time. The buildings were all made out of metal and glass. Behind a large shop was a dome-shaped roof. Even the clothes in the windows looked better and closer to my taste. I even saw a mannequin wearing black jeans and a top that resembled mine.

I looked at the price tag and almost couldn't breathe. It was three times the price of the outfit I was wearing now. Then it hit me. I needed to find a new job. My old one was good because of the flexible hours. It meant I could get my uni work done and still get money. I could never rely on my parents for help.

Judging by his apartment, I could probably borrow some from Keith, but I wasn't that kind of person. Would much rather earn my money. I was about to walk in and ask if they had any jobs available when I smelt it. So far, I had only just smelt the usual smells. The fumes from cars and the slight smell of perfume from the girls walking past. Nothing really stood out until now. It lingered around me like it wanted to tease my nose. It was so thick it blocked out everything else. Not only could I smell it, but I could also feel it against my skin.

It was a strong smell of mint. Somehow it smelt warm as well. I looked around me trying to find the source, but it was no use. I was surrounded by crowds of people. Even if I knew what I was looking for I still wouldn't be able to find it. For some reason, I started feeling warmer. The temperature hadn't gotten hotter, and the sun was still hiding behind the many clouds in the sky.

I took one last look around me then just carried on walking. The new shopping complex was built in the shape of a horseshoe. As I got to the curved part the mint smell slowly dissipated into the air. I put it to the back of the mind and concentrated on the world around me. Coming down the other side of the horseshoe I noticed that most of these shops were electronics or housewares. I looked into some of them, but really, all I could think about was the rumbling in my stomach. I needed food, and the smell of a chip shop from down the road hit my nostrils. It seemed a little weird that I could smell it so easily when earlier there was no hint of it around.

I was tempted to walk down and get a portion of chips with a large battered sausage only I couldn't. Keith was expecting me back for take-out. That wasn't the only reason though. I was really craving some pizza right now. But the bigger reason was the need to find out where he got all his possessions from.

So I walked back through the town the way I had come. I walked past the same shops and the same groups of yobs still hanging around. My feet started getting a little tired by the time I got back to the alleyway. On the way down the road, I noticed the group of men outside the café shop had dwindled down to just a couple. The man that had peered up at me was still there reading the same newspaper.

I ignored him for the second time and walked into the darkness. The alleyway didn't bother me the last time. This time it felt different though. The hairs on the back of my neck seem to be standing up on end like a warning. I came out the other side. That's when I heard the scrape of a shoe. It came from somewhere in the small car park. I froze right there with my eyes darting around the area. I could have easily turned and fled. That was until I heard another footstep.

I turned my head a little and saw a figure out of the corner of my eye. That exit was blocked, and it was the only one I knew of. The only other safe place was the apartment. That would mean I'd have to get up those rickety steps. However bad they may seem, the two men around me right now made them seem like stairs to heaven.

I took a deep breath and forced my feet to move. My heart was pounding so hard I could see my top moving with every beat. I had only taken three steps when I heard the same foot scrape from ahead of me. This time I did the opposite of freezing. I made my feet move faster. I managed to get to the wooden steps before it all went drastically wrong.

My foot was on the bottom step for a second before it was ripped away. I felt the hands on my hips pulling me back further and further. Both my arms and legs were stretched out in front of me as I flew back through the air. My body hit the ground with a massive thud. The air was knocked out of my lungs like a lightweight boxer in a heavyweight fight. With the force of my landing, my vision went blurry. All I could see was a shape leaning down towards me. I did all I could do. I curled up into a ball, bringing my arms up to cover my head. Three powerful blows to my side and a kick to my head and then the beating suddenly stopped. I was in no state to fight in the first place let alone now.

Nothing in my head made sense, I couldn't think straight from the hits. It felt like the punches, and the kick had beaten my thoughts into an unrecognisable mess. I felt my arm being tugged on. My body left the ground and landed in the arms of a man. I hoped it was over. That they would just take anything in my pockets and leave me alone. But I was suddenly pushed back. I felt the metal of a car behind me. It was the only thing stopping me from falling to the ground. I tried to open my eyes, but only the left one obeyed. My vision came to me as two more men came along for the fun. In my mind, I wished the fighting was over. It probably was, but I doubt I was going to like what they had in mind. Especially with the way the guys were looking at me. My clothes weren't very revealing, but the way these guys were staring at me made me feel naked. This turned my stomach into a knot and made me feel sick. I would take hours of them beating me over what they were clearly thinking.

I looked over to the stairs leading up to safety. My cousin was on the other side of that door and yet he seemed so far away.Reality hit me like a sledgehammer to the gut when my jeans were tugged on. I looked down at the hand trying to slide inside. My body tried to back away, but the car wouldn't allow it. My hands went to the wrist but were easily brushed away.

My next action was impulsive and stupid. I swung my fist as hard as I could. I felt the sting as it connected with something hard. He immediately attacked in response. My cheek felt like it had been hit with a brick. My balance was lost from the force, and I fell to the ground for the second time. I didn't want to get up. I just wanted to close my eyes and be back in the apartment. Only I knew this wasn't a dream. This was far from over, and I could feel a tear sliding down my cheek.

Rough hands picked me up again. This time I was pushed against the car face first. My jeans were tugged at, and I could feel them slowly dropping lower exposing some skin. I pressed my face against the cold metal and shut my brain off. I didn't want to feel anything, but it wasn't that simple. His hands on my skin were hard to ignore. The dirty feeling they left behind as they slowly moved around the front. More tears slid down my cheeks as I did my best to endure what was happening and what was going to happen.

Then all of a sudden, the grimy hands were gone. I heard a loud bang and then gasps of shock. The smells and odours coming from these people were replaced by a strong smell of mint. I breathed it in not really knowing how but I was quickly feeling a little better. Within a few more seconds I felt a lot better. My sides weren't aching so much anymore, and my left eye was blinking open.

I turned around to see what was going on. Only all I saw was a slimy looking man giving me a slimier look. When his eyes dropped to my knickers showing over the front of my jeans he pounced on me. Instinctively I shot up my arms, and my elbows dug into his chest. To my surprise, he stopped there instead of crushing down on my petite frame.

Gritting my teeth, I pushed as hard as I could and managed to move him further back. Then I started moving my feet to get some space between me and the car. With this new- found strength I stepped aside and yanked the guy into the metal of the vehicle. His body crashed into the car making a dent in the frame.

I didn't wait for him to react. I thought about what the first guy had been doing and what this guy wanted to do. This filled my body both with anger and even more power. I grabbed some hair and pulled his face up from the car. He let out a cry of pain which brought out a smile on my face. Then I silenced him as I brought his face down onto the metal. Blood splattered on the glass window giving me an idea. Pulling his head back again, this time I aimed for the glass. His cranium smashed through the glass with ease sending pieces everywhere.

I left the body where it was, half hanging out of the window. It dawned on me what I had done when I stepped back and looked at the scene. I didn't feel guilty or sick about what had happened. He deserved what he got. I was more concerned about the sudden gain in strength that was coursing through my muscles. I had never been particularly strong in the past, and I had just beat a guy twice my size in a fight.

Too preoccupied with my thoughts, I didn't notice the presence behind me until a strong whiff of mint hit my senses. There was no thought in my next action. It was simply instinct. I twisted my body around, and my right hand shot out in a fist with speed that surprised me. My target was a tall guy with almost black hair down to his shoulders. His features were strong looking and masculine. This matched his body. The tight black t-shirt he was wearing emphasised his muscles. I wanted to take back my punch, but it was too late. All I could do was watch it hit that handsome face of his.

Luckily to my surprise, he was quicker than me. My fist was stopped inches from his face. His hand around my wrist was both strong and gentle at the same time. I could feel his grip tight against my skin. It wasn't hurting, but it spoke of power that was being held back. He was able to stop my punch with ease and without any discomfort to myself or him.

He slowly lowered my hand which fell to my side. For plenty of seconds, I just stood there looking at him. Studying his face a little but mainly his body. I couldn't help it. I had the sudden urge to grab him and throw him up against the car. I couldn't believe it after the mayhem that had just happened.

Four guys had just jumped me and tried to do to me what I was thinking about doing to this stranger. The glint in his eyes had me wondering if he was thinking the same thing. Then he moved closer to me. The heat coming off of him was unnatural. It made me ready for a kiss and more. It made me ache for his lips to be on mine.

I took a step towards him. Hands cradled around my arse. It felt good but not as good as his lips looked. I wanted them and him. It didn't matter if I was in a car park. It actually seemed to heighten my arousal. His breath blew against my lips, and it was the final straw. I leaned forward, but at the last minute, I heard my name being shouted. My head whipped around automatically. The stranger in front of me mirrored my action with a hint of disappointment in his eyes.

There stood Keith standing at the top of the stairs. His face was a picture. It was filled with disbelief at me and the man I was about to kiss and confusion with the bodies on the floor. I turned back to the man in front of me. Only he wasn't standing there anymore. I looked around until I saw him disappearing through the alleyway. I hadn't even realised his hands had moved from my butt or the lack of heat. That still burned on my skin like I was being doused in flames.

I was bummed out that we didn't get to share the passion that was clearly felt by both of us. Then there was a small part of me that was made up of common sense. I had no idea who he was. I looked at the four injured men who more than likely knocked out. The one sticking out of the car was still not moving. I turned around to the other three. The one that had been pulling on my jeans was lying face first on the bonnet of a nearby car. The metal had been hit so hard, it was molded around the man's top half. He must have been dropped with a lot of force.

The amount of force in the attacks could be seen on the others as well. The last two attackers were lying on their backs. Their bodies were littered with blood and broken bones. My eyes dropped to the nearest guy. Blood was covering his entire chest. It looked thick and dripped onto the floor. The man's face looked almost broken like it had taken repeated blows from a shovel.

Next to them was a bundle of splinters that used to be something whole. I hadn't even heard the sound of wood smashing into someone's face. I was too busy trying to protect myself.

I took another look around at my surroundings. My eyes soaked up the mayhem and I could feel my heart beating faster as I did. I didn't hear the footsteps behind me until a hand touched my shoulder making me yelp. My whole body twisted around to find Keith standing there. He still looked confused. "What the hell happened?"

"They followed me down here. They jumped me, and they wanted to…" I swallowed to stop my body from throwing up, "They wanted to do things to me. That guy, whoever he was, saved me."

I looked over at the mouth of the alleyway hoping he would be standing there but I was disappointed. "Well, who … what the hell …?" He had no idea what to say. He gave up and just blew out a long sigh. "I was just about to order the pizza. You hungry?"

"Starving."

He softly squeezed my arm, "You okay?"

I started walking towards the apartment with Keith beside me, "My sides were hurting from the fighting, but they seem okay now. I'm sure it will bruise up nicely in the morning." I rubbed my side where it had been hurting. It felt smooth, and there was no pain. Not even a dull ache of something healed.

We were silent moving up the steps. Once we were inside the apartment, Keith grabbed the phone and dialed for our takeaway. While it was ringing, he turned to me, "What kind of pizza do you want?"

"Anything with meat." All of a sudden my body wanted meat. I'd never been a full-blown vegetarian, but I'd always leaned in that direction.

"Okay." The low ringing from the other end stopped, and I could hear a faint voice. Keith ordered something called a meat feast and a pepperoni pizza for himself. A price was given and a time. He placed the phone back on the receiver and walked over to the kitchen area. I followed him, trying to think of something to start a conversation. Luckily, Keith beat me to it, "So are you going to elaborate on what happened or should I just label it as one of those things?"

"Probably best if you just label it as one of those things. I'm not completely sure I understand what actually happened."

"Okay." He seemed to think as he leant against the counter in the kitchen. "I'll do just that, as long as you tell me about one of those nights."

"What nights?"

"The ones at the holiday cabin our families used to go to. The ones when you used to disappear and come back in the morning."

"Oh. One of those nights."

"If it's a problem to talk about, then don't worry about it."

"The only problem is I can't remember those nights. I would wake up somewhere and not have any memories of the night before. I've even woke up naked a couple of times, other times my clothes have been ripped." I was about to tell him about the last time, but I remembered what had happened to the truck driver. I decided against the idea. It wasn't going to be an easy thing to explain. So I steered away from that subject. "So, how can you afford all this stuff?"

"Bit of a subject change." He smiled at me. "I just have a high paying job."

"Which is?"

"I just work for a company. Working in an office is pretty boring but pays really well." He turned his back to me and got a glass out of a cupboard. I watched him pull a carton of orange juice out of the fridge. He offered me a glass, but I didn't take it. I took another glance around the apartment at all the expensive things. I found it weird that it didn't match the car sitting outside. "How come you can afford all this stuff but have that rust bucket?"

"If you're referring to the car then you clearly don't know your classics."

"Classic? It was lucky enough to still be in one piece."

"Well, the car is a little like this apartment. It may look a little rough on the outside, but I have re-built the inside. It would beat any of those useless cars down on the industrial estate."

What was Keith talking about? Maybe there were more interesting things to do here than I first thought. "What cars?"

"There's a group that does street racing down there. The estate is just one long stretch."

"You ever take your car down there?"

"Once or twice. They don't really like newcomers. Especially when they lose against them."

"Did you win often?"

"Of course. As if you would doubt my car."

"Well, it does look like it would lose against an old lady on a scooter."

"One more insult about the car and you won't be getting any lifts anywhere." He smiled at me letting me know it was a joke. At least I hoped it was a joke. I didn't particularly want to be walking to the university every day. We stood in the kitchen for ten more minutes chatting about random things. Nothing important came up, and Keith didn't ask about those nights again. I was happy he had dropped the quiz. The more I thought about them, the more worried I got. I didn't need Keith worrying about me as well.

When the pizza came, my stomach was making weird noises at the thought of food. Another plus, Keith wasn't able to ask questions with a mouthful of pizza. This meant my mind stretched out back to the car park. I thought about what had happened while munching on my meat feast. I had managed to grab the guy and smash his head through that window. That had taken a lot of strength, strength that I never had before. Then I thought about the last night in Branswell. The finger I had broken felt like a toothpick. I never thought about it until now. I never even felt bad about what had happened to that truck driver. I still didn't at the moment. It was at the back of my mind, and I kept it there. No point dwelling on things that have already happened. Worrying wouldn't change a thing. This was a new place for a new start.

We finished the pizzas. He asked if I wanted to join him for a film. I wanted to see the television in action, but my head was starting to hurt. I excused myself, and by the time I got to my bedroom, my head felt like it was going to split into two parts. My body was burning up as well. My skin felt like it was on fire. My insides felt like they had been dipped in acid. I fell onto my bed. My mouth clamped down on my quilt so I wouldn't alarm Keith as I screamed in pain.

Beads of sweat started building on my forehead when my bones felt like they were breaking. First, my arms felt like they were gone. The sensation of the bed on my skin was lost in the pain. My vision started out blurry but was quickly becoming filled with darkness. I had no idea how long it would last, but I was filled with fear. I had never felt this much pain before.

I don't know when I did, but I passed out not too long after I heard some kind of cracking noise. It went twice before my mind shut down. I remember nothing after that moment.

CHAPTER 3

When I woke up in the morning, the first thing I felt was a massive headache. My brain felt like it was too big for my skull. It pounded at the sides made out of bones like a caged animal. I opened my eyes to see my bedroom. It wasn't how I had left it the night before. A couple of the shelves on the wall had been smashed to the floor. One of the wardrobe doors was lying in two pieces. Some of my clothes were just shreds of cloth now. Even the set of drawers to my left was damaged.

I got off the bed only just realizing that I was naked. My body had been covered in clothes when I had fallen asleep if you could have called it that. I turned around to the bed. To my shock, it was a mess. Not only was the quilt thrown about. It was also ripped to pieces. My room looked like a bomb had gone off in it. I had no idea what had happened after I blacked out. Somehow, I made all this mess. I wondered if Keith had heard me. The door didn't look like it had been opened, but then would I really notice? I almost walked out the room before remembering my lack of attire.

I tried opening the top drawer, but the front came off in my hands. Placing it by my feet, I grabbed some underwear which didn't match. Then rummaging through the clothes in the wardrobe I found a pair of black trousers, a blue vest and a blue flannel shirt that were still intact.

Before exiting the room, I picked up some of the mess from the floor. Unfortunately, the shreds resembled the top I had been wearing the night before. It was one of my favorite ones as well which frustrated me more than my lack of memory. Would I have to wear my least favorite clothes until I figured this all out?

As I left the room, I had an image of Keith lying on the floor like my clothes. Skin ripped to shreds like my clothes have been. Luckily, he was standing in the kitchen cooking some breakfast. From the smell of it, there were sausages, eggs and some beans cooking in the pot. My stomach rumbled at the thought of food. I didn't know what to say. Did he know what had happened last night? Did he see something or just stay out of it? Surely, he must have at least heard me.

He noticed my presence and smiled, "Hey. Fancy some breakfast?" Breakfast? That's what he wanted to talk about? I walked forwards to stand next to him. This amplified the smell. The juices running around the food in the pan made me want to take it all. "Breakfast?" He asked again.

"Umm."

"Are you okay?"

"Not really." I looked back at the entrance to the hallway. When I turned back around Keith looked at me with confusion. "Did you stay in last night?"

"No, I went to the bar down the road. Why what's up?" He went back to prodding the food with his spatula.

"Nothing. Nothing is wrong. Just had a restless night that's all."

"Oh, I just remembered. There's a message on a post-it near the phone."

As I made my way over to it, I kept him talking wanting to keep my own mind occupied, "Who's it from?"

"The head of personnel at the university, she wants to chat with you about your start in the middle of the year."

"Cool." I lifted the note off the wall and scanned the words Keith had written. It was simple and short. I had an appointment at ten o'clock with someone called Sarah Greene. I folded the piece of paper and put it in my pocket. I joined Keith back in the kitchen looking for a clock on any of the walls. I couldn't spot one. I looked at the cooker, but Keith was blocking my eye-line to the digital clock. "What's the time?"

He leant back and looked down at the red digits. As he was pre-occupied, I noticed three cuts just below his rolled-up sleeve. They looked very recent. "The time is just before nine."

"Thanks. What happened to your arm?"

He looked down at the red marks, "Had a rough night last night that's all." I wasn't too sure if it had happened down at the pub or if it had been me. If he had come into my room last night, then it could have easily have happened. Except, judging by the state of my bedroom, I would have done more damage. I didn't want it to have been me. With the cuts jumping out at me now, I just wanted to get out of the apartment. Despite the lovely smell of the food, I could just pick something up on the way to my appointment. "I think I'll pass on the food after all."

"Okay, more for me. Do you want a lift? I doubt the food will last very long."

"Nah, I'll walk it. Let me see the town a bit more."

"You remember how to get there?"

"Pretty much straight then over the roundabout, right?"

"Correct." He waved me goodbye with the spatula, showing me the cuts again. I ignored them as much as I could before leaving. Picking up my purse and my keys from the table next to the door. I couldn't remember putting them there, but I was glad they were safe. Keith got another wave before I exited the apartment.

Once at the bottom of the stairs I looked around. There

was no sign that yesterday had even happened. There were no bodies on the ground. Even the smashed window in the car had been replaced. No tape with police written across it. No sign that anyone had noticed anything. I was about to walk over to the car I had been pushed up against when I smelt a slight whiff of mint. It was nowhere near as strong as yesterday, but it was there, teasing me. Taking a strong sniff, I could tell it was recent.

Maybe the guy had come back to see if I was okay after his disappearing act. I walked out through the alleyway and onto the path by the road. This is where the mint smell got mixed in with the car fumes and the perfume lingering in the air. I pushed the mint trail out of my mind. Time to not only forget what had happened in the car park but also that mystery man. Even though I could smell his minty scent, for some reason, I was certain I wouldn't be seeing him anytime soon. Could have been wishful thinking but it was something I was holding onto.

It didn't take as long as I thought it would to get to the university. I did stop off on the way to get some chips from the chip shop I saw the day before. They tasted just as good as they smelt. I walked up the university steps half an hour after leaving the apartment. I would have gotten here quicker if the old woman in front of me at the chip shop hadn't taken so long counting out her change.

I stopped at the top step and stared up at the large building. It didn't look as impressive as my last one. The building itself was just one big cube. It had five floors. Windows lined the whole side from left to right. Double doors led into the lobby beyond them. The road behind me turned straight into the car park which sat just beside the building entrance. There weren't many students around. Not surprising since it was a Saturday.

Off to the left was a large building twice the size of this one. Using the signs in front of me I knew that DORMITO-

RIES took up the top half of the levels and the others were for APPRENTICESHIPS.

I walked through the double doors. Ahead of me, stretched out a long hallway. To my right were some vending machines and a set of elevators. To my left was a fold-out table. Sitting behind it was a girl. She looked around my age maybe a little older. Her blonde hair was hanging down to her shoulders and looked straightened. Her glasses just sat on the end of her nose. She lifted her head up and smiled at me as she pushed them up with a finger. I walked over to her not really sure what to say.

She wore a black and white stripy top. Her feet were crossed over showing off her black shoes with inches of heel. As I got to the table her smile went wider before she spoke, "How may I help you?" I was about to speak when I got a sudden odour of ash. It was weird how it came to me suddenly. The girl kept smiling until she edged me on to answer her question, "Are you okay?"

"Yeah. I'm fine." I quickly smiled back at her. "I have an appointment to speak with someone called Sarah Greene?"

"You must be new." I nodded. "I'm sorry. I don't have anything written here." She lifted a clipboard up from the table and scanned through the list again. She did it once more before returning to me. "I have checked, and I don't have anything. But, let's take a walk down to her office and see if we can find her." She was awfully helpful. I did find it weird that my appointment wasn't on the list though.

She picked up her clipboard and placed her glasses down on the table top. As she walked out from behind her desk, I saw her faded blue jeans. I wouldn't have put them with the black heels, but on her, they looked beautiful.

I followed her down the long hallway. A cantina appeared to our left with plenty of seats and tables, but the counter area looked more like a little coffee shop. We kept walking, passing a set of stairs on our left. We took a left at a T-junction, and that's when she started talking. "So when are you going to be starting?"

"Monday coming up will be my first day I think."

"Really? You're being transferred half-way through the year then?"

"Yep. Issues at home meant I had to move." I wasn't too sure why, but I felt like opening up to her. It might have been to do with her great smile that didn't seem to be going anywhere. It looked so friendly. "My parents basically chucked me out of the house. Sent me here to live with my cousin."

"Wow."

"Tell me about it."

"So, do you know anyone around here apart from your cousin?"

"Nope. Just him and I don't really know him all that well."

Then she asked me a question I was totally shocked by, "Is he cute?"

"Excuse me?"

"You know. Cute, handsome. Does he have an arse that you just want to bite? I know he's your cousin but give me your honest opinion." She had a little grin on her face.

"I guess you could call him cute."

"Might keep an eye out for him then." She winked at me.

"Okay." I wasn't too sure what to say to that. I was still shocked by her initial question. I hadn't even noticed that we had travelled so far through the halls. There was no way I could tell someone where in the building we were. I only caught glimpses into classrooms since we were still moving. All I saw were chairs and tables. Some even had expensive looking computers in them.

I sniffed, expecting to get the same kind of smell as my last university. Instead, that ash smell was still lingering around me. It had even gotten worse. It felt like it was trying to invade my nose. I felt like it was trying to surround me and take over my body. Every time I breathed in, I felt a little of it move through my nostrils. I tried to shrug the feeling off, but it didn't work. So I ignored it as best as I could. I forgot all about it and left it behind me in the hallway.

Instead, I decided to concentrate on this woman beside me. She was a little weird, especially asking me if I think my own cousin is handsome. She was being nice to me though. It was that last thought that made me speak up, "How long have you been here?"

She looked into nothingness while doing math in her head, "Around five years now."

"Five years? Doing a long course?"

"I keep changing my mind about what I want to do. Maybe I'm just afraid of what happens after all this. I like it here, so I don't see the problem with it. Did you enjoy your old uni?"

"It was okay. It looked a lot flashier compared to this one. The people there though, they were very pompous. They had their groups, and I didn't seem to fit into any of them. I didn't really have many friends."

"You've got nothing to worry about here then. Everyone gets on with everyone. It's very friendly. You got me as a friend at least." Her smile got bigger somehow. She seemed harmless enough. Maybe she could be a good friend. No alarm bells seemed to be going off in my head about her. "In fact. I'm going to be at a bar in the next town over tonight. Fancy joining me?"

"I'll have to think about it, but I can't see why not." I really couldn't think of a reason not to go. I wasn't doing anything, and I didn't think staying in with Keith for a movie night would be as much fun as he thought.

We only walked for a few more seconds when we approached a door. As we stopped that ash smell came back to me. I tried to push it away with a big huff, but it didn't work. I looked at the simple brown door with a pane of frosted glass with Sarah Greene stuck in gold letters. The girl next to me knocked, but there was no answer, so she tried again with the same result.

"That's weird. She's usually here on a Saturday catching up on some work."

"Maybe she went to grab some coffee?"

"Maybe." Cassie stuck out her hand and twisted the doorknob. The door wasn't locked, and it swung open after a little nudge.

The inside of the office wasn't very big. It had a simple desk sitting in front of a large window. I could see tops of trees like the ground behind the university sloped down drastically. To the right was a large bookcase filled with dust-covered books. I ignored them because I wasn't much of a reader. The door blocked any view of the left wall. Other than the furniture it was completely empty. There was no sign of a person or any indication that someone had been in there all day. "Looks like no one is here."

"Seems that way. How did you get this appointment?"

"My cousin took this note." I pulled out the post-it and handed it to her.

"Huh. Don't get why she isn't here then." A noise came after her words that made me jump. We both turned in unison towards the noise maker. A man stood there in the hall-way. He had a hand resting on the door next to him. Most likely what had made the noise. He looked a little familiar. I wasn't too sure where I had seen him from, but he was there somewhere in my mind.

Footsteps echoed through the hall from behind us. I didn't want to take my eyes off of this man, but he didn't seem to be going anywhere. As I turned to look over my shoulder, I noticed my escort looking ready to fight. Two against one was good odds for us, but as I looked down the other end of the hallway, I noticed two more men coming our way. Now the odds had changed for the worse. The need to flee hit my legs and they were ready to move.

I looked back around to the first man, the man I sort of remembered. My eyes scanned his face then down over his suit. I moved down to his shoes and back up to his sunglasses. He looked like a spy for the government. There was something poking out from under his arm. I tried to focus my eyes, but it didn't work. It was simply a blob of white.

A sudden bump on my back made me jump a little. The girl with me leant in close and whispered into my ear. As she did the ash scent invaded my nose. It filled my senses almost blocking out everything else. "Run or stay and fight?"

"You're kidding, right?"

"Yeah, I didn't know what I was thinking." Thank God she was finally thinking straight. She actually thought about fighting these guys. I wouldn't have been any help so the odds would have actually been three against one. I didn't hold much hope for my new friend. That was until she seemed to disappear in front of my eyes. One second she was standing there, so close, then the next she was gone. It was only when I heard the grunts behind me that I knew where she had gone. How the hell she had done it was beyond me.

I turned around to watch the noises in action. She was super-fast. She dealt with one guy so easily. A single dodge and a quick jab sent the man flying in the wall. Not only speed but also strength? Who the hell was this girl?

The second guy had his arm wrapped around her shoulders. His face was covered with a big smile. He clearly thought he had won. Two simple moves and it was apparent he was wrong. My friend shoved her elbow into his gut. This made him release her from his grip. Next, the clipboard she was holding was swung upwards. It connected with the man's forehead, snapping into two pieces. This sent the attacker's body flying into a backflip. He knocked a notice board onto the floor before slumping down into a sitting position. The second piece of the clipboard was chucked onto the floor, no longer of any use.

She turned towards me. I was expecting her to be happy that she just took out two guys with so much ease. Instead, she looked worried. I suddenly knew why when I was grabbed from behind. An arm came across my throat. I gasped, breathing in a lot of the ash smell that was still hanging around in the air. After a few breathless gasps, I started feeling stronger.

The breathing that was hitting my ear was becoming unbearably loud. I could also hear some loud beating from close by. I couldn't pinpoint it, but it was close. Strong aftershave blinded my nose to everything else. I crumpled my face up at the potency of it.

I felt my feet being dragged back. My instinct sent my arm out to grab hold of the closest door frame. I watched my hand move so fast it was nothing but a blur. As soon as my fingers gripped the wood, we stopped. I felt him tugging on my body, but my hand wouldn't let go. His arm was digging into my throat too much now. With my eyes, I was pleading for some help, but the girl just stood there. Since she didn't want to help me, then I would have to try something myself.

I grabbed the man's arm and tried to pull it from around my neck. Only managing to budge it a couple of inches, it then snapped back against my throat. I remembered her moves and matched them quickly. I pulled my arm forwards and shot my elbow back into his stomach. Annoyingly it was like hitting a brick wall. I tried again. This resulted in a small painless grunt. I mustered up as much power as I had in my arm and hit him again. This time his grip on me broke, and I heard his pain filled groan. I turned around to face him expecting him to be leaning over in front of me. Instead, he was still skidding across the floor only stopping as he hit into a display case. There should have been no way I could have done that. It was impossible. I didn't know what was happening with me lately.

The man got to his feet and ran away from us. His eyes

were filled with fear, and it also swam around in the air. The beating I had heard earlier had quickened for a few seconds. Now it was a very faint noise that was threatening to go quietly.

It did so as I listened to his footsteps do the same. I heard the scraping of feet, so I twisted around to see Cassie walking towards me. She had a big smile on her face like we had just won a race. "I can't believe you're one as well. I should have realised."

"What? One of what? What do you mean?"

"You're fast and strong like me."

"I don't know what you're trying to get at, but I have to go home." I started running before I even knew my feet were moving. A few metres and I kicked something on the floor. It was sent flying down the hallway. I caught up with it as it skidded into the wall at the end. It was a newspaper. The memory of a man wearing a suit while reading a newspaper popped into my head. They were the same people. The man that had just attacked me was the same one I saw outside the café near Keith's apartment. I had seen him just before I had been attacked. It was too much of a coincidence, but I couldn't think about that right now.

I left the newspaper on the floor and started running again. My pounding footsteps took me through so many corridors, and I had no clue where I was. I managed to burst outside, but I was on the opposite side of the main building where I needed to be.

Expecting to be out of breath I was worried that I felt like I had just been walking instead of full speed running. I walked around the wall slowing down my pace as I came to the car park at the front. I joined the few pedestrians on the path and walked all the way back to the apartment, thinking about what had just happened. No explanations came to mind. I was walking blind still lost in my thoughts which meant I almost bumped into the girl from the university. As soon as I saw her friendly face that smell of ash came flooding back to me.

I stopped my feet from moving inches from standing on top of her. She was smiling like nothing had happened. I was starting to find her frightening. What she had managed to do. Her sweet voice came out of her mouth, "Why did you run off like that? I could barely keep up."

I didn't think I had been running that fast, "I was freaked out. Why were those men there?"

"My guess, for you."

"Why me?"

"I don't know why but don't you find it strange that you have an appointment with someone who's not there. Then all of a sudden, they appear in the same hallway?"

I thought about it, "I suppose so." I thought about the guy who had grabbed me. He had been there last time I was attacked. The two incidents had to be connected? I found myself angry at my actions. Why had I let him go? He was the only person who could give me answers. I doubt this girl could give me them. She was as much in the dark as I was. "Anyway. I have to go." I didn't, but I just wanted to get home and forget about it all.

"Go? But, we have to talk about this. I haven't met someone like me, well not a female anyway. Not for a very long time."

"I don't know what you mean. I really have to go. Thanks for your help."

"Okay, are we still going to that bar tonight?"

"Sure." I just wanted to get out of there. I didn't want to go to the bar but wanting my own space was more important to me right now. I wanted to shut out the world and just think about something that made sense. "I'll meet you here?"

"Sure. I'll pick you up around eight."

"Cool." There wasn't much enthusiasm in my voice, but she didn't look like she minded. She still had that smile on her face.

"My name's Cassie by the way."

"Beth." I simply walked past her when no more words came out of her mouth. I took a look behind me. She headed back up towards the university. She was going back to work or whatever she was doing after the events that had happened? She was definitely different to anyone I had met before.

I decided to leave her out of my thoughts right now. I could make up my mind about her later on tonight. For a while, I didn't notice that the ash smell had lingered around me. Not leaving me to live a normal life. As I neared the apartment, I was starting to get hot. I was wearing baggy clothes, and the wind was hitting my body with force, and yet I was getting even hotter.

I looked up at the sun. It didn't even touch my face with much heat. The warmth I was feeling seemed to be coming from inside my body. I didn't care about it much. I was nearing the road that would lead me to Keith's.

I walked along until I came to that little café place. I looked over to where the man with the newspaper had been sitting. There was no one sitting outside in the little metal chairs this time. I wondered when I would be seeing that man next. If the pattern were correct then tomorrow he would appear in my life yet again. Maybe next time he won't be trying to grab me. Maybe he would just want a chat. I hoped that last thought would be true instead of the worse one that followed with the image of him shooting me before I knew he was there.

As I neared the alleyway entrance, I could swear people were looking at me weird. Their faces were distorted in the smallest of ways. People had bigger eyes that didn't match the rest of their faces. Their foreheads seemed abnormal. As each one passed me, they gave me looks. There was a mixture of anger and concern. I didn't know what was going on, but I was glad I was in the car park now. The heat seemed to die down as I stepped into the shade. The darkness almost felt welcoming. Almost like I belonged there. I must have some kind of bug. This is the second day in a row that I've felt weird. I've had blackouts, but nothing has happened this close together before. If tomorrow weren't an ordinary day, then I would have to go to the doctors or the hospital. Just to get checked out. It's always better to be safe than sorry. Who knows, they might actually be able to find out what is wrong with me this time.

The trip up the stairs was quicker than usual. Maybe I was getting used to the rotting look of them. I thought about the codes that are locked inside my head. I punched them in and unlocked the doors. To my delight, I had them right and was allowed entry to the luxurious home of my cousin. As soon as I got in, he was there. He had a huge smile on his face and was immediately asking questions, "How did it go?"

"She wasn't there." I was tempted to tell him the whole story. There was the need to be close to at least one person in my new life. Keith would be a good one but then again, how would he take it all? Would it be too weird for him? Would he involve the police? He was a sweet guy, but it wasn't a good idea to get him involved if there was more danger ahead. The less he knew, the better things would be for him. "She had to leave quickly. Emergency at home or something. I've got another appointment tomorrow." Bugger. Why did I have to tell him that? Why the hell would she work on a Sunday? Plus, now I would have to spend the day out somewhere. Especially since I don't have a clue what her phone number is or where she lived. Maybe Cassie will know. Maybe meeting her tonight wouldn't be such a bad idea.

"Cool. What have you got planned for the rest of the day?"

I was going to say I would walk around town but then I remembered how I felt under the sun. "Might just stay in and watch some films."

"Sounds like fun. I have to meet a buddy in town. Something to do with a delivery I have to take. Should be gone for a while so you'll have the place to yourself."

"Okay. Oh, I was invited to a bar in a town nearby tonight. Is that alright?"

"You're asking me for permission? This isn't your parent's house. You don't have to ask me. You're old enough to make your own decisions. Just make sure to be careful, okay?"

"Yeah, of course, I'll be careful." Since the last night I had out ended in a car crash, I doubted this one would be as dangerous. "Will I see you before I go? I'm meeting Cassie at eight."

"I should be back around six."

"Good, I'll need your opinion on my outfit," I said before I remembered how destroyed my clothes were. Maybe I'd catch a break in my bad luck, and there will be something nice in one piece.

He laughed at me, "No problem. Catch you later." He twiddled his keys around his finger as he left the apartment. I heard both doors close and automatically lock. As I looked around the vast apartment, my eyes fell on the large, flat-screen television. I was looking forward to watching some films on it. First, I needed to grab a shower though. I was sweaty from my walk, more than I should have been. I hadn't noticed how my baggy clothes were clinging to my skin until now.

I walked to the bathroom shaking the front of my top, trying to cool the skin underneath. Entering the bathroom, I saw the light shining in through the small window. The white tiles looked shiny and new like Keith spent his spare time cleaning them constantly. In the right corner, there was a shower that was so big it would hold four people comfortably. The sink was larger than the kitchen sink back at my parent's.

I walked in and shut the door behind me. It was a weird gesture since Keith had left the apartment. With it closed though I felt safer. Like the smaller room wouldn't hold any threats compared to the large apartment.

I stripped off my clothes and got inside the shower. The knobs were turned, and I was covered with warm water. I fiddled with the temperature to get it a little hotter and just perfect. Using the scrubber and some of Keith's shower gel I washed from top to toe. Sticking the black scrubber back to the wall I shut my eyes and concentrated on the water hitting my skin. It felt good, my body tingling everywhere it hit. I stood there for a few minutes in the peace of the shower. The sound of the water hitting my head blocking out any other noises that would disturb me.

Running my hands through my wet hair, there was a sudden presence behind me. My body jumped around as I heard the door of the shower opening. Somehow the bathroom was shrouded in shadows. A dark figure stepped into the steam that the hot water was creating. I couldn't see his face, but I knew him. I had met him before. There was no explanation of how I knew it was him. It was just the certainty of it in my mind as I lifted my hand up without a second thought. My fingertips were about to touch his chest when my eyes snapped open.

The light pierced through the steam filling the room. I turned around actually expecting someone else to be in there with me. To my dismay, there wasn't. With disappointment from being alone filling my head, I turned off the water. The presence had felt so real.

Once I had dried myself and got dressed in a pair of shorts and a vest top I used for sleeping I headed out into the kitchen. Without Keith around the massive apartment seemed even bigger. With a few hours to kill I grabbed some cold pizza that had been left over from yesterday. As I munched on it, I walked over to the television. Pulling out the massive drawer I found his DVD collection.

Instead of cases, all the discs were in plastic sleeves, and there were so many of them. It rivalled his music collection in size. After flipping through the first column, I smiled when I found my favourite movie trilogy of all time. I pulled it out and slid it into the futuristic looking player. Grabbing a plate and a few more slices of pizza I lounged into one of the super comfy sofas. The cushions dipped down, giving me a cocoon-like feeling. The DVD menu came up, and I pushed play and prepared to watch the film in quiet.

I was halfway through the third film in the trilogy when Keith came back home. He looked run-down and severely pissed off. I paused the film and turned around to kneel on the cushion. I watched him drop a backpack onto the floor and walk straight to the fridge. He pulled out a bottle of vodka and started gulping it down. I quickly jumped over the back of the sofa and jogged to the kitchen. "Hey, what's wrong?"

He took a short pause between gulps to answer, "Bad day." He carried on drinking like he was planning on passing out within the next hour.

"If you keep drinking like that your day won't get any better." I had seen, my parents, doing it for years.

"Trust me nothing can make this day worse. Are you still planning on going out tonight?"

"Yeah. Oh damn. Still, need to get dressed." Looking at the cooker timer which told me I only had a half hour before Cassie would be here. Without listening to Keith's comment, I ran off to my bedroom.

Managing to find a dress that looked killer on my body I slipped it on and checked myself out in the mirror. As I did, I found myself looking forward to a night out. My shower had washed off any bad feelings I had, and my problems didn't seem so bad at the moment, and I decided not to think about them. I needed to make new friends now, and Cassie seemed like my best option. And everyone had their little quirks. Why should she be any different?

Curling my long brunette hair into loose twirls and laying a thin layer of makeup over my features and I was ready. Jogging back out into the kitchen Keith was still there drinking vodka out of the bottle.

"Take a break from drinking for a moment and tell me how I look." I did a little twirl for him.

"Very nice. Only, is there a possibility that you could stay in with me tonight?"

"Was your meeting really that bad?" He nodded. "I would, but Cassie seemed to be looking forward to it. She would be crushed if I didn't go." Would she? I didn't think she would. Maybe I was going out tonight more for me after all. To let some steam off. Maybe even to relax in a young person's kind of way. "I'm sorry."

"It's okay. I'll see if I have some mates free for a drink or three."

"Sounds good. Now since you got home a little later than you said. I have to leave you now. Try not to get too drunk okay? Don't want to come home and find you passed out on the bathroom floor covered in sick."

"Can't promise anything. Hell, I might not even make it out of the apartment. This vodka is being very friendly at the moment."

"Well, make sure the vodka puts you to bed at a reasonable time."

"Hey, you were sent here so I could look after you. Not the other way round." He flashed a smile. His eyes were still screaming from the bad day he had. I didn't want to leave him in this state especially with a vodka bottle in his hand. A bottle that was quickly becoming an empty one. But he was a grown man, and I needed to look after myself.

I turned around and left the apartment. As I stood at the top of the stairs, I checked my purse. There was enough cash in there to get me drunk and buy a few for my new friend. I walked down to the car park with an optimistic look on tonight. Might be exactly what I need.

I was only standing beside the road when Cassie came pulling up in her car. She jumped out giving me a good look at what she was wearing. Her body was clad in casual clothes which made me feel a little over-dressed.

It was a simple pair of black jeans that showed off her skinny legs and a long-sleeved top. Her top didn't show any skin, but the tightness of it showed off all her curves, and she had plenty in that department. I found myself a little jealous given my much smaller cup size.

Her fingers twirled her long ponytail as I walked up to her. Even lazily leaning up against her car she looked good. Nearing her the ash smell that had appeared last time came again. This time I ignored it and locked it far away from me. I didn't want anything to do with it. Her arms were spread out and quickly wrapped around me like we were old friends. "Hey, I'm glad you came. We're going to have lots of fun tonight."

As I breathed in, I got that scent of ash again. I blew out a breath trying to send it far away, "Great. Definitely what I need right now."

"Jump in then." Cassie ran around to the driver's side as I gave her vehicle a quick look over. It was a small black thing, but it didn't look like it was in bad shape. I would feel safer in this car than I did in Keith's for sure.

I looked up at the sky as a large black cloud lingered above us. We exchanged a look then quickly ducked into the car just as the first droplets of rain started falling. Cassie concentrated on her driving as the droplets pounded against the metal roof. We were soon out of town and on our way to our night out. Then she opened her mouth, "You're looking great tonight."

"Thanks. Feel a little over-dressed."

"Please. You'll have all the guys after you looking like that." She gave me a quick smile before looking back at the road.

"Thank you." I wasn't too worried about getting guys to hit on me at the moment. Maybe just the one guy but I doubt I would be lucky enough to have him show up. "So where are we heading?"

"It's a little bar called Moonlight. It's in the next village over, Northwall. Not exactly close to being called a local but it's my favourite place. You're going to love it." I noticed her sideways glance and her grin again.

"Yeah? Just as long as it serves alcohol, then I'll be happy." I laughed just before Cassie started laughing. "How are we going to get back?"

"I'm not drinking. I find I don't need to drink to act stupid. Plus it's a lot cheaper."

"Good point. How long have you been going there?"

"For quite a while now. Can't remember the first time. The guy who owns it is cool. Makes the place what it is."

"What kind of place is it? Just an ordinary bar?"

"Sort of. Like all bars though, it has some interesting regulars. You'll soon see." She pulled another smile, showing off her white teeth. I noticed her canines were unusually sharp. Before I could get a better look, they disappeared behind her red lips.

We chatted about random stuff the rest of the way. It didn't take long at all to get to the bar. We had just entered Northwall when she pulled the car to the left into a small car park. We both climbed out of the vehicle to be hit with a cold wind.

Luckily the rain hadn't reached here yet. I stepped away from the car and looked up at the building. It didn't look like that big of a place. I could hear the thumping bass of the music coming from inside. From this point, it sounded more like a club than a pub. The building was dark blue. The two windows along the front were blacked out and didn't give anything of the inside away.

When another gust of chill hit my body, I was annoyed I hadn't thought about a coat. The two of us jogged over to the front entrance, happy I was sensible and wore flats. I could feel the bass of the music vibrating through my body from outside.

As we neared the entrance, I saw the doorman. He was huge. I doubt he would have been able to fit through the door to the bar. He was wearing black jeans and a tight black t-shirt. He had more bulging muscles than I knew possible. His look made him seem dangerous and completely un-friendly. That was until he saw Cassie and his face immedi-ately changed from dangerous to happy. "Hey, Cassie. Back so soon." The doorman even spoke with a slight lisp which made him seem more cuddly.

"You know I can't keep away from you." She let out a gig-gle before he wrapped his arms around her small body. She looked like she would have snapped in half if he squeezed too tight. Her arms were fully stretched, but they still didn't reach all the way up around his neck. "Is there a good crowd in tonight?"

"The usuals plus a few colourful gentlemen. Just keep an eye on your friend here."

"She can take care of herself, trust me." He gave me the once over and didn't seem to believe her. Cassie looked over her shoulder at me as I felt her fingers take my hand. "Come on." The large doorman moved to the side and let us past. He towered over me as I moved in front of him. He smelt strange like he'd been hiking up mountains all day. It wasn't sweat but the crisp air I imagined you got from that kind of height. It was refreshing but still strange.

As soon as the door was moved the music hit me like a solid barrier. The bass suddenly created ringing in my ears. I couldn't even hear the music. It just sounded like beats and random lyrics to me. It did have a heavy rhythmic beat to it though which already had my hand tapping against my thigh.

The medium sized dance floor to the left was so crowded, people were dancing next to the bar and around the tables as well. The DJ sat in the corner dancing behind his decks. He played around with buttons and dials as he did. The lights coming from his equipment covered him in luminescent colours. Lights scanned the dance floor throwing people into light then plunging them into darkness.

The rest of the bar was cut off from the dance floor by some large brick pillars. They didn't look like they were holding the roof up, but they looked extremely heavy and gave the place an old feeling. The wall ahead of me had the bar. It came out towards me giving the barman lots of room to work. He even had a small table that looked like it was for mixing drinks. Like most bars the back wall was lined with liquor and spirits, taunting the drunken patrons.

Over to the right sat a pool table and a few chairs. The little wooden chairs seemed to be the only ones in the whole place. Surrounding the pool table were three doors. Two at the end of the room which, judging from the signs, seemed to lead to the toilets. The other one had no sign by it, but it did have a heavy-duty lock on it. Cassie leant in close to my ear, "What do you drink?"

"Anything will be fine." I went to grab some money out of my small purse, but she had already disappeared into the crowd. I stood there looking for her blonde ponytail, but she was so short. So I just looked around at the people. The dancing was pretty wild. Along the bar, there were people doing shots after shots. The mellowest area was around the pool table. Unfortunately, the limited number of seats were already taken. My eyes picked up Cassie as she was being served. God knows what she was going to get me, but I needed to have some fun.

I looked around a little bit more until some guy came

into my view. He was extremely tall and was toned. His long legs were covered by some simple black trousers that seemed to be clinging to his thighs. His top half was inside a long-sleeved red top. He would look yummy if it weren't for his dead eyes. He didn't look alive. He stared his blank expression right at me and shouted over the music, "You look good enough to eat." He pulled a devil smile. I just felt sick inside. He carried on staring at me waiting for some kind of response. If that was his best chat-up line, he wasn't going to get anywhere with me. "Can I buy you a drink?"

"No thanks."

"Do you want to get out of here?" He pulled another devil smile. His eyes narrowed as he stared.

Wasn't he getting the message, "Definitely not." I quickly moved past him, getting a strong whiff of ash. It quickly mixed in with the rest of the bar smells and was gone as I moved closer to Cassie. She had just got her change back from the barman when I arrived. I slid in between two people to get to her. As I placed my hands on the bar, she slid over a shot and a bottle of beer. She had to yell for me to hear her, "Hope you like beer."

"Not my favourite but it's got alcohol in it." She laughed at my very poor joke. We clinked our shot glasses together and downed them. "I had a guy come up to me and give me a really bad chat up line."

"Was it, you look good enough to eat?" I nodded. "Surprised you haven't heard that one before." She gave me a little nudge with her elbow.

"Suppose I don't hang around places like this very often."

"I'm sure that will change." She bumped me again and giggled. "Another shot?"

"Sure. Why not." I took a few gulps of my beer to get rid of the vodka taste. As Cassie got the attention of the barman, I turned to look around at the rest of the bar. I scanned the people again, watching the dancing, bobbing a little myself. There was a wide selection of people. A few bikers, both male, and female were standing at the side of the dance floor. Most of the ones dancing were dressed in tight clothing using dance moves to attract the opposite sex. Women weren't shy about showing some cleavage or skin. The men's toned bodies were shown off by their clothes. It was a feast for the eyes for both genders. Some were even wearing leather trousers. My eyes dropped down to check out the shapes of their arses. A small smile hit my lips at some of them.

After I had finished checking the males out, I moved my eyes further around the room until I found that creepy guy again. He was leaning in the corner keeping his creepy gaze on me. His eyes didn't move. He would never get anywhere with me unless he changes his game plan. Even then it wouldn't do any good. He had done too much damage so far. I moved onto the next guy who was looking at me. He had just walked through the door, and his eyes were locked on mine. His face didn't show any emotion, but his eyes betrayed that. I wasn't too sure who he was, but I had seen that look before. I wanted to look behind me and carry on drinking with Cassie, but I was frozen. Neither my eyes or my body would budge.

He started walking towards me. I had no idea why I couldn't move, but deep down I didn't want to. If he walked right up to me and took me in his arms, I wouldn't care. I wouldn't care where he took me, just as long as he did take me. I wanted his hands on my body. Needed to feel his skin on mine.

He was a few metres away from me, and I could swear I could feel the heat coming off of him. I didn't even feel Cassie's tap on my shoulder until she did it for the third time. I turned slowly, keeping my eyes on the hunk. At the last second, I whipped my head around. Cassie had a shot held up in front of my face. I took it and gulped it down without even tasting what it was. We both placed our empty glasses on the bar. I forgot about her for a few seconds and looked for my hunk again.

My heart sunk when he was nowhere to be seen. I searched the dance floor and the pool table but couldn't see him. He could be in the toilet or maybe he left. I would definitely have to keep an eye out for him tonight.

I returned to Cassie who had ordered yet another shot. I hadn't even finished my beer yet. The barman placed them on the wood and slid them over to us. As we went to clink them together, I noticed that Cassie's was a different colour. "What's that?"

"It's a non-alcoholic shot. The owner makes them for me."

"I totally forgot you were not drinking. Think the music is making me dumber." She smiled. "You and the owner good mates?"

"Pretty good. Gotten to know him over the years."

"Cool. Seems a little harsh that I'm getting drunk and you're not, but, oh well." I snapped my head back, and the shot went down smoothly. It tasted a lot better than the vodka shots she had ordered before. The empty glass joined the rest still sitting on the bar. Cassie grabbed her bottle of beer, "Fancy grabbing a game of pool?"

"Sure. I'll warn you though, I get better the more I drink." All the way to the table we were laughing. I was having a great time already, and it was just the start of the night. Cassie seemed like a cool girl to go drinking with even if she wasn't getting drunk with me.

We arrived at the pool table as the current game was ending. Cassie quickly got a coin from her pocket and slotted it inside the table. Cassie racked up the triangle as I picked up a cue. Feeling the effects of the shots, I steadied myself against the table. "You should break while my eyesight stops going blurry."

Cassie didn't do anything but laugh at me. She leant down

and blasted the cue ball. She had hit the thing so hard it was hard to follow. Balls bounced off the sides, and two striped balls dropped into pockets. She walked around the table a little and took her next shot potting another striped ball. This went on, without me having a shot until she was onto her last.

I wasn't very happy about not actually playing pool. I was just standing there making sure I didn't fall over. So I decided to play dirty. I walked around to where she was chalking her cue. I slid my bum onto the edge of the table facing her. As she leant down to line up her shot, I breathed in to speak. Only I got a strong whiff of ash again. It was weird how it came to me now and again.

Once again I ignored it and concentrated on my plan. As I saw her arm pull back, I spoke into her ear, "Wow, really cute guy." Her head turned quickly sending her cue ball bouncing around the table until it bumped into a spotted ball. "I guess it's my turn now."

She stood up still scanning the room, "Where's this cute guy?" I couldn't help smiling as it slowly dawned on her and she gave me a look. "That's just mean." I simply shrugged and bent down to take my shot.

My next three shots were perfect. The fourth one just missed the pocket. I placed my cue back into the slots where they lived and started drinking my beer. "Take the shot. You've beaten me."

"Maybe." I could tell she didn't believe herself. She didn't even look like she really had to try. A simple tap and the two balls moved across the green material, and the black eight ball dropped into the corner pocket. I saw Cassie's mouth move, but it wasn't her voice that I heard, "Fancy a game?" I turned my head to face the gorgeous guy that I saw earlier. "I'm not that great, but I'm sure I could give you a run for your money."

I tried to think of something cool to say, but I was drawing a blank. "Sure. If it's okay with my friend."

I looked over my shoulder, and she just gave me a wink, "Sure. I'll be over on the dance floor meeting my own cute guy." I mouthed the word thank you to her. She smiled at me, giving the guy a once over before dancing off into the crowd.

I twisted back around and looked at just how cute this guy was close up. His long hair was pulled back over his head. He had bright green eyes which were hard to look away from. His lips were juicy, and I just wanted to bite them. A few more heated ideas made my cheeks blush.

His black shirt was tight on his body and showed off his biceps. My eyes traced down to his legs. The baggy blue jeans he wore didn't give much away. I could always check out his arse when he bends over to take a shot.

When my eyes moved back up his body, my scan locked with his stare. Just like last time the bar melted away with the heat of it. Then all of a sudden I could smell a hint of mint and the memory of this guy came flooding back. This was the man who saved me. The one that I had found so irresistible. As the next few seconds passed, he somehow got even hotter. My attraction to him was becoming unbearable. I would have grabbed him and played with my new toy, but he was holding out a pool cue for me to take instead of something else. I took it from him with a smile. His voice came out a little rough. "You're break, cutie."

"Okay." I walked up to the end of the pool table. Waiting up by the white ball I happily watched this guy set up the balls. He removed the plastic triangle allowing me to line up my shot. Using more power than I thought I was capable of I slammed the cue into the ball. It smashed the triangle apart, and I was happy to see a spotted ball slowly drop into a pocket.

My next few balls were potted easily. It wasn't until my fifth shot that I started losing my concentration. I lined the shot up fine, but I noticed my opposition standing directly ahead of me. I couldn't help but let my eyes move past my ball and land on his stomach. I thought I could see the slight shape of a six-pack under the material. A trickle of sweat slowly moved down my back. I didn't even look back down when I took my shot.

I tore my eyes from him and quickly followed my ball's trajectory as it missed everything on the table. I heard a little snigger from my competition. I didn't mind too much. He had said he wasn't very good and at least I could check out his bum when he bends over.

He moved around the table, quickly hitting his balls into the pockets with ease. As I watched, I started to feel a little light headed. Putting it down to the drink and the atmosphere I ignored it and carried on watching, not wanting to miss anything. A grin curled my mouth as he came to stand right in front of me. My eyes were glued to his arse as he bent over. I had to resist the urge to reach out and squeeze it or do something worse. It was harder than I thought because the way the denim pulled tight to his cheeks made them look delicious.

He potted the next lot of his shots allowing me to check out his buttocks two more times. I had already put my cue back as he potted the eight ball easily. He laid his pool cue down onto the table and turned round to face me.

I stood up and closed in on him, "I thought you weren't very good?"

"I must have just had a good game." He pulled a really cute smile. It just about melted my heart and lit a fire under my hormones. He was getting cuter and cuter the more time I spent with him. He inched closer. I could feel his breath on my lips. This made me want him right now. I was almost about to kiss him when he spoke. Speaking was not what I wanted him to do right now especially with his lips. "This isn't going to work out."

It's not going to work out? What the hell was that? This was only the second time we had met. The first time wasn't what I was expecting to happen when I met such a cute guy.

This time was much better. I was having a great time, and he looked like he was too. Then all of a sudden he says this. I was definitely confused, "What do you mean?"

"We're just too different. Before I thought we were the same but I was wrong." He leant forward. I pursed my lips, ready to receive his. Instead, I felt his on my cheek. A simple peck and he turned and walked away. I watched him all the way until he disappeared out the front door. There I was alone, gobsmacked at his actions. The night had been great up until that point. That heart crushing point. What the hell had I done wrong?

I was still deep in thought when Cassie came and found me. My feet had moved me off to the side so people could play. She basically skipped up to me with a great big smile on her face. When she saw my expression that smile disappeared, "What's wrong?"

"Nothing. Just don't feel very well."

"Oh, well I'll take you home, come on."

A tall, well-built man walked up behind her, "I think you have company." She turned around. Her head just reached his chest. This meant she had to stand on tiptoes when he leant down to kiss her. I quickly cut in, "Look, you're having fun. I'll get a taxi home. I'll see you around uni." I didn't wait for her to answer me. Every part of me just wanted to get out of the bar, so I darted out the entrance. On my way out, the doorman gave me a nice smile and hoped I came back soon. I gave him a half-hearted smile in return.

As soon as I was in the car park, I looked around. There were no taxi's sitting about, and there were no people around either. I pulled my phone out and was ready to dial Keith's number to get a taxi firm when I heard footsteps. They weren't coming from the pub's door, so that ruled Cassie out. They were coming from the car park. I looked over there but saw nothing but shadows.

I forgot about the noise and went on with bringing up

Keith's number. It came up on the screen, but my concentration was cut off by another noise. This time when I turned around, I could see a slight figure in the shadows. I blinked a couple of times. With each blink, the shadows became lighter. I managed to make out the tall shape of a man. As I stared at him, I could feel his eyes on me. After a few seconds, he moved out from his cover. It was the creepy guy from earlier. He obviously wasn't taking no for an answer.

He walked straight up to me with his mouth in some kind of crooked smile. It didn't help his looks. He looked creepier if that was at all possible. I pushed Keith's name and hovered my thumb over the dial button. My eyes quickly scanned around for anyone else in the area, but we were alone. He caught on to what I had done, "Don't worry. We won't be disturbed." He seemed to walk with such grace. It made him just that little bit creepier. Every second standing there stretched out into horrible minutes.

He looked straight into my eyes. With his stare, there was that ash smell again. It filled my nostrils, but there seemed to be something there stopping it from invading my brain. He smiled again showing his teeth. His canines were extremely sharp. It was like he could read my mind. He ran his tongue over one of his pointy teeth like it was going to seduce me. If anything, it made me hate him more. I was about to make up a poor excuse and leave when his arm shot up to my face. It happened so fast I didn't notice until his fingers grazed my cheek. They were as cold as ice and sent chills across my cheek. I whipped my head back to get away from him. My cheek still held circles of cold from his touch. He didn't look happy about the rejection. His arm fell down to his side, "So when are you going to stop this whole hard to get act?"

"It's not an act. I genuinely don't like you." I looked down at my phone.

He seemed to find that hilariously funny, "Come on. Give it up. I promise you it'll be fun." He moved a little closer. I could feel his chill all around me like it was a cloak. "I know you want me."

"No, I don't. The complete opposite actually." He slowly nodded his head. Then he moved his arms out to grab my hips. I tried to move back, but I wasn't quick enough. His fingers were bruising me as he pulled me close to him. I brought my arms up as I crashed into his chest. Even though it felt hard and ripped, it wasn't attractive on this guy. His fingers were locked together behind me, and he wasn't letting me go. "If you give me a kiss and don't get turned on I'll let you go."

"How about, you let me go now before I smash in your teeth." I put a little anger into those words, but it didn't seem to affect his attitude. In fact, he started laughing again. It was a horrible sound, and it wasn't a very good idea. I don't know where it came from, but a large ball of anger started growing inside me. I had never felt this kind of thing before. It was getting hard to control so I let him have it.

I raised my palm and jammed it into his chin, so his head snapped back. Then I rammed my phone into his exposed throat. A soft gurgle came out of his mouth. His hands behind me started grabbing at my dress. Not in a sexual way but in a need to hurt me kind of way. I heard a rip as the material gave way under the pressure. This fuelled my anger. With my phone still lodged in his neck, I dropped my other hand and grabbed his crotch with pure hate. His gurgle turned into a pain filled cry. Although something in his eyes told me he was slightly enjoying it as well. That made me squeeze harder. The arousal in his eyes quickly disappeared, and they turned cold and dark.

I didn't see his fist until it hit me on the side of the face. It sent me tumbling to the ground. As I hit it with a dull thud, my phone slipped away from my grasp. I opened my eyes to see the man pouncing on top of me. His teeth were showing, and he was snarling at me like an animal from hell. If this was what he was like in bed, I couldn't see how anyone could find him attractive. Instinct shot my arm forward, and my fist cracked into his jaw. The force of it sent him back onto the hard concrete.

I scrambled to my feet at the same time as this weirdo. He crouched ready to fight. That scared me to my core and sent a shiver down my spine. How the hell was I supposed to fight this guy? He clearly wasn't on the same sane planet as me. I tried to think of something to do, but unfortunately, he didn't give me time to think.

He ran at me so fast his body was no more than a blur. He crashed into me square on. I brought my hands up to try and protect myself. It was useless against the force of his attack. We travelled back a few metres until one of my heels caught on something. We dropped so hard I felt my skin being scraped from my arms by the gravel. The other guy went flying over me skidding across the ground face first. I wanted to get up and be ready for the next attack, but the pain I felt was too much. All I could do was roll over and stare at the man already on his feet. He slowly sauntered over with an arrogant look on his face. He got within a metre of me and stopped. The smell of ash surrounded me. I gasped it in along with precious air that I needed inside my lungs.

The ash seemed to fill me up with new found strength. Managing to get my feet back under me I stood tall. He bared his teeth and prepared to attack again. I didn't want to fight anymore, but it looked like I had no choice.

His arm flew through the air, but I never felt the hit. I took a step back to see the man holding this monster back. Even though I had felt this guy's power in his attacks, the man behind him was holding him still with minimum effort. My enemy was still snarling at me like a beast trying to catch its prey. I was terrified and unable to do anything apart from stand there and watch.

The two guys suddenly burst into wrestling for a little while until my opponent got an arm free. He swung it back and smashed my saviour in the side of the head. Even though I could feel the impact, the one on the receiving end didn't even make a noise. Instead, he breathed in and then flung the body he was holding into the building. It was like he weighed as little as a feather.

The body cracked the wall, and a few bricks fell to the floor along with the lump of flesh and bone. He tried getting up, but the hit must have done some serious damage because he fell back to the floor with a grunt.

I walked over to the man who had saved me. The side of his head was already bruised from the elbow he had received. "Are you okay?"

"Yeah, I'm fine. It'll be gone by the morning. Are you okay?"

"I suppose. I don't know why he attacked me though."

"They usually don't like being said no to. They get a bit rowdy sometimes. I assure you, not all of them in here are like that."

I smiled at him. "Guys, huh?"

"Yeah, guys." His voice held a slight hint of sarcasm. "I was actually talking about vampires though."

My mouth dropped so fast it could have made a crater in the floor, "Huh?"

"You know. Vampires are quite territorial and think once they find something, it's there's."

"Wait. Go back. Vampires?"

"Yeah, vampires. Why do you look so shocked? Cassie mentioned you."

He was reading my face perfectly. My mouth was wide open, and I was confused beyond belief. I looked down at the man still lying on the floor. I remembered his snarling and how sharp his canines had looked. His touch was ice cold. He was super-fast and strong. Then again, if he was such a powerful vampire, how the hell was I not dead right now? I looked back up at the thoughtful man standing in front of me. "I don't believe what you're saying."

"Why not? I'm surprised he went for your kind though."

If it could my jaw would have dropped even further, "What are you talking about?"

"Well, the fact that werewolves and vampires don't get along."

"I'm sorry. Werewolves?"

"Yeah."

"You're saying that I'm a werewolf?"

"Well, yeah." He was the one to look confused now. "I saw the attraction you had with that guy in the bar. It was clear that it was a werewolf thing."

"But...." I didn't know what to say. I didn't know if he was telling the truth or was some kind of crazy person. There was no way I could be a werewolf. Werewolves didn't exist, and neither did vampires. Above all things, I'm human. Who the hell did this person think he was? Making stuff up like this. He had been smoking too much weed or was dropped on his head as a child more than once.

I wasn't going to listen to him anymore. He was wrong about me. I wasn't a werewolf. Out of anyone in my life, I would be the one to know. That anger boiled again, and I shouted. "You're wrong!" I started backing away from him. He took a step forward towards me which sent me running. I wasn't about to stay there and have him tell me more lies. I had no idea where I was going, but I wanted to be anywhere else but here. I ran and didn't stop. I wasn't even paying attention to the buildings whizzing past me. Tears trailed down my cheeks then got lost in the wind. I don't know why I was crying. It's not like I was hurt by what was said. Maybe it was a delayed reaction from being attacked by that maniac. Maybe my body had just had enough of the last couple of days.

Soon the buildings gave way to trees, and the concrete beneath my feet turned to dirt. I stopped running when my feet started to ache from pounding the floor. My shoes dug into the loose dirt as I spun around slowly taking my surrounding. A small clearing with a few rocks. There was no scent in the air. No sounds from any nearby bugs or animals. The wind was silent as it slipped between the branches. The large brown trees blocked my view of everything. I felt completely alone, isolated in my tree fortress. I slumped down next to a tree and leant my back against it. More tears came down my face, and after a few seconds, I was falling to pieces. Tears filled my vision, and I sobbed for what seemed like forever until I fell asleep.

CHAPTER 4

I woke up to birds chirping high up in the branches. The sunlight coming through the leaves hurt my eyes to start off with. After they got used to the brightness, I took a better look around. I was still in the forest but in a different spot than last night. The clearing was nowhere to be seen. This time I was lying naked underneath a bush. The twigs beneath my belly dug in sending shooting pains down my legs.

I pushed myself to my feet and looked around. The trees around me made a much bigger clearing, and I could hear the distant noise of traffic. As a soft breeze ran across my nakedness, my eyes scanned for my clothes with no luck. The area around me showed no signs of my purse either. That had all my belongings inside it including my keys.

I looked down at the ground where I had been laying and found some scuffs. They carried on going out of the clearing and into the woods. I decided to follow them, hoping I would find my things along the way. I hugged my arms around my body to fight off the cold, but it didn't do much to help.

I had no idea how long I had been walking until I found the first sign of hope. Sitting on the floor was my dress. Luckily it wasn't a mess. I couldn't see my bra anywhere, so I slipped the dress on without it. Looking around a little more I found my thong. Following this trail of bread crumbs, I came upon the small clearing I had sat in the night before crying. I looked around for my handbag but couldn't spot it anywhere. However, I did find some marks on the tree that seemed weird.

It looked like someone had sliced into the bark with a knife. A few of the trees around me had these marks. I was about to start walking some more when I heard a twig snap. Immediately I had the image of that guy following me and spouting more nonsense.

I whipped around when another snap came, and there he was. He wasn't even trying to hide. He was just standing there in the clearing at the tree-line. His head and face were covered with the same length of stubble. He was wearing the same thing he wore last night like he had been chasing me this whole time. The black jeans and the plain, black t-shirt was joined by a black leather jacket now. I remembered the lies he had spouted last night, but for some reason, I didn't get as angry.

However, I was very tempted to walk up to him and punch him in the face. Something inside me stopped my feet from moving. There was something about what he had said that suddenly clicked in my head. I hadn't thought about it last night but what he said sort of made sense. The blackouts I had been having for most of my life. The cut that had healed on my forehead. The strength and speed I've been gaining lately weren't normal. The ripped clothes and what had happened to my bed the other night. I couldn't believe I was thinking this, but maybe he had been right. I looked down at the marks on the tree next to me. Three marks. They were claw marks, not knife marks. He had been right, and I've been one all along. How the hell didn't I know this about myself? It took a complete stranger to just say it for me to realise it.

Then my brain came back to reality, and I started battling my thoughts with common sense. Telling myself that it couldn't be true. Those things didn't exist in this world. They were all make-believe.

As my head fought, my body did the same, and my legs buckled. My knees hit the dirt, but I didn't fall. Something was wrapped around my shoulders, stopping me from hitting the ground fully. He had been so far away, what was going on?

Looking up at him he pulled a smile that reached his green eyes. He looked cute whereas before he just seemed crazy. His arms felt strong as they held me. I had a sudden leap of arousal. I pushed it deep down though. It wasn't something I needed to deal with right now. I didn't want anything like that happening. At least, not until I knew exactly who he was. I wanted to know, more than anything in the world, was he right about me? Also, was he the same or something different entirely?

I didn't know how long we had been sitting there. When he moved, I was sad to feel the source of heat moving away from my body. Luckily, he knelt next to me and removed his jacket and slipped it around my shoulders. The warmth of it right now was the best thing in the world. I slipped my arms into the sleeves and zipped it up. As I stood up, I felt a twig snap under my bare foot. The snapped ends stabbed into my sole sending pain up my left leg. I had a quick look around, "I don't suppose you saw any shoes on your way here?"

"Sorry, I didn't." I went to take another look around when I smelt something riding on the breeze. It came again with the next soft gust. It was a slight hint of mint. I looked around to see if that cute guy was standing in the trees but couldn't spot his attractive features. There wasn't anyone to be seen out in the woods with us.

Another gust hit my body making me huddle my legs together. Sniffing the air I could smell a few layers of mint. I didn't know how I knew, but there was definitely more than one person out here. I turned to the man standing next to me. He too was looking around at the trees. I didn't want him knowing I could smell something too. Instead, I played dumb, "What's wrong?"

"I smell something. At first, I thought it was you, but now I'm sure we're not alone. Stay here."

"But, what's going on?"

"Just stay put." I did what I was told as he walked off into the woods. He soon disappeared behind the trees, and I was alone in the clearing. I kept sniffing the air like a dog. The hint of mint still lingered but it wasn't getting any stronger. I put it to the back of my mind. Letting my back rest against a tree, I let out a long sigh. My mind went through all the things that were said last night. About me being a werewolf. I looked down at the marks that were next to my shin. I thought about all those nights that I couldn't remember. Thought about the morning I woke up and my entire bedroom was ripped to shreds.

I moved from my life and into the myths. The moon and the power it had over the werewolves in the stories everyone hears. Different movies would say different things about the beasts. I decided to forget about them and went back to books. Silver was the main thing that always popped up. I couldn't think of a time when I was in contact with silver. The entire collection of cutlery in my parent's house had wooden handles. Maybe they knew all along and never told me. I had always preferred golden jewellery.

I forgot about the silver thing and thought back to the moon. Images of the monsters werewolves turned into popped into my head. I didn't like the fact that I might be one of those uncontrollable animals. In some stories, the human part could keep control but in others, they couldn't. They would run around all night killing animals, and people then wake up with no recollection. Maybe that would explain my blackouts and the lack of memories. I was getting a little used to the thought, but I definitely didn't like it. I didn't want to become a beast with no control and kill people.

Maybe I had been killing humans all along. The number of times I woke up covered in blood. I can't believe I hadn't heard about bodies popping up. Then again, they would think that the truck driver had been an accident. Even though the broken finger was my fault, it wouldn't look out of place in a car crash.

I was snapped back to reality by the sound of a twig breaking. The wind carried the sound that held the same minty scent. Now it smelt a lot closer. As I breathed in the mint, more twigs snapped. I followed the sounds as they drew closer and closer. I was really hoping it would be my new friend but the man who moved out from the trees was not him. He had long blonde hair swept back into a ponytail. He was big, but it wasn't all muscles. His stomach pushed out against the material of his t-shirt distorting the design. The clothes were all black. This guy didn't seem to mind the heat of the sun on him. He stopped in the middle of the clearing and stared at me. I could hear him breathing in deeply from where I stood. After a couple of sniffs, he smiled at me baring his sharp teeth.

All of a sudden he ran at me with extreme speed. His footsteps were bare whispers on the forest floor. I was frozen, not able to move, not even able to scream. The man got half way to me and leapt into the air, a deep growl creeping up his throat. I watched both in fear and wonder at the man's jump. It all turned to fear as he drew so close I could smell his breath. I tried to step back, but the tree stopped me from retreating.

I clenched my eyes shut and waited for my impending death. Suddenly I heard a loud thud that sent a gust of wind through my hair. A deep growl and then a yelp of pain. My eyes shot open to find a sight I couldn't believe. The man that tried to attack me was there. However, he was rolling on the floor with something that wasn't entirely human. I could only see parts of it as they fought in a flurry of movement. One second I could see a hairy arm sticking out of a stretched black t-shirt. The next I was looking at a foot that had hair all over it. The foot's claws dug into the ground trying to get leverage in the fight.

The two figures rolled around, knocking into trees and kicking up dirt. I took a step back hitting the massive trunk of the tree again. My nails dug into the bark. I tried to pull my eyes from the fight, but it was so impressive to watch. The pure power of these two made cracks in the trees.

The fight only lasted for a minute longer. The only attack I saw properly was the last one as the hairy creature clamped its jaws around the man's neck. I saw the gleaming teeth dig into flesh. As they were ripped out, blood splattered over the ground. The gouged skin was so torn I was surprised the head didn't fall off. The elongated hands dropped the body to the ground. His face turned to me, but I wasn't looking at anything I recognised. Its eyes were the only human features, and even those had short hairs surrounding them. They looked so familiar to me.

The rest of the face was covered in longer hairs. Some of them hung underneath the chin almost like a beard. The chin that was sticking out like a snout. Lips pulled back in a snarl showing off the blood covered teeth. The red liquid trickled out of its open mouth and onto the ground. I stared into the eyes that were locked on me.

The creature slowly stood up on its hind legs. With the stretched feet, it towered over me. It took a step closer, and I still wasn't budging. I was putting as much effort as I could into it, and it wasn't working, my body refused to listen. I was about to become this thing's second meal, and I couldn't move an inch.

Another step, I could feel my heart beating so hard I was expecting it to explode at any second. The third step and something was happening. It had nothing to do with my feet though. The beast's body was shrinking. The hairs on its arms were getting shorter until the pale skin underneath it was visible. Its face became more human as those hairs slipped back into the skin. All that was left was a barely visible chin of stubble. I finally realised why I recognised the eyes. It was the man from last night and the one that had found me here. The one whose jacket I now wore. It wasn't possible.

Limbs and body parts became human. He shrugged off his ruined t-shirt and was fully naked by the time he walked to me. "It's okay. I'm not going to hurt you." He was clearly reading the terrified look on my face. I didn't know if I should be afraid or not but that was my automatic response to what had happened. Then again, if he was right and I was a werewolf, then maybe I could trust what he was saying.

He turned around as another breeze hit the clearing. The mint smell filled the area like we were surrounded by it. My head darted in all directions not able to spot anyone. Because of how close the trees were, I couldn't see any further than ten metres. The sun was a little higher now, sending beams of light through the gaps it could find. The naked man was looking around but with more precision.

Suddenly he bolted. Dodging between the trees and was out of sight leaving me alone once again. I kept looking at the trees around me, hoping I would spot someone. Hopefully someone friendly.

Lifting my nose up to the air I sniffed. I knew that smell wasn't going to leave me alone just like the person it was coming from. Not getting anywhere with my nose I started getting bored of waiting. Trying to calm my heartbeat I took a few deep breaths. The mint smell became stronger. With it came a new scent. It was the smell of cologne, and it was strong. Breathing again I noticed another scent behind it. It was one of sweat. The two smells were coming from two different directions. I didn't know which one was which. I just wanted my guy back. I don't know why but for some reason

I felt a little safer with him around.

That's when I heard footsteps. They weren't close, but they were moving towards me fast. The person was running, I could hear his breathing. The footsteps didn't sound hard like it was barefoot on the soil. It must be my rescuer. I looked in the direction they were coming from. I concentrated harder. Hearing the breathing getting heavier.

I was so distracted by this person I only smelt the cologne when a sudden wind hit my face. It was so strong, so foul, so close. I slowly turned my head. Standing next to the body on the floor was another. Unlike the other attacker, this one was thin. I could still tell he worked out in his spare time, but he was nowhere near bulky. His head was completely shaved which showed off his weirdly shaped skull and a strange tattoo. His clothes reminded me of a hobo. They were baggy and dirty with holes. He looked like he had just woken up in an alleyway from a night of binge drinking.

He was staring at me like I held his next drink. He bared his sharp teeth at me and roared just like the last one. The very sound vibrated my bones and hurt my ears. I couldn't stop staring. He took his jacket off and threw it to the ground. His t-shirt was then ripped to pieces showing me his muscles and bones. He didn't bother taking his trousers off for which I was grateful. I couldn't believe what was about to happen.

He roared at me again. With the sound came some other noises. As he got taller, I heard a noise that sounded like trees bending in the wind. His feet grew a couple of inches, and big claws ripped his shoes apart. His waist shrunk, getting thinner but his rib cage grew. It stretched his skin until it got buried behind fur. The hairs grew longer and darker. His arms grew, and those muscles became something a weightlifter would be jealous of. Right before they were covered in fur.

As his roar slowly dwindled to a moan his face grew outwards. The bone beneath his eyebrows stuck out. A snap of bone in his jaws made me cringe as his mouth came out into a snout. His teeth were sharp before, but now they looked like they could cut through metal. Each one gleamed with saliva that dripped from his lips. The hair on his face was the last to form after his ears grew to points.

He let out another roar. This time it was a low rumble of power which had me shaking with fear. Unlike the last one I saw, this one wasn't going to be helping me. This one was going to rip me apart with those massive claws. He took a few thudding steps. I thought this was it. I thought I was going to be eaten by something out of a book.

I gripped the tree behind me even tighter feeling my nails sinking into the bark. Those dark eyes kept my stare as the animal stalked towards me. I prayed to god that I would be helped. That somehow the beast I saw earlier would come back. Deep down the fear slowly made space for a small amount of hope when I heard a noise. To my right, I could hear some leaves being trampled. I tried to move my head, but I was stuck staring at the massive beast of death. I didn't know what was going to happen until a massive bang ran out in the forest.

I felt a sting in the air that crept all over my skin before it was quickly followed by a howl. It was ear-shattering, and I had to cover my ears, but it didn't help. I watched the beast drop to its knees. It held clawed hands up to its chest where I could see blood squirting out of a hole. Another bang made me jump before I felt another sting creep over skin. I watched the animal's head snap back suddenly. The howling stopped as the body fell back onto the dirt, dead.

Footsteps to my right made me jump. The bald man who had saved me three times now came into view. He was holding a black gun in his hand. As he came close, I felt something tingling across my skin. It was neither pleasant nor painful. It just felt odd. A smooth voice came out of the mouth, "Are you okay?"

"I think so. Just don't think I can take much more of

this."

"You'll be fine. The adrenaline will keep you going." He dropped the gun to the ground then walked over to the beast he had shot twice. He moved its head to the side with his foot. As he held it there, I watched. The hairs moved back into the skin, and the form of the body changed back into a human. It was the second time I had seen it, but I still couldn't believe it. One second it was some kind of beast, and then it was human again.

I dropped to my knees as my body couldn't take standing anymore. My hands covered my face, and I shut my eyes, willing all this to be a dream. As I slowly pulled them away, I froze. I looked at my nails. Bark was sticking out from underneath them. That wasn't the problem though. They were no longer pale and short. They were pitch black and two inches long. They didn't belong on the end of my fingers. They weren't human. Everything has been pointing to what this guy had said. Every step closer to that conclusion was a step away from being me. I had grown up to be twenty-two years old as a human. Now just because of what happened one night, I'm no longer going to be me. I was some kind of monster. Couldn't I have gone on ignorant to this truth?

As tears slowly moved down my cheeks, the nails moved back into my fingertips. They changed from black to the usual pale colour of human nails. Once they were gone, I looked up. I saw the bald man putting on a t-shirt. He was already wearing a pair of trousers. Once he was fully dressed again, he offered me a hand. I took it and shakily got back to my feet. He leant down and picked up his gun. I watched him slip it into the back of his trousers. I was confused, "Why aren't you wearing your own clothes?"

"They ripped when I changed. Hate going through so many clothes." I wanted to laugh, but my body wouldn't allow me. I think I was still in shock about everything. "My name's Logan by the way."

"Bethany."

"I know. Cassie told me about you. She was the first one to tell me you were different."

"Oh?" He ran his hand across his face and sniffed it. Suddenly his face changed. He no longer held a friendly presence. He sniffed again. I did the same thinking he was smelling another attacker. The problem was I couldn't get a hint of anything. The only two things I could smell was the forest around us and the sweat coming from Logan. I thought I would be able to smell the blood, but the sweat seemed to cover that up.

I turned back towards Logan only I was no longer looking at his face. Now I was looking down the barrel of his gun. What the hell had happened? Why was he now pointing a gun at me? His sharp voice came to me from behind the gun, "Who sent you?"

"What?" I had no idea what he was going on about. Had he lost his mind? "What are you talking about?"

"I know what you are now."

"You told me last night what I am."

"Stop playing games with me." He raised his voice. "You are not a werewolf, and you know it."

One minute he was telling me I was one, now he was changing his mind, "I don't know what you're talking about."

"Fine." I didn't see what happened next because he moved so fast. All I know is that I felt a massive pain in the side of my head. It was so painful I blacked out as I fell down to the floor. I didn't even feel the ground against my body. Blackness enveloped my mind blocking everything out. I couldn't even think.

When consciousness was starting to come back, the first thing I heard was a conversation. The first one voice I recognised. The second one was female, but it wasn't Cassie. I cracked an eye open. The bar from last night surrounded me. I had no idea how long I had been out, and it was still hard to know thanks to the covered-up windows. I wiggled my bum, the creak of the wood told me I was sitting on one of the chairs. Judging by the pillars in front of me, I was in the middle of the dance floor. I tried moving my arms, but they were tied together at the wrist. The rope was rubbing against my skin making them feel on fire. I settled and listened more intently to the words being said, "Look, Logan. I can keep her contained for you. Other than that, what am I doing here?"

"Well, if things turn out to be on the bad side, I'm going to be leaving. I'm leaving the pub to you either permanently or temporarily. That's up to you."

"What are you talking about?"

"If she turns out to be one of them and in my opinion, that's exactly what she is, then I have no choice. I'll have to start somewhere new."

"But you can't leave. You've been here for a while now. How would they have found you?"

"I don't know. I don't think I've left any signs of my presence here. Maybe they're just guessing, or someone has seen something and blabbed. Either way, if she's a problem, then we'll have to get rid of her before I go."

"Wait, what? Get rid of her?" I was glad this female sounded against the idea.

"Yeah."

"How?"

"I'll leave the how to you."

"What! I didn't come here to get rid of some girl like she's a bag of rubbish."

"Well, then scramble her brains or erase my existence from her mind. You got plenty of tricks up your sleeve. Just use one of those."

"Okay. Only if she's bad news though. If not then I'm not touching her, and you're going to release her."

"Agreed." The bald man walked into my line of sight. Even with my eyes only slightly open I could see the bandages lining his left arm. I don't remember anything happening to him before. Must have happened after I was knocked unconscious. He was carrying his phone in his other hand. He was looking down at the blank screen with intent. Maybe he was waiting for a phone call. This phone call was no doubt the thing that will determine whether I'm an enemy or not.

Since the mobile phone wasn't ringing, he looked in my direction. I stared at him as he looked at me. After a few seconds, a loud ring bounced around my ears and the room. He quickly answered his phone. "Well?" I couldn't hear the other side, but whatever was said, Logan felt it was good news. His smile was clear through my cracked eye.

After a few words and grunts, he hung up. He slid his phone onto the bar behind him and turned to his friend. "Good news. We don't have to get rid of her. I still might have to leave though. I have to get a file from my office."

"What about her?"

"Cut her lose. Just be wary. She might not have any werewolf in her anymore, but she might attack all the same."

"Okay." As Logan walked out of sight, a woman came into view. She had long blonde hair tied up in a ponytail. It hung freely until the tips kinked in touching the bottom of her spine. Her face was cute. She looked just a little older than me. Her height was much like Cassie's short frame.

Her black knee-high boots made her look even shorter. She wore tight black trousers that traced her buttocks perfectly. Even I couldn't help a quick look at them. She wore a black leather jacket that hid her top. As she walked around me, her high heels clicked on the floor. I watched her as she rested her hand on my shoulder. I pretended I was just waking up from sleep. My eyes were opened slowly, and I looked up at her. She gave me a friendly smile. "Hi, my name's Jewel."

When I spoke, my voice sounded a little rough, "Hi."

"I'm going to untie you, okay. I told Logan that he overreacted. Everything's going to be okay."

I nodded, "I just want to know what the hell is going on."

"We can wait for Logan to come back and he can tell you. It's probably best that way." I nodded. She moved around behind me. I heard a slight singe before my wrists were released from the ropes. Pulling them round in front of me I looked at where the ropes had rubbed. There were slight marks that I rubbed gently.

I looked up at Jewel as I slowly got off the chair. She motioned for me to move through to the other side of the bar, so I followed. Stools lined across the front of the bar that I hadn't noticed the night before. I took one looking at the mirror that sat on the back wall. My mirror image looked in bad shape, but I had looked worse.

Jewel sat on a stool nearer the door. It wasn't long until Logan came back from his office. He came walking through a dark brown door that sat on the wall behind the bar. As he came to stand in front of me, I noticed a folder under his arm. He placed it on the bar between us. He then looked into my eyes, "I'm really sorry about the head. At least you healed yourself quickly." His mouth kept moving before I could comment. "You probably have a bunch of questions about what I've been talking about. I admit I was confused when I first heard about all this." He took a short pause before carrying on. "Now I have all the information about the current predicament, I can answer any questions you have. So let rip." He placed his fists on the bar and stood there waiting for the first question. I really didn't know where to start. I just looked at him trying to think of a good question, but there was so much I wanted to know. I opened my mouth to speak, but it wasn't my voice I heard. "Can I get my payment for using my gifts, please? Before you two get into a deep conversation and you forget about me."

Logan answered her, "Sure. Do you want the usual or cash?"

"The usual, please." I was curious to know what the usual

was since the other option had been cash.

"Sure." He walked down a little and got a bottle from under the bar. It was placed on the bar, and I stared. I was definitely confused since it looked just like water. Logan placed a shot glass next to it, and I watched with interest as she unscrewed the lid and poured herself a drink of the clear liquid. She placed her right hand on the top of the shot glass and grabbed it with her left. She mumbled something and tapped the glass on the bar. As she did this, the clear liquid quickly turned into a shade brown. It was quickly chucked back into her throat. She pulled a face then filled it up again and repeated the actions.

I turned to Logan with a look of interest. Luckily he answered that question without me having to ask, "She's a witch." Although I got an answer, it left me with more questions. "The bottle of water has been treated with a spell. I have a few bottles of it, and I hear there aren't many out there. I can't remember the spell she's using, but it turns it into whiskey."

"Are the bottles expensive?"

"Let's just say I acquired them from someone who won't miss them. It's cheaper than paying her in cash, so everyone wins."

"I'm sorry. All of this is a little hard to take in."

"I know. I was like that when I was younger. You just have to let it sink in before trying to process it."

"Okay." I stopped talking and just thought of nothing. Only, it wasn't working. "Earlier, when she said she had contained me, what did she do?"

"She was using a spell to cut off your smell. Before you ask, I'll explain everything."

"Thank you."

I just sat there on the stool ready to listen as Logan began his explanation, "To explain what I'm talking about, I need to begin at the very start. The world was once how you used to see it. Humans were the only ones on Earth, other than animals of course. I think it was the year 1686 when it all changed."

Jewel's voice cut through the conversation, "1684 actually." She downed another shot of whiskey.

Logan cleared his throat and carried on with his story with a smile, "Okay, 1684. There was an influx of practiced witchcraft that used a supernatural source of power which came out of nowhere. Most of the witches stayed away from it, but the ones who used it said it gave their spells extra power. They couldn't resist the urge, and the world can't live without balance. The supernatural power of the witchcraft mixed with the spiritual power of the planet and then something happened similar to a big bang, just on a much less destructive scale. To everyone but the witches, everything seemed normal. Behind the scenes though, supernatural creatures began popping up. Witches were the ones who found them and named them, researched them. More and more creatures popped up through the years. To this day no one really knows how many species there are. New ones keep being discovered each year."

I sat there intently listening to his every word. I wasn't too sure if I believed him yet. Then again, what I've seen so far has been evidence of his story. Logan continued, "There were three main witches behind the sudden shift in species upon the planet. The most powerful one was Luana. She was also the evilest witch alive at the time and the one responsible for how the world is now. She got the other two witches to do a spell with her. But she tricked them. Instead of using the spiritual power of the planet. She used the supernatural. She betrayed them, and that's what created the change."

"You said she was the most powerful? How did she die?"

"Well, there are two myths which are told to this very day. The first is that her body was possessed and taken to hell for punishment. As you could probably tell, that was welcomed by religious members and The Church. Especially by the people who conducted the Salem witch trials which started in 1692. They called themselves believers, but really they're just a bunch of vigilantes that use the name of God as an excuse to punish the wicked. Anyway, the second myth is that she lives to this very day under a different name. She keeps herself to herself because when the shift in the spiritual force happened, she was stripped of her powers. No one knows for sure what happened or even if one of the myths is correct."

"What about the other two witches? Wouldn't they know?"

"You would think. The problem is they disappeared through the years as well. There is no recording of any sighting." Logan turned around and pulled a pint glass off a shelf. He motioned to another and looked at me. I guessed he was offering me a drink to which I declined, so he just filled the one with beer. It frothed over the edge of the glass as he walked back to me. "You sure you don't want a drink? I have water."

I smiled back at his friendly offer. "I'm sure. How do you mean they disappeared?"

"Well, there has been so many stories surface after the big event. It's hard to figure out which ones are true and which are false. So many of them tell how they've blended into our way of living but who knows? Some people are convinced that Luana killed them at the start of the new world. Only those specific witches know the truth, and without finding them, there would be no way of anyone knowing for sure. The two other witches were known as Rankord and Amara."

He paused, and it gave me a chance to think about my next question. "Where does a witch's power come from?"

"Ley lines. They flow through the planet. Witches are able to tap into the spiritual energy flowing through these lines. Hence we have people like Jewel here." I looked over at her, and she gave me a smile before having another shot. I turned back to Logan who was downing a few mouthfuls of beer. He finished and placed his half-empty glass on the counter. "That's the story of how everything became how it is."

"How do you know all of this?"

"Jewel managed to find a history book that depicts the whole thing up to that point." He disappeared back to his office without a word. When he came, he was holding a book. It wasn't very big, but it looked very old. It was covered in dark brown leather. He slid it onto the bar. "This thing holds all the information you need to know about the history of witchcraft. It goes all the way back to the first witch and stops at the big event with an extra bit explaining what had happened."

"It doesn't look big enough for all that."

"All because of magick." He lifted the book up and opened it to a random page. I stared at the page at nothing. They were completely blank. I thought he was kidding. Then I saw the pages changing. A soft golden glow swept down from top to bottom. As it passed over the page words started forming in that glow. It didn't stop until both pages were filled with tiny writing. He picked up the left wedge of pages and flicked through them. I watched them go by, but the pages in Logan's hand didn't seem to be getting any smaller. He went and went until his hand should have been empty three times over. Then the last page finally flipped over.

On the page was a large title that just simply said, THE BEGINNING. I couldn't feel my face I was so shocked at the book and how amazing it was. "The book used to write all by itself through magick from the ley lines. Ever since the planet was put out of balance, it can't do it. There's too much interference or something. Not too sure about the details." He turned to Jewel. "Isn't that what you said?" She nodded as another shot went down her throat. The bottle was almost empty now. "So the last piece of information, after what had happened with the three witches, is about what we are."

Now he was getting to what I needed to know. "So what are we, exactly?"

"Well, because the world has to have a balance to it. We were created out of pure spiritual energy by the gods."

"The gods?"

"Well, the gods for witches. It's a whole religion, but you'll have to find that out another time. The way things were with all the new creatures, it was unbalanced. We tip the scales back to make it all even." He paused again and had a few sips of beer. "We're like witches. We are still human but with gifts."

"And what is that gift?"

Logan looked at me intently before continuing. "We can smell when supernatural creatures are close by, and we use that smell to leech off of their powers. Obviously, when you're not trained to use that power, it becomes too much for you to handle and you black out which I'm sure has been happening to you?"

I nodded, "So there are people running about with this power without knowing they have it?"

"Not exactly. The government has gotten good at finding people like us before it manifests."

"Manifests?" This was getting confusing now.

"Yeah, when the body goes through puberty, the special gene wakes up and changes the body along with the usual ones."

"Okay. Now going back to what you said before. What do you mean leech off of their powers?"

"Say for instance you leech off a werewolf. It means you will have the same strengths as them but also the same weaknesses. It's a great gift if used properly. Obviously, if you don't think about what you're doing, then it becomes very dangerous. Which is why I'm surprised they left you for this long?"

"Left me? Maybe they don't know I'm like this."

"The government calls us leechers, and according to this file they know about you, and they're very interested in you. According to a friend I have, they've been keeping a close eye on you. They've purposely not trained you to use your gifts."

"Why would they do that? Isn't it dangerous?" I was starting to get angry that I was left to fend for myself. People have been hurt. That truck driver could be dead.

"Well, the longer we go without being trained, the more powerful we are. It also means vampires and other creatures don't know what you are. To them, you're just a human. Unless of course, they see you do something very supernatural. By the sound of it, the only reason the government has done this to you is to capture me."

"Capture you?"

"Yep. I've been a rogue agent coming up on seventeen years now. I've kept off the grid or used fake names as much as possible and every attempt on my life I've fought back and escaped. Clearly, they thought their best bet would be to get a leecher up to the same strength as me and then use them."

"Are you sure?"

"My friend says so, and I believe him. They've been keeping a close eye on you as well. They had a whole team with you in Branswell. Now they have an agent very close to you." He leafed through the stack of papers in front of us. A piece from the middle was placed on top. I looked at it as it was turned around to face me. The name at the top wasn't familiar but the face staring at me was. It was my cousin, Keith. Only, that wasn't his name. According to the information, he wasn't even my cousin. It didn't make sense. Wouldn't my parents have known? "My parents told me he was my cousin. Why would they think that if it's not true?"

"This explains it." He pulled another sheet out of the pile and covered my fake cousin's face with it. This was a simple letter to my parents. The symbol at the top was similar to a coat of arms. I read through it then looked up at Logan. "The government lied to my parents? They think I've gone off to a special university for delinquents?"

"Instead you're living with an agent for the government section who is trying to kill me."

"I don't believe it. Don't they care what I want?"

"It's the government, they take people's lives and use them for their own benefit. That's one reason why I got out."

"So why do they want to kill you?"

"I do the opposite of what they do. Sometimes anyway."

"I don't understand."

He leant forward resting his elbows on the stack of papers. "The leecher unit of the government are trained to track down and fight supernatural creatures. Their main objective is to kill them and rid the world of them. The only time they change their tactics is when they want to capture them. If a new one comes along, they have to take it back to headquarters and examine it. Find out the weaknesses they can use against them. Gives them an edge in battle. Whereas, I try and help them. A lot of them, if given a chance would adapt to their surroundings and not be a problem. Like your friend Cassie. I found her on the street feeding off of the homeless. True, no one would miss them, but it's no way to live. I helped her, and now if she comes across any supernatural creatures, she sends them my way. Unless of course they try and kill her."

"Is that it? Hardly seems worth going to all this trouble to get to you."

"Well, my friend on the inside slips me cases sometimes. They're like jobs. I get the money instead of the government. It bugs them, and it keeps me afloat money wise."

I had taken everything in, but it wasn't being computed, not yet. My mind would need much more time to process all this. Even then who was to say if I would be okay. One question was still floating around in my head, "So what happens now?"

"I would like it if you didn't help the guys after me." A soft chuckle escaped his lips, but I could tell it was at least semi-serious.

"What, help you?"

"No. I wouldn't put you in that kind of danger. Just go about your usual life. Be a friend. I know Cassie would love that."

Something was stopping me from having a real life though, "What about the guy pretending to be my cousin?"

"Ah, yes. I almost forgot about him. That makes things a little trickier doesn't it?" He stood there thinking for a little bit. He didn't even touch the rest of his pint for this period. Then I could tell a light bulb went off in his head, "I'll ask my friend to do some research on him and we'll see what he finds. Call me at this number tomorrow morning, and I'll tell you what we can do about it."

"Wait!" I stood up so fast my stool wobbled threatening to topple over. "I can't go back to him. I got attacked outside his apartment and another time at the university in Ingleford. He was the only one to know about the appointment time."

"You've been attacked? But, I thought they were just after me. This can't be right. Maybe we should have a sit down with this fake cousin. See what details he can add to the mix."

"Why? What are you planning on doing to him?"

"Nothing bad. I just want to talk to him to find out what's going on. Get to the bottom of it all. That way the next step will be clearer. Don't you agree Jewel?" I didn't hear her say anything, but I saw her nod out the corner of my eye. "There, then it's settled. We'll go talk to him and then decide what we should do."

"What, the three of us?"

This time, Jewel did say something, "Of course he doesn't mean the three of us."

"Actually, I do." Jewel was clearly about to protest this statement, but Logan cut her off. "If something bad happens

I need you there. I can't do anything if there are no super-natural creatures lurking about can I?"

"This is nothing to do with me though. I got my pay-ment, and I can walk out the door, right now."

"I'll double your payment. We'll be quick. Just a little chat. I promise." I could tell Logan thought it would be a quick job. For some reason, there was a knot in my stomach saying otherwise. Logan lifted two bottles of water up from behind the bar. He waved them in front of Jewel trying to get her to say yes. She eyed the bottles as she moved off her stool. Her high heels clicked on the concrete floor as she moved towards us. As she approached, the smell of smoke moved around me like a cloud. She was only a few metres away from me when I heard Logan's voice. It sounded almost like a whisper as it tried to fight through the smoky smell. "Wait don't get too close to her."

I felt his hands on either side of my face. He pulled it round to look at him. His face was almost a dark silhouette in my foggy vision. His voice came again, stirring the fog, "Focus on my voice. Follow the sound of it through the smoke." Follow his voice? I was sitting on the stool in front of him. Where was I going to be following him? Despite my thoughts, I tried what he had said. I focused on his voice and tried to move towards it. Moving through the fog was like walking through water.

As I got closer to Logan's voice, the fog started to dis-sipate. A few seconds later and I could see his smile and hear him perfectly. I looked to my right where Jewel had retreated back to her stool. I turned my confused face to Logan for answers, "What the hell just happened?"

"Maybe I should train you to control it first before we go anywhere."

Jewel quickly piped up, "Then you don't need me. It would be too dangerous if it goes wrong. Bye." She was walk-ing out the door as the last word hit my ears. The door closed behind her with a soft thud. I looked at Logan who spoke, "Looks like it's just us for the moment. I'll ring Cassie and get her to come down. It's Sunday so it's not like she'll be busy in church." He walked off with a chuckle. I didn't know if vampires could enter a church or not. Logan walked into his office, and I heard him on the phone.

I sat on my stool still recovering from the fog attack. I pictured a vampire inside a church. It just didn't look right. The scene in my mind slowly slipped into chaos with every-one running away in fear. In my mind, even the statues inside the building looked scared. I giggled to myself at the image I had created.

The rest of the time I passed by thinking about what I was. For some reason, I kept looking at my reflection. Expecting to see something different but I looked the same. I felt the same.

Logan burst back through the door. He strolled up to his pint and downed the rest of it. The empty glass was placed inside some kind of dishwasher by his leg. He gestured to a drink and asked me if I wanted it with just a raise of an eye-brow. I shook my head, "Is Cassie coming?"

"Oh, yeah. She'll be here in fifteen minutes."

"What is the time?"

He looked down at the watch on his wrist, "It's just after three."

"What? How long was I out for?"

"About four hours. Again, I'm sorry about your head."

"It's fine. It doesn't hurt anymore." I thought about the time of day and the sun. "How is Cassie getting here? Surely vampires die in the sunlight. Turn to ash or something?"

"I guess this gives me the perfect amount of time to ex-plain vampires for you."

"Great. Is there much to explain?" My first lesson in vampires. My life had definitely changed for the weirder.

He started the conversation off while pouring himself

another pint of beer. I had no idea why he hadn't just reused his previous glass. "First things first. Some of the stories you find in books and films are true. Some of them of course, are false. For instance, the sunlight thing. The only time during the day that vampires burst into flames and turn to ash is at noon. At that time the sun is at the highest point in its arc, and that's when it's at its hottest. Other than that particular time they can go out in the sun. The only problem is, the more time they spend in it, the more it boils their brain. This in time will send them mad and will end in bloodlust. That is when you don't want to be around them."

"Why? What's bloodlust?"

"Just what it sounds like. In this state, the vampire doesn't remember who people are. If Cassie was out in the sun too long, then she could look at you and just think lunch."

A shiver ran down my back at the thought. To think someone as friendly as Cassie could turn into something like that. "How will I know when a vampire is in bloodlust?"

"Their eyes will be bloodshot. It's the only way to know for sure. Other smaller signs will be looking lost. They seem to just look around for blood. They will even stay out in the sun looking for it, even if it's noon."

"That's pretty mad."

"It is, so you have to be careful if you leech off of one. Just think about the situation you're in before you do it."

"Do you mean if I leech off of a vampire in bloodlust. I'll also be in that state."

"Exactly. I mean, vampires in bloodlust are naturally stronger and faster than usual. Then again, if a vampire has trained, they will be even faster than one in bloodlust."

Huh? "What do you mean train? I thought vampires were just that much stronger and faster than humans. I thought their speed and strength were based on how old they were. Obviously, the older they are, the stronger or faster they are, right?"

"Wrong." He took this chance to pause and start on his pint. It was now a third of the way down from its original, frothy line. "The older the vampire, the more chance they have of being better than others. The problem is, when a vampire does the ritual of turning a human into a vampire, they transfer some of their power along with their blood. Think of it like a pint of beer. When a vampire turns a human, a percentage of his power goes to that vampire. The more they turn, the smaller the percentages will be. The first youngling will be stronger than the rest. Sometimes, that first youngling can become stronger than its maker. That rarely happens, usually when the vampire isn't very clever."

"Younglings? Maker?"

"A youngling is a baby vampire. A vampire's maker is the vamp that turned them."

"So, if a vampire turns a load of people, they would be weaker than one that didn't turn anyone."

"Exactly. This is why the world hasn't been over-run by them."

"How will I know how strong or fast they are?"

"Don't worry. With the smell of the vampire, you'll be able to tell how strong they are, how fast they are. If you come across a gang of them. You could leech off of the most powerful one and be stronger than the rest, but I would recommend running away."

"Because I would be outnumbered?"

"Yes. Normally if you're stronger and faster, in a fight with humans you could win. Vampires are completely different though. They're fast enough and cunning enough to get behind you in a split second and snap your neck."

"If I die while leeching off of a vampire will I die as one?"

"That's correct. When we leech off of a supernatural creature, we become that creature. Every part of us becomes one. Get staked as a vamp, and you will turn to ash."

"Staked. Like a piece of wood through the heart?"

"Anything through the heart would do the trick. Although they are allergic to wood. Wood on their skin isn't a problem, but when it comes into contact with the blood, it is like a chemical reaction. For instance, if you stab or shoot a vampire in the leg with wood, they wouldn't be able to use that leg because it would be infected. Also once the wood is in contact with their blood, their gifts become weaker. Enough of it and they become paralyzed. The same happens if you break their necks. It won't kill them, but it'll paralyze them long enough to finish the job properly."

"All of this is pretty hard to take in. It's just so weird to hear."

"There's more. Garlic doesn't do anything, and neither does holy water. A bunch of nonsense created by idiots to sell movies. Silver does squat as well. Fire on the other hand. Set one alight and they will burn to ash like a match. It won't take long, and they will be in so much agony."

"What happens if one bites me?" I thought about all the gruesome scenes from films where they turn humans into monsters.

"It'll hurt like hell. Nothing would actually happen though. For them to turn someone, I'm guessing that's what you're talking about, they first drain a human of most of his or her blood. Then they cut their wrist or whatever and feed the almost dead human their blood. I think the guys in the lab back with the government said it takes fifteen hours for the human to turn completely. If the human isn't asleep somewhere, then they will walk around in complete agony as their body tries to reject the vampire blood." He took another gulp of beer and swallowed it down.

"So, I don't need to worry if I get bitten."

"Don't worry but I would get pissed off if I was you."

"Obviously." I suddenly paused. "Is it hard to kill one of them mentally? I mean, they look like humans. Is it hard to get over that fact?"

"They look like humans most of the time. In a fight, they show their fangs. With their fangs out they would be hard to mistake for a human being."

"Are they that noticeable?"

"Noticeable?" He looked around the bar. He walked off and came back with his hands behind his back. As he stood in front of me, he asked, "Tell me if you think this is noticeable?" He lifted his hands and placed two toothpicks inside his upper lip. They shot downwards like vampire teeth, almost reaching the bottom of his chin. "This is what a thirsty one looks like. Roughly."

"Okay, a little out of the ordinary. By the way, they look good on you." He yanked them out and flicked them at me with a smile on his face. "Anything else I need to know?"

"Let me see. Oh right. They have a gift called glamouring. To achieve this, they need direct eye contact. It doesn't matter about the distance. They could do it up close or across a crowded room. As long as there's eye contact for a period of time."

"Can one vampire glamour another?"

"No. I don't know if anyone has found out why, but they can't."

"Okay, so what does glamouring do?"

He held his pint in his hand like he was going to drink it at any second, "It's a way of hypnotising a human. They can make them do whatever they want. The human will even do what they're told when the vampire leaves. The human who gets picked doesn't remember a thing after. It's like they black out. Vampires can't do it to other supernatural creatures either, it's not specific to vampires. It's just humans."

My mind thought back to the night in this very pub, "What about that vampire that attacked me. Why didn't he just glamour me to sleep with him?"

"He's an arrogant vampire. You'll come across a lot of

them, but that one is especially arrogant. Unfortunately, he comes here now and again. He obviously thought he could win you over without his gifts. I think that's everything. Do you have any questions?"

I nodded, "If I leech off of a vampire? Can I then turn someone?"

"Yes, you can. When we leech we change into that creature completely which includes our blood. No power is drained off of you or the vamp you're leeching from though. The human you change will be very weak. The government used to use that technique to recruit new members. The problem was, they would have to train constantly for a long time to become as strong or fast as a normal vampire. They ended up scrapping that idea."

"What about us? Is there anything else I need to know about leechers?"

"Well, the better the leecher the further away they can be from their target. How old are you?"

"Twenty-two. How old were you when you learnt about all this?"

"I was sixteen. Your range is bigger than mine since you haven't been trained yet. What you do is concentrate on someone. You will be able to smell their essence better the more you concentrate. You suck that essence in through your nose then it takes effect. It's naturally slow but once you're trained, you can either push it away or suck it in quicker. Now once you have changed into that creature, you will still be able to use your leecher abilities."

"Has anyone leeched off of two creatures before?"

"I have never heard of anyone leeching off of two sources at once. Even two of the same species."

"What do you think would happen if someone achieved it?"

"I have no idea. Anyway, once you want to stop leeching off of a creature. Say it has run away or been killed by you or something, then you can still use the power you have. Of course, if you want to stop you can just let go of the essence." Logan finally drunk some of his beer before setting it down.

I giggled which he frowned at. "You have a little froth moustache."

He frowned at me before rubbing it off. "Anyway. If you touch a supernatural creature than you get all their essence in an instant. It's not like you'll steal it but it's a very quick way of going full throttle. Do you understand all of this?"

I nodded, not really sure if I did or not. "Anything else I need to know?"

"Other than you can't leech off another leech's power. That's the last one I believe." He looked down at his watch. "Perfect timing too. Cassie should be here any second."

"Cool." I had all the facts in my head. The problem was, would I remember it all when it came to a sticky situation? Plus, I had no idea what this training is going to entail. I was both looking forward to it and worrying about it, all at the same time.

Cassie walked through the doorway five minutes after Logan had explained things. She was wearing a simple white dress with flowers blooming all over it. She looked very summery. She didn't look like a vampire. No dark goth clothes or anything.

She walked up to me and gave me a hug. I could smell the ash again, but it didn't invade my senses like the smoke had. It just hung under my nose ready to be sucked in if I allowed it. I breathed through my mouth and gave her a hug back. As soon as she let go, I backed away a few steps. She looked a little hurt, "Are you afraid of me?"

"It's not that. It's the smell."

"Oh my gosh. I'm so sorry. I don't think sometimes." She turned to Logan who was patiently waiting for his hello. "Hey, Logan."

"Hey. Thanks for helping."

"I'm always here to help." She turned to me and smiled. "So, how are we going to do this?"

"I say we dive right in. I'll be here just in case things get out of hand. Beth, all I want you to do is to concentrate and sniff out the ash smell. Breathe it in and see how you feel. Just try a little bit of it. Don't go overboard."

I nodded, feeling really nervous at the thought of becoming a vampire. Even if it was just for a few minutes. Cassie stayed where she was, leaning against the bar looking very casual. I stared into her eyes searching for that smell in the air.

It took me a little while to find it since it was mixing in with the usual bar smells. I found it frustrating that when I hadn't even been trying it had been so easy. As I identified the smell, it seemed to swarm around me. I couldn't see it, but I could feel the presence of it in the air. I slowly sniffed until I could feel my nostrils were filled with the essence of ash. It didn't make me cough like I thought it would. It smoothly slipped inside. I had no idea where it went, and I couldn't feel it anymore. All I knew was that I felt better. I felt stronger and more agile on my feet. I felt like myself. Nothing major had changed. I had expected to feel strange. Feel completely different. It wasn't what I was expecting at all.

I moved closer to the bar. As I put my hand on the wood, I slipped onto the nearest stool. Logan moved down to stand in front of me. He still had his pint in his hand. There wasn't much of the beer left now. "How do you feel?"

"I feel fine. Probably better than fine. Feel stronger and more confident."

"Feel anything else?"

I sat there thinking about it, "Not really."

"Okay." He leant down and pulled out a metal baseball bat from behind the bar. Logan must keep it behind there in case there's trouble. "Bend it."

"Excuse me?"

"Bend it. Remember you're a vampire. Cassie is a very strong vampire so you can do this easily." He slid the bat off the bar and chucked it over to Cassie. She caught it with a blur of speed. I watched as she used both hands at either end and bent the metal into a hoop. The sound of it sounded horrible. She chucked it at me with surprising speed. My hands shot up without me having to think. I was amazed at myself when my hands turned into nothing.

I sat there staring at the metal in my hands. Giving both of them a look before staring back down at the distorted bat. I can do this. My fingers curled around the metal, and I pulled. It was as easy as snapping a twig. The loop was changed with a moaning creak. Once it was back to its original shape, I threw it back to Logan. I had purposefully put some effort into it. His hand shot up, but the force of it almost sent him stumbling into the bar behind him. I gave him the best innocent smile I could.

He gave one back as he replaced the bat under the bar. "Now what I want you to do is run to the other side of the bar and bring back a ball from the pool table. Run as fast as you can. Just watch you don't run into something."

"Um, okay." I got off the stool and stood on the floor. A few deep breaths to prepare myself and then I pushed off. I pumped my legs as fast as possible. I was shocked by the speed that everything flew by me. It was more of a shock when my shoulder came into contact with the wall. Pain shot through my shoulder. I looked at the dent the impact had created. When I checked my shoulder, I saw no scratches. I apologised to Logan as I walked back to my starting position. "I'll try it again."

"Okay." Logan looked like he was fighting back laughter. I couldn't blame him. If it had been someone else, I would have laughed as well.

I prepared again and shot off. My bare feet gripped the concrete floor better than I thought they would. Turning the corner, I saw the pool table in a blur and stopped. My legs slowed down quickly to end in a slight jog in the short space. The pool table stood next to me, looking very small for some reason. I picked up the eight ball and ran back around the corner. I slowed my feet down and came to a stop where I had started. Placing the eight ball on the bar, Logan seemed impressed by my second attempt, "Very good. How's your shoulder feeling?"

"It's fine. Barely hurts anymore. What's next?" My smile grew as I felt quite good.

"I need you to have a flavour of something."

"Not blood I hope."

"No, but it's something you might have to get used to."

"Okay. What is it?"

"The thirst. If you leech off of a vampire who hasn't eaten in a while or if you become one for a long period of time, then you'll have to fight it. For the moment I want you to keep leeching off of Cassie until you start feeling hungry. Then I want you to stop and just wait."

"Sounds easy enough."

"It'll be harder than you think, I promise you." Something in his words had me thinking he knew all too well what happened if the thirst won. "If it gets too much for you then just let go of the vampire essence inside of you. It's not like blowing out of your nose, but if you think about it, then it will happen."

"Okay."

"If it feels bad than push it out as quick as possible. Let me know if you can't control yourself."

"What will you do?"

"Hold you back." He walked around from behind the bar and stood next to me. "Ready?" I nodded because my throat was starting to feel dry because of my nerves. I swallowed trying to clear the feeling, but it clung there. Ignoring it, I focused on Cassie and her scent of ash that was much easier to find this time around. I sucked it in through my nostrils in a steady stream.

It kept coming and coming until no more would come in. I stopped sniffing the air and concentrated on the feeling inside of me. It started out small and barely noticeable. That was until I suddenly heard beating in my ear. It got louder as it was all I could think about. I followed where the noise was until I looked over my shoulder at Logan's chest. He noticed my stare, "It's my heartbeat you can hear. I totally forgot to tell you about that. Vampires are attuned to the sound of the heart and the smell of blood. Also, their eyesight is a lot better than humans." I could hear his words and was understanding them. However, they were at the back of my mind since the beating had me entranced. It was weird how a sound could be delicious to my ears.

I wanted to rip open his chest and suck his heart dry. It felt weird having the urge and the need but not wanting to do something about it. "I'm starting to feel a little different. I want to taste blood. I feel like I need it."

"You do need it. You've become a vampire. I need you to let go of the ash smell. Push it out." I did what he said. As I could feel the smell coming back, moving back through my nose and out into the air, the beating slowly got quieter. The need diminished as the ash smell vanished out of my body.

After a few seconds of feeling drained, I felt my normal self. I felt human again. I no longer had the need to taste Logan's blood. Looking over to Cassie she gave me a big smile. As she looked at me, the ash smell began skulking its way back to me, but I ignored it. I felt a little easier being around her now since I could cut it off with a barrier of will. I turned my head as Logan spoke, "How are you feeling now?"

"I feel fine again. I don't feel like a vampire anymore."

"That's good. You're a natural at this. The fact they left you for so long is making it easier for you to control your gifts. Now, let's go visit your supposed cousin."

"We're finished?" He nodded and gave me a smile. "Sure, let's go. Cassie is coming right?"

"Of course, I am." She stood up from her stool and shoved her hands in her pockets. "You'll need me just in case there's trouble, right Logan."

"Exactly. Come on, Cassie you can follow us in your car. Save you leaving it here." She nodded and pulled her hands out of her jeans pockets along with her car keys. Logan leant over the bar to retrieve his massive bundle of keys. The three of us left by the front door. Logan locked the building up behind us, and we walked around to the car park. Cassie had parked her little car next to Logan's old looking muscle car. The bodywork on it looked good, it was just the paint. It was so faded in some parts that the metal was visible. It didn't look nearly as bad as my cousin's car.

As I climbed in, Logan started up the engine. It roared like a lion, and I could feel it vibrating the seat. If it was going to be like that for the whole trip, the vibrations would knock off some more of the paintwork.

Luckily for the whole trip, the car purred like a kitten. We pulled into the little car park behind Keith's apartment. To my surprise, the only car that was here belonged to the liar posing as my cousin. The rest of the spaces were empty. I looked over at the area where my fight had happened. The feeling I was having when it was going on was explainable now. The speed and power I had relied on were all because of that guy showing up. I'm sure I will find out what kind of creatures smell like mint. Then maybe I can track that guy down and at least find out what his sudden problem with me is. He had barely said any words to me, and even the ones he had weren't great. His face was completely emotionless and yet I had felt such a connection with him. I wouldn't be able to explain it if anyone asked. It was just there in my stomach and in my heart. I wanted him, and I wanted him despite his rejection last night.

We all got out and wandered over to the steps. Cassie laughed before saying, "Those steps don't look like they can take our weight."

"That's what I said. They creak so I'd watch your step if I were you."

She gave me a nudge which seemed to send ash smells across my skin under the leather jacket I was still wearing. "Watch yourself, Cassie. Beth hasn't mastered her gifts yet and touching her could give her more than she can handle at this point."

I turned my head to him as we climbed the stairs. "Thought I was a natural?"

"A natural you might be, only this isn't the time or the place for you to be winging it."

"Oh. So, what's the plan here?"

"We're going to wing it." He gave me a huge smile and banged on the door before I could give him a sarcastic comment. I heard shuffling footsteps coming from the other side. The first door was unlocked and opened. My stomach starting knotting itself up. With each second that door stayed shut, it got worse. It felt like I was about to lose everything I had eaten in the last day until the door flung open. The man standing there looked horrible. The apartment was doused in darkness which matched his look.

He was wearing a black bathrobe with his jogging bottoms and a plain white t-shirt. His face was scruffy with his chin unshaven and his hair all messy. When he spoke it was with a gruff voice like he had smoked a whole packet of cigarettes today, "I wondered if this would happen. They've always underestimated you, and with Beth, in the mix, I knew it would go belly up. You might as well come in." He turned on his bare feet and started shuffling back into the dark. I walked in with the other two behind me. I noticed the two empty bottles of vodka sitting down by the sofa. The third I saw in his hand. He was pouring himself a drink at the kitchen counter. The air seemed to hold a hint of vodka. It was too bad I couldn't shut off my nose to those kind of smells. It was one I could do without.

Logan got straight down to the job at hand, "Look, pal, how do we get them to leave Beth and me alone."

"Don't you get it? They can't leave you alone because of what you know."

"What!? What I know? I don't know anything that would bother them. I know supernatural beings exist but so do all of them. I know they're trying to kill every single one of them, but I didn't think it was for that reason."

"You know what they want even if you can't remember it. They're not going to take a simple, 'I forgot,' from you."

"If they want what I supposedly know, why would they try and kill me?"

"Because there is more than one way of getting information out of someone's head. They don't have to be alive."

"Well, I guess it's just a pain in the arse when you have your best agent leave you."

"I wouldn't know. I was just a desk jockey, and then I got lumped with this job. I had no idea of what I was getting into and sadly no choice in the matter."

I stepped forwards, "What do you mean, 'getting into?' All you've done is lie to my parents and me."

"That might be all I've done. I didn't want to be part of murder though."

"They won't kill me. Not now I can control my gifts, and with Logan and Cassie's help, I'm sure I'll be fine."

"It's not just you I'm talking about." He downed the vodka in one go and poured another one. "They have started tying up loose ends. Once they found out you weren't going to be of any use to us anymore, they started killing anyone who's involved."

The picture was starting to get a little clearer. The drinking he's been doing, and his new attire was pointing towards the end of his mission. I had no idea what they would do to him. After all, he is just a desk man. Would they kill him or give him another job? Maybe they would send him back to his desk or wipe his memory somehow. He said that there are ways of getting information out of someone's head. Maybe they have ways of making people forget. "What loose ends are they tying up now? You?"

"I'm next. Then it will be you three. Oh, your werewolf mate has already been put under observation."

"What does that mean?"

Logan moved a little closer to me and whispered, "Don't worry about him."

"What do you mean?" Then my head clicked a couple of puzzle pieces together. They're tying up loose ends. My parents were the only other people who could possibly know something. Is he saying they're the ones being taken care of now?

That was the last thing that passed through my mind. The next thing I knew I was out the door and running down the street. I was breathing in the last of the ash smell I had stolen from Cassie on the way out, and then I was blurring. I stuck to the empty spaces, and most of the journey was done through the woods. It was starting to get dark by the time I got to Branswell. My legs weren't tired, and I wasn't out of breath. I suppose being a vampire had its advantages.

I let go of the vampire inside of me and pushed it out of my nose. The smell was finally gone and the slightly weird feeling I had also been getting went with it. It might not be near noon, but I wasn't used to the feeling of the sun on a vampire brain. As I walked in the direction of my house, I thanked Cassie for being as fast as she is.

I walked around a corner at the top of a hill and came out onto the green outside my parent's house. Nothing seemed to be out of the ordinary. A part of me expected to see a flaming house as my parents screamed out from the inside.

My next thought was hearing screams as I look through the window in time to watch them being executed. Luckily that wasn't the case.

I walked in through the front gate like I was coming home early from the local pub. As I walked past the patio doors, I saw my parents sitting watching television. I was here in time to save them. They were sitting there so normally even though they could be killed any second now. I quickly walked to the front door and burst through it. It was a strange feeling to be happy to see my parents. I walked around the corner to look down into the lounge. They didn't even turn their heads to look at me. I know we have our differences, but they could at least say hello since I'm not supposed to be there. Maybe ask me why I'm not with my fake cousin in Ingleford.

I took a step forward to try and get their attention. Still no movement. This was getting weird. They were being too still. Neither one of them had taken a swig from their wine glasses. Their glasses weren't even in their hands. They were carefully placed on the table between them. I took another step forward, and that's when the television shined a bright light on them. It was only for a few seconds, but it was long enough to see the dark red on their faces. Another flash came, and the deep bullet wounds in their foreheads made my stomach churn. It threatened to rebel, but I managed to keep the contents down.

My feet were planted to the spot. I couldn't move forward to touch them, and I couldn't walk away. The wooden panels beneath my feet were acting like glue. A tear was about to trickle down my cheek when a smell filled the room. Mint seemed to fill the area, even the corners that hadn't been touched with a duster in some time. It couldn't be my hero that I wanted to see so badly. He didn't know I even lived in this town let alone if I lived in this specific house. I forced my body to turn.

Standing at the other end of the room in the dining area

was a short man. He was wearing a black, short-sleeved shirt over a white vest. His black jeans were held up with a brown belt. His face was mostly covered by his goatee, and his long hair fell down to his shoulders and looked almost like it had been wet recently. I looked again at his clothes until I realised they were ones from my dad's wardrobe. He gave me a crooked smile, "I'm sorry. I couldn't walk around naked now could I?" My throat was so dry I could only squeeze out a gurgling sound. "I'm also sorry about their arms. I was really hungry after my run down here." I whipped my head around. Blood was covering a hand on each body. Just at the end of my mum's blouse sleeve was a rip on her arm. A rip that could have only been done by an animal. In this case, it was this man that did the ripping.

Anger surged inside me. It filled my limbs with it and encouraged them to move and to tear his limbs off. I agreed with that feeling. I sucked as much of the mint in through my nose as I could. It filled my head and my body with such power it fueled to my anger. It was almost uncontrollable. It built and built until I couldn't take anymore. My limbs starting creaking. My bones in my feet got longer, and so did the ones in my legs. I grew a couple of inches. My arms were getting heavier as I felt hair pushing through my skin.

I didn't watch the rest of it as I threw my head back and cried out in pain. I felt my mandible bone stretching outwards turning my cry into a howl. My nose moved out until it filled half my vision. My teeth no longer felt small in my mouth. Big, sharp teeth lined my gums, and I wanted to taste flesh. I hunched over and supported myself on my back legs.

I moved forwards hearing the claws on my feet scrape against the wood flooring. The man in front of me smiled and roared. Before he could start to change, I rushed forwards. My claws on my hands dug into his shoulders as I pushed him back against the dining room table. A chair fell to the floor as his limbs flung out to brace against the impact.

With claws dug into his shoulders, I pulled him to me and then slammed him into the table again. It shifted across the floor. I felt a punch on my side, but it felt little more than a fly.

I let my anger out, and I dug my teeth into his right shoulder. His pain was screamed in my ear. I let go of him as blood filled my mouth. It dribbled out as I bared my teeth to him. I didn't see the chair being swung at me. I did, however, feel it smash into the side of my head. Wood splintered into small pieces. The blow didn't hurt me and didn't distract me. I had no idea if it was just being a werewolf or it was the amount of anger I felt.

Pulling my left hand free, I swung it through the air. My claws sliced into his chest sending him sideways. I turned to watch him slam into a desk. The front of it came down like a drawbridge. Some of the contents spilled onto the floor including a letter opener. Judging by the stinging I suddenly felt all over my skin it was made of silver. I wouldn't like getting too close to that thing.

I stood back, waiting for my fighter to attack me. He ran forwards getting up to a fast speed. My speed and strength matched his so he was easy to track. I moved just as fast and managed to get out the way of his first two attacks. The third was a kick to my leg. It connected with my knee making me drop to the ground with a grunt. He tried to follow up with a punch aimed at my head. I got my hand in the way first. I didn't grab his flying fist like I hoped. I did do something better though. Half-way up his arms were my claws dug into his flesh. Blood was pouring out, wetting the hairs on my forearm. I pushed him back feeling the sting of silver. His back hit the desk again. I had damaged this man enough. It was time to end this fight.

I pushed my werewolf half out of my body. As it left the sting of silver went with it. The claws on my hand slowly moved out of his arm allowing even more blood to fall to the floor. Once it was almost out, I saw a punch. I used the very last part of the werewolf essence and moved out the way. As I bent my fingers snatched the letter opener from the floor and I attacked. To my advantage, the pain my opponent was feeling was distracting him. If he had been one hundred percent, he could have dodged out of the way easily. Instead, the point of the letter opener plummeted into his chest. It pierced his heart sending pain all through his body.

I watched him scream as steam started coming out of his chest where the weapon had hit. I backed away, afraid of what might happen. I carried on watching happy he was in as much pain as he was. I wished ten times more upon him.

As the screaming slowly died down, I was happy to see no exploding body parts. It was almost like the silver only kills the werewolf side of the man. Although upon checking his pulse I was sure he was dead. Both parts of him.

I turned to face my parents. The wounds were clearer now I knew they were there. I started feeling faint. I didn't think it was the power I had just leeched because it wasn't for long. I didn't know if it was the sight of my parents like that. It didn't matter at this point because my body was falling down to the floor whether I wanted to or not. My eyes were shut, and my brain was empty before my side hit the wooden floor panels.

CHAPTER 5

W hen I came to, I was no longer on the floor. My head rested on a big pillow. The smell of it was so familiar. I opened my eyes to verify that I was lying in my bedroom. There was no one else in the room, just me. As I shifted my body, I felt my covers rubbing over my skin. When I changed, I must have ruined Logan's jacket and my dress.

Then my thoughts went to what was sitting in the lounge. Not the dead werewolf. It was more the couple sitting on the sofas. My stomach hadn't lost it last night, but it wasn't going to hold back now. I bolted upright and threw my head to the side. It splattered against my carpet changing the colour quickly.

After I finished and wiped my mouth, I got off the bed on the other side. I walked across the floor and placed my hand on the doorknob. I caught a quick glimpse of myself in the mirror that hung on my door. Seeing my skin on display.

I turned to my bedroom and threw on some underwear and a black, short-sleeved top and a simple pair of jeans. Since I didn't know what had happened to Logan's jacket, I picked out my black denim one. The next step was to leave the room. I just forgot about the pool of sick by the bed. My parents weren't going to be moaning about it now.

It hurt less than I thought it would. The thought of my

parents being dead. It probably hadn't been processed yet. As I drew closer to the rest of the house, I started hearing voices. By the time I walked into the large room at the front of the house, I had realised it was Cassie and Logan.

As I walked in, they gave me a concerned look. I apologised to Logan about his jacket when I saw the pieces of it on the floor. "Don't worry about it." I pulled a big smile, but it didn't seem to ease their looks. I looked down to the floor where the werewolf had fallen. The two of them must have moved the body and cleaned up as well. I next looked down to the lounge section of the room. There were now two lumps sitting on the sofas. One of them had chucked the table cloth over them. Small red dots seeping into the material.

Logan slowly stepped forward. "What happened here?"

"I came in. Saw my parents and then got attacked by a werewolf. His body was there?"

"We took it to the woods just up the road. Anyone finds it, it'll just seem like a random killing. Nothing to worry about." He held out his hand. Inside it was the silver letter opener that I had used to kill my attacker. It was clean and looked brand new. I took it and stared down at the pointy end for a few seconds. I had used it to stab someone through the heart. It didn't matter if he was a werewolf. He still looked human. I had found it so easy to do it.

The weird thing was, even without the werewolf essence, I didn't really care. It was the same with the truck driver that had possibly died in the crash. I still didn't feel remorse for what happened. I looked over to my dead parents again. There was slight sadness inside me, but it wasn't all-consuming like it should be. They were my parents. Anyone else would have fallen to pieces and yet I had been in a fight and won. Things weren't normal anymore. I wasn't normal anymore.

Logan's voice made me jump, "If you're wondering why there's no guilt, it's natural for leechers. I guess we're programmed that way. Makes it easier to do what we're here to do."

"How did you know?"

"Your first kill." He pointed to the letter opener that was still in my hand. "I thought the exact same thing."

"What was your first kill?"

"A vampire. It was my first assignment. Got told it was a routine check. Instead, when I got there, I was ordered to kill the vampire. In vampire years he was over two hundred years and very powerful. The problem was, he was turned when he was twelve. He had evaded us for so long because of this. They didn't tell me. I had to find out the hard way. It was the first time we knew where he would be in twenty-three years. I had no choice, and to this day I hate myself for what I did." Logan blew out a long sigh before continuing, "After a few years I started getting a new view of what the government does. It took me a while to get out and get off their radar. I don't plan on getting back on it without a fight. After this is all done, then I'm off again. Moving and getting off the grid. I don't blame you for the fact they have found me again. I realise that you were just a pawn in this game."

"How did they manage to find out where you were in the first place? It couldn't have been a coincidence I was taken to a town near your bar."

"Your buddy back at the apartment gave me the answer to that. They had tracked me down to a wide area with descriptions and using police help. Then they just deployed you and hoped for the best. They staged attacks to get me to notice you or at least one of my friends."

I hadn't seen people following me all the time though which didn't explain how they knew where I was, "How do they know where I am?"

"They're very good at following people without being seen, but you're right. They've implanted a tracking device inside your heart."

"What?!" My hand shot up to my chest. I didn't know why because I wouldn't be able to feel it let alone do something about it. "How the hell did they get one inside my heart?"

"It's fired out of a rifle. You were most likely given it during one of your blackouts. Since you weren't human, it most likely would have sped up the healing process making it impossible to see where the implant was shot. Also means you wouldn't remember it since you hadn't been trained. They just had to wait until you led them straight to me."

"Sorry about that."

"Actually, that's my fault so it should be me to apologise." It was the first time Cassie had spoken in this conversation. It wasn't going to be her last. "So what are we going to do about her implant?"

"That gets a little complicated."

"What do you mean?" She lowered her voice, but I still heard it, "You heard what happens to it if they see fit."

I took a step forward, "What?!"

Logan blew out a long breath before speaking, "To shut the implant off someone has to break into the government facility and destroy your folder on their servers."

"What does the implant do if they see fit though?"

"When I say someone that means me…."

"And me!"

Logan ignored Cassie, "Which would be basically handing me over to them. I've spent all this time on the run, and I'm not going to be walking straight into their home."

"What does the implant do? Logan, tell me!" I didn't like shouting, but it was needed. He wasn't listening, and I wanted the answer. I was seconds from punching him to get his attention.

"If they feel you're completely useless, they initiate some kind of self-destruct measure which means the implant spits out jagged blades. These will dig themselves into your heart, and the person dies very painfully."

"Oh." I wished I hadn't even asked. My fingertips rubbing over my heart as I thought about it happening.

"It also secretes a sort of gel that seems to stop a leecher from using their abilities. This means you won't be able to heal yourself. If it's tampered with, then it does the same thing. The only way of it not being a threat is to destroy the folder at a leecher headquarters."

"I'll help as well, obviously."

"I'm sorry you can't expect me to do this. I'm really sorry." Logan looked sorry, but it didn't matter. He was the only one who could help me.

I was about to start pleading, but then I realised he was right, "Okay. Would you help me out as much as you can though?"

He seemed shocked by my sudden change in attitude, "Of course. I can get my guy on the inside to get some blueprints."

"Can't you just get him to destroy the files himself?"

"He's not allowed to be in that area. Special clearance is needed. He would be tortured and then killed if he was spotted. I will help any way I can with anything else that's needed."

"Thanks." Cassie went to open her mouth, but I spoke again, "Are we ready to go?"

She looked down at my parents, "Don't you want to organise things here?"

I thought about it, still finding it weird how I was not feeling distraught, "I'm sure the government will send some kind of cleaning crew, right Logan?"

"It is what they do."

"There's nothing else I want to do so I'm ready to go."

Logan dug his keys out of his pocket, "I've got my car." He walked towards the front door.

Cassie walked up to me, "Are you sure you're alright?"

"I really am. It's hard to explain." I smiled at her and

walked out of the house after putting the letter opener back in the desk. Cassie shut the door, and we left the village in Logan's vehicle. It would no doubt be the last time I set foot in Branswell since there was nothing there for me now.

I sat in the car looking out the window for the whole journey. My current predicament ran through my head many times. There were no family members who lived nearby. My cousin is a fake and I didn't know if I could stay there. I mean, if I did the government would know where I was. It didn't sound good. I could go on the run with Logan, but I would have to sort this tracking device out first. All I can do is concentrate on that. I can forget about the university for the moment. No point in trying to sort that out if I could be going on the run or maybe end up dead.

I got lost in my thoughts until we arrived back at the Moonlight Bar. Cassie started speaking, but I was distracted. There was a smell in the air that shouldn't be there. I recognised it as the mint scent of werewolves. My eyes searched for the beast. There weren't many people in the area which made it easier.

As I turned to face the green across the road from the pub, I saw someone who wasn't walking anywhere. He stared back at me. From this distance, his stare still hit me hard. I could feel his eyes piercing all the way down to my brain. He knew who I was, he couldn't be just a random werewolf. He was there for a reason. I turned to tell the other two, but I felt a soft puff of air across my skin. I heard Logan cry in pain as he fell back, clutching at his chest.

There wasn't any time to check if he was okay. The werewolf I had spotted suddenly bolted, and I quickly followed, launching myself into a run. I sucked the mint scent into my lungs, and the essence sped up my feet.

My nose kept sucking on it as I followed. The more I took, the quicker my feet moved. People kept looking at me with quick glances but other than that I didn't get much attention. I kept sniffing the air. Not only for the minty smell but also the unwashed scent that ran along the same trail.

I got into the centre of town when the trail hung in the air like a beacon. He was still here, hiding amongst the crowd. I forgot about his essence since it was everywhere and just concentrated on that unclean part of him. It was as easy as following a glowing gold line. I walked past a pub and found the very centre of town. There was a small market going on. Lots of people and lots of smells. It got harder to follow the scent the more I ventured into the crowds. I lost it when I passed a fish stall. I had to stop sniffing because the stink of the fish was too much. I guess a werewolf's sense of smell isn't always a good thing to have.

I carried on walking looking all around keeping a keen eye on everyone. I was concentrating so hard I almost lashed out at someone who quickly turned around holding a jacket.

I was almost out the other end of the market when I got a strong whiff of mint. It flowed around me like I was surrounded by werewolves until it hit me on the back. I turned around as quick as I could. My fist was brought back, but the face I saw wasn't one I wanted to hit. It was the complete opposite, I wanted to kiss it. His eyes looked at me like he was looking into my soul. I watched as his eyes moved down my body. He was handsome even when he was checking me out. His eyes were brought up to meet mine. As soon as our eyes met, my body heated up. It felt like his eyes were covering me with fire. Sweat trickled down my back, and I was finding it hard to breathe. The small urge I felt to kiss him was now amplified. I wanted him now, and I didn't care where. I could see the lust in his eyes. He wanted me just as much.

He stepped closer, letting his breath hit my lips. It sent chills all over my body that got followed by a tingling feeling. He opened his mouth to speak but didn't say anything. I kept looking into his eyes until it looked like he was suddenly snapped out of a trance. His face quickly changed. The happiness was drained away and replaced with confusion.

His fingers gripped mine tightly, and I was yanked away from the market. I hoped I was being pulled somewhere nice, somewhere isolated where we could be alone. My heart skipped a couple of beats when he pulled me into a dark alleyway. My back was pushed up against the wall, and my hormones jumped to life. I moved my lips forward to grasp his, but he backed away. I was confused but not any less turned on. I gave him a smile, but his confusion stayed. He finally spoke, "What are you?"

Now it was my turn to be confused, "Huh?"

"First, I have such an attraction to you I'm positive you're a werewolf. Then you seem to be human. Now your aura is so strong it rivals mine. I was attracted to you even when I thought you were human. It's not just a werewolf aura thing. The problem is you can only be one thing. If you are, then I can't see you ever again. I wouldn't want to see you again. Now tell me, what are you?"

He suspected what I was. I couldn't lie because he would find out sooner or later. "I'm a leecher." I searched his face for any sign of how he felt. Despite the situation, I still wanted his lips on mine. My hormones wouldn't calm down even when I saw the blood drain from his face. He didn't look angry, but he definitely didn't look happy. I wanted to make it all better, but no ideas came to mind. I tried moving my hand to grab his, but he moved away. His eyes dropped to the ground then back at me. He opened his mouth, but instead of speaking he sped away into the crowd. I was frozen by his reaction for a few seconds before my feet listened to my mind. I followed my werewolf out of the shadows.

I looked both ways as the sunlight hit me. Nothing to the right, so I started running to the left. I only took a few steps when I saw him being dragged off around a corner. So I sped up and turned the corner only seconds after. The werewolf was falling down with a feathered dart sticking out his neck.

His body hit the side of a bin sending a metallic thud through the alleyway.

I stared at the man holding a gun. He was the smelly man I had spotted across the green. He was the man I lost in the market, and he had just knocked my man unconscious. The animal side of me smashed around inside my head, wanting to be let loose. I could already feel my body changing. A roar crept out of my throat, and I let it come out. My foot moved forwards, but my body froze in that stance. I felt a little prick of pain in my chest. My fingers searched and found the same kind of dart. I heard this man's voice a little muffled, "Sorry I shot your friend. He wouldn't be involved if it wasn't for you." That was the last thing I heard. The sounds from the market disappeared along with my sight. I felt the concrete of the alleyway hit my face.

I woke up to the taste of blood in my mouth. It flowed around as I moved my tongue to my lip. Before opening my eyes, I spat. I heard it splat against something hard not too far away. As my nerves woke up, I felt the thin mattress underneath me. My eyelids slowly moved allowing a small amount of light in. A white ceiling hovered above me. A single fan idly spun round keeping the air around me cool. I could no longer feel the power of the werewolf inside me. This meant I was human and vulnerable.

I lifted my head up and opened my eyes fully. Apart from the bed and the fan, there was nothing else in my small white room. There were three opaque walls and a transparent one. Through the clear window, I could only see a hallway. There was nothing on the wall opposite my cell. Nothing else I could see or use. I was stuck in this room with a bed and nothing else. That was until someone came to speak to me. Since I had no idea where I was, it could be months before I see another person. Or it could be seconds. In this case, it was the latter.

I had just sat up on the side of the bed when I heard

footsteps echoing through the hallway. I quickly ran up to the glass and pressed myself against it to get a better look. The footsteps got louder until a guard walked into view. I couldn't smell any funny scents, so I guessed he was human. Unless the glass barrier between us was cutting off my leecher gifts. I would need to have another talk with Logan about all the ins and outs. I was about to bang on the glass to get his attention, but he stopped in front of my cell anyway.

He was wearing black trousers with a grey shirt. The black baton in his holster looked like a painful weapon. On the other side of his belt, I could see the top of a pepper spray can. Luckily he didn't seem to be in possession of a gun. In his left hand was a clipboard. He was looking it up and down, lifting the top page now and again. A pencil was brought up, and a line was written across one of the pages. He then lowered it, holding both objects in his left hand. With his right, he grabbed a key card which was attached to his belt by a line of cable. He swiped it through a contraption to the right of my glass wall. The whole thing slid to the side giving me an opening to run. As the guard was placing his key card back in his pocket, I saw the opportunity and took it.

I burst through the gap and sped down the hallway. It wasn't as fast as a werewolf, but I was surprised by my own speed. My bare feet were hitting the floor with soft bangs. Wait a minute, bare feet? I shouldn't have bare feet, I picked up some trainers from my parent's house on the way out. I quickly looked down at my body, and I was completely naked. No wonder my cell had felt so cold.

As I looked up, I felt a sharp pain in my right calf. Pain then shot through my whole body as I fell to the ground. I hit it hard but the pain didn't stop there. I started having spasms from the taser. I rolled over and looked back at the guard. He had his baton in his hand only it wasn't what I had thought. My eyes shot down to the hooks poking into my skin.

Suddenly the pain stopped and so did the spasms. Blood

was seeping out around the hooks. Before I could yank them out, they shot from my skin and back into his baton. Holstering it, he walked towards me and pulled out a simple bandage from a pocket. He pulled off a layer of plastic film and placed it over all three wounds. I watched it suck onto my skin until it was airtight. I could feel some kind of cool gel mixing in with my blood. It was soothing the stinging pain.

The guard lifted me up to my feet and started pushing me along the hallway by my elbow. We came to a large metal door. He swiped his key card making the door slide up into the ceiling. We walked through another corridor until we came to a small door on the left. It was dark brown, unlike the grey ones we had been walking past so far. He leant forward and punched a code into the number pad to the left of the door. I watched, but his hand blocked most of the numbers.

The door opened and what I saw was one hundred percent different than the hallway. It was a big office. The metal floor gave way to dark red carpet. The walls were painted dark brown with a black pattern making it look like wood. The only piece of furniture in the room was the large desk that dominated the middle along with two chairs. The closest one was a small black one. It didn't look very comfortable, and it was no doubt there for me. The one behind the desk was a large leather chair. It had a high back, and I could imagine sinking into the padding on it. Unfortunately, it was already occupied.

The guard escorted me in leaving me in the small chair and turning his back. I wished there had been a supernatural creature to leech off of. With his back turned it would have been a perfect time. This drummed the point into my brain, Leechers are useless around humans.

I've had no training to fight or use weapons. I can't leech off of a human because there's nothing there to leech. The fight would last two seconds, and I'd end up losing. So much for keeping the world in balance when it's the humans who are in charge.

I heard the door to the office close, and I locked eyes with the man behind the desk. He didn't look like he was an enemy. He had a friendly smile which made wrinkles all over his bald face. He wasn't wearing a suit like I thought he would be. Instead, he was wearing a pair of blue jeans with a white t-shirt. He didn't look like he belonged in this office. The picture sitting on his desk of him shaking the hands of a movie star gave him a different look. Who the hell was this guy? Did he just have lots of money or was he important to the world? Questions I would not be getting the answers to.

He spoke, letting out a soft Scottish accent with his words, "You no doubt have questions, but that's not why I'm here. I've been called up, on my day off because apparently, the person who will change the world is here. But, unfortunately for you, I'm not going to be treating you any different. So." He stood up from behind his desk. His figure was easier to see now. He was a lot bigger than he looked when he was sitting. It wasn't fat either. He must work out every day to get a body like that. It was a shame he was so ugly. Good body, bad face. "First we're going to send you down to check your brain waves. If they're good, then you'll be sent down to the training room. Then the fun will begin." He flashed a horrible grin.

I wanted to speak, but my mouth wouldn't move. The fear in my body was so great it wouldn't allow it. I just wanted to be home. I wished that none of this had happened. If I could go back in time, I wouldn't go out all the time. I would trap myself in my room and stay away from people like this. There were no supernatural creatures in my room.

I focused back on the bald guy. His eyes were no longer piercing into my mind. They were moving up from my feet. I was more aware of my nakedness now than before. His eyes lingered on my chest before another horrible grin appeared on his face. My skin crawled at that moment. Pulling my arms across to hide my body didn't seem to stop that disgusting feeling. I wanted to get away from this man.

My wish was granted but not in a good way. Two men came through the door. Both of them were big. Shaved heads and they were wearing the kind of suits you would find in a mental hospital. White trousers, white shirts. They chucked a boiler suit at me. The uglier one spoke in a gruff voice, "Put that on." Then his eyes made the trip down my body then back up to my chest. I would get dressed even if they handed me a bin bag.

The blue boiler suit was baggy, but at least it covered me up. I was dragged off out of the office and down the hallway. The two big men didn't mind throwing me about. Clearly, I'm still valuable with a few bruises. They put me in an elevator, and the three of us rode it down a few levels. It was cramped with the two big bodies on either side of me.

The doors opened. This level was different from the last. A single corridor stretched out in front of us. The floor was still white like the others, but the walls were all glass. It gave the impression of one big room cut into smaller ones. In fact, that was exactly what they had done. I was moved until we almost got to the wall at the end. They pushed me through a glass door on the left. It was hard to see where the glass was because it was so clear.

Standing in the room in front of me was a short man. He only came up to my chest which made me even happier for the boiler suit. He had a smile painted on his face. His hair was thinning, and it was slicked back showing the weird shape of his head. He had glasses perching on the top of his forehead. He wasn't wearing a white lab coat like some of the others. Instead, he was wearing black clothes underneath a black apron. It looked thick, and I could see small stains of red on it. It reminded me of the aprons you would see butchers wearing just a different colour. It had my fear tripling in magnitude.

He motioned towards the chair sitting behind him. It looked like a dentist chair. I hated going to the dentist, but I was betting I would hate this even more. The two big escorts didn't move to make me sit. The three of them waited patiently. It quickly dawned on me I didn't have a decision in the matter. I slowly plodded forwards and slipped into the seat. My eyes went to the vent above me. Something to concentrate on and hopefully distract me.

I heard small wheels squeaking from behind me. The short man wheeled around a small table. On top was some kind of monitor with two wires coming out the back. It looked like a scientific car battery, and I hoped they weren't going to be electrocuting me.

I looked over at the two men by the door. They weren't moving or showing any facial expressions. They might not know what's about to happen. The more horrible scenario is that they like to watch what is going to happen.

The doctor shuffled over to me with the wires in his hands. He placed them on either side of my head. They stuck to my temples like they were caked in glue. I watched him play with the box as sweat started gathering at the edge of my hair. My whole body was getting warmer with each second. He flipped the switch, and the black screen came to life. Green lines were flowing across it. They looked like they were dancing to some unheard music. He fiddled with a few of the knobs now and again, but the only thing I felt was a slight hint of warmth.

He flipped the switch to turn it off, and the wires were removed from my temples. I was so relieved it was over. All that worrying for nothing. I let out my breath which I had been holding the whole time. A slight smile tweaked the edge of my mouth.

That was until I remembered the next part. The training room. The doctor tapped me on the shoulder. "Please sit up." I did so, swinging my legs over the edge. He pulled a stethoscope out of a drawer. Without warning, he tugged down the zip of my boiler suit. My cleavage was on display, but he didn't look at all interested. Maybe he swung the other way. He placed the metal circle of the stethoscope against my skin. It sent chills all over my body making my nipples hard. He listened intently and then put the thing away. As soon as I could, I zipped my suit back up. I was getting eyes from the two by the door.

The man cleared his throat before asking, "Have you been experiencing any discomfort in your chest?" I couldn't seem to find the words in this situation, so I just shook my head. "Good." He motioned to the two by the door. They walked forwards and practically lifted me off the chair. My feet landed on the floor, and I was pushed out the door.

As we took our walk back to the elevator, I took quick glances into the other rooms. Some of them were empty, but a few were occupied. One person had his chest cut open, and the scientist looked like he was removing something from his heart. Maybe it was the same kind of tracker I had. I could see the pieces of metal attached to it that had killed him. It was dripping with blood, and the blades had pieces of heart still attached. It must have been so painful.

The last room on the left, near the elevator, was filled with scientists. As we were almost inside the suspended box, I caught a look at what they were looking at. A man was lying on the chair topless. I ignored his six pack and saw his hairy arms. His mandible bone was protruding out like he had leeched off of a werewolf. Were they seeing the effects of the leeching on the body or was he stuck that way? If he was stuck, would that happen to me? More questions without answers filled my brain.

We rode the elevator up. It took longer than the last trip as we moved higher than before. As we moved I wondered where I was. They could have taken me to a completely different city or country, and I wouldn't be any wiser. They could have stayed in the same place for all I knew. It wouldn't matter unless I escape. That was the first thing I needed to focus on.

The doors opened again. A corridor moved away from us, ending in a corner. The floor was carpeted, and the walls were painted blue. I could see the white wall underneath it, but at least it was a break from the colour. I was pushed out onto the carpet with a harsh shove. The carpet felt soft and fluffy under my feet.

We walked through the corridor. The whole right wall had a long window. I looked down onto the training room. It looked like an ordinary gym. The floor was white, but most of it was covered in thin, black mats. The far wall had punching bags, and pieces of wood positioned ready to be broken. Beside the wood were pieces of metal set-up in the same manner. Against the right wall was gym equipment. Most of it was weight lifting machines, but there were a few running machines and rowing machines as well. The left wall had a pair of double doors. The left ones were normal looking. The ones on the right were padlocked. There was a sign above it saying EQUIPMENT. I would have to wait to see what the wall under the window was. There were small windows dotted around near the ceiling. I could see dark figures standing in them. They held big, black rifles in their hands. By the looks of it, anything out of line happens then you get taken care of.

We took the right corner and walked down some stairs. I was grateful I wasn't pushed because I would have fallen and broken a few bones. The stairs ended in the double doors I had spotted from the window. I didn't wait for the doors to be opened for me. I figured chivalry wasn't around down here.

The smell of the mats and sweat hit me as I walked in. I heard my own footsteps but not the others. I looked back as the doors swung shut leaving me alone in this big room. I heard a lock sliding into place. The knot in my stomach told me to get ready for danger. Anything coming into this room was only going to have me to play with.

I moved into the middle of the room and peered up at the men with guns. They had a clear shot so there couldn't be any misbehaving. I looked at the wall I couldn't see before. It was filled with doors. There were six of them in total. No windows or handles. Electronically locked and opened of course. I heard bangs from above me. I shot my eyes upwards, but the room was so big covering the ceiling in darkness. More bangs came with no clue what was making them which had my heart pounding faster.

My focus was brought down as a voice filled the room. "First of all, we want you to leech off of the vampire and show us what skills you have." It wasn't a voice I recognised from the two who had spoken to me so far. How did they know I now knew what I was? Had they just guessed that Logan would have told me? Plus, where was this vampire I'm supposed to leech from? Only I stood in the gym.

Of course, I spoke too soon. A bang came from the ceiling then I watched a cage plummet toward the gym floor. It stopped inches from smashing to pieces. It swung a little as the vampire inside it bashed against the metal bars. It wasn't happy about being imprisoned in such a small space. If they let it out, it was going to be taking all that anger out on me.

I quickly leeched off the ash smell now filling the air. It filled my body until I could feel the vampire's gifts. The voice came again giving me a command, "Run." I did as I was told and ran as quickly as possible. I made it around the room four times in a few seconds. The vampire they had in the cage was very fast. Judging from the power I could feel in my arms, he was very strong as well. "The punching bag, destroy it." My feet skidded a little as I shot over to where they hung. At first, I just used my strength. I could feel the sand giving way to my power, and the material got weaker with each hit.

I added the speed I had gained with my strength. Five punches later and the sand started pouring out of the holes I was making. I mustered all my power in my right arm and swung my fist. I aimed to punch right through the bag. My fist hit the leather breaking it apart. Sand moved over my skin as my fist broke through the other side. Sand covered my feet as it poured freely. It felt like walking on the beech when I backed away from it.

Back in the middle, I checked out my fists as I felt the stings. Small cuts covered my skin, but I watched as they closed up. There weren't any scars left behind, and the stinging soon disappeared as the redness faded quickly.

The cage still swinging from its angry contents was pulled back up into the darkness. The next second another one fell down. This one was bigger to accommodate the large werewolf standing inside of it. He too was angry, but he wasn't lashing out at the bars. He held his anger and his power inside ready to unleash it when he was in a smarter situation. He had scars down his face. He looked like a fighter, and I was glad he was inside that cage. I wouldn't stand a chance against him. Even with his werewolf powers inside of me, he was more used to them. Plus his anger would be a weapon I wouldn't have.

The voice came again. "I want you to leech off of this werewolf and change into your wolf form." I heard muttering before the microphone was completely shut off. I didn't get a chance to understand it, but the other man didn't sound happy.

I turned to face the caged beast. Allowing the vampire essence to leave my body the mint scent moved in. I felt more powerful than last time. This werewolf was stronger than the vampire, but my legs didn't feel as nimble. I would bet the vampire could outrun this man easily. Then again, looking at the size of him, most people could make that assumption.

I paused for a bit, thinking about what I was about to do.

The last time I shifted it was because of the anger. Was that the trigger or was it more mental? Then there was the question of what they were going to do after. Would they release someone to fight me? I had no idea how good I was at fighting in my werewolf form. It wasn't something I had been practicing and last time was more instinct than anything else. Despite my worries, I did what I was ordered. I set my mind to the werewolf shape and forced my body into the change.

I felt the power of the wolf fill my body. My feet and my legs grew out of shape. My arms spread out a little, my muscles grew and stretched the boiler suit. My fingers grew twice the length, and black claws appeared on the end. Cracking of ribs and my spine filled my ears as I started to hunch over. Before it was uncomfortable, but now the pain was filling my every thought. My neck grew out a little and then my ears started changing. I could feel them grow into points. Hair grew on my body. I could see the long strands on the back of my hands. They were black as the night.

My forehead moved outwards along with my mouth. It grew into a pointier snout than last time. I heard my boiler suit rip and felt it slide over my body. I could see my whole body covered in hair. This was different than the last time. I felt different. The very shape I was in was more hunched over. I felt more beast-like than human. My mind seemed to be smaller. I could still control my movements. The difference was, it felt like something was there trying to get in. I could feel something banging against the walls of my mind. Luckily I could hold whatever it was there inside my mind. I just didn't know how long my willpower would last.

I ignored that wild side and looked around. Different brands of aftershave swam down from the windows above. I breathed in the past that smell and got into the base scents. In this form, I could imagine their bodies in my clawed hands. Ripping them apart. I could feel my sharp teeth sinking into their flesh and the blood trickling down my throat. It wouldn't quench my thirst like a vampire, but it would dampen that anger I felt building inside. It was like if I let out the beast, the anger would fuel its power. That feeling would keep me going until all my enemies were dead by my hands.

The voice came again, "Change back." A soft growl came out of my snarled lips as I followed these orders like a puppet. Hearing my bones creak with the strain of changing. Soon my body didn't resemble the wild animal but was back to being the dainty female I was.

My arms flung around me hiding my indecency. I looked around at the men standing in the windows. I couldn't see their eyes behind their black visors, but I could feel their stares. All these looks I was getting were making me sick. I looked down at the wrecked boiler suit on the floor. Luckily I was able to slip it back on and kept my intimate parts covered up. I just hoped it would stay like that.

Finally pulling up the zip the werewolf cage went back up to the ceiling. I expected to hear the voice again, but instead one of the electrical doors slowly opened. On the other side was a small room with a simple man inside. He came walking out of the room in casual clothes like he was picked up off the street. Blood was dried up on the side of his head, but there was no cut visible. He looked at my ragged attire and smiled. When he spoke I was surprised to hear the sexy voice that didn't suit him at all, "I see I've been brought dinner. Room service is a little slack, but you will do nicely." Many swear words came to mind. I quickly sucked on his supernatural scent and filled my whole body with his gifts. It was just in time too. He rushed forward with his arms reaching for me with a crazy look on his face.

I blurred to my right, his hands just breezing past my face. He spun around and gave me a sneer. I threw my fist at his chin, but he could tell it was coming. It missed him by an inch and left me open for his fist to crack into my jaw. I fell to the floor from the impact. Pushing up I spat out some blood before looking up to see his boot coming down at me. I rolled out of the way, hearing it thud into the ground.

He walked slowly towards me as I climbed onto my feet. I re-arranged my boiler suit to cover myself up again. When he was close enough, he lashed out. I managed to move out of the way of the next two attacks and throw one of my own. I caught him in the face, and his head snapped back. I brought my foot up between his legs. It hit him so hard his feet lifted off the ground before he collapsed to the floor. His face was filled with pain as well as his words, "I'm going to kill you."

"You have to get on your feet first." He lifted himself up onto one hand, but I kicked it out from underneath him. His face smacked into the mats. Blood splattered under his face. The voice came over the speakers around the room, "You have three seconds to kill him." That was it? I looked down at the vampire lying near my feet. He didn't seem like a great guy, and he was going to kill me.

He looked up at me with blood trickling out of his mouth. "I'm going to rip you apart."

I was about to speak when the voice came over the speakers again, "Time's up." Shock filled me when the room started filling up with smoke. It stopped once there was a thick layer surrounding us. I could only see a few metres in front of me. As I looked down, I saw the massive grin this vampire had. I was about to lift my fist up, but I blinked, and he was gone. The smoke seemed to wrap around him and make him vanish. I looked around but couldn't see anything. No shadows or movement.

Suddenly I felt a whack against my spine. Pain flared as I stumbled forwards. I spun around, but no one was there. Somehow he could disappear into the smoke. So I willed it to hide me as well. If he could do it then so could I. I willed it to cover my body, but nothing was happening.

Another hit came in my gut making me double over. I breathed in big gulps of air trying to get rid of that burning pain in my lungs. I saw the mist move, and a dark figure walked towards me. As the smoke moved off his body, the vampire came into view. He stared at me like I was dinner presented to him on a plate. His finger was raised, and he rubbed the blood on his chin. I watched as his tongue licked the blood from his skin. It made my stomach churn. If this is what most vampires are like, then this is the last one I wanted to see.

He opened his mouth wide. I looked up at him as the canines on the top row came out of his gums. They didn't stop growing until they were an inch long. He closed his mouth letting the tips meet the bottom of his chin. He looked horrible. For a split second, I wondered what Cassie would look like with her vampire teeth out. I wondered if they would be different or if they would be the same.

The vampire leant down and grabbed a handful of my hair. He snarled at me. His breath stunk of dried blood. I tried to break his grip, but my strength was temporarily lowered from the pain running through my body. He clearly didn't think it was enough, so he delivered another punch to my gut. The only thing keeping me upright was his grip on my hair.

He opened his mouth, ready to feed on my blood. His eyes glinted with pleasure as I saw my horrified face in their reflection. I wished he didn't have hold of me. Just wanted to be anywhere else but here. I shut my eyes tight and just hoped that it wasn't real. That I could disappear.

With my vampiric hearing, I heard his snigger. His delight in beating me. Only this filled my body with the last amount of strength I had left. I shoved my hand under his chin. Those teeth poked into my hand, but I didn't care. My hand was better than my neck.

I pushed harder drawing his head back, and I saw his neck. Immediately the thought of sinking my own vampire teeth into his flesh popped into my head. It was washed away with the sanity of my humanity. I didn't want to taste this man's blood any more than a cat likes swimming.

I brought my hand back and slammed my fist into his exposed throat. He immediately let go of me and dropped to the floor coughing. He looked up at me with his mouth gaping. I saw him start to slowly disappear into the fog, but I was too quick for him. I grabbed a handful of his hair and pulled him up to my level. As he climbed I spotted his crooked leg. I lifted my foot up and brought it down onto his knee. The crack was louder than his moan of pain. I let go of his hair, and he fell to the floor, beaten. The voice came again, "I said kill him." Unfortunately, it seemed like I had no choice in the matter. He was a bad vampire. I had to keep that thought in my mind. Make sure I think of that before I rammed something through his heart.

I looked around the room for something to use as the smoke started to disappear. The walls and the contents of the room started to come back into sight. I noticed the pieces of wood next to the punching bags. One of those would be perfect. The wood came away from the metal bracket very easily. I wielded the piece of wood as I walked back to my enemy.

As I got to him, he looked up. His eyes were filled with the horror of the realisation he was about to die. I ignored it with a lot of difficulty.

Kicking him over onto his back I pinned him down with my knees. One on his hip and the other on his shoulder. As I brought the wood over my head, I swallowed past the lump in my throat. I looked away from the vampire under my knees. Before I could change my mind, I slammed the wood down into his chest. The scream he made wasn't natural. It was ear- shattering.

I fell back off of him in shock. Moving away as I watched in horror as the screaming got louder. His skin started to bubble. His cheek bubbled up, the skin slowly turning to white and peeling off, showing burnt skin underneath. His teeth stuck out further. The white of them shining as saliva came out of his mouth with his yelling. Flames started to come out of his open mouth and his eyes. It was like someone had lit his brain on fire. The flames were getting bigger and bigger until his whole body was covered in them. I couldn't stand his screaming anymore. I covered my ears, but it didn't help. The sound still bashed at my ears trying to get in. I couldn't tear my eyes away from the display either. With every bubble in the skin and every flame licking the air around him, he got closer to dying.

Still frozen there as the body started to disintegrate on the floor. Bits of his skin were falling off after turning to ash. As more and more of him spread out on the floor, the screaming slowly died down. At the point of it completely stopping, his head had gone. His body was just a lump of ash that was still glowing with heat. The flames slowly died down when there was nothing left to burn.

I finally removed my hands from my ears and used them to stand up. Moving over to the pile I kicked the stake I had used. The ash fell apart spreading into a wider circle. I looked up at the guards once more. Still, there was no reaction. I looked over at the five doors that were still closed, wondering what was on the other side.

Using the essence still inside me I focused on my hearing and that part of me deep down that wanted blood. Listening to the heartbeats around me. I could hear the werewolf's beating from the rafters above me. It was beating in unison with another. That made three cages up top since a vampire's heart didn't beat. I could hear three more hiding behind the doors. That meant there was at least one more vampire to have fun with. Either that or another supernatural creature that didn't have a heartbeat. Then again, maybe one of the rooms was empty. Who said they all had to be occupied.

The voice that came again made me jump, "Very good. Your training is coming along nicely. Next, I want you to leech off of this creature." The third cage, suspending from the ceiling, dropped down to my level. There must be some kind of mistake. What was inside the cage wasn't a creature. Not an obvious one by any measure. It was a young girl. She looked like she was sixteen.

Everything she wore was black from her jeans to her hair. Her vest top showed off her arms. They weren't massive, but they were toned. Her biceps flexed as she pulled on the cage containing her. She seemed calm. She didn't seem bothered by the situation she was in.

I did what I was told. Allowing my gifts to search for her specific scent. The only one I could find that didn't belong in the room smelled like rain. It smelt like the room had been drenched in it. It was such an odd scent to have.

Despite this though, I leeched off of her not knowing what I would turn into. I focused on the feelings I was getting. I to, just like her, became calm. The situation wasn't bothering me as much anymore. It felt like all my worries had been lifted from me.

The next feeling was strange. I felt lighter on my feet like my body weight had been cut down by half. I moved my feet still feeling agile like a cat. Next, my eyes got sharper. The colours of the room brightened. The mats stood out from the floor.

The girl looked at me like she knew what I was. Not what I had become but what I was all along. "Shift shape." The voice was very direct. It only gave me small information on the woman. She had another shape. Her scent ruled out a werewolf. The problem was that left the whole collection of supernatural creatures. I had no idea how many there were, and I had no idea what kind of ones there are. For all I knew, she could shift into a rat or something I wouldn't be able to control.

The voice came again, ordering me to shift. I pushed my rat idea out of my head. Pulling more of her scent into my body, I felt even lighter. I concentrated on shifting shape. Instead of imagining myself changing into the animal I thought of the scent changing my body. It took longer than before.

After the first set of limbs started changing it came quicker. I just let my body morph into the shape it wanted to. My legs got shorter becoming only six inches long. My toes moulded into three points. Talons appeared at the end of them. My body started sprouting feathers. They were big and dark brown and felt horrible as they pushed through my skin. My neck shortened and my whole body shrunk. Not only was I getting shorter, but I was getting thinner. My fingers seemed to disappear amongst the many feathers lining my arms. My head morphed into the size of a bowling ball. My face poked outwards, my eyes becoming black marbles. A pointy, yellow beak changed from my mouth and nose.

I opened it and let out a high-pitched squawk. It was the noise of a massive eagle. Flapping my wings, I bounced around the mats. My claws shredded the material with ease. I stretched my wings out. They were a metre wide each, and they look so beautiful. I flapped them twice, feeling the breeze that blew up around me.

I liked this form. Not only was I big and able to fly but my eye-sight had gotten even better. I could see further with a lot more detail. If I looked hard enough, I could see the beads of sweat sitting on the woman's neck. It must be so amazing to be able to shift into this at will. Although it didn't seem to help her with getting caught.

The voice came again, a little clearer than before, "Very good. Change back and prepare for the next fight." I changed back into my human shape. My bones stretching out into a human shape. I watched the tip of my beak disappear, and my nose appear. The feathers moved back into my body, and my skin showed through. I no longer stood a metre tall. I was back to my original height. Just like the last time my boiler suit had seen the worst of it. I managed to get it to stay on my body by tying a few stray ends together. It would have to do though until I was given something better. They might be nice enough to supply some after the training was over.

I would have stolen the ones on the vampire, but they had been burnt away by the fire. My eyes went to the eagle shifter as she gave me a weird look before being raised up into the rafters. The darkness swallowed her, and I was alone on the mats again. As the voice boomed into the room, I turned to the doors, wondering what they would reveal, "Find a way of killing the next test."

No more instructions than that? No hint of what it was going to be? With no information, I chose the best thing to do. I stretched my gifts up into the darkness above me. Finding that minty smell, I sucked it in and allowed my body to take on the form of the animal.

Once I had changed into a werewolf, I readied myself. I thought about the gifts inside my body and looked down at my fingertips. They couldn't be classed as weapons, so I thought about the black claws of the werewolf. Willing them to grow I was happy to see them extend out and blacken. They looked sharp enough to rip through metal. Ready for my fight I looked at the doors and let out a rumbling growl.

The door in the middle slowly opened. I wasn't prepared for what was inside. Just like the last one, the room was very small, and it was cramped. What came strolling out was a large animal. Its paws were the size of my head. Its teeth shimmered under the lights. Its tongue hung out of its open mouth. Black eyes surrounded by bright yellow looked out at me. Its whole body was covered in yellow fur except for the orange mane framing its head.

I had no idea if a werewolf could kill a lion. The only way I was sure to win the fight is to get it back into its human form. That is if it has one. Would they be sick enough to make me go against a real lion? I didn't know, and I had no time to think about it. The large beast lunged at me with those massive paws out in anger.

I just managed to roll out of the way, feeling the breeze as a paw came close to taking off my head. I got back to my feet. The massive lion landed with grace and slowly turned around to lock its eyes on me again. The lion moved closer. I prepared for a fight not sure what I was going to do. Then the lion moved with surprising speed. I tried to move out of the way, but I saw teeth slashing into my arm. Red blood dripped down onto the floor. As the lion gnawed at it, my arm started going numb.

I shook it trying to get the beast off of me, but it didn't work. The lion pulled me down to my knees. My fingers grabbed its mane, and I pulled back hard. It roared as its teeth slid out of my arm. With my arm free, I took two handfuls of fur and swung the massive beast. I sent the four-legged animal into the weights making them crash over the floor. It flattened one of the machines under its immense weight.

With the animal on the other side of the room, I looked down at my arm. The cuts were deep, and even though I could feel them healing already, it would take a long time. I forgot about my arm and concentrated on the fight.

I pushed into a run, my claws kicking up pieces of matting as I moved. The lion charged at me with its teeth ready to attack. It lifted up those massive paws again. My eyes saw the claws extending out as we met.

Dipping down under those dangerous weapons I crashed my shoulder into its chest. With my momentum still going I pushed it into the wall. I felt the force of it reverberate through my whole body. I didn't wait to feel the pain of an attack. My hands moved out and grabbed the first thing I could find. Using it to swing the lion again I turned and used all my strength and made a big dent in the metal wall.

It let out a whimper like it was a kitten. I quickly pounced on the body and pulled on its neck. I hadn't used much power to do it. It made a dull thud as I dropped it to the floor. I stood back and changed back into my human form. There was no point trying to sort out my boiler suit. After that last shift, it was little more than a tattered piece of cloth.

I moved my attention from me to the lion on the ground. Watching as the fur disappeared and the body shifted into a man. The claws were now nails, and the paws were now hands and feet. The man who was before me now didn't look like it could change into something so powerful. He looked like the kid that would be picked on at school and have his head dunked into the toilet. His head pointed in a broken direction.

I had killed this man. It was easier to think I had just killed a lion. I wished that was the truth. Before the voice came again, I knelt down next to the shifter. I pulled his clothes off and dressed. The clothes were a little snug, but it would do. I took this quiet time to look around the room and think. I wasn't allowing them to depict what I do anymore. Becoming a murderer that kills on command wasn't something I wanted to become. It wasn't going to happen. I had to find a way out of here and quick.

Nothing in the room was jumping out at me. There was only one way in this room, and that was through the double doors. I had no idea what was through the windows even if I could get past all those guns.

I had almost finished looking around when the speakers leaked the voice into the room. "You have another fight to get through. Do whatever you can to survive." The room went silent. Once again I was left alone to fend off another attack. I wasn't planning on waiting for it though. My eyes picked out a spot where smoke had been bellowing out before.

Using the naked body, I threw it like a wrecking ball. It hit with enough force to break the pipe behind the panel. The damage punctured a hole sending smoke into the room. I got rid of the werewolf inside of me and leeched off the vampire that was hanging from the ceiling. The ash smell filled my body as the smoke filled the room. I thought about disappearing and wrapped the mist around me.

My willpower brought the smoke around my body, and when I looked down, even I couldn't see my own hands. I was lost in the smoke. This would buy me some time but not a lot. I had to think quickly. Nothing came to mind until I heard a bang from above my head reminding me of the eagle shifter. If I leeched off of her, I could fly out of here. I would need some help so the first step would be to get her out of her cage.

The vampire scent was of no use to me now, so I got rid of it. As the gifts leaked out of my body, I became visible. Luckily the smoke was thick enough now for me to disappear from the guard's view without help. I reached up with my leeching gifts and sucked in the rain smell that was hanging up in the corner. The feeling of being light came again. I slipped my clothes off quickly and jumped into the air. I forced my body through the change. It was becoming easier to shift into different shapes, and I was flapping my huge wings within seconds.

I flapped them harder, lifting myself up to the rafters easily. My talons wrapped around the metal beam running across the ceiling. Around it was a chain that held the cage in its suspended state. I followed it back to the wall where there was some kind of pulley system. I looked down. The smoke hadn't made its way up this high. I could see the very top of the metal cage underneath me. I shouted down, "Shift shape and I'll lower the cage." In my head, that's what I heard. What actually came out of my beak was a high-pitched squawk. I had no idea if it was the right noise until I heard a squawk come back. The sound was completely different in my head, "Hurry. I've been locked up for too long. I need to fly."

Using my wings, I hovered slowly over to the electronic pulley system. My talons wrapped around the chain, keeping me stable. I brought my beak down and started pecking the casing around the electronics. It dislodged on the fourth making it fall to the ground, getting lost in the smoke. I dug my beak into the wires and started ripping at them almost singing my feathers with sparks. I pulled at one, and the cage suddenly dropped into the thick mist. I tipped forwards and tucked my wings back against my body. As I plummeted the wind, I created pushed the mist out of my view. It cleared a little path so I could see the blue mats. At the last second, I spread my wings out, catching the air underneath them. My claws came to rest on the mats without so much as a sound. I had no idea how I knew what to do, but flying came so easy to me like it was all in my head.

It must have stopped just above the ground since I hadn't heard a loud bang. I felt like I was going round in circles until I came across a piece of it. It was a small piece that changed into a trail leading me to the cage. I raised myself up into the air and landed on the bottom of the hole that had been created. I peered inside but couldn't see another person or eagle.

Dropping back down to the mats I heard a soft noise behind me. I turned my head, my long neck making it easy. Through the thick fog came an eagle shape, hopping along. It came to a stop next to me. It opened its beak, and a noise came out. It wasn't loud, and I could only just hear it. It made sense though which was starting to weird me out, "Let's go through the windows. I'll meet you on the other side."

Next thing I knew I was feeling the wind created by her wings. I looked up as she vanished into the mist. I followed her example and started flapping my wings. My talons left the floor, and I kept going up and up.

Finally, I heard a loud scream. I followed the sound and finally came across the wall. There was movement coming from behind one of them. Next, I heard gunfire and then yelling. I knew it was my turn, so I flew a little higher and then swooped down towards the window in front of me. I tucked my wings back and lowered my head.

My flight was shortly ended as I smacked into the side of a helmet. My wings shot out, and I frantically flapped them to correct myself. I looked at the helmet as it turned towards me. He lifted up his gun to aim at me. If I tried to fly away, he could easily shoot me.

Bringing up my sharp talons I pierced them into his shoulder. Blood coursed out of the woods as I slammed my beak into his visor. It cracked under the pressure and smashed on the second attempt. My small eyes picked up the look of fear, and I squawked loudly at him bringing out a cry of horror. He shook my talons free and started running off down the hallway. I watched as he sped into the next guard along with enough force to send them both to the floor.

The runner stayed on the floor too afraid to move. The one he knocked over was now getting up. His eyes were locked on me. I looked behind me, and more guards were heading my way. I looked back down the other way and found the guard raising his gun. I started flying towards him, but I knew I wasn't going to get there in time.

Flapping my wings as hard as I could I was only a metre away when I was staring at the barrel of his gun. I thought it was over until I felt the air around me stirring. Her wings flying her over my body hitting the guard beak first. She smashed the visor and started pecking at his face. I saw blood dripping down his face. I made my way past the two of them hearing the footsteps behind me. I carried on flying through the hallway.

Suddenly I heard wings coming up behind me. My eagle friend had caught up with me. I squawked at her, "Thanks."

"No worries. Follow me." She sped up, overtaking me and taking the lead. I matched my movements to hers. She was more used to her wings and knew exactly how to use them. A few times I would lose control in the small space and have to kick off the wall with my claws. By the time we came to a door, I was getting the hang of it.

The large metal door down the end looked thick. The hand scanner was the only way through it. I thought we would have to shift back to humans, but my friend just kept flying, picking up more speed.

At the last second, she curled up into a thin object and pierced through the small glass window sitting in the middle. A puff of feathers came up in front of me as some of them got caught on the glass. As I neared the hole, I wrapped my wings around my body. I stretched my legs out behind me and lowered my head. My body spun giving me more accuracy as I passed through the hole. I felt the jagged glass take off some of my own feathers, but I didn't feel any pain.

Bursting out the other side I brought my wings back out and glided. We flew through the hallways for a little bit longer. Beyond the metal door, there were no guards and no scientists. There wasn't anyone to see us flying around the corners. After a few more turns the hallways seemed to change. They were less cold. There was wallpaper instead of the metal walls. Carpet zoomed past below us. It seemed like we were flying through the corridors of an office building.

Hope burst inside me when I saw light streaming through a massive window at the end of the corridor. The flying finally finished when we came to that office. We landed on the grey carpet and shifted back to our human forms. I could feel the feathers move through my skin. I didn't think I would get used to my mouth turning from a hard beak to soft lips. It felt too weird.

I looked behind us, and there was no one following us just yet. I hadn't seen any people sitting behind any desks doing work either. It was completely vacated. I turned to the woman standing in front of me. She ruffled her short punk haircut as the last of her feathers slipped through her skin. Her features were cute and her eyes were a bright colour of blue. She also didn't seem bothered by the fact she was standing there naked. I could tell that she was cold from her nipples, but she didn't seem to show it any other way. I noticed her eyes running down over my naked body. It felt like she was checking me out, but I thought that was stupid.

She shot her hand out for a handshake, "My name is Helen. It's nice to meet you." Her eyes darted down to my chest and then back up to my eyes. A little smile moved her lips.

"Beth. Do we have time for pleasantries?"

"I suppose not. Where are you heading?"

"I guess that depends on where we are."

"Right." Upon saying this, she walked over to the floor-to-ceiling window. "It appears we're in Twindlewood."

"Twindlewood? Where is Ingleford from here?"

"That would be west from here, I think." She paused for a few seconds. "West is…."

I cut her off, "That way." I pointed off into the distance. "Yeah."

"How did I know that?"

"It's a gift that comes with the eagle shifting." She picked up the office chair next to her. From her petite size, I didn't think it would have been possible, but she managed to shatter the window. "Nice to have met you. I'm heading a different way so be careful, and again it was nice to have met you." She held out her hand for another shake. I took it this time unable to stop my smile. As our palms met, I noticed her eyes moving down my body. They moved back up paying close attention to my breasts. It felt weird to have her look at me like that. What was stranger was the way it had me feeling. My heart picked up, and I could feel my nipples harden at the attention.

I put it down to shock and smiled back. It did make a change from having all the guys look at me like that though. She gave me a cheeky smile and then dived out of the window. I watched her body fall until all I saw was wings. She used the momentum of her fall to zoom off into the distance.

I took a few steps back and looked through the hole she had created. The cool breeze coming in called to the eagle inside. There was no fear about what I was going to do. In fact, as I ran and dived through I let out a cry of enjoyment. The air slammed against my body as I fell. I let the animal inside take over my form, and I shot off west gliding with my huge wings out.

It was night time when I arrived back at the pub. I landed in a shadowed corner of the car park, using this to morph back into a human. I didn't allow the essence of the shifter to leave my body just yet. Who knows what had happened here when I ran off. The eagle form would give me a chance to fly away if there was any danger.

I walked between the cars and found the spot where Logan had fallen to the ground. There were a few drops of blood on the concrete, but there were no other signs of what had happened. I walked around the back of the pub since it was covered in darkness just in case someone was watching.

I found two doors. One of them was made of wood and seemed to lead into the back of the pub. The other one seemed to be reinforced with metal. It must lead to an important part of the building. I knocked on it, ready to fight or fly. When I heard footsteps, I reached out with my leecher gift and got the whiff of ash. I had no idea if it was a bad vampire or if it was Cassie. Sniffing again I tried to find other scents, but I guess I didn't have the kind of smell you get from being a werewolf.

The footsteps finally stopped on the other side. Suddenly the door was thrown open, and something rushed out and hit me. I didn't know if it was an enemy or a friend. I threw my fist up anyway. I connected with hard bone. The body staggered back from my sudden defense. I looked and was relieved when I saw Cassie standing there holding her jaw. "Sorry about that."

"Sorry I tried to attack you." I followed her as she motioned for me to follow. The metal door led into a small room. This, in turn, led into Logan's office. He was lying there on his desk. His eyes were closed, and his arm was lying on his chest. I could see bandages covering a wound in his chest. I turned to her about to ask what had happened when I saw her. "You look terrible."

"Well, thanks. You look like you've had some trouble yourself." I looked down at my naked body. "There are some clothes in the cupboard over there."

I followed her finger. "Thanks. What happened to Logan?"

"He was shot with a tracking device. The same one as you have. Now I'm going to grab some sleep."

"Sleep?"

"Vampires do sleep." She laughed.

"I didn't mean that. What about the tracking device? Shouldn't we be leaving here?"

"Don't worry about it. Jewel managed to put a spell on it. And yours."

"How?"

"She found a strand of your hair in the bar. She used that to block the signal."

"Won't they come and raid this place anyway?"

"Jewel did something about that as well. She sent off trails for them to follow. Very talented girl. I really do need some sleep though."

"Okay. I was just hoping I could find out what happened." I pointed to Logan.

"A guy tried to attack us, but I managed to beat him into submission. I got him to phone his superiors and tell them we had gone off somewhere. They shouldn't bother us, at least for a little while with that and Jewel's spells."

"Okay." I still didn't want to wait until the morning to know everything, but Cassie did look rough. I went to the cupboard she had pointed to and grabbed some clothes. They were Logan's and very manly. I pulled on some jeans and grabbed a belt so they wouldn't fall down. I slipped my feet into some socks and my arms into a black shirt. It was so baggy I tied the loose ends into a knot. It made it tighter, but it still left me enough room to move. I grabbed a leather jacket and pulled it over my body. It reminded me of the one he had given me that cold morning in the forest. I didn't slide my arms through the sleeves. Instead, I dropped down into a chair and used it as a blanket. It was quite warm in the office, and I fell asleep quickly. My arms were tired, and the chair was comfortable. I was very happy to greet the darkness of sleep. It felt good as it cleared my head so I could dream.

CHAPTER 6

I woke up to the sweet smell of coffee. It travelled up my nose and gave my brain a kick start to get me up. I opened my eyes and found myself with my feet up on Logan's desk. My back ached from the awkward position I had been in. Cassie and Logan weren't here so they must be where the coffee smell was coming from.

I dropped my feet off the desk and slowly got to my feet. Putting on the jacket, I walked out of the office. Logan was standing behind the bar, and Cassie was sitting on a stool in front of him. I moved around to the patron's side of the bar and perched myself next to her. Logan slid over a cup of coffee. It smelt so good I had to have some of it right then. Unfortunately, when I lifted it up to take a sip, Logan started speaking. "What happened to you?"

I lowered the cup and inhaled the smell of it, "I got caught by the government. At least I figured it was the government."

"What!? How did you escape?"

"They had me in some kind of training room. They had an eagle shifter there. I helped her escape her cage. We flew out of there together."

"Where is this eagle shifter now?"

"She went her own way."

"Oh. Could you find your way back there?" He saw my

145

confusion. "They might have the servers we need to find. To delete our tracking files."

"I thought Jewel took care of that."

"That's only temporary. They'll figure out what she did at some point."

"Okay. I could probably find my way back there. It's in Twindlewood."

"That helps. My friend hasn't got back to me yet. He did, however, send these over." He dropped a folder onto the bar next to his cup of coffee. I took this chance to take a few gulps from my own cup. It didn't taste as good as it smelt but it was good enough.

Logan opened the folder and pulled out the few pages that were inside. The top piece showed what looked like a blueprint of a computer. "This is the computer system that we'll have to get to. I have instructions on how to disable the files that are tracking us."

I turned to Cassie, "Are you still helping?"

"Of course." She gave me a smile. "It's what friends are for."

"Thanks." I hadn't known her for long, and she was willing to help me out with people who hunt her kind. She must really hate them. "So how do we get there?"

Logan put his cup down after finishing his coffee, "We can drive to the place. Park down the road from the building. That bit is easy. It's the getting in and out that's the problem. I do have an idea though." He moved the top page off the pile and grabbed the next three. He laid them out facing Cassie and me. They were all photos of people. One male and two females. "These are people who work for this specific part of the government. Jewel can make us look and sound like them. We use their disguises, and that's how we get in. We find the computer system and destroy our files. We then either walk out or fight out. Depending on how long the disguises last."

Cassie spoke, "Sounds easy enough."

I wasn't so convinced, "Easy? Do we need these people to use them as disguises?"

"No, we don't. It would be better if we got them out the way but we don't have that amount of time. We just have to keep an eye out when we're there. Other than that, it's pretty much sorted."

"Okay."

"So, when do we get started?" Cassie was clearly eager to get going.

A voice came from the office door, "We can start right away." I turned around to see Jewel standing there. She had her hair up in a ponytail again. She was wearing tight black trousers with a long-sleeve top. She walked around to my side of the bar. She placed three bottles of liquid on top of the three photos. "Each of you drinks one of these. You will have two hours before you change back so wait until the last minute before taking it."

Logan interrupted her speech, "Any side effects this time?"

"None and the last time wasn't my fault. I told you not to take that potion with alcohol."

"Fair point." Logan gave her a wink.

I was intrigued, "What happened last time?"

"You don't want to know." I did, but I doubt he was going to be telling the story anytime soon. I would have to try and get it out of Jewel another time. "Okay. We take the potions when we get there. Break in and delete our files. Then we can move on from this situation. Oh, I almost forgot. I found your phone out in the car park. You must have dropped it during that fight with the vampire a couple of nights ago."

"Thanks." He slid it over to me. I was about to check it for any texts or missed calls when something else caught my eye. Jewel handed Logan a book. It was made out of brown leather. It looked battered and worn, and the pages looked stained.

Logan caught my gaze. He flicked through the pages quickly and then placed it near the bottles of alcohol at the back of the bar. He turned back around to me, "It's a spell book. Witches call them chronicles. They're chopped up versions of the witch journals that were written by the three main witches, Luana, Rankord, and Amara. Each of them wrote their own set of journals. Each set holds different kinds of spells."

"What do you mean different kinds?"

Logan gave Jewel a look letting her carry on the witch lesson. She sat down on the stool next to me. "There are three categories of spells. Luana excelled at destruction spells. Offensive and the most powerful out of the three. They range from fireballs to spells used for torturing. Rankord's spells consist of illusions. That's what kind of witch I am. Those kind of spells are like disguises or changing water to alcohol. Amara's spells were defensive ones. Healing spells or shields. The three witches were supposed to be three sides of a pyramid. The most powerful ones from each group of witches. It was balanced until Luana took too much power. You know what happened after that."

"How many chronicles do you have?"

"I give all mine to Logan. I've lost count how many we have."

Logan chimed in, "We've only got four or five."

Jewel nodded in agreement. "Only two of those contain illusion spells though."

"How come you give them to Logan?"

"Well, being a witch means I soak the knowledge of the spell into my brain. Once I've learnt it, then I have it in there forever. Logan can only use the spells when he leeches off of a witch, so he needs the books to remember the incantations."

"Oh. Do you know how many chronicles there are in total?"

"No one knows. I haven't even heard of anyone owning a novel from the actual journals. Just have to keep an eye out for them. Would be an amazing find." Her eyes twinkled at the thought.

"Cool." I turned to Logan who had started looking through the chronicle again. "Are you going to let me learn some spells?"

"Maybe. You will have to be careful though. When us leechers learn spells, we take in the spiritual power of the spell. Since we were made from the spiritual energy of the planet, you would die if you take too much of it. So, maybe in the future, I will teach you. When you have better control." He softened the verbal blow with a smile. It didn't help.

It wasn't the answer I was looking for, but I suppose he knows best. I went back to my phone now the lesson was over. There had been three missed calls from an unknown number and a voice mail. I punched in the voicemail number and lifted it to my ear. The usual robotic voice came on and explained when the message was left. The beep came then a voice that I had been hoping I would never hear again came out of my phone.

"I have left this message to ask for your forgiveness. When I signed up for this mission, I had no idea what was going to happen. I guess I was naive. I hope you can forgive me for the part I played. This message isn't just to ask for this. I also want you to come back to the apartment. I can tell you this isn't a trap, but I know you won't believe me. All I can hope is that you listen to my plea. I have left you something that should help you. Please come back. I want you to have it. Please. Goodbye."

I couldn't speak. The message was over, but I could still hear Keith's voice in my head. I could hear him apologising, trying to get me to go back to the apartment. The sincerity in his voice made me think he was telling the truth, but then again, he was part of the government. I may have seen too many films, but they could have faked his voice. Either way, I would need to tell these guys about it.

Cassie noticed my confused look as I stared at the phone, "Is everything okay?"

"Um, I don't know."

Logan stopped his conversation with Jewel and asked, "What do you mean?"

I looked at Logan as he carried on cleaning some glasses. "I just had a message from Keith."

"What?" I swear Cassie had almost fallen off her stool at the news. "What did he say?"

Logan had leant on his elbows, "Yeah, what did he have to say for himself?"

"He wants me to go back to the apartment. Apparently, he's left me something there that will help me. He kept saying sorry, and he sounded sincere. Said he didn't know exactly what they were going to do."

"It's a trap." Logan sounded so convinced like there would be no wiggle room in the matter.

"Maybe. I guess it's more curiosity that is making me want to go."

I heard the high heels next to me, "I can go and do a spell. If there's anyone there, it will tell me. You two can sniff out any supernatural creatures, and between the four of us, I think we can handle any trouble. What do you think?"

Logan turned to her, "How come you've become interested all of a sudden?"

"Can't I change my mind?" Logan pulled a face at her "Okay. I went home and looked around my place. I realised the amount of help you've given me. Think it's about time I do the same for someone in need. Starting with the apartment."

"So, you're going to help us delete our tracker files?"

"I've hidden them for now. Forgive me if I don't walk into that place."

"I understand your position on that. Plus, thank you for offering the help you have given us so far."

"Thank you for the help you've given me in the past." They shared a smile. I could see something there between them. It was only something small, but I could sense it like electricity. It wasn't a leecher gift. It was something that came with being female. Jewel was the one who broke the smile first. She looked at me and smiled. "Let's get driving then."

Logan walked from behind the bar, "I'll drive."

Cassie hopped off her stool, "I'll take mine just in case. We can head off to the government building straight after. We might need an extra car."

"Good idea."

We all left out the back door. The windows were still bordered up like before. It looked dead. If the government did come looking for us here, they would certainly believe the building was deserted.

The few seconds it took to walk over to Logan's car I wondered if he would really move after all this. I hoped he wouldn't. I liked having someone around that could help if I had any leecher problems.

I was about to get into the passenger side, but Jewel stopped me. "Hold on a second." She placed her hand on top of Logan's car. She closed her eyes and started speaking in a weird language. She whispered the words like she was talking to an invisible friend.

As she chanted, I noticed the colour of the car changing. The back moved out and the front pulled in. Changing from a classic muscle car to something an old man would drive. "I'm going to change the look of Cassie's car as well. I'll just grab a lift with her. See both of you at the other end."

"Bye." After Logan replied we climbed into his new trick. "Amazing isn't it?"

"Sure is. Is she going to turn it back?"

"I don't know. When I leave, I can just buy another car.

Not a problem." The car was pulled back, and he revved the engine a couple of times. "Luckily it still has the same engine." He slammed the accelerator down, and the car sped out of the car park after a quick wheel spin. I clung to my seat as Logan maneuvered down the road.

I allowed him to concentrate on the road until we were out of the little town. He slowed down once we were on the long road to Ingleford. Here is when I allowed my curiosity to come out, "How did you and Jewel meet?"

He maneuvered a roundabout without lifting his foot off the accelerator and then answered my question, "I bumped into her at a bar in Kendell."

"Kendell?"

"Where she was born. I used to hide out there. The only problem was the number of supernatural creatures. Anyway. She was hustling people out of money. When she ran into trouble, I helped her out. To start off with she wasn't that appreciative. I bumped into her again a few months later."

"Was she in trouble again?"

"No, this time she helped me. This made us even so we went our separate ways. When I opened a bar up, she turned up one night and was hustling people again. When I confronted her about it, we got talking. It was clear she needed help, so I offered her a job. She, of course, said no."

"She said no?"

"At first at least. She came back when she lost her apartment. I let her crash on the sofa at my place. Been mates since then really. She does her own thing now though. Hasn't worked behind one of my bars in a while."

"Where does she work now then?"

"She does a few jobs for her friends now and again."

"Friends?" I wondered what kind of friends a witch would have. I was positive they were also witches, but I wondered what they were like.

"Fellow witches. There's a small group of them, and they

help each other out with various things."

"Have you met any of them?"

"Nope. They refuse to come anywhere near me."

"How come?"

"Because of what I am. You'll find that people will react to you in the same way."

"I guess the government hasn't treated people all that well."

"Every supernatural creature they've come across they either kill or imprison and study. It keeps their leechers informed with what they'll be able to do when they leech. It also means they can create weapons to kill them. Wooden bullets for vampires. Silver ones for werewolves. They even got things like silver knuckledusters and knives. They obviously have their own library of chronicles they have stolen over the years. It's even said that they have a few of the journals. No one has been stupid enough to try and steal them though."

"High security."

"The highest. I can't believe we're going to be doing what we're planning. It's suicide."

"We have to do it though don't we?"

"Yeah, unfortunately. If we want to have a life, then it's a must."

At the mention of a life, my mind went to the werewolf. He was caught because of me. I owed him, and maybe if I set him free, we could talk. "The creatures that they capture. Do you think they would be in the same building I was held?"

"I have no idea. Why do you ask?"

"When I was taken they took a werewolf."

"The one I saw you with that night at the bar?"

"Yeah."

Logan paused before asking, "Does he know what you are?"

"He figured it out, yeah. He wasn't too happy about it."

"What happened?"

"He ran away. It's why he was caught." I started thinking about him. I thought about what he had said about me. "He told me he was attracted to me."

"What about when he found out you're a leecher?"

"We didn't exactly talk."

"So, you didn't see him at the building then?"

"No."

"I'm not a hundred percent sure about this, but my mate is stationed at a facility in Morton. They have a study lab there."

"I was held in Twindlewood."

"Right. Still, I can ask my friend if he knows of any werewolves being brought in anywhere."

"Didn't you used to work for them? Wouldn't you know?"

"That was a while ago. After a while, I started re-visiting facilities and disabling them. I mostly did the small ones, and unfortunately, it didn't do much damage to the government division." Logan seemed to go quiet after that. I didn't want to push him for information. Logan's history still seemed to haunt him, and he was going to help which is good enough for me.

The trees around us suddenly gave way to houses. I remembered them immediately. I recognised the shops that appeared ahead of us. We came to the roundabouts and were driving down the alleyway within minutes. Logan followed Cassie into the small car park then blocked off the alleyway with his vehicle. Making sure no one could follow us in easily if they were watching.

I looked around for any signs of trouble. There were no extra cars apart from Keith's beat up vehicle. There was no one outside the cafe across the road. We all climbed out. Jewel started chanting, and the middle of her palms began to glow orange. She finished speaking, and they slowly turned back to skin colour. She turned to Logan. "There's no one else here."

"Good. Let's go." We walked from the cars to the stairs. They creaked with every touch of our feet. With all four of us on it, I was more certain it was going to break and crumble under our weight.

We got to the top safely. I went to unlock the doors protecting the apartment, but I didn't need to. The outside one had been left ajar. I froze waiting to try and hear a sound from inside. The four of us all looked at each other. I noticed Logan breathe in through his nose. He must be leeching off of Cassie. I did the same allowing my body to change into a vampire's.

As soon as the change happened, I started heating up. I looked up at the sun, feeling the heat on my face. My eyes dropped to Cassie. She must be feeling the same way, but she wasn't showing it. Maybe she had long enough to get used to the burning feeling. I quickly checked my phone. It was just before eleven. An hour and the three of us will be bursting into flames. That was a disturbing thought.

Logan seemed to see my worried look at the sun. He moved towards the door and opened both of them. The apartment was dark. We stepped inside and out of the sunlight. I felt better as the shadows welcomed me like I was an old friend. Cassie closed the second door behind us bringing the apartment into total silence. I heard Jewel chanting behind me. It lasted a few seconds and then the silence came back. "There's nobody here."

I was confused, "What about Keith?"

"He's here." Logan lifted his arm and pointed. I looked in the direction, but the darkness made everything invisible. I couldn't even see the kitchen ahead of us. "Blink a couple of times and think about seeing the heat in the room."

"Huh?"

"Trust me." I had no idea what he was talking about, but I had learned not to question his advice. When I blinked, nothing happened the first time. The second time all I saw was darkness. I blinked twice, quickly and thought about the heat in the room. When my eyelids lifted, I saw the apartment differently.

It was no longer dark. It was filled with bright colours. There were yellows, oranges, and reds. I still couldn't make out the kitchen counters, but there was something bright orange hovering ahead of us. It was completely still.

The four of us ventured deeper into the apartment. I looked around just making sure no one was here. I wasn't going to let my guard down even if Jewel had used her spell. There were no flares of colour. Most of the space around me was made up of shades of grey. I listened intently, waiting to hear a scrape of someone's foot or the beat of someone's heart. There were only our feet and Jewel's heart beating. It was soft and steady. She wasn't nervous one bit. If I could have heard my own, it could have been a different story.

Moving towards the orange blob of heat I heard Cassie's feet moving away from us. Then suddenly the whole place was filled with bright yellow, burning my eyes. They instinctively blinked twice bringing my normal sight back.

Cassie was standing over in the corner. She had found a switch that operated the windows. Light was now flooding into the room. The shape we had spotted had been what I was dreading. Keith was swinging there with a rope wrapped around his neck. His face was a horrible shade of blue. On the floor was one of the chairs from the table.

I looked around. The rest of the chairs were kicked over, and the living area was a mess. Cupboard doors were left open. Put that with the open doors, and it would seem someone had broken in looking for something. I saw Logan reach up and touch Keith's hand, "He's warm. This didn't happen too long ago." He looked around at what I had already spotted. "Someone was looking for something, clearly."

"Then they took whatever Keith left me."

"We need to get out of here just in case they're coming back."

"I just want to grab some of my stuff."

"Hurry." I turned my back on the hanging body and moved down the hallway. My door was open, hanging crooked on the top hinge. The drawers ahead of me were slightly pulled out, and the wardrobe doors had been chucked onto my bed. They weren't very careful when they were looking.

I looked at the shelves to my left. What I was looking for wasn't there. Looking around I found it on the carpet. I bent down and picked the ring up. I thought about slipping it on my finger, but instead, I put it in my pocket.

Grabbing my bag from the wardrobe, I filled it up with anything that was in one piece. Then I unloaded the drawers, placing my socks and delicates with my clothes. I went to slide the bottom one back in, but it stopped a few inches from closing. I tried it again, but it wouldn't budge past that point.

I slid it out the whole way and felt underneath. As I slid my hand to the right, I felt something slim. I yanked on it and heard the tape come loose. As I pulled it out, I saw my name scribbled on the envelope.

There was no time to open it now, so I dropped it into the bag with my clothes. Once I had everything I went to leave the room. On my way out I caught a glimpse of the photo of me on my family holiday. They must have gotten it somehow because it was a real photo. Was there no limits to their resources.

On my way out I knocked the picture to the floor in anger. Clearing my head before I moved into the kitchen. The three of them were waiting for me. I wiggled the bag in my hand, "I'm ready."

Logan clapped his hands together, "Okay, let's go." He turned to Jewel. "Are you coming with us?"

"I might as well tag along. Got nothing else to do, have I? But I won't be entering the building." She smiled at Logan.

"Okay then. Let's get going. Beth, you're riding with me. Try and keep up Cassie." He laughed at her. She stuck out her tongue in return. "Beth, do you need help with the bag."

"No, I got it." I walked past him to the door making sure I didn't look at Keith's body again. He may have been lying to me, but he was pushed into the position. What happened wasn't his fault. I let go of the vampire inside of me and walked out into the sun. As Logan and Jewel joined me, I looked down at the time on my phone. It was just after noon.

I looked back at Cassie as she appeared in the doorway. I lifted my wrist up and showed her the watch. She just shrugged and said, "I'll be fine. Right Jewel?" I turned to Jewel who was nodding her head. The next second Cassie walked past me and out into the sunlight with a massive smile. Nothing happened. No smoke or flames. She just walked down the stairs and got into her car. Jewel followed her leaving Logan and me at the top of the steps.

He just smiled at me and took his own trip to the car. I followed him down onto the tarmac. Logan opened the boot, and after pulling out the envelope, I placed the bag inside and went to the passenger's side. Climbing in, I placed the envelope on my lap as I did my seat belt. Once we were ready to go, I explained. "Keith left me it."

"I gathered that. What's inside?"

"I don't know yet." I turned the object over as Logan turned the ignition. The engine noises were joined by the ripping of paper. I got one side open and looked inside. There were a few pages folded up. There was a thin slip of paper and a gold key.

I pulled the key out first. There was a small tag attached to an address, 114 Mason Street, Twindlewood. I looked across at Logan and held the tag so he could read it, "Where's that?"

Logan thought about it for a few seconds, "Twindlewood."

"Really, I hadn't read that part."

He gave me a smile. "We can head there after the facility."

"But Keith said in his message he left me something. This must be it."

"What about the rest of the envelope?" I looked down at the contents. Maybe I should keep looking. I slipped the key into my trouser pocket, and I pulled out the wedge of paper. The top slip was a cheque made out in my name. It was worth nine thousand, three hundred pounds. Did Keith leave all his savings to me? Why would he do that?

I folded the cheque in half and slipped that into one of my back pockets. The next piece was a deed to an apartment with the same address on the key. Keith had already signed his signature at the bottom. All it would need was mine, and I would own the property. It seemed too easy and too good to be true.

The second page had a list of names and numbers next to them with no other information. Then there was only one thing left to look at. It was a note. I unfolded it and started reading as Logan's car zoomed towards our next destination.

Dear Beth,

First things first. I just want to say sorry for the part I played in this whole thing. I know I said it plenty of times in the message I left on your phone, but I want to make sure you know I really mean it. Next, I hope the contents of the envelope makes up for what I did. The cheque can be cashed anywhere. The list is of account numbers and the names associated with each account. This will filter the money so the government won't be able to track it. This will make it safe for you to spend.

The deed I have put inside the envelope is for you to sign. I have an apartment in Twindlewood. It isn't in any file anywhere. No one knows I have it and you will be safe there. Sign the deeds, and it's yours. The key inside is the only key for the locks. You will be the only person who has one. Inside you will find a hidden room in the bedroom. Inside I managed to store away some weapons and some specific items. Along with some blueprints and a map of the building they were holding you in.

Also, out the window, you will be able to see the headquarters. I hope it will help you get a fresh start from all this. I wish I could do more to help. Again, I'm sorry. If I could go back, I would choose a different path.

Yours sincerely Keith

Many things were going through my head, but I couldn't put them in order. They were all muddled up and didn't make sense. I couldn't think of anything else at the same time as not being able to make sense of it. He left me loads of money and an apartment. I was going to own an apartment. Was it just to help us attack the building or was it forever? Would I be able to keep it?

The only thing I could say for sure is that Keith was sincere when he said sorry. Why else would he do all this for me? The word trap didn't even enter my mind. I couldn't say for sure why not but it didn't.

I looked to my right because I could feel Logan's stare every now and again. We looked at each other for a few seconds. I didn't know what to say. No words were forming in my head. Logan spoke after checking he was on our side of the road still, "So what was in the envelope?"

"A few things." I looked through them again as I spoke, "The key obviously. There's a cheque for me. Papers for the deed to an apartment in Twindlewood. A list of accounts and names for the money to be filtered through and a note from Keith."

"What did it say?"

"Just that he was sorry and he's left me the money and an apartment to say this. He also explained that the apartment is opposite the building the leecher headquarters in Twindlewood. He says there are plans of the building inside the apartment. He says he's tried to help as much as he could."

"He's given us that kind of information? Would have been good to get some more information out of him whilst he was alive. Could have found other buildings housing the headquarters of different units." There was a short pause of silence in the car. "Is that everything?" I nodded. "Since this facility is likely the headquarters he is on about they'll no doubt have the files on our trackers. What's the address for the apartment again?"

"It's at 114 Mason Street in Twindlewood."

"I'll get a route up on my phone. I'm not too sure where that is from here." He pulled out his phone and started playing with it. It wasn't long until he had some maps up and the route from our position to the apartment. We would arrive there in about an hour. It would be a long journey with my mind all crazy. "I'll send a message to Jewel to tell them our change in direction." I nodded not really thinking about what he was saying. I needed to talk about anything, but nothing came to mind.

Suddenly I was saved when Logan asked me a question, "What was it like to morph into an eagle?"

I was a little shocked at this sudden change in topic, "It was weird. It's different from changing into a werewolf. The feathers feel weird coming out of your skin."

"I bet. I've never come across an eagle shifter."

"What shifters have you come across?"

He started listing off the ones he had met, "I've come across all the common ones. Bear shifters, puma shifters. The rarer ones like shark shifters and monkey shifters I've only seen a few times. There are some like the eagle shifters that I've only heard about. I wasn't too sure if they existed or not."

"Like?" I was giving little input because I wanted to listen to his voice. It helped my head.

"They go from one extreme to the other. I've heard about polar bear shifters and horse shifters. Of course, there are so many supernatural creatures there are no doubt some animal shifters that no one has ever met. The world is extremely big with lots of places for them to hide."

"True." I thought about anything that would fill the time up with conversation. "Can you tell me about werewolves?"

"Anything in specific?"

"Like you did with the vampires. Just things I should know if I leech off of one."

"Of course. I'm here to help you."

I wondered who I would ask if Logan did leave. "Cheers. Can you try and think of everything though? I had to fight against a vampire during my so-called training, and he disappeared into the fog."

"Oh yeah. Sorry, sometimes my brain can't think of everything at once. If I do forget anything though I'm sure your werewolf friend will fill you in."

"That's if he wants to talk to me again."

"If you break him out of that place I'm sure he'll manage some words of gratitude." That was the problem though. I didn't want just words. I wanted everything he could give me. I wanted his hands and his body totally at my submission. My mind drifted off into my thoughts as Logan started speaking. It was important I listen so I pushed my werewolf to the back of my brain, for now.

I locked him there, out of sight but definitely not out of mind. "First thing you should take notice of is the moon." I turned to face him to give him my full attention. "If it's nearing a full moon, the less control you will have over your other form. Also, the more you will resemble a wolf."

"How do you mean?"

"Well, you remember what I looked like that day I found you in the woods." I nodded. "That was after a full moon. Now if I would change today, then I would look a little different."

"That's why I felt different." It was his turn to be confused, "I turned into a werewolf during training. I felt different."

"Yes, that's probably why. It would have only been a small change. If you change a few days on either side of a full moon, then you would be a pretty large wolf."

"How large?"

"Not much bigger than a normal wolf. Maybe a few inches higher but your claws and your teeth will be sharper and a lot bigger. You will also look fiercer. And it will be almost impossible to control that fierceness."

"Okay then." I locked the information away in my brain. "What happens if I change on a full moon?"

"You wouldn't have a choice about it. All werewolves change on a full moon whether they want to or not. If you leech off of a werewolf during this time, then you won't have a choice either. As soon as midnight hits they go through the change. The duration they stay in that form depends on how old they are as a werewolf. The older they are, the shorter the time. However, age has no difference to the lack of control."

"No control?"

"It's like the shifting. The more wolf-like you are, the less control the human part of you has. The animal side starts taking over your brain, stealing the control from you."

"Does it feel like something is trying to get into your head?"

"Exactly."

"I was able to feel it slightly. Like someone else was in my brain."

"Unfortunately, there is a spell out there that as far as I know, no one has been able to find. It will make a full moon appear on any night. They can unleash the werewolves' true forms any night of the month."

"That sounds so dangerous. Who would want to do that?"

"Anyone wanting to create chaos. The government for one."

"They want that spell? How would they use it though?"

"They have plenty of witches under their control. Some are volunteers whereas some are blackmailed and made to help. It's a dangerous world out there."

"No kidding. I wonder if I'll ever be able to have a normal life?" Logan locked eyes with me, and I saw that same feeling in his. "So, do I. Wish I was never born this way. We don't have a choice on what we are though. We do have a choice how we use our gifts. We can use them for good and help people like us and Cassie and Jewel."

"Sounds as good as it could be. I don't know where I would be if you three hadn't helped me."

"Let's call it even after this." We sealed the deal with a handshake. He smiled at me and continued with his lesson on werewolves. "Getting back on track. Even without changing into your animal form, you will still have werewolf abilities. For instance, you can have wolf claws to help you fight. They come in handy if you don't want to change completely. You will also have werewolf speed and strength. Werewolves can give a good fight against a vampire even if they have been training. A werewolf's only weakness is silver. If you get silver in your heart or your brain, then you're dead."

Logan paused as he maneuvered around a few slow drivers. "If you get it in your bloodstream then it will hurt like hell and work its way to your heart. The only way to get it out of your system is to morph into your wolf form. This will also quicken up the healing process of any injuries you've endured. Just remember the moon. Even during the day, it can affect your mind in that form."

I thought about the interaction I had with my werewolf, "What happens if two werewolves meet?"

"Do you mean your auras?"

"What's one of those?"

"I'm sure that's what you're talking about. Werewolves have heightened auras. Like pheromones that other were-wolves pick up. This means if two werewolves are attracted to each other they have to fight hard not to show it right then and there. Doesn't matter where you are. It even works on other creatures, especially humans."

"Is there a way of controlling it?"

"Yes, but it will take training just like everything else. You just have to switch that part of you off. A mental cold shower if you will." I laughed at his reference. "It gets easier obviously but if a werewolf has its on high then clearly it's even harder to ignore it."

"Could I use it to my advantage?"

"Sometimes in the right situation, it can be just as effective as a vampire's glamour technique. If you need to get past a male security guard, you can drench him in your aura. Then you just knock him out when he's trying to get in your knickers."

"Right."

"I think that's everything you need to know about werewolves. At least it's the important things."

"I'm sure if there's anything else you'll let me know. Thanks."

"No worries."

We moved into Twindlewood, slowing as the traffic thickened. "Can you tell me about witches?"

His face suddenly got serious, "What do you mean?"

"The same thing you just told me, just about witches."

"I can only give you one piece of advice, and that's not to leech off of one. Especially at this early stage in your training."

"Why not?"

"You're not ready yet."

"Okay." Not ready yet? I only wanted to know about them. It's not like I was going to go off and leech off of

Jewel when we arrived. All I wanted was information. Wasn't I ready enough for that? What would happen if I came across one and needed to defend myself? I had a feeling a witch could easily kill a simple human. Judging from his still serious face, I shouldn't push for it right now.

With the new atmosphere in the car, I stayed silent. We travelled the rest of the way without speaking another word. It went all the way until his phone came up with a notice saying we had arrived at our destination. We turned into a multistory car park that was the bottom three floors of a building. We circled around to the top floor and found a spot between a van and an old truck. The car fitted in nicely with its surroundings. Blending in with the old vehicles like it belonged.

We got out and saw Cassie parking in a space a few metres up from us. The four of us rode the elevator up into the apartment portion of the building. The doors parted, and we walked out into a small, circular room. In front of us was a door labeled, STAFF ONLY. We walked out of the circle and down a shiny hallway.

We came out into an even larger room. The floor stretched out into a massive circle. From the left, I could hear laughter and chatter from the restaurant attached to the side. Cars whizzed by the front entrance on street level.

The area in the middle of the circle was dominated by a beautiful fountain. Standing in the middle was a small group of kids pouring water out of jugs and watering cans. The sound it made was soft and gave the whole room a nice touch of serenity. It was surrounded by black leather sofas.

Over to the right of us was a desk. A single person was standing behind it wearing a black suit. He smiled at us as we looked over at him. Just to the left of the desk was a staircase that ran around the walls, spiraling up. The ceiling was hard to see it was that far away. A large chandelier was hanging from the middle sending light beams all over the walls. Jewel spoke, "So what are we doing here? This doesn't look like the kind of building that the government would hide in."

I looked at Logan who turned towards me, "I didn't tell her the details. Beth was left money and the deed to an apartment here. A note that was also left said it would hold information that will help us."

Jewel understood, "Sounds good. Any help will be good."

"Apparently it will help us a lot." I wanted her to know this. Hopefully, with this extra help, we can delete our files and get my werewolf out of that place. I really did hope he would forget what I am and just like me. He said he was attracted to me before he knew so I can't see why he couldn't. Has the government really made that much of a bad name for us?

"I'm going to just ask the guy at reception." No one seemed to disagree with my idea. I walked across the floor looking at my reflection in its shiny surface.

I was greeted with a very polite hello. "How may I help you, miss?"

"I was just wondering what floor this apartment is on." I handed over the key, but he didn't take it from me.

"Ah, old school. That would definitely be for the seventh floor. You can either use the elevator or the stairs."

"I think I'll use the elevator."

"Everyone does. The stairs are more for decoration than anything else." I smiled at him and walked away from his desk. I looked up at the stairs running up against the wall as I walked. They were a weird form of decoration.

I got to the other three who had been watching. "The apartment is on the seventh floor."

Logan seemed impressed, "That was simple." I pulled a big smile, and we walked over to the elevators. The button was pushed, and the box arrived quickly. We all climbed inside and made our way up to the seventh floor.

By the time we arrived, I was starting to get sick of the little jingle being fed into the box. Why did places like this insist on putting that kind of music in a small tiny box? It just wasn't right. At least feed in a radio station or something more tolerable.

The doors opened, and I expected to see a hallway. Instead, we stepped out into a tiny room with the one door. I unlocked the door, and we all moved into the apartment.

The flooring was made up of black and white squares. They led straight across the apartment to a wall made up of windows. We all walked around, gobsmacked at the vastness of it all. I looked over to the left. Attached to the wall near the door was an extremely large television. It was bigger than the one in Keith's fake apartment. Sitting in front of it was a square of white sofas. They looked like they were made more for style instead of comfort.

I walked to my right, moving around the curve of the building. A kitchen lined the left wall. It had a cooker with a vent above it, a microwave and a toaster all in view. Cupboards lined the bottom and the top of the wall. They had shiny black fronts, matching the flooring and the appliances.

There was a door further around on the wall. No doubt a bedroom or a bathroom. I followed the other three as we moved further around the place. The wall opposite us was another one made up of windows. The view out of this one was better than the last.

At the edge of the city, there was a large green area. It looked like a picnic site, but it was massive. Beyond that, there was a large river that came into view from the right and disappeared behind the wall on the left. The rest of the view was made up of fields which were both green and brown.

Around this side of the apartment was a glass dining table. Six seats sat around it with black upholstery. These unlike the sofas on the other side looked nice and soft. Hanging from the ceiling right above the table was a tiny light fitting. It was only made up of one bulb, but since it was the only one along this side, I bet it was bright enough to light the whole area.

Moving along the curve of the apartment I found another door. Moving through it I found a large bedroom. Sitting over to the left was a massive bed. It looked so comfortable that it made me feel sleepy.

Walking along I let my fingers drag across the mirror doors of the built-in wardrobe. It slid across smoothly revealing the suits hiding behind them. My eyes followed the thread down to the floor where I spotted a big black bag.

Sitting on top of it was a thick envelope with my name scrawled across it in black ink. Figuring it was our help I took it from the bedroom and back into the bigger section of the apartment. They all looked over to me as I plopped it down onto the glass table.

"This must be the help he mentioned in his letter." As Logan unzipped the bag, I took a step back and ripped open the envelope. Inside was a simple piece of paper. Pulling it out I saw the drawn map of a building level. A line went from a box labelled elevator and went to another which seemed to be some kind of cell.

Across the bottom was a short note written for me. Telling me that if I wanted to get my werewolf friend out of there, this would show me the way. I thought about telling Logan about it but instead just folded it up and slipped it into my back pocket. My fingertips brushed across the deed sitting in my back pocket.

As I did this, I felt the things I had already put in there. I pulled the deed out of my pocket seeing the line I needed to sign. There wasn't anything for me to do right now, so it's as good a time as any.

I managed to find a pen sitting in a little pen pot on the kitchen counter. The pen was put to paper, and I signed at the bottom. As soon as the last point of my signature was done a sudden shriek sent the pen flying out of my hand as I jumped around. Cassie was kneeling on the floor with her hands clutching her head. I ran over to her just as Logan was kneeling down beside her. No one could get close to her without risking one of her hands swinging for them like we would hurt her further. Logan looked up at me, so I asked, "What's going on?"

"I don't know. What were you doing over there?"

"All I did was sign the deed for the apartment."

"Quick, invite her in."

"She's already in."

"Just do it!" The tone of his voice had me obeying his command. I had to yell just so Cassie would hear me over her screaming. "Cassie, I officially invite you into my apartment." As the last word left my lips, the apartment was thrown into silence. Cassie was still cradling her head in her hands, but at least she had stopped screaming. I knelt there still not knowing what the hell was going on. I looked at Logan who seemed to be waiting for Cassie to say something. Jewel was standing by the table. She didn't seem too bothered by what had just happened.

After what seemed like forever, Cassie finally lifted her head up. She looked first at Logan than at me. A smile slowly appeared on her face. "Thanks for inviting me in." She placed a hand on the table and pushed herself upright. She gave me another smile, then sat down on one of the seats. Her head was placed back into her hands. I was still confused, and I wanted answers. "What just happened?" I was directing my question at anyone. An answer from either one of my new friends would do.

Logan spoke first, "Vampires aren't allowed to enter someone's house without being invited in first."

"Then how was she able to enter the one I was staying at before. Plus, my parent's house, she was there too."

"She can enter them if the owner is dead. Your parents were dead, and the guy pretending to be Keith was dead when we arrived. This apartment was also owned by Keith. As soon as you signed the deed, it became yours. You're not dead, and you hadn't invited Cassie inside. That's what was happening."

Cassie's weak voice came from behind her hands, "I've never had it like that before."

"That's because usually the place you're trying to enter is already owned. You would usually get a pain when you try to walk through the door. Since you were already inside the apartment when it switched hands, the pain was far more aggressive, and you couldn't escape it as easily." Logan place a hand on hers. "Your fine now though. It doesn't leave any permanent damage." Logan smiled at her and then went back to his piece of paper when Cassie smiled back.

I moved around to stand beside her, kneeling back down to get her face in my vision. "Are you okay?" She nodded her head. "Are you sure?"

This time she lifted it up from her hands, "I'm fine. Just have a little headache that's all. It'll pass with time." She pulled another smile and then put her head back into her palms. I moved away, letting her have her own space to recover. Moving away from the table I watched the three of them. Two of them at work and the third recovering. So far this trip isn't what I thought it would be.

I spun on my heel and stared out of the large window. As my eyes moved over the fields, I remembered something in Keith's note about the view of the building. I quickly moved to the other side of the building. The whole landscape was covered with buildings. Some shorter and the others towering over this one.

My sight focused on one of the tallest ones. It had blacked out windows. There was one, in particular, I was concentrating on. It had a smashed hole in the middle. Workmen and their tools stood in the office space. It couldn't be a coincidence. That had to be the building Helen and I had leapt through.

I didn't know how long I had been staring at the building,

but I jumped when Cassie's hand landed on my shoulder. My head whipped around to face her. Right then I only noticed that I couldn't smell the ash scent. A small part of me worried I had lost my ability suddenly for no reason. But I slowly sniffed and thought about her essence. It came quickly, teasing my nose with its scent. I guessed my abilities were just becoming easier to control. Leaving it to mix in with the other normal scents that were around me I asked, "You feeling better now?"

"Much. We're ready if you are."

"Cool. There's the building." I pointed out the window. Cassie saw the hole in the side. "How come you've come this far?"

She seemed shocked by my sudden question. "What do you mean?"

"How come you're so willing to help. I'm sorry, but I don't think anyone is that nice."

"I suppose I have an ulterior motive."

"What is it?"

"How come you're so interested?" She smiled at me.

"Just being curious I suppose." I gave her a smile back.

"Fair enough. Can we step away from the window for a little bit? Been in the sun quite a bit today."

"Yeah, sorry." We continued our conversation as we moved into the kitchen. "So what's your reason?"

"The government leechers attacked my family to get to me."

"What do you mean?"

"Maybe I should start at the beginning. Obviously, I haven't always been a vampire. I had a normal life. Going to school and all that. Had a lovely boyfriend. Going out with mates. Then it all changed when I was turned. She wasn't a bad vampire. She wasn't the kind of vampire that would go around killing people whenever she wanted. She may have fed on them now and again but not maliciously."

I leant against the counter ready to hear her story. "Why did she turn you then?"

"She found me. I had been arguing with some guy after a night out. He wouldn't take no for an answer, and I didn't want to say yes. When I left to walk home, he followed me and dragged me into an alleyway. He tried it on, and we soon got into a fight. He beat me within an inch of my life. If Janus hadn't found me, I would be dead. I begged her to help, and she did. It wasn't what I expected, but she still saved my life."

I was hooked, "What happened next?"

"Well, it took me a while to get used to it. I had Janus helping me though. It was easier with her by my side. I tried to fit back into my original life, but my family became afraid of me."

"Why?"

"Because I told them what I was. They didn't even hear me out. Just told me to get out of the house. They thought they knew all about vampires thanks to the movie business. Thinking I would kill them if they got a paper cut. But who could blame them? If they had heard about some of the things I have done, they would have every right to be afraid of me."

"I thought you had Janus by your side. I thought she wasn't like that?"

"She wasn't, but the government took her. They chained her up and studied her. Then she was killed. Like I said, they took my family away from me. Janus was my only family by the end of it. After that, I lost my way until Logan found me. It took me a while to trust him, but he has a way of making you feel safe around him." She paused, taking a couple deep breaths. "I guess that's why I'm doing this."

"Sounds like a good reason to me." She smiled. "Thank you for your help."

I heard footsteps approaching from behind us, "We're

ready to go Beth."

I gave Logan a firm nod. "Did Keith give us everything we needed?"

"He did. We got a blueprint of the server level. Map to the security room and instructions on how to disable the alarms and other security measures they have in place. Also, he has written down how to delete our files. So we are all set."

Logan sounded like he thought this would be easy but something in my gut was knotting up. Nothing was going simply anymore since my life had changed. I didn't think this would be any different. "I'm ready to go. That's the building." I pointed over to the window.

He nodded, "Can you hold this?" He held out his hand. I took the card from his palm. It was completely blank, the black plastic shining from the light. "It will get us into the server room. It acts as a master key."

"Cool." I slipped it into my pocket.

Logan then handed a key to Cassie, "This is the key to the security room. When you're in there try and find the security feed and find out where it's recording. Destroy them, so they don't get our faces if we take too long." She nodded after taking the key off of him. "Okay, time to go." He turned around and walked over to the entrance. The three of us joined him as he walked out into the elevator.

I tried my hardest to get the jingle out of my head, but it wasn't working. It was still going round and round when we were standing on the side of the street. The lights went red, and the little green man appeared. The large group of people, including us, walked across the tarmac.

We arrived on the other path and slipped over to the side of the entrance. Finding a hidden section amongst some decorative pillars. Jewel pulled the little vials out of her jacket pockets. She passed them out to us.

I pulled the bung out and stared down at the clear liquid. Before I could question the taste, both Logan and Cassie downed there's without hesitation. My confidence in the liquid didn't spike when they both showed disgusted faces. Cassie looked at me and smiled, "It's really not that bad." For some reason, I wasn't trusting her statement.

It didn't matter though, I had to do this. I tipped the bottle up and felt the cold liquid trickle down my throat. Hitting my stomach, it sent a chill throughout my whole body. The taste was horrible. It was as strong as having a shot of absinthe mixed with motor oil. The aftertaste hit my stomach almost making the potion come back up my throat.

Swallowing that gagging urge down it made the aftertaste even worse. I looked up after trying to cough away the taste in my mouth. I looked over to who I thought was Logan. Only I no longer saw that man. Instead, he looked older, just like the man in the photo from before.

I turned to my left where Cassie had been standing. She no longer had her blonde hair, and it was even longer than before. She looked at me with the same eyes that stared up from one of the other photos. The potion sure does work quickly.

I put my hand up to my hair. It was no longer hanging down past my shoulders. It was short and spiky at the back. I could feel the fringe hanging down to the right. Looking down at my body I saw the change in attire. I now wore a grey skirt with a grey jacket. The potion not only changed my appearance but also the clothes I was wearing.

I looked up again and noticed the change in the other two. They were wearing suits themselves now. Magick really was amazing. Jewel was standing there, the only one that looked like herself. She just smiled at us. She leant forwards then flicked her hair back into a massive arch. When I looked at her, she no longer had those cute features.

Her mouth and her nose were bigger. Each feature had been changed only slightly, and yet it made her look completely different. She then ran her hands down her ponytail.

As her skin rubbed over the strands, it changed from blonde to black all the way down to the tips. I was gobsmacked for the second time today. "You can change your hair colour without worrying about your roots."

Giving me a wink she then wiggled her body, letting her clothes flow around her. I carried on staring with a gaping mouth as they differed. They changed from her original clothes to a nice suit. Her trousers wrapped around her hips tightly but flowed down to become baggy by her feet. The jacket cut in, emphasizing her hourglass figure. She looked good, and I found myself thinking how cool magick was again. She smiled at us, "Ready to go?"

"You're coming with us?"

"Might as well. I'm here aren't I."

Logan nodded, "Okay then. Let's get going before we all change our minds." He looked around at everyone. He took in our new looks and our new clothes.

A problem suddenly popped into my mind, "What about the leechers inside? Won't they smell Cassie and Jewel?"

"Don't worry about that. Have you noticed that you don't smell the ash or the smoke as much anymore?" I sniffed the air, I could barely find a trace of them around me. "It gets like that. Once you are in control of your ability your body automatically keeps the scents out of your nose. You would have to be looking for them to notice them now. We can walk straight past a leecher, and they wouldn't notice in a place like this. They will feel safe with no need to be on guard. So don't worry about it." He smiled at me. "Let's go."

The four of us walked out of our corner and entered the building with the rest of the traffic. We fit right in just like we belonged. I looked around at my surroundings once we got through the entrance. We were walking through a wide corridor. Paintings lined the walls on either side of us. I didn't bother to take too much detail in.

We came to where the hallway bent into a corner, moving

over, so we didn't get bumped into. I looked further down the corridor. The hallway kept going all the way to the other end of the building. On the left, halfway down, was a large reception desk. A woman sat behind it wearing a very white shirt which was clinging to her body like a second skin. She was busy tapping away on her computer.

On either side of her desk were sets of stairs. They moved up then across, meeting in the middle. The rest of the stairs moved up to an elevator high above her. It had the usual steel doors that I was seeing on all elevators lately.

Logan moved ahead and then started walking up the stairs. He was suddenly stopped by the receptionist. "Excuse me, sweetie. You need to sign in." That was going to be for all four of us.

Taking our turns, we all wrote a name down. Doubting she would even check I just wrote down the first one that popped into my head. She wasn't likely going to check them since she had already gone back to tapping away on her computer.

As we followed Logan up the stairs, he pressed the little circular button on the wall. Whilst waiting for the elevator to arrive I turned around and looked at the people walking past the desk. I wondered where they were going and what they would do once there. There were so many things they could be up to in this building.

A soft ping came from the doors behind me. The four of us slipped through people coming off. I was happy to hear no silly music being fed into the metal box. Logan pushed the button for the twelfth floor. The elevator doors shut, and it started rising up the shaft.

It didn't take long for the elevator to stop at the right level. Moving out onto the soft carpet. I looked to our left then over to the right. The left corridor was short, ending in an office door. To the right, it carried on going, and that's the way we needed to go.

With Logan leading us we passed little offices. Now and again I saw someone working behind a desk. They didn't look up from their work, didn't pay us any attention.

I followed the other three through the lefts and the rights. It wasn't long until we came to the first stop. The door to our right had a black sign on the wood. It sat just below the frosted glass saying, SECURITY ROOM. "Remember Cassie, no killing anyone."

"I remember, don't worry. I'm not a killing machine."

"I know. That's not what I meant."

"I know you didn't." When she grinned, I was able to see her personality shining through her disguise.

Jewel knew we didn't have time for this, "Guys, we can sort this out later on. We have to be quick, remember. Get the key out Cassie." She did so and slowly turned it in the lock. Once the soft click came, she and Jewel slipped inside quickly.

"Time for us to find our own room." Logan and I walked off as I heard two grunts followed by soft thuds.

It was a longer journey for us, but we managed to get there with no problems. We looked around before trying the door. The doorknob rattled, but it was locked. I pressed my face against the glass. It was frosted just like the last one making it impossible to see anything. I didn't know what I was trying to do.

When I moved back, Logan was leaning against the wall with a slight smirk on his face. "What?" He didn't say anything. All he did was nod towards the wall to my right. I looked down at the metal contraption. It had two slits, one at the top and one at the bottom. A little blue arrow glowed above the highest one.

I turned back to Logan. "The key card you gave me?" He nodded, keeping that smirk on his face. Giving him a glare I used our gadget on the contraption. It shot out the bottom as a green light blinked twice. Logan moved in and held the door open for me. He gave me a nice smile as I entered past him.

With the door shut behind us, we stood and stared at all the blinking lights around the room. Both sides of the room were lined with glass cabinets. There were twelve of them with god knows how many servers inside them. At the end was a lonely computer sitting on a desk. A single light bulb shone light onto it. Sitting against the wall to the side of this desk was a large box. It looked like an old-fashioned fuse box only much bigger.

Logan sat down on the computer chair. When he turned on the monitor, it helped to light up the room. Logan laid out a piece of paper in front of him. I peered over his shoulder at the list of instructions Keith must have left us. Waiting behind him as he scanned through the list twice before tapping away at the keyboard.

My eyes watched the screen as he worked but it wasn't too long until I lost interest. I ended up looking around the room. The blinking lights were almost hypnotic as they blinked at me in green and red. My feet took me back to the room, peering through the glass at the servers.

By the time I made my way back to Logan, he was just finishing up. He tapped a few buttons then switched off the monitor. He had a big smile showing when he stood up, happy with what he had done. "It's all finished. The trackers are deactivated, and the files have been deleted. Now it's time to get out of here whilst the potions are still working."

"Go? Things are going well aren't they?"

He seemed to know exactly where I was going with this, "Yes I suppose we are doing very well."

"We still have quite a bit of time left, and no one knows we're here. Cassie is even getting the tapes. It's the perfect time."

He sighed, "We'll see what's what when we get back to the elevator. Okay?"

"I can live with that." Could I? I didn't believe my own words and Logan's look meant he didn't either. It didn't matter to me though. I wanted to break the werewolf out, and my mind was set on that. I have the plans, a disguise and I'm already in the building. It was now or never, and I wanted it to happen.

I didn't care if all I got from the werewolf was a look before he ran away and out of my life. One of his looks could melt my heart in seconds. That's one thing I could live with. Him melting my heart.

"Beth. Snap out of your little fantasy." He laughed at me.

"I wasn't fantasising."

"I'm sure." He pulled a cheeky smile. It wasn't Logan looking at me, but that was his smile. "Let's go get the others and get back to the elevator."

"Alright." We walked out of the room. I checked both ways, and we both started walking towards the security room. "I wasn't fantasising." Logan didn't even bother with a reply. I could see his smile out of the corner of my eye.

When we arrived at the door to the security room, Logan knocked. The door was slowly opened, and I saw half of Jewel's changed face come into view. Once she realised it was us she opened it all the way. Cassie was in the back of the room sorting out the two guards she had knocked out. By the looks of it, she was making it looked like they just fell out of their chairs. I don't know if they would believe it, but it was worth a shot. Once she was done, she walked over to join us. Logan got straight down to business and asked, "Did you get the tapes?"

Cassie replied with a nod, "It's all just recorded, so I deleted it from the hard drive. If they have a back-up somewhere, then we're screwed."

"It's alright. It was just a precaution wasn't it, just in case we ran out of time. You two ready to get back to the elevator?"

Jewel looked behind her at Cassie before answering for the both of them, "Yeah, we're ready."

"Good, oh thanks for sorting out the security box for the alarms."

"Piece of cake." My eyes went to the box on the wall. Two wires had been cut and linked together via a black box.

Cassie finally joined us at the door after placing two hats by the heads lying on the floor. The four of us back together, we started heading for our exit. The whole way all I could think about was getting my werewolf out of here. We were almost back to the steel doors when we had an unexpected guest blocking our freedom. It wasn't a guard or even one of the office workers. When I sniffed the air, he didn't smell of anything in particular. No special scents. He was human, and he didn't look like he belonged.

He was wearing black leather trousers with a black vest. His black jacket gave him an evil look, but his soft face didn't. His hair was slicked back with grease. A thick gold chain hung around his neck. When he spoke, I could feel his sleazy voice rubbing over my skin like oil. "So we meet again, Jewel." He grinned like he was looking at a date he was taking out.

Jewel sounded surprised, "How did you know it was me?"

"I've been watching you since you arrived at the building across the street."

Logan butted in, "I'm sorry, who are you?"

"Why don't I allow Jewel fill you in on that." He locked his eyes on Jewel. "Jewel?"

She let out a big breath. "He's Michael Grey. He works for a guy called The Saracen."

"The Saracen?" That name didn't sound like one a mother would give her child.

It was Logan who filled me in instead of Jewel, "The Saracen is the man Jewel owes money to. He's a big crime boss."

The human carried on talking, "That he is. He's sent me not to collect the money."

"He hasn't?" I couldn't blame Jewel for being surprised by this. I was not only surprised by this man but confused by the whole situation. "I've just come to give you a warning. If you don't pay the money, then he will send his best man to finish the job."

"Who's that?"

"His name is Gerald. You may have read about him in some books lying about the world. Although you may have seen him under a different name. He used to go by the name, Kellan."

Logan gasped. I turned to him, "What's wrong?"

"Kellan is an extremely old vampire, extremely dangerous. I can't believe he's turned to debt collecting after all he's done."

"What do you mean?" I looked back at Michael Grey. He was casually leaning against the wall with his arms crossed over his chest. "What has this vampire done?"

"He's been moving behind the scenes for almost three hundred years. Each major book about the history of the supernatural creatures, you'll find at least one of his names. He was a major player in the war between vampires and werewolves. The truth was that there never was a war. It was all fixed through books and information. Kellan did that."

"What do you mean?"

Michael finished the story off, "It was all faked. People believe what they read in those things. Now vampires and werewolves will never be allies. Witches are known for being loners anyway plus the rest of the creatures out there are just minorities. No one really cares about them at this point. Pitting the two largest supernatural creatures against each other was ingenious. He's a great man. Now he's your worst nightmare. Plus, if you three are sticking by Jewel's side, then he's your worst nightmare too. Call this your final warning." He lifted his hand up and waved like he was saying goodbye to an old friend. He turned around and started walking back to the elevator.

I didn't know about the others, but I was definitely in

shock. I understood about Jewel's debt despite not knowing much about them. The thing that concerned me was why would he risk coming into this building? Is this Saracen bloke that big of a crime boss?

Once he was sure this Michael guy was out of the area, Logan spoke quickly, "I thought you said you only had debts with the guys in Rumsey?"

"I didn't tell you about this one because it's not as big as the other."

"I helped you out the last time. I trusted you, but you kept this from me?" Logan was clearly hurt by her secrecy.

"I thought I had got away with it. They used to be in Jamestown, but they must have moved. I wasn't planning on going back, I didn't think they would have come after me for so little."

"How much do you owe?"

"Just over five."

"Five thousand? That is a lot of money."

"Not to these guys. They wouldn't miss it."

"Obviously they did. Especially if they're sending this Kellan guy after you. You and now us. You've dragged not only me into this like the last time, but you've dragged Cassie and Bethany into it as well. This is worse than last time Jewel. You need to sort this out."

"I don't have five thousand pounds to give them. I have some, but if I come up short, they still won't accept it."

"Well, then you need to start getting some money and fast." Logan was raising his voice and was getting angry in the wrong place.

"So you're not going to help me this time?"

"Last time I offered the help. This time I'm chucked into the deep end along with you. It's not a choice."

"I didn't think they would find me and I'm sorry you're in this too. All of you."

"That's not good enough Jewel. Last time I almost lost

my bar."

"Look, I'm saying sorry." Tears were starting to form at the bottom of her eyes. She was sorry, but Logan didn't seem to be hearing or seeing her sorrow.

"Jewel!"

Cassie moved closer to Jewel, "Logan, chill for a bit."

"Jewel!"

"Guys, can we talk about this somewhere else, please? Any place where we won't get killed." My sudden outburst was a surprise not only to them but to me as well. I had to do it though. Logan's voice was getting too loud, and it wasn't getting us anywhere. So I kept that authority in my voice. "Let's get going."

"Beth is right. We need to get out of here before we carry this on. Okay with you Jewel?"

"Okay." She walked off practically stumping her feet. Cassie and I exchanged looks of worry before walking down the corridor after her. I turned to Logan. He didn't look happy, but I couldn't help but ask, "When you say get out of here do you mean the level?" He turned his head and stared at me. He didn't have to say anything. I knew exactly what he was thinking, and I didn't like it. I also didn't want to listen to him. Just because some guy shows up who wants money from Jewel doesn't mean we should leave. The government still didn't know we were there and our disguises were still intact.

I felt the folded up map in my pocket. It seemed to be jabbing me, making sure I still knew it was there. Prompting me not to listen to Logan's angry stare. We had got to the elevator, and I hadn't come up with a plan yet. All the way down to the bottom level. They opened showing me the traffic of people again.

The other three walked out onto the stairs. I was about to step out when an idea popped into my head. It probably wasn't the best, but it was the only one that I could think of.

I quickly stepped back into the suspended box and pushed the button for the fifteenth floor. They didn't notice until the doors were closing. I managed to get a glimpse of Logan's angry stare before the doors shut.

I was alone in the elevator, and soon I would be alone in a building run by the people searching for me. If this disguise wore off too soon, then they wouldn't have to search very hard. Then I would be locked on that floor again, ordered to kill more people. The number of thoughts that ran through my head was astronomical. Most of them about being caught and all the things they would do to me.

The doors opened again, and I found myself staring at even more offices. The hallway stretched out ahead of me like all the rest have. It wasn't long before it ended in a t-junction. I moved out of my metal surroundings and started walking. I heard the doors behind me close. It must be off to transport more people around this building. I hoped it was going back down to the bottom level so my friends could help. I doubted that was the case if Logan's look was anything to go by.

I carried on walking, pulling the map out of my pocket. As I walked, I followed the black line from the elevator to the cell block. There was no one around which slowed the pace of my heart. On the map, it didn't look that far, but my feet were starting to hurt when I finally came to a door. It was marked on the map but it looked just like the doors around me like it would lead into a standard office. It even had a name on the glass in black stick-on letters.

I looked down at the map and thought about the route I had taken. There had been no deviation from the trail. After looking around for people, I put away my map and tried the handle. Slowly pulling it open I peered inside. My hope dropped when I saw that it was just another office.

As my eyes moved around my mind noticed that this one was smaller than the others. The walls were covered in white plastic sheets that were almost see-through. Moving into the tiny room, I shut the door. As soon as it clicked shut I started hearing a hissing noise. Horror filled my mind as my head shot around, looking for gas leaking into the room. But there was nothing to be seen or feared. As the hissing stopped a doorway opened up in the wall.

Moving cautiously through the new door I found myself in a room. I stared down a hallway that stretched ahead of me. Each side of it was covered in metal doors. They were grey, standing out from the white walls. Each one had a grated window, half metal, and half glass.

Looking over my shoulder as I was shut in this hallway. I put my mind back to the doors. Lifting myself up onto my tip-toes, I peered through the glass. Inside the cell was horrible. The walls were built from stone. It looked cold. There was only a bed against the back wall and nothing else. There was someone lying on it. It wasn't my werewolf, so I forgot about him and moved along the line of doors.

Each cell either had no one inside it or they weren't my werewolf. It was the eighth one along when I found him in. He was sitting on the edge of the bed in some kind of blue jumpsuit. He looked defeated and not how I remembered him. He didn't look like the strong werewolf I liked so much.

This, however, didn't make my hormones any less happy to see him. I could see his arm muscles fighting against the restraints of his sleeves. I couldn't help but let my eyebrows perk up. I let my hormones do a little dance whilst I figured the door out. There was no handle to just open it. There wasn't a card slot or a number pad either. There was no way for me to open it up.

Not able to figure it out by myself, I banged on the door and got back on my tiptoes. The occupier looked up. He didn't seem happy to see me, but he did reluctantly get off his bed and walked over to me. "What are you doing here?" His words were filled with anger like it was me who had put him here.

"I'm here to get you out."

"What? Why would you do that?" I was confused. That was until I caught my reflection in the glass. He wouldn't recognise me behind this magical disguise, would he? "It's me. The girl from the pub."

"The leecher? You here to get some training?"

"No. I have someone helping me control my abilities, but we can talk about it later. Do you know how to open the door?"

"I don't know. The doors open before I see or hear anyone." He seemed to be reluctant to talk to me even though I was here to break him out.

"Then how come you haven't escaped?"

"There's a silver lining in the doorway. The door opens, and I become weak. All they have to do is shock me with their sticks. Believe me when I say I know what it feels like."

"You didn't seem like the kind of guy to take things lying down."

"I'm not!" His hands came crashing into the door with anger. He blew out a breath to calm himself and stared at me before saying, "Have you checked the walls for anything?"

"There's nothing around the doors."

"What about further back."

"Hold on." I moved back from the door smiling at the sound of his voice. Quickly jogging back a little way I couldn't see anything like a button or even a panel. As I turned back around my foot scraped across something on the floor. It was small, but it was something that shouldn't be there. Bending down I let my fingertip trace the outline. Trying to push it like a button didn't work.

So I got back to my feet and placed my foot in the perfectly sized section. Letting my weight push down it dipped in. A soft puff of air came out of the wall as two sections came out, forming a horseshoe of computer consoles.

Slipping in between them I let my eyes move over the screens. Most of it I didn't understand, but hope appeared when I saw the camera feeds from the cells. Looking at the bottom corner, I saw a green button. So I pushed it without thinking, wanting my werewolf out of that room.

Hearing a loud, metallic thud, I rushed out of the horseshoe of consoles and stood at the mouth of the cell block. I stared down the hallway, but I wasn't happy. A door had opened, but it was on the other side of the hallway. Running back to the screen I hit the view of my wolf in his cell. With it now highlighted with a green glow I hit the button in the corner again.

Moving back to the doorway I saw him walking out of his cell. He looked so much bigger than I remembered and it made him look even hotter. I slowly walked forward. His eyes were locked on me. I was about to reach out to grab his hand, but something crashed into the side of me, making me crash into the wall.

I felt fingers clamping around my throat, squeezing my windpipe. Sucking in enough air to stop me from blacking out. I tried to look up, but my head was being pushed against the wall. Then I felt whoever this was, sniffing my hair, then my neck. His hair tickled my skin as he moved. Then I was looking into his eyes. They started off cold, but then they filled with the same heat that was building inside of my soul.

His arms wrapped around my waist and I was pulled to his lips and kissed with passion. They felt so good against mine. His body felt beyond good as I felt it against mine. I would die happy right at that moment.

I got very annoyed when we were abruptly interrupted. A body impacted into our sides, sending us sprawling down onto the floor. My werewolf's arms around me cushioned my fall. I looked up as a grunt escaped my mouth. A man was looking down at us with a mad look in his eyes. This man bent down and yanked me up by my hair. I couldn't move because my hair felt like it was going to be ripped out if I resisted. My vision was filled with his fist swinging for my face. I shut my eyes and waited for the impact and the pain.

A breeze came from my right. I shot my eyes open, but it was little more than a blur. I fell to my knees as the grip on my hair let go. I watched the men wrestling. Using my sense of smell, I found two scents. Both of them were mint; they were strong werewolves. Analysing those scents, I smiled as it turned out my werewolf was the stronger of the two.

I felt my body being filled with the strength and speed of my werewolf as I sucked in his minty essence. As those feelings filled me, so did the urge to fight and to rip apart my enemy. With the man leaning over my werewolf, I rushed forwards and grabbed his hair like he had with me. The way he grunted and moaned made my actions feel even better, payback for the pain he caused me.

A blur of fists hit his ribs. I heard a few cracks and a cry of pain with each punch. Once my friend was finished I dropped the body like a bag of bricks. He crumpled on the floor holding his stomach. I felt the heat in the air around me. It was climbing to an unbearable temperature. I turned to find my man's face inches from mine. His eyes seemed to glow golden with need. This time the desire seemed to be something physical pushing me towards him. Not with my heart but with the urge to have him inside me. Something so primal and animalistic.

It frightened me so much that I placed my hand against his chest and pushed him at arm's length. Pushing out his essence, that urge slowly faded to the normal way I felt around him. His eyes didn't change until he was finally able to break his stare. He blinked a couple of times and then turned away from me. I backed away from him feeling the gap between us like a chasm. "That was unexpected."

"The fight?" Drew asked.

"Yeah." I found myself wondering what else could have

been unexpected. "Let's get out of here whilst we still can."
I didn't get a chance to turn around towards the door. My
ears were filled with a high-pitched squeal. A little bulb came
out of the ceiling spraying red light all over the walls. "No.
Follow me!" I had to yell just so he would hear me over the
hear piercing alarm. I started jogging for the door. My ears
just made out the thundering steps of his feet behind me.
Moving into the small office and we both paused at the door.
I took a few glances at the werewolf standing by my side. I
then realised something, "What's your name?"

He seemed surprised I would pick a time like this to ask
him. "Drew."

"Beth."

"Cute name."

"Cute butt." It slipped out before I could stop myself but
I smiled when he did.

"Thanks." I smiled at him as I could feel my cheeks heating up as I blushed. I turned back to the door and quickly
pushed it open. Luckily, there were no red lights making it
hard to see. "This way." I started jogging back the way I came
like I was following imaginary breadcrumbs. We were almost
halfway back when we had to come to a complete stop. Running down the hallway towards us were guards. They were
heavily armoured with assault rifles. Drew's hand grabbed
me, and I was pulled back around the corner before we were
spotted. Our backs were pressed against the wall, making our
arms touch. I could feel the heat of his skin through our
clothes. "What are we going to do?"

"They've got silver bullets. I think we can take them
though. There are two of us."

"Wait a second. How do you know they have silver bullets?"

"Can't you feel them? You're still leeching off of me,
aren't you?"

"No." I blew out a sigh and started leeching off of him.

With the usual feelings of my body changing, I felt the urge to have him once again. Swallowing down a dry throat I pushed that urge away and felt for what he was talking about.

I could hear the footsteps coming down over the carpet. Chatter coming through their earpieces was so clear I could have been wearing one as well. I could smell the sweat building up under their black uniforms. Then there it was. The stinging against my skin. I could feel the presence of those special bullets. "You think we can take them do you?"

"Yeah, they smell like humans. We can do it, we just have to be fast about it. And don't get shot."

"Okay." I quickly reached out but not with my werewolf side. I used my leeching gifts and sniffed the air. Drew was right. I couldn't smell any special scents apart from his. They were definitely human. Maybe we could do this. It was going to be a big fight. I turned back to Drew who gave me a quick smirk like he was looking forward to the battle.

"Ready, Beth?"

"Sure." I really wasn't, but it had to be done.

He was about to run around the corner when he turned back towards me, "Don't hold back. You have to let yourself go and just attack. Don't think about it. They might be human, but they chose to work for this unit. They aren't any better than the people who run this place."

"Okay." I tried to put his words to work in my head. I decided not to think about it. Whether it would last during the fight was another thing entirely.

I was about to start thinking of what I would do when I looked beside me, and Drew was gone. Next second there was gunfire and grunts of pain. Bullets riddled the wall in front of me. I quickly darted around the corner low and fast. Drew had a guard's arm bent in a very broken direction. He hid behind the body like a shield.

Empty clips banged along the floor as the guards started reloading their guns. I moved forwards not really knowing what to do. My heart was beating so fast I thought it would jump out of my chest just to get out of this situation. I saw Drew peering around his human shield. I also spotted the handle of an office door moving to his left. Next thing I knew I was at that door kicking it down.

With my werewolf strength, the wood easily splintered into a thousand pieces. Through the cloud of wood, I saw a shadowy figure beyond. Moving quickly, I jumped onto this person. I felt the butt of a rifle smack into the side of my head. The pain didn't even register in my brain. The only thing I felt was the anger that filled me.

As I climbed to my feet, I pulled this guard right into my face. My heavy, angry breathing fogged up the visor. Growling low just before I pushed him back into the wall. The plaster crumpled but didn't give way. The guard pushed back at me making me take a step back. Using this momentum fingers curled into his uniform, and I swung him around.

His feet flew out from under him as his body crashed into the desk. Releasing him, he made a nice mess of the furniture like a wrecking ball. The man groaned and rolled over but wasn't getting up anytime soon.

I walked over and looked out of the doorway that no longer had a door attached to it. Drew was further down the hallway beating the hell out of someone else. The rest seemed to have retreated around the corner. Moving back to safety I made a hole in the wall to move into the next office along.

I tuned my werewolf hearing up and found the chattering of the other guards. Judging by the different tones there were four, maybe five left. Then again, there could be some not even chatting. I had to take the risk if we were to win this fight.

Stepping back through my hole I quickly turned and shot off into a sprint. I crossed the room in a split second. Dipping my shoulder down I sent myself through the other wall.

I swung my arms and grabbed the nearest guard through the dust.

Through my head, a list of things popped up. Kill or knock them out quickly. Move fast and hit strong. Keep aware of my surroundings and don't die. That last point stuck in my mind.

My eyes hit his as we stared at each other. I moved fast, seeing my own fist as a blur in his visor. It crashed through the plastic and into his nose, breaking it beyond repair. Before the body could hit the floor, I was moving again.

Guards were positioned along the corridor in a line like they were waiting for me. Some were kneeling by the walls, some had taken shelter inside doorways. Ordering my legs to pump faster I picked up speed. I was moving so fast that the guards seemed like they were going in slow-motion.

The first guard I came to was kneeling. He received my knee to his face breaking his helmet in two before his cranium smacked into the wall, hanging in the hole. I moved further down the line of enemies.

Feet carried me quickly to my next target. I grabbed his gun and used my muscles to smash the metal into his unprotected chin. The guard flew up and back into the office. I heard his body hit something smash-able as I arrived at my next enemy.

The barrel of his gun was being lifted as I arrived. Knocking it up, keeping me from danger I planted my fist hard into his gut. He let out a deep groan as he crumpled down to the ground. The next guard was running up to me. As I grabbed his shoulders, I felt a breeze rush past as Drew ran down the corridor to help. Gripping one shoulder, I slammed my hand into the side of his helmet. The dome of his gear crashed through a window, and the body flew through following it. He rested in the office, out of the fight.

As I ran down the corridor, I watched Drew deal with two guards at the same time. There were two more further down trying to follow our movements. Drew hadn't noticed the guns pointing down towards us. I heard the triggers being pulled back. My body kept moving, and I crashed into Drew as he finished off his two guards. We went moving through an open doorway, my shoulder hitting into a filing cabinet as we fell to the floor.

My shoulder ached a little from hitting the metal, but it was a better feeling than a silver bullet. We both placed our backs to the filing cabinets. I wondered if they would stop a bullet, but it was our only protection right now. My ears picked up their conversation, "Get the wolf bane ready."

"Right."

"Hurry." Suddenly my hearing was filled with gunfire. I felt the sting of silver on my skin as it pounded into the walls and the metal. I shielded myself with my arm even though it wouldn't do much to protect me from the bullets. The gunfire stopped when I heard a metallic click. I turned to Drew, "The gun is empty." I was around the corner quickly, not hearing something Drew was saying to me.

I froze to the spot when I saw a rifle pointed at me. The click of the trigger hit my ears, but instead of a sharp pain of a bullet, I felt a dull thud in my side. Drew sent me down to the floor and out of the way of whatever flew past us.

My protector stood there in the middle of the hallway, baring his teeth at the guards. In my mind, I could see Drew's bloody body lying on the floor. It filled me with dread. I tried to get to my feet but Drew threw his hand up. My head turned back towards the guards. I expected to see the flash at the end of a barrel, but that's not what happened.

Next thing I knew, there was a big blur. One of the guards was dropped to the floor with a powerful punch. The last guard was being held up against the wall by his throat by Cassie. A short, skinny girl holding a guy who probably weighs twice as much.

I looked up to Drew. His hand position had changed and

was now offering me help to get up to my feet. I took it, and we both walked down to the end of the corridor. Cassie gave me a friendly smile, "Glad to see you're okay."

"Thanks for coming to help."

"Of course I was going to help. Wasn't going to let you have all the fun." She squeezed a little harder on the guard's throat. I could hear he was having trouble breathing, but I didn't care at this point. Drew grabbed the gun out of his limp hand. I watched him eject the clip which was holding the weapon they called wolf's bane. The gun was dropped, and Drew popped out a bullet from the clip. He held the bullet between his thumb and forefinger. Both Cassie and I stared at it.

It was a glass bullet containing a weird yellow liquid. Drew asked, "Can either of you two venture a guess at what this is?"

I shook my head, and Cassie spoke, "Not a clue. Pocket it. Might be able to find out later." Drew did so. Cassie looked back up at the guard. She didn't hesitate another second. Her hand twitched, and the guard's head snapped into an impossible position. Cassie let go of him, and the dead body dropped to the floor like a brick. I had just seen Cassie kill someone in cold blood and yet I didn't feel sorry for him. I wasn't too sure if it was the emotionless feelings of the leecher inside of me. Or maybe it was the werewolf essence that had changed my body.

But I was ready to leave and get out of this place when Cassie spotted something. She knelt down by the dead body she had just created. "Look at this." Drew and I both joined her down on one knee. She had a finger on a part of the uniform. I looked at the words written across the man's chest, Wolf Squad.

I voiced my thought, "He can't be a werewolf because I would have smelt his scent."

Cassie voiced her opinions, "That might mean he's part

of a unit trained to kill werewolves. That wolf's bane you're carrying might be a weapon designed just for you guys. You better let me carry it."

"Good idea. The last thing I need is something eating through my leg." He pulled it out and offered it to her. "My name's Drew by the way."

She took it with a smile. "Cassie. I can see why Bethany went to all this trouble. We better get going. Logan and Jewel are waiting for us in the apartment."

"Who?"

We started jogging back to the elevator as I explained it, "Logan is another leecher. He's on our side. He owns the bar in Ingleford."

"He's a leecher?"

"Yeah. Jewel is a witch."

"What kind?"

"Huh?"

"Um, illusion, healing or destruction?"

"Oh right. She's a witch of illusion."

"Okay, hence the disguise."

"Exactly."

"And the apartment?"

"That's a longer story. It's just better if you know it belongs to me now and it's a safe place."

Cassie piped up throwing a spanner in the works, "Actually, they're waiting in a different apartment. Sorry."

"What happened to my apartment?"

"That one has been compromised now thanks to Jewel's debt. As soon as we're back, we're leaving. I'm sure Logan will be fine with Drew tagging along."

I was speechless. There was no settling down anymore. I couldn't just relax and think about things. We were going to be on the move a lot now if not all the time just to stay ahead of the government. We had deleted our files but would they ever stop looking for us. Then there were people popping up from the past.

We got to the elevator and climbed in, starting our descent down to the bottom level of the building. Cassie turned to us. "We've got a lot of things going on, don't we?"

"I know. We've deleted the tracker files though. We can just run and get away can't we?"

"True, I don't think they'll stop looking for Logan though. Or you."

"He managed to hide away from them last time. We all can get away and hide out."

"I suppose. Then we have Jewel's past catching up with all of us. Could be big trouble if we don't get it sorted."

"How is Logan with it now?"

"He hasn't really calmed down that much. You running off didn't help much."

"Yeah." I felt guilty about it, but it was something I needed to do. Giving Drew a glance before continuing my questioning. "He'll help though, won't he?"

"I don't know. He did almost lose everything last time."

"But, what about that vampire guy? He has to help otherwise this vampire debt-collector will be after him as well."

Cassie started nodding her head, "I'm sure he'll come around. He's a nice guy through and through. Don't think he has a bad bone in his body."

"I've noticed that. Looks like we have a little group going on here."

"We have to stick together. If the government got Logan than I wouldn't have any help when things go bad."

"When things go bad?"

"If I get into trouble or if I'm not feeling like myself."

"Oh. Must be hard being a vampire all the time." I gave Drew a quick glance. He was standing there silently taking in all this information. "You become accustomed to it." I noticed a sad look she had, but I decided not to push it. There was clearly more to being a vampire than the thirst they could feel.

The doors opened up, and I was happy to hear no alarms going off. I flicked my eyes over to Drew again and smiled. He gave me a cute one back, and the three of us exited the elevator like we belonged. The receptionist was on her phone as I moved down the stairs. As we stepped onto the bottom step, she looked at us. My heart stopped as our eyes met.

I listened intently using my werewolf hearing. To my pleasure, she wasn't talking about us despite Drew's blue jumpsuit. Clearly, she didn't know what the prisoners looked like. She was on the phone complaining about some kind of order that didn't get delivered. We moved into the traffic of people and walked out of the building.

We had managed to get in and get out with relatively no trouble. The fight was just a small hiccup that we managed to get past. We were out of the building, and because we deleted the tracker files, we were off the radar now. Unfortunately, even though we got rid of one problem, we still had another. We have to get Jewel out of this debt with The Saracen.

CHAPTER 7

The walk across the street and the journey in the lift was silent. I couldn't even think of anything. My mind was filled with worry that we were being followed. That somehow they had gotten security footage of us. I kept looking over my shoulder, but there was nothing to see. Just an ordinary crowd of people going about their lives. No one rushing to capture us.

The three of us moved into the same building as my apartment, but the elevator took us three levels higher. Its doors opened, and we walked out into an exact replica of the apartment three floors down. The only difference was the colour. The flooring was white, and so were the cupboard doors in the kitchen. The counter was the same colour as well. Logan and Jewel were standing there by the cooker. They were chatting which stopped when they noticed us enter. The gang was back together, but I saw Logan's stare that was filled with anger, "You should not have run off like that."

"I survived."

"What if you hadn't? I'm sure it was just pure luck." His look went from me to the tall werewolf by my side. "You must be the hunky werewolf she ran off to rescue." He wasn't giving Drew the happiest of looks either.

Drew didn't take notice of it, "My name is Drew." He

held out his hand. I didn't expect Logan to shake it, but he did. "I would be dead if it wasn't for Beth."

"I'm sure being locked up there was horrible." Logan managed to keep the sarcasm out of his words, but I was sure it was there.

"No, I mean we had to fight a unit of guards. I would be dead if it weren't for her. You have trained her well."

"How do you know I have been training her?" His tone sharpened a little.

"I'm a werewolf. I have a very good nose. You should know that...... leecher."

There was a sudden scowl on Logan's face, "Do you have a problem with me being a leecher?"

Drew paused which seemed to draw on forever. "As long as you're not on their side. By the sound of it, you're one great guy."

Logan pulled a big grin, "I am a good guy. So what are you going to be doing?"

"I don't understand."

"Are you sticking around and helping us without trouble or is this just a quick stop before you disappear?"

He turned around to face me. His eyes were so deep. I could drown in them. "What kind of trouble are you in?"

I answered, "Well, I'm not really the one in trouble, sort of."

"Yeah. From the way you and Cassie were talking, it's Jewel who's in trouble." He turned to the only one left, "I guess that's you." She nodded in response also not looking happy. Likely to do with her situation more than the new edition to the group.

Logan filled Drew in with the rest of the story, "That also puts the rest of us in trouble. This Michael Grey guy saw us with her. Now we're all marked for the debt." Logan was making sure Jewel knew what he thought of it all.

"How much are we talking about?"

"Jewel?" Logan gave her a stare that would have frozen my blood.

"If I remember correctly, I owe around five thousand, two hundred and five pounds."

"How the hell did you run up that kind of money? Are you a gambler or something?"

Jewel looked away looking ashamed of her past. "I stole it."

"From who?"

"The Saracen."

Drew scoffed at the name. "That was dumb."

Suddenly everyone was paying attention to Drew. I asked what everyone was thinking, "What do you mean?"

"Well, The Saracen is a large crime boss. He has hands in almost everything. He owns God knows how many businesses in various cities. He has some very unsavoury friends, and he doesn't mind getting his own hands bloody. He's a very distasteful man. You don't want to get on his bad side."

Logan stepped closer to Drew. "How do you know so much about him?"

"I was hired for a job of his. I backed out at the last minute when I found out it was for him. Even though I never told anyone or betrayed him, he still burned me. I couldn't get a job anywhere, and I had to move."

Jewel spoke to Drew, "You used to live in Greystone?"

"Yeah. You?"

She nodded her head, "That's where I got all my debt from. I moved after that but then got into more debt. Why would The Saracen move?"

"I heard it was because the police were getting too close to shutting him down and arresting him. He paid them all off then moved to start up some new businesses."

"Great, so finding me was just pure luck then."

"By the looks of it. I'm guessing he's moved here then." Jewel nodded. "Great. Hopefully, I won't have the misfortune to run into him.""

Logan talked with an impatient tone in his voice, "This isn't helping us get anywhere. We need to think up a plan to get ourselves out of it."

I decided to throw my idea in first, "What about the money Keith left me? There is plenty there to clear the debt. I would have loads left over after."

"That's not an option. It takes too long for cheques to clear. I have a feeling he will only accept cash."

"What about one of his rivals?" Cassie smiled at her own idea.

Logan didn't seem so sure. "What do you mean?"

"I imagine he has made enemies doing the kind of business he does. Why don't we ask one of his rivals to help in exchange for getting rid of their competition or something?"

"It's a good idea, but I don't know anything about this kind of thing."

"I do." Everyone turned their heads towards Drew for the second time. I also was wondering how he knew all this since surely it was a while ago he was involved with him. "I know the perfect guy who could be interested in helping us."

"And who might that be?" Logan crossed his arms over his chest, waiting for a response.

"There's another businessman with his own unsavoury interests. The one thing that holds most his interest is trying to beat The Saracen. They've been trying to beat each other for years. When one of them buys a nightclub, the other must buy two of them. One owns a building then the other one buys a street. It's almost putting The Saracen's rival out of business. It appears he would be the one with deeper pockets. So if you tell this guy that we are willing to help him get rid of The Saracen, then he'll help."

Logan was getting suspicious of all this information. "How do you know this?"

"He will help me."

"Why?" Logan was starting to get impatient. His nostrils were flaring.

"Because I know him. I've known him for a long time. If I ask for his help and give him a good reason, he will help us."

Jewel stepped forwards from her standing position, "Then that's what we'll do. Logan?"

"It's our best shot." He turned to Drew, "Where will this guy be?"

"He owns a club in Jordanna. He hangs out there mostly. If he's not there, then I can find out from the manager."

"It's our best option. Let's get going."

"Um." Logan stopped at Drew's noise. "I was wondering if I could grab a shower. I haven't had one in a while. I must smell." He pulled a great big smile. If he had directed that at me, I would have had a hard time saying no.

"Okay but make it quick." I checked if anyone was looking then sneakily sniffed my armpits. Unfortunately, Logan seemed to spot what I was doing. "You don't have to worry. Leechers don't smell. It's something to do with our gifts. I never really thought to ask the government about it. I suppose they wouldn't know much about it anyway. No one seems to have many details about leechers."

"Okay." With my last word, the apartment fell into silence. In the distance, I could hear the shower being turned on and the removal of clothes. I then realised I still had the essence of a werewolf in my lungs. I listened to the far away noises as Drew removed his underwear and stepped into the water. After a few more seconds and just after he started singing out of tune, I allowed the essence to leak out of my nose. With that and the sounds gone my mind was able to wander.

I started looking at my life and how I could get it back to normal if that was even possible. I have a crush on a werewolf, and my closest friend is a vampire. I don't think a normal life is waiting for me after this unless I was willing to turn my back on everything.

We all sat on the sofas that were around the corner from the kitchen. None of us were talking. We couldn't really talk about what we were going to do because Drew had all the information. Logan seemed to still be upset with Jewel. The tension was so thick between them it was like a fog. Cassie wasn't even saying a word, which was very unlike her.

Jewel had taken to sitting there with her knees up to her chest. I had been staring out of the window ever since we sat down. The world out there still looked the same. Buildings were the same, and so was the sun. I could see it preparing to disappear behind the horizon. The buildings were positioned, so I had a great view of this between two skyscrapers. I could sit there watching the sun vanish completely and watch the moonlight come across the sky.

Then I remembered the werewolves. Then the vampires. I thought about the number of supernatural creatures that are out there. The world might look the same, but it wasn't. Not to me anymore. Humans were no longer the only ones on the planet. I could never have a normal life. The only thing I had that was anything to do with my life before was the ring in my pocket.

I took it out and stared at it. Memories of my friend came flooding back. He was the only thing I had from my old life. Even now I couldn't be friends with him. Would he except me for what I am and with my new friends, would he hang around? I breathed out heavily and slipped the ring on.

It still fit snugly around my middle finger. It reminded me of my original life. I remembered the night he had stayed with me. We laid there hugging after I came to. I felt completely safe. I would give anything to have that feeling right now.

I looked down at the ring. It was starting to feel a bit too tight against my skin. I tried slipping it off, but it wouldn't budge. It was like someone had applied super glue to the inside. I pulled as hard as I could, but it still wouldn't move.

I lifted my finger up to eye level and examined the metal. Nothing seemed out of place. There was no change to the look of it. I couldn't find anything that was different which made the squeezing feel even weirder.

I turned my hand over and suddenly got a pain in my head. It was gone as quickly as a prick. Then another one came, this one was more painful. With the third sharp pain, I got an image in my head. It was very blurry, and it was too quick to really see what was happening. Again pain came, this time sticking around. It felt like a knife was being pushed through my brain from the front. With the pressure of pain, the image came again, this time for longer.

It was blurry to start off with, then it became clearer the longer the pain stuck around. I didn't like what I was seeing. My friend was down on his knees. His wrists had chains around them, and they were bolted to the floor. His top was ripped, and I could see three claw marks on his skin. His face was battered and bruised. My friend's head hung. I could see a small trickle of blood dripping from his face. A person stood in front of him. He was harder to see. He seemed to be shrouded in darkness whereas the rest of the room was clear as crystal.

It seemed to be some kind of freezer. A place where a restaurant would keep its larger pieces of meat or their frozen desserts. I suddenly remembered that my friend used to work at the local food place. I looked back at his clothes and could just make out the logo on his ripped polo shirt. Why would anyone hurt him? Why would I be seeing it like this?

I looked down at the ring. It wasn't getting any tighter, but I still wouldn't be able to get it off. I tried to look back at the scene, but it was going blurry again. Slipping out of my mind like sand through my fingers.

As the image disappeared so did the snug feeling on my finger. The ring was loose enough, so I took it off and chucked it onto the seat next to me. I scowled at it and rubbed my finger trying to get colour back into it. Once it felt normal again, I rubbed my head. The sharp pain was no longer there. It had been replaced by a dull throb. It would no doubt turn into a headache. Something I didn't need right now. Logan's voice made me jump, "Are you okay?"

I didn't want him having something else to worry about, "I'm fine. The ring just brings back memories." It didn't feel good lying to him. However, I didn't really know what just happened. It couldn't be a vision. All I did was put on a ring. I wasn't thinking clearly. I don't think I had a great night's sleep since my blackouts started.

I heard Cassie's voice, "Hey, Logan. Do you know what this is?" He turned around to face her. She was holding out the bullet containing the liquid. Logan plucked it from her grip carefully. "The guards we took it off said it was called.... What was it, Beth?"

"Wolf's bane."

At those words, his jaw dropped, "Did you say wolf's bane?" I nodded. "They finally managed to weaponise it."

"What is it?" Cassie sounded eager to find out. I was as well, but Jewel didn't seem bothered. Her gaze was out the window.

"Well. This is a weapon specifically designed to kill were-wolves. The liquid is a mixture, the main ingredient being an extract from a plant called wolf's bane. The glass breaks upon impact and the liquid mixes with the werewolf's blood. The essence of the plant reacts with the blood and kills them slowly and painfully. Here you go Cassie, perhaps keep hold of it just in case we need it." I saw Logan look towards the bathroom. I didn't like his look. I was going to say some-thing, but Cassie spoke first, "Cheers Logan. It will come in handy if we come across any nasty werewolves."

Logan looked over to the bathroom again. I decided not to say anything about it, it was too much hassle to start a fight. It would no doubt lead to an argument, and that was something we couldn't afford to have right now. Instead, I simply started a new subject, "Are you okay?"

"What do you mean? I'm fine."

"You seem pretty angry at Jewel."

"It's just an emotional response. It'll pass." His eyes moved to her as she gave him a glance. "She knows it."

They both looked away. "Do you think this plan is going to work?"

Logan shrugged, "It's worth a try. Your boyfriend seems to think it will." I was about to correct his assumption that we weren't going out, but Drew chose that time to walk in. He had changed out of his jumpsuit. No doubt took some of Keith's clothes. They were a little tight on his body, but he still looked good in them. Because of this, his muscles were pressing against the material trying to tear through.

I tore my eyes from his body and looked up into his stare. They were deep depths of desire. Then he blinked and it was gone, locked behind his self-control. But I couldn't keep mine under that same control especially when he smiled at me.

"All clean now?" Logan's voice wasn't holding any less tension than the room.

"Yep. Ready when you are."

"Then let's get going." We all made our way towards the elevator. As I passed Drew, I got a whiff of the body wash he used. It smelt good enough I would be willing to lick it off his body. The aura he was no doubt projecting wasn't helping me keep those thoughts out of my head. I had to keep my thoughts straight. I couldn't afford to get distracted. It could get not only me killed but the others as well. I wouldn't allow that to happen. I wouldn't be able to live with myself if something happened.

We got into the elevator where Drew's smell was amplified by the small area. I tried to distract myself from it by looking at the numbers changing above the door. It wasn't working. I was almost about to turn around and take more than just a sniff of him when Logan started speaking, "Jewel, can you switch off the potions now."

She replied, but her voice sounded so quiet, "They should wear off soon."

"All the same can you just do it. Been this person for too long now." There were a few seconds of silence, and then the air was filled with some chanting. A few sentences of the gibberish and I felt my whole body tingling. As I looked down, the suit I was wearing slowly changed into my clothes. They felt older now and a very big change from the suit. I turned to look at my distorted image in the elevator wall.

It wasn't a clear reflection, but I could see I had changed back. I looked around at the rest, and they too had gone back to the way they looked before. Even Jewel had morphed herself back.

With all of us now back to normal, Logan carried on talking as the tension in the small box didn't lighten. "So where is this guy's club?"

"It's in Parke." Parke was the smallest of areas within Jordanna. It was mostly made up of run-down houses. I was surprised to find out the nightclub was there.

"More specifically."

"Cray Park."

"Cray Park? You have to be kidding me. Your friend owns a business in Cray Park?"

"I know it's rough, but we'll be fine."

"How can you be so sure? How many killings have happened in the last month?"

"Trust me." For some reason, I was willing to trust him. I had heard about the reputation of Cray Park, but I was willing to go there on his word alone. I knew Logan wasn't going to be that easy. I hope he would still come along. Even though I had Drew with me, I felt safer because of Logan. "I can get us in and out of there safely."

"But we're not just going there for a night out. We'll be going into the club of a businessman who I'm guessing doesn't use golf clubs for the sport."

"He doesn't like golf actually."

"Well, how the hell do you know?!" Logan looked like he was ready to throw Drew up against the elevator wall.

"Because he's my father."

"What?!" My high-pitched voice seemed to bounce off the metal walls. That, I didn't see coming. "So this business-man is a werewolf?"

"No, my biological father."

Now I was confused, "Doesn't the werewolf gene stay in the family?"

Drew turned to me, "It doesn't work like that. A pack picks people that they want. They go through a ritual where you drink the alpha male's blood just before a full moon. It's simple, but it's a ritual that's taken seriously."

"That's enough with the lessons. What's your father's name?"

"His name is Griffin Gaynes."

"You're Gaynes' son? Unbelievable. When were you going to tell us that?"

"I didn't see it as a problem."

I was yet again confused, "Who's Griffin Gaynes?"

Logan didn't answer, it was Cassie instead, "He's a large crime boss. Apparently not as large as The Saracen. But he is a dangerous bloke, and you've fallen for his son. Have fun meeting the parent." She pulled a face at me, so I pulled one back. Drew smiled at us both. "So when do we meet this guy?"

"Now," Logan said abruptly. "We need to get this all sort-ed so I can go about getting lost again." I put my hands into my pocket and noticed the ring wasn't there. While I cast my mind back, trying to remember if I had left it behind, my hands started patting my pockets. I was about to speak up when I saw Cassie's outstretched hand. The ring was stuck between her fingers. I took it off of her and shoved it straight into my pocket, "Thanks."

"Don't mention it." My eyes flicked from Cassie to Drew. As his stare met mine, the elevator stopped, and the doors opened. I could feel his eyes burning into my back as we made our way to the cars. Since Logan had mentioned wanting to have a private chat with Jewel, Drew and I took Cassie's car. I hoped Logan was going to apologise for his behaviour. Part of me understood his reaction, but it wouldn't help the situation.

As we set off, Drew started giving Cassie directions. He had informed us it would only take forty minutes. I looked up at the sky as the buildings whizzed past us. I guessed it would be getting dark by the time we arrived. There would be more people hanging around, and during the night people tend to get a little crazy. Yet it didn't bother me. Having Drew with me in the car made me feel secure and protected. A small part of me knew he wouldn't let any harm come to me.

Drew had pointed Cassie in the right direction and we were on our way out of the city. I checked through the back window if Logan was following. I could see his face behind the wheel, but it wasn't the car we took last time. Jewel must have changed it again. Logan was being very paranoid. I know Michael Grey knows where we were, but I very much doubted he saw the cars. Then again, Logan had survived this long being careful.

I turned around to look at the two sitting in the front. A werewolf and a vampire sitting next to each other. All the films and books had it wrong. Then again they were most likely based on the lie that Kellan had made up. Because of him, they would always pit the two species against each other, claiming they arch-enemies. Just like humans, it depends on the person themselves. I'm sure there are gangs of vampires out there that would get a lot of enjoyment out of ripping a werewolf apart.

I looked into the side mirror. From this angle, I could see Drew's face. He had no clue I was looking. Drew looked so soft, so sweet. If I had a thousand guesses, I would never peg him as a werewolf. I wouldn't say he was anything but human. My heart skipped a beat with the way I felt about him. At the moment, I knew it was pure lust that made me want him. His werewolf aura might have something to do with that. But there was a throbbing in my heart that seemed to pulse to something deeper.

I hope this all worked out so I could have some kind of relationship with him. Then again, could a relationship be called that when it was between a werewolf and a leecher? Wouldn't be able to hang out with him on a full moon. He will always have that animal side of him that will want to get out. Would he lose control of his anger at those moments if we argue? In the moments of passion I wanted to share with him, would he lose control? So many thoughts ran through my head.

As I looked out the window again, I decided to forget about Drew and my feelings. I had to keep my mind clear. We could deal with a relationship after all this was cleared up. If there was a relationship to have. He had once said we couldn't be together because of what I am. Does that still stand or could he put that behind him? I hoped so.

We were ten minutes away from Jordanna when the first word was spoken. It was such a loud change from the silence. My eyes went to Cassie as she asked, "So, Drew. Tell me a story about yourself."

"A story?"

"Yeah, like a childhood one."

"Oh." Drew pulled a smile which showed off his white teeth. "I didn't have a great childhood. Having a father in control of a lot of businesses and not doing things legally all the time was tough. When I grew older, I thought I lucked out by getting a second chance with being a werewolf. I would get a new family who I was bound to with werewolf blood. I would get brothers and sisters, as well parents that cared about me."

"How come you're not with your pack now?"

"I was kicked out."

"What?" My voice cut through their conversation. "How do you get kicked out of a pack of werewolves?"

"Apparently there are a whole bunch of ways to get kicked out of a pack. I obviously broke one of them."

"What happened?" I leant forwards in my seat like it would help me hear him clearer.

He opened his mouth like he was going to say something then seemed to change his mind, "It's not a happy story. I don't feel like telling it right now. Anyway, we have more pressing matters to deal with."

Cassie with her comedy timing, "Like your real dad? How come your relationship isn't great with him?"

"I don't want to talk about that either." For some reason, the last two points seemed to be connected. Maybe it was his father's fault he got kicked out. "What about you?" I thought he was talking to Cassie until I saw him looking at me via the side mirror. "What happened to you when you were younger?"

"It was very boring. No werewolf packs or being turned into a vampire."

"Surely you have some interesting things to tell. You are a leecher after all."

"There's a problem with that. I can barely remember things from nights where I accidentally used my leecher powers. The first night I remember was just before I moved away from my parents. Woke up naked in the woods. Got into a car crash after breaking a guy's finger. Wasn't that much fun."

Under normal conditions, telling such a story would have brought gasps of shock and surprise. However in a car with a werewolf and a vampire, it must have been so tame compared to their life stories.

"Sounds it. Cassie?" A mumble came out of Cassie's voice but Drew suddenly spat out a sentence of words, "Turn right here." I looked up to see the turning coming up quick. Cassie threw the wheel to the right. The car curved around the road with a sharp squeal from the tyres. A lorry beeped its horn as it just missed our back bumper. Cassie managed to stop the car from swinging into the opposite lane but only just.

I swung my gaze through the back window. Logan manoeuvred the corner a little slower than Cassie. Now that we were no longer in danger of having a car crash and Drew's instructions were coming in plenty of time, I looked out my window at the city around us. A hospital whizzed past. The entrance doors were blocked by an ambulance. A bed was half sticking out of the back. A paramedic in his green uniform was yanking on it with all his might. The white sheet was draped over a heavy looking guy. The other paramedic standing by the front of the ambulance looked like he wasn't going to be helping anytime soon.

After the hospital, the scenery gave way to a large green area. It was covered in picnic tables and trees. Beyond that were smaller buildings. A line of businesses like a pet shop and a grocery store.

The road curved left in between the buildings. A skyscraper sat on the corner. We took another left and passed under a carriageway. Following the four-lane road above I could see the thick wires of a suspension bridge in the distance. We slowed down for the red light hanging from the pole above us. As we came to a soft halt, I checked behind us again. To my shock, I wasn't looking at Logan and Jewel. Behind the wheel of a red banger, was a guy with long hair. It was dark brown and looked extremely greasy. He smiled at me, but there was nothing nice about it. I quickly turned back around not wanting to look at it anymore. I wanted to look again to see if Logan was in the car behind, but I didn't want to see that smile again.

That idea got left behind at the junction when we started moving again. I heard the ticking of the indicator, and we started turning right. The buildings we were leaving behind were tall and modern. These ones we were now driving past looked rundown. They were dark, and some were in ruins. Not the kind of place I would place a nightclub. It would be my luck that we had to visit one in the decrepit part of the city.

We drove through streets lined with gangs and loud exhausts on cheap cars. We veered around a right corner, and then Drew's directions turned us into a little parking lot. It wasn't a large one, and there were only a couple of spaces left. Cassie drove around the little one-way system and parked facing the way out. I watched Logan drive in and park in the last space a few seconds later. Drew got out of the car, "This is it."

"Great." I tried to put as much sarcasm into my voice, but Drew didn't seem to hear it. Cassie, on the other hand, sent a smirk my way.

"Don't worry. You have us with you. Plus your boyfriend is the owner's son."

"He's not my boyfriend."

"Yet." She pulled a massive grin, and I heard her little giggle as she got out the car. I exited out of the passenger side door after moving Drew's seat forwards. It was nice to be able to have my legs fully stretched out again. I looked over the cars as Drew met Logan and Jewel where they had parked. I looked up at the building to my left. It was like an apartment block. I didn't know anyone who would want to live there though. They did have garages so the cars wouldn't get destroyed, but I doubt a simple lock would persuade people around here not to do naughty things.

My gaze went to my right, seeing the entrance of the

nightclub lit up like Vegas. However, the rest of the building was just as run down as the neighbourhood. Once we were all in a bigger group, we started walking to the neon light that spelt the name of the club, Night Stalker. It didn't make the club sound very nice. In fact, it made me not want to go inside even more. Unfortunately, that was our plan.

I cleared my head of all worry as we walked the last few steps to the doorman. There was a short queue lined up outside. They were stopped by a red velvet rope linking two golden poles which looked more expensive than the building.

The doorman took one look at Drew and just stepped aside. He didn't say anything to any of us. The only time I heard him speak was to shout at the queue to shut up. If the inside of the building was anything like the outside, I couldn't understand why people were waiting to get in.

A thick wooden door that looked like it belonged on a medieval castle led us in. As soon as we walked into the little cloakroom area, I could hear the music. It sounded just like any other club. A heavy bass line that vibrated through every bone in your body along with some voice singing. I could never understand what the singer was saying because of the loud sounds on top.

A blonde behind the reception desk looked disinterested in us as we came in. Everything on her was fake from the extensions in her hair to the breasts in her dress. She didn't give us any kind of acknowledgment until Drew slipped some money across the counter. Not only were we walking into this kind of place but now we have to pay to enter.

Even with the money, she didn't act human until she looked up and saw Drew's face. She pulled a great big smile and started playing with the end of her hair. There was no way it could be any more obvious without jumping over the desk and mounting him. All that Drew did back, much to my delight, was give her a quick nod. This didn't seem to hurt her in any way. As Drew walked past her, she didn't stop staring at him. More precisely, his arse. I couldn't blame her, in the trousers he was wearing it did look delicious.

I peered back at the blonde, but she was no longer looking at Drew. She was giving me the evils big time. If all the girls were going to be like this here, I was going to dislike it even more.

We moved past the desk and the toilets. Black stairs led the way up to the where the music was being pumped out of large speakers. As we ascended further, the music got so loud I couldn't hear my own thoughts. I guess that was the idea. Only let the people here think about dancing and drinking.

We walked through a pair of double doors, and the music hit us with full force. I looked around. To the right were a few little stools creating a tiny seating area. The rest of the level spread out to the left. Immediately in front of us was a large dance floor. Stairs led up to the left to another level holding a smaller dance floor. Over to the left led up to a bar and a few poles. All I could really see in that direction were neon signs in the shape of beer names.

We moved further into the room, just standing on the edge of the dance floor. People were dancing like idiots like no one could see them. Jumping and flailing their arms about. Looking past them to the bar. One side was quiet and calm, the other had multiple bartenders running around. Seemed like one side was to serve the normal people and the other was for the erratic dancers. Although, judging by what some people are wearing, there aren't any normal people in here.

I looked over to Logan and Drew. Their mouths were moving, but the music blocked my ears from hearing them. After they had cleared something up Drew looked my way. Then he carried on talking to Logan. The only thing I could make out was that they were talking about me. After a few sentences Drew nodded. He threw a worried look my way before walking off. Logan and everyone else followed. I was at the back of the line which allowed me to keep looking around the club.

We went up the stairs on the left and up to another bar. From below I hadn't noticed the two walkways that ran around the walls up here. They were covered in darkness with the odd splash of colour from the moving lights. Up here people were dancing even weirder and for a moment I could swear I saw a couple doing more than dancing together.

Looking away quickly I saw the glass booth where the DJ was dancing just as bad as the others. He had glow sticks hanging from his clothes. I couldn't believe I hadn't noticed him before since he was lit up like a Christmas tree. The wall above the glass booth was one big window. On the other side, I could see a luxurious office with a man sitting in a green leather chair. I saw the illumination of a screen on his desk. It showed the queue outside and a few of the areas inside.

We left the bar and walked up a short hallway. A man standing behind a red velvet rope stopped us from progressing any further. He didn't even speak. As soon as Drew came into his vision, he just lifted the rope and stepped aside. I heard the soft metal clink as he placed the rope back across blocking anyone else from following.

Ahead were two doors. The one ahead just had a toilet sign on it, and the other had "Private" written across in shiny gold letters. I was expecting Drew to knock on the door. Instead, he just grabbed the handle and walked straight in. As soon as we got through the door, a man rushed forwards to grab Drew. He was big, but I couldn't smell anything in the air. He was human and Drew could easily toss him aside. However Drew just stood there. The large man pulled his fist back. It stopped when the man at the desk shouted. "Let him go!" All of our attention went to him as he practically ran across the room. He slammed his hand into the large man's chest. "Don't you know who this is?" Another hit sent the man back a step which was weird considering the size difference. The man from the desk turned to face Drew and smiled, "Haven't seen you around here for a while. What's up?"

"Nothing. Where's Griffin?"

"Your dad is at his new club. It's not far from here. I can give you the address if you like."

"That would be great." The man smiled and jogged back to his desk. He seemed to be rushing about to help Drew without asking any questions. Either he was a nice guy, or he was afraid of what Drew's father would do if he didn't.

The man came back with a piece of paper. Drew took it from him and turned around. He didn't say thank you or wait for the man to speak. He came walking out making the rest of us retreat back into the little corridor. It happened so quick I almost got pushed into the toilet behind me. My bum hit the wood, and the door swung open. Hands landed on my hips.

I turned my head around to see a blonde guy behind me. He smiled showing his white teeth and the small gap where one of his canines used to sit. He let me get my balance back and then let go. I slid to the side to let him through which was hard due to his massive size. He was wearing a suit just like the big man in the office. After a short sentence from the man that helped us, this new guard shut the office door behind him.

We had what we needed, and I didn't want to stay in here any longer than we had to. The man by the velvet rope let us out, and we made our way through the busy crowd. Whilst elbowing my way through the dancers my nose picked up a scent. It smelt so weird. I found it hard to place where it was coming from and what it reminded me of. With all the sweat lingering in the air I would have to stand around concentrating on it to find this person. I had a quick look around me, but there was no way of pinpointing it. So I stopped. I refused to let my feet move until I found the source. Cassie noticed and tapped me on the shoulder. "What's wrong?"

"I smelt something weird."

"I didn't smell anything."

"A leecher something."

"Oh, what did it smell like?"

My eyes darted around the large room again. "I don't know. It smelt strange like I was in a jungle or something. The smell of strange plants and trees. I can't be sure though."

"Sounds strange to me." She looked at the door. Everyone else had already moved out into the cool air. "We should go. Catch up."

"Yeah. It's just." I looked back towards the two dance floors. The person I smelt could have been right there in front of me, and I wouldn't know it. I took a big sniff of the air, but it seemed to have been lost to the room. I did, however, smell mint, ash and something else. It was the smell of fresh ice like someone had shoved two ice cubes up my nose. I looked at the crazy people moving to the music, but I couldn't see anyone who stood out. Just like the werewolves and the vampires I could smell, the ice cube smell was from someone who looked human. Someone who could blend in and you would never see them coming for you.

Cassie's voice came again, more like a whisper, "Beth." My feet moved at her voice automatically, walking past her. Our footsteps tapped the steps as we moved back to the entrance. The others had waited at the bottom for us two. The blonde behind the counter was staring at Drew again. He wasn't the only one though. Her eyes were also checking out Logan. She didn't seem too fussed who she looked at.

As we left the building, I noticed the bright shine of the moon in the night sky. It illuminated the clouds around it like something from a book cover.

Drew caught my gaze and looked up as well. "The full moon isn't too far off now.""What does it feel like?"

"Haven't you felt it before?"

"I don't have many memories of what has happened."

"Maybe one night we can take a run together. When we

don't have other things to do, obviously."

"Obviously."

We smiled at each other which was quickly broken by Logan's interruption, "Come on you two." Everyone including Cassie was already near the cars. As we went to join them, Jewel gave us a little smile.

She was very quiet lately. I guess Logan wasn't the best conversationalist in the car. Could imagine how cold the atmosphere was in there with them. Happy I would be enjoying the warmth of Cassie's car.

A stupid grin came to my lips as Drew opened the door for me. I gave him the cutest smile I could muster, and I got one in return. My knees went weak at the impact it had on me. Climbing in first I made sure I got a quick look at his butt as he climbed into the front. I could see why the blonde in the club was checking it out. It did look good.

As Cassie started the engine a question popped into my head, "Doesn't Logan need the address?"

Drew turned to me, "I already gave it to him."

"Oh."

"I did it when you were still in the club. What were you doing by the way?"

"I thought I smelt something, but it was nothing."

He looked over his shoulder at me before saying, "Okay."

"Time to go." Cassie slipped the car into gear and left the car park after Logan and Jewel. "So where are we going, Drew?"

"It's just a few roads away, follow Logan. It won't take us long. A few rights and lefts if my memory serves me well and we're there."

I leant forwards in my chair, "Is it in the same area then?"

"Almost. Why?"

"It's just, this place doesn't look that friendly." Staring out the window, I saw the mucky looking neighbourhood we were leaving.

"You mean it's rough looking."

"I suppose." Drew laughed. "It's not funny."

"Don't worry, I'm sure you can look after yourself."

"Maybe." I wasn't too sure if I could. Surviving the training room had been pure luck and instinct. Drew was there to help me out with the guards in the office building.

"You've survived this long." He turned around to face me. A great big smile was on his face. "Besides you have us to protect you."

"Nothing to worry about, Beth. You have a witch, a werewolf, a vampire and another leecher as friends. Nothing is going to happen."

"You two are right. Shouldn't worry about things so much. Hey."

My eyes met Cassie's in the rear-view mirror. "Very true. Now I'm curious about what happened in the club."

"I told you I smelt something."

"Not that. I'm talking about what happened in the office. What was that all about Drew? You were very short with that guy."

He sighed, "It's complicated."

"Stories are never complicated. They're either too personal or embarrassing. Now I have loads of stories that are embarrassing. I think you should tell us yours."

"Okay." He blew out another breath. "You're right, it's not complicated. It's actually very simple. It is personal though." I was both intrigued and worried. He was a werewolf. Anything to do with his past was going to be supernatural. Would I want to hear this? Would I still see this man the way I do now after this story? "It happened a few months after I was officially turned into a werewolf." It seemed I was going to be hearing it anyway. "There was a girl in our pack that I was fond of. She felt the same, and we got authorisation from the alpha of our pack. I took her home for dinner to meet my father. He met her and liked her. On the business side of things, he was used to taking whatever he wanted. It never occurred to him that his personal life should be different. About twenty minutes after we arrived he went missing as well as my guest. When I went looking, I found them both upstairs in the toilet. He had her perched on the edge of the sink. Their clothes littered the floor. They both seemed to be enjoying themselves."

Cassie quickly interrupted, "We get the picture. You can skip past that part."

"The problem was that she hadn't been turned long. Maybe a couple of weeks. This meant she couldn't quite control herself. The heat of sex for a werewolf is like a drug and can be very hard to control in the first few months. When my father said no, she kept going until he hit her. She lost it and attacked him. Rage is another thing hard to stop in those months. I tried to stop her, but she turned and swiped my dad's arm. Horrible gashes that went deep into the muscle. She went to kill him, but he shot her first."

"With what?"

"A silver bullet."

"He knew you were werewolves? That they exist?"

"I never told him. He, however, not to my knowledge, had been working for the government. The head of a special lab creating ways to detect supernatural creatures. He had one on his wrist at the time which told him she was a werewolf. Anyway, he obviously had the silver bullets made just in case when he learnt about the species. When I went back to the pack and explained what had happened, they kicked me out. Because he was connected to me by blood, I to, had her blood on my hands. I had only been there for a few months, and then I was out. I never forgave my father for doing what he did. He cost me, my new family. That is why I act the way I do when it comes to anything connected with him."

"Sounds fair." Those two words were the last ones said for the rest of the drive.

I wasn't sure if I wanted to hear that story or not. It was part of his past, and I would need to hear things about it if I wanted to get to know him. My past is boring compared to his, but my future was going to be the complete opposite. I was glad to have him around as well as Cassie. I leant back in my seat and got comfortable for the last few directions.

Since there wasn't any parking along the street, we went down a ramp into an underground car park. Not only was there a large entrance to the club up above, but there was also a smaller one down in the underground parking lot with its own neon sign. It wasn't as flash or as big as the one above us, but it had a large bouncer guarding it all the same. The glowing neon-lit that area of the level with a soft blue glow. The squiggly glass spelt out the name of the club, The Four Elements.

Climbing out I watched as a small group of girls walked over to the bouncer. They weren't wearing much. It made me feel a little overdressed for heading into a club. It didn't matter though, and I turned to give Jewel a smile. She raised her eyebrows in an unasked question. So I motioned towards my clothes. I was happy to see her smile and saw her fingers click. I felt the material around my body shifting against my skin. When I looked down, I saw the change in my attire. Now wearing a tight pair of black jeans and a top that gave off a good look at my cleavage. She had even changed the kind of bra I had on. Making my breasts push up and together.

As Jewel came walking past me, she sent a wink my way. "I figured Drew would like the look."

"Thank you." Turning around I saw Drew looking. Watching as his eyes slowly moved up from my jeans and over my cleavage. Smiling at the sexy grin that hit his lips. "Like something?"

"You have no idea." He wrapped an arm around my waist, and we all moved closer to the bouncer. Since the club was new, the bouncer would no doubt be fresh to the job.

Meaning he wouldn't know who Drew was like the last place.

My werewolf went to say something to me but then his eyes went back down to the top stretched over my chest. His face was a picture that I wanted to remember forever. I didn't say anything. All I did was pull a cute smile and punched him in the shoulder. He smiled, but his eyes didn't move. That was until Logan brought us back to the mission at hand. "Let's get going. I don't want to be here any longer than is needed."

"Sure, Logan." Drew took the lead. The bouncer, after letting the girls in, watched us all the way. He pulled a fake smile at Drew, then asked for his name. When Drew gave it to him, he checked the list in his hand. He clearly didn't know who he was working for if the last name didn't ring a bell. "You're not on the list. How about the rest of you?"

"You don't understand. I'm here to see my father."

"Is his name on the list?"

"He owns the place so probably not."

"He owns the place. Like I haven't heard that before. Get out of here."

"You don't understand. I want to see my father. Scratch that, I don't want to see him, I need to see him."

"That's nice buttercup. Out of the way."

"You don't understand."

"You've said that already."

"Look!"

"Keep your voice down or I'll…"

"What? You'll do what?" Drew stepped forwards, staring up at this large man. If he had been human, it would have been a stupid thing to do. However, knowing he had that hidden beast inside him meant the bouncer was in trouble if he didn't listen.

"This." Drew was grabbed roughly by his shoulder. A quick sniff told me that the large man was human. So when Drew moved so quickly, it shocked him. Despite his size, he was lifted up off the floor by his throat. His feet dangled there inches from the concrete. Taking a few side steps, my werewolf moved the bouncer out the way of the door before sending him flying off into the wall.

The man wasn't knocked out, but he was shocked. He got to his feet and towered over Drew again. This time he chose the better option and simply stood aside. "In you go and have a good time."

"Not likely." We all went into the darkness of the club.

A hallway stretched out with mirrors on either side of us. They reflected our twin images back upon themselves. I looked on either side seeing the many reflections of myself getting smaller and smaller as they moved back into the distance.

As we neared the end of the mirrors, the music started pounding into our heads. It was the usual kind of music you would expect in a club, but it was quieter. The bass wasn't shaking my bones, and I could hear the vocals of the song. I could also hear people chattering. Now and again, the speaking was covered by cheering. Even the music became backround noise when this happened.

When we moved into the main room of the club, it was not what I was expecting. The lighting was not dark with strobe lighting flashing around the place. Instead, it was well lit. The lights on the ceiling were stylish. Over to the right was plenty of seating. Small tables were dotted about in between the chairs. The rest of the room was a large dance floor, but not much dancing was going on. None of the seats were filled with people either.

Everyone that seemed to be here for drinks or fun crowded in front of the bar. A few movements came from the barmen, and the whole crowd cheered like a famous band had just walked on stage. We all moved closer with our curiosity.

As we neared the back of the crowd Drew seemed to spot someone. His breath touched my ear making me shiver a little. It wasn't necessary because the music wasn't loud, but I wasn't going to complain. "I'll be back soon. Griffin is over there." He gestured over to the end of the bar. I looked and saw a man standing there in a suit. It looked expensive and made him stand out from the rest. He had a red hand-kerchief sticking out of the jacket pocket lending him some class. The light from the ceiling created a white curve on his black shoes. The strands of hair he had left on his head were long and were slicked back leaving a round bald spot covered the dome of his head. He had a gentle face which didn't fit his persona as a crime boss.

As he saw Drew walking towards him, he seemed to not know what to do. At first, he stepped away from the bar and looked happy. Then his smile disappeared, and he moved back to his leaning position. Then he was shuffling his feet about. He looked everywhere except at Drew. By the time the werewolf got to his father, the man had moved away from the bar again. He held out his hand for a handshake. I wasn't surprised when Drew didn't take the offer. Neither of them looked very happy about the conversation they were having.

My attention was torn from them when another cheer from the crowd made me jump. I slowly moved a little closer, weaving in between people. Coming out I found a small gap up at the end of the bar. Perching my elbows on the shiny wood, I watched the bartenders at work. They were amazing at their jobs. I found my eyes watching with wonder as the bottles and glasses were flung around in the air. Chucking them to each other and mixing drinks without a drop spilt on the floor.

The two nearest to me were similar in looks. They were tall, both with a little chub on their stomachs. Their white shirts showed this to all the patrons, but they didn't seem to care. The one with brunette hair had a vacant look in his eyes. He had a cheeky smile that went well with his baby looks. The blonde one had a wicked smile like he had stolen it from the devil himself. He wore black sunglasses, blocking my view of his eyes.

The two down at the other end were different. They were both short but the difference was one being skinny, and the other was larger. It wasn't fat. It seemed to be rock hard muscle. His shirt was so tight I could see it ripping if he turned the wrong way. The other however was almost drowning in his. Both had receding hairlines with their hair gelled up in style.

Their looks and their skills with the bottles wasn't what amazed me though. Each of them was showcasing a special gift. The big guy at the far end was crushing chunks ice the size of snooker balls with his bare hands. Turning them into nothing more than slush.

His friend beside him was moving things around the bar without touching them. Like he could control them with some kind of invisible force. The two nearest to me were easier to see. The blonde was making drinks of water for him and anyone else who wanted one. With his tricks and movements, it seemed like he was bringing these drinks out from nowhere. Turning an empty glass into one containing water.

Forgetting about him I noticed the fourth setting shots alight without the aid of a lighter. It was interesting, to say the least. I couldn't smell anything until I started looking for it. Allowing the usual scents to drift into the background and looking for something different. As my eyes focused on the muscular one, I felt a cool breeze of smell entering my nose. Made me feel like I was atop a tall mountain with clouds forming below me. The clear, crisp air you would get at the summit.

The second bartender's essence moved up my nose like a gush of wind. The coolness of it hitting my brain. As I stopped the smell kept breezing up my nostrils like it was a constant wind. As I stared at him, he caught my glance and smiled. He then quickly went back to getting drinks ready for the customers.

I moved onto the blonde who was spinning a bottle of vodka around his back. He smelled like a vast body of water. Like an ocean surrounded me at this very moment.

The last guy alone smelled warm. He smelled like he was on fire right there in front of me. Thing is he wasn't. He was moving around pouring shots along the bar. They were all supernatural and were using the powers in the open. The question was, is this all they could do, simple tricks or were they hiding something bigger.

I stood there watching them work until the one that had smiled appeared in front of me. "What can I get you?"

"Nothing thanks. I'm not here for the drinks."

"Here for the show are you?" He didn't wait for me to answer. Plucking some ice cubes from a bucket, he placed them on the bar in front of me and waved his hands above them. I heard a very tiny gush of wind and the cubes started sliding over the wood. They moved in a pattern, just missing each other like a choreographed dance. Shooting his hand up the cubes lifted from the wooden bar and into his grasp. Allowing them to slide back into the bucket he smiled at me again. "How was that?"

"Very impressive."

The bartender's eyes narrowed slightly, "Not impressive enough?"

"I didn't say that." His smile appeared again. He looked over my shoulder at some of the candles sitting on the tables at the back of the room. He sent my attention that way with a nod. I heard him blow out sharply. As he did one of the candles snuffed out with a puff of smoke. Blowing again another went out suddenly. I turned back around as he dropped his hand from his mouth. "So can you do anything bigger or is it just small magic tricks?"

"We're all capable of so much more." He winked before walking off to attend to a customer. I squeezed my way out of the crowd when I saw Drew chatting with the others. As I came up to them Drew spoke, "He's going to help us. He said he would do it as a favour to me, but I know he just wants to get rid of The Saracen."

"Did he say how he's going to help us?"

"He said he would set up a deal for one of the buildings he owns. The Saracen's been after it for a while so he'll be more inclined to accept the deal. He wasn't exact with the details of the meet. Wherever it is we can deal with The Saracen and everything else should get sorted. My father is going to call me when it's set up." Drew held up an expensive looking phone. I didn't recognise the name of it. "All we have to do is wait."

"How long?" Logan seemed impatient. "Did he give any clue when he would be getting things going?"

"He said he was going to make the call now. Whether The Saracen will take the bait straight away is just something we'll have to wait and see."

"We don't have time though. We need to get this sorted so things can be dealt with permanently."

"I talked about that as well. He said he might be able to help with the government. He's still got some pull with some friends in his old department. He might be able to get us some gadgets as well."

"Let me guess, we'll have to wait and see how that goes as well."

"Yes."

"How many times do I have to say this, we don't have the time to wait."

"Saying that doesn't mean things will go any quicker. We need to calm down and wait."

"We don't have time!" Logan blew out a long breath and walked out of the bar.

"I'll go after him." Cassie followed him out quickly.

I turned to Drew, "How long do you think it will take?"

"I'm sorry, but I really don't know. Can never tell with

my father." Drew did carry on talking but I stopped listening. That smell I had noticed in the last club was now teasing my sense of smell. I concentrated on the smell and tried to find its source. Following it like an Easter egg hunt. My gaze moved around the room and past the crowd. The person producing the scent wasn't in that mob of watchers, but he was close by. Drew finally realised I wasn't listening to him. He touched me on the arm to get my attention, "What's wrong?"

Jewel moved closer as I replied, "There's a strange scent here. It was at the other club as well. I can't pinpoint it though."

"That could be one of my father's toys. He might have been worried the government would send their leechers after him. He might have other gadgets in this place so you should be careful."

"So what do we do?"

"I'm not an expert. Just concentrate and look around. See if anyone jumps out at you."

"I'll try." Before I could even get a sniff of the air, I saw the guy from the other club. The one that had helped us in the office. He was in a heated discussion with Drew's father.

They were still going at it as they walked through a door marked private.

Grabbing Drew's attention I nodded over to the slowly closing door. The werewolf seemed surprised to see the visitor, "How did he get here so quick?"

"I don't know, but now the smell has gone." Drew turned around as the door shut behind them.

"Did you get this smell in his office?"

"No, it was on the way out."

"Strange. You sure the smell was coming from him?"

"Not sure but it went as soon as he went through that door." I gave the air a quick sniff but couldn't find a single trace of that strange smell. "Yeah, it's definitely gone now.

"There's only one thing I can think of."

"What?"

"No way. There hasn't been any documented case of it." Jewel cut in.

"What?" Was either of them going to fill me in?

"Just because there isn't a documented case doesn't mean they don't exist."

"Drew, Jewel, what are you two talking about?"

Jewel's eyes locked on mine, "What Drew is saying, is that the person you are smelling is a shapeshifter. He can take on people's looks. Become them if you will."

I didn't understand the problem, "Why are you saying this can't be true?"

"No one has ever really met one. There's only rumours about them. Nothing solid."

"Nothing about what a leecher would smell or anything?"

"Nothing."

"It doesn't mean they don't exist. It's the only thing that comes to mind with this situation. It's the only thing we have to go by." Jewel aimed her determination at Drew, trying to convince him.

"Say this is all true. What do we do? If that person in there isn't the guy from the other club, what is he doing here?"

Drew's face dropped, "It can't be anything good." He turned on his heel quickly and jogged over to the door labeled private. His fist was quick, knocking loudly, the force making the wood creak. When there was no answer Drew tried again. This time the door swung open and there stood a bear-sized man wearing a nice black suit. This person blocked both the path and the view, "Jewel, go get Logan and Cassie. Tell them what's going on. I'll try and help Drew."

"Okay. Be careful."

"You too." Jewel quickly moved over the carpet and headed towards the underground parking. I walked over to help Drew not sure of how exactly I could. The two men were arguing. "I don't have time to explain again. I need to see my father, now." Drew tried to move past the big man. He managed to budge him a little to the side, but the man was solid. He placed a hand on Drew's shoulder just like the last one did. I watched as Drew grabbed the man's wrist and twisted sharply. The suited guy dropped to his knees, his face was filled with pain. Drew twisted a little harder to get his point across. "I'm sorry, but I needed to do this. My father is in danger." The man nodded. I was sure he was just nodding so his wrist wouldn't get broken. I was about to move forwards but Drew moved so quickly. He brought his knee up and smacked it into the bridge of this guy's nose. The man's head snapped back, and the large lump fell back onto the carpet. "Help me." Drew grabbed the man's arms and started dragging him through the doorway. I grabbed the feet but wasn't much help. There was no way I would leech off of someone since Griffin Gaynes was so close. I had to be careful if the stories about him were true and the gadgets he had at his disposal.

Looking out into the bar as I shut the door I was happy to see no one had seen us. Letting it click shut I turned and followed Drew. There were no doors apart from a glass one at the end. It was frosted glass keeping the other side a mystery. All we could make out were two blurry shapes.

One of them was standing, and the other seemed to be sitting in a seat. Drew moved faster, his feet hitting the carpet harder. I quickened my own feet to try and keep up with him. As we neared the door, Drew didn't slow down. He just launched himself through the air, shattering the glass window. Taking a deep breath, I jumped through the hole left behind. Impressed by my own agility as I landed on the other side. Under our feet, hardwood flooring stretched out to a massive desk ahead of us.

We rushed forwards, but there was no point. The man standing was Mr. Gaynes. The supposed shapeshifter was slumped over the desk with his eyes closed. I spoke before

Drew got a chance to, "What happened?"

"He pulled a gun on me, so I hit him."

"With what?" Drew asked.

He held his fist up to show us, "It's a special knuckle duster. It shocks them like a taser. Comes in handy when you're old like me." He smiled, but it was all slime. I wasn't going to be trusting this man anytime soon. "He was saying something about one of my other clubs."

"So you know this man isn't one of your employees then?"

"Yes. I've known the real person for quite some time now. I asked about his three kids. The real man only has two. I have to be careful when trusting people."

"Did he give you any information?" I hoped it was going to be a short answer. I didn't want to listen to any more of his voice. It seemed to slide across my skin leaving a trail of slime. "Did he say anything else?"

"Not before I hit him. I'll interrogate him when he wakes up and find out what he was up to. You should all get out of here. Find somewhere safe to lay low. I'll ring the phone I gave you when it's all set up. Then both of us can get The Saracen out of our lives for good."

"Right. Let's go, Beth." As Drew turned around, I thought about how Mr. Gaynes was going to interrogate this person. Then again, it would be best not to think about it. It would undoubtedly make my stomach churn.

So I followed Drew back to the others. As we all walked back out into the underground car park Drew mentioned laying low. "There's a motel just outside of the city that we should stay at until the meet is all set."

Logan nodded in agreement, "I hope this motel has a shower and a bed. I desperately need one."

"I need something to eat." Cassie didn't look hungry. Then again I didn't know what a hungry vampire looked like. "Haven't eaten anything in almost a week."

"You can go that long without blood?"

"I'm old enough to last almost two weeks. I just don't like going that long."

Realising there was still things I knew nothing about I looked into the deep eyes of my werewolf. "What about you Drew?"

"I can go a few days without meat before feeling hunger. But I don't need to eat to survive."

"What do you mean?"

"I'll explain as we walk." We did so, and he carried on explaining his eating habits. "Werewolves don't need to eat to survive. If we don't eat we become weak and are easy prey though."

"So the more you eat, the stronger you are."

"To a certain point, yes."

"Same goes for us vampires as well."

"What about leechers? I haven't eaten for a while now, and I don't feel that hungry. I mean I could eat, but my stomach isn't aching from it."

"You would have to ask Logan about that. Unless Drew knows."

"I don't know, I've tried to steer clear of leechers." He smiled at me. "Up until now." He rubbed my arm as we neared the cars. Logan was sitting in the driver's seat playing with the sat nav. Sticking his head out the window, "I think it would be best to stick to one car. Got the motel logged into the sat nav." Drew walked around to the passenger side door, so it looked like it was going to be us girls in the back. But before getting into the vehicle I only now noticed that someone was missing. "Where's Jewel?"

Logan blew out a long sigh before replying. "She took off. Was too scared to come to the meet in person. As usual, leaving it up to someone else to clean up her mess."

I was about to say something, but I could tell from his face that it would be a terrible idea right now. He needed time to calm down before this situation was discussed.

Logan handed Drew the sat nav. "Is that the right place?"

Drew gave it a quick look, "Yep, that's the one. Only five minutes down the road."

"Let's go then." Logan started the car and sped out of the car park. We got back onto the main road and zoomed past the trees lining the edge of the roads on our way out of the city.

"Logan, do we need to eat?"

"What do you mean? We can grab something when we're at the motel if you're hungry."

"No, I mean do leechers need to eat? Like a vampire or a werewolf", I saw his eyes meet mine in the rear-view mirror.

"We leechers need to eat like any human, but we don't need to eat as often. Our bodies get weaker after a few days. Then we need to eat. Obviously, you can eat anytime you want, and you will feel hungry now and again. It all depends if you can handle the hunger in your stomach or not."

"Oh." I looked away from the rear-view mirror and looked out the window. With all this talking about food, I was starting to feel that ache in my stomach. I couldn't remember the last time I had eaten anything. There should be something at the motel for me to have.

Sitting in the back with a space in between Cassie and me made me think of Jewel. It seemed like there was a gap in the group just like there was in the car. I wondered where she had run off to.

We pulled off the concrete road and followed a dirt track up to the motel. It looked like it belonged in the woods. The reception area was made out of wood like a small cabin. The longer building that housed the rooms was a little more modern. It still looked like it belonged to a mutated family from a horror film. The empty car park told us we were the only ones here. The open sign on the reception door was the only sign anyone was working.

After parking, we all walked into the little cabin. In the window was the usual stand of pamphlets. It was only just big enough for the four of us. A weird musky smell was coming from somewhere. This was accompanied by a radio in the back and some poor singing. Logan tapped the bell that sat on the desk which didn't give off the normal ping. So he knocked on the counter a few times. Seconds later the bad singing stopped, and a short man popped his head out from the office.

The thick-rimmed glasses he wore were almost covered by the greasy curls that made up his fringe. There was a look of surprise before he pulled a crooked smile. His dirt covered jeans and shirt made it look like he had just come back from hiking in the woods. Or rolling around in the mud.

"How may I help you?" I was shocked to hear how squeaky his voice was. Then my eyes dropped to his hands as he rubbed them together like they were dirty.

Logan spoke quickly, "Any rooms free?"

"They all are. You get your pick today." Pulling up a big book, he flopped it open before us. "You just need to sign in. How many rooms would you like?" His eyes darted between what he must have thought were two couples.

"Four."

The motel worker didn't seem hurt by Logan's stern tone. "Four it is." Our keys were pulled from the little pigeon holes on the wall. "You pay when you leave. I will need a credit card for insurance purposes obviously."

Drew moved forward, "Just in case we make a run for it?"

"I don't like to say that but yeah." A squeal came out of his mouth like it was supposed to be some kind of laugh.

"It's alright." The man studied the card Drew handed over. Once happy he placed it in a small box for safe keeping. Logan scooped up the keys and tossed one to each of us. My eyes looked at the yellow three dug into the redwood of the tag. I turned to Cassie, "What number did you get?"

"I'm in four." She looked at my key and smiled, "You better keep the noise down lady." She laughed and walked out the door. Logan gave me a little smile as he walked past me to get to the door. I heard it shut as Drew turned around. He had a large smile aimed my way. "Looks like I'm on the other side of you." He held his tag up so I could see. "Number two." His smile got bigger as he walked towards the door. I couldn't help but show my own.

Looking at the worker, he gave me a grin. I lessened my own smile and aimed it his way. "Thank you." Moving out of the small room quickly I saw Cassie and Logan disappear into their rooms. As I made my way over to my room, I let my eyes run over Drew's figure. With the way it looked and moved I wondered if I would be able to stick to my own room.

Just as I was about to slide my key into the lock, I had a bad thought. I couldn't remember if Logan or Drew turned the sat nav off. Could we be tracked through that or was I being paranoid? Either way now that we were laying low I didn't want to take any chance.

I jogged back to the car and opened the door, thanking Logan in my mind for not locking it. I bent down and picked the little box up. Holding down the power button, I watched the screen go black. Then I decided to take it one step further, pulling off the back and yanking out the battery.

Once I was happy my paranoia had been looked after, I put it back in its home. I was about to leave the car alone when I spotted something sticking from under the passenger seat. Feeling curious I pulled out a yellow envelope from its hiding place.

Turning the object over in my hands I listened to the gravel under my feet as I made my way back to my room. I kept my leecher smell on high, seeing if I could pick any scents up that shouldn't be there. There was nothing there, so

I used my key and entered the safety of my room.

Locking it behind me and putting the chain across made me feel safer. It made no sense since a supernatural creature would turn the wood into splinters or could even smash through the big window. There was no logic behind my actions, but it made me feel safer. It was stupid, and I knew that, but it didn't change that fact.

Plopping down on the bed I heard a voice from the other side of the wall. I doubt Cassie would be chatting with anyone so it must be her television. I picked up the remote for mine and switched it on. I didn't care what channel it showed, it was to give the impression I was watching it. I didn't know if we had been followed or not. There could have been someone with that shapeshifter.

With my cover as an ordinary occupant secure, I opened the envelope and tipped out the contents. It was a single wad of paper folded up. Unfolding it, I almost dropped it out of shock. On the front page was a stapled photograph of me. It must have been taken at my old university.

My photo had a red stamp on my face. I could feel my heart pounding harder in my chest as I read those letters. Spelling out the primary target. Why was I the primary target? Surely they were using me to get to Logan. Why would I be the primary target and not the secondary? It wasn't making sense.

I flicked the pages frantically, picking up any information I could. It seemed the government had been keeping track of me for years and years. Almost my whole life. Pages held logs in here that dated back to when I was twelve. I seemed to remember my blackouts starting around then. They weren't very often, but I was definitely twelve when they began.

Reading on I noticed the gap between each episode was about a year when it all started. More and more logs were recorded as it happened more frequently. This was getting weird. It was like they were more concerned about me than they were Logan. He was the more important one, not me. He had information on them and has been a thorn in their sides for a while now. I was a nobody. I had only just got used to my ability. Surely they had leechers in their unit that are more capable.

I just want to have a normal life where I can go to university and get a part-time job and have some friends. I could have a small apartment, but it would be mine. That's all I wanted. Now I was on the run from not only the government but a very old vampire who was hell-bent on collecting a debt for this Saracen bloke.

All of that and it didn't include what had happened with the ring. That was something very out of the ordinary. It was beyond abnormal for it to squeeze so tightly around my finger. Now we were resting it would have been the perfect time to ask Jewel about it. It was a shame she wasn't here to do that.

A sudden knock hit the door making me drop the papers onto my bed. Taking a quick look down at the horrible information I answered. "Just a minute." Flicking the cover over the papers, I walked up to the door. A quick look through the peephole revealed my surprise visitor was Drew. My lips moved into a big smile making me forget all about what I had just read. Even through the distorted glass, he looked yummy.

Unlocking the door and unhooking the chain I opened the door. He smiled as he saw me. I couldn't help but smile back. It was infectious. Even if I tried my hardest, I wouldn't be able to stop my lips from curling. "How come you've decided to pay me a visit?"

"Just thought I'd come by and offer you some help."

"What would I need help with?" I was trying to make myself not seem interested. My body language wasn't helping. My hip was stuck out to the side, and I was twiddling the ends of my hair. I had noticed the small traits I have when I am flirting. I would always try and stop them, but a minute later

I would be doing it again. I had learnt to just live with them, and with this particular guy, I didn't care if he noticed them.

"You said you hadn't really been told much about were-wolves. I've come to change that."

"In that case, I would like to say thank you and take you up on your offer."

"Great." He took a step inside the room. I placed my palm on his chest. My thoughts were briefly jumbled as all I could think about was the strong muscles pressed against my palm. His body felt warm even through the material of his top. Right then I wanted to rip it open and feast my eyes on his flesh.

I wanted to touch him, skin on skin. Those seconds of heat I felt had my mind swimming with so many thoughts and ideas. But it wasn't the time for daydreaming. I slowly slid my hand down his body feeling every ripple and bump of his body. My tongue licking my bottom lip involuntarily. My hand kept going until it hung freely by my side. "What's wrong?" A soft smile curved the corners of his mouth up towards his twinkling eyes.

"There's nothing wrong. Let's practice in your room."

"Maybe we should do it outside. Take a walk in the woods." His smile grew mischievous.

To my own disappointment, I said, "We should stay in our rooms. Just in case we're needed."

"Good point. My room it is then." Drew didn't look dis-appointed. He was still smiling which was making it hard to behave. I could easily jump into his arms and forget about the rest of the world and judging by his look, he felt the same way.

My hormones calmed down a little when he stepped back allowing me to shut my door and check to make sure it was locked. Then my werewolf led me over to his room. When we entered, I noticed he didn't have the television on. Since he was on the end, I could no longer hear Cassie in her room.

one else seemed to. It was no doubt another thing that leechers didn't have to worry about. After all, if we don't need to eat much then maybe we wouldn't need the toilet as much. The thought was destroyed as Drew came back into view. He finished rubbing his hands on a white towel and tossed it back into the bathroom. "Okay, first challenge. The soap in my bathroom is a scented bar. If you can guess from the smell of my hands what the scent is, then you can pick the next challenge." I smiled. This was going to be fun.

I looked at his hands, not knowing if it would help or not. Much like when I use my leecher abilities, I let my sense of smell reach out through the air. I sniffed around for the smell of the soap. He just stood there staring at me. I could see a slight smile, but I ignored it. Instead, all my concentration was on his hands.

It only took me ten seconds longer before I was getting something. It was almost like I could see the wisp of smells rising from his hands. It floated into the air. I drew it closer to me. As it rose up my nostrils, it gave me the answer to the challenge. "Jasmine."

"Correct. I thought you weren't going to get it for a second. Fancy heading outside for the next one?"

"If we stay close to the motel I can't see it being a problem." I got off the chair as Drew walked past me. I still had my senses locked onto Drew. As he passed by all kinds of smells kicked up around me. Not only was the jasmine smell heightened at this short distance, but I also got his natural scent mixed in with that. My hormones sat up and took notice immediately.

I saw Drew's massive grin like he could smell my heightened arousal in the air. It was annoying that he could sense my hormones when I had no clue about his. As I walked towards the door he was now opening I was starting to feel a little hotter. Sweat started to trickle down the back of my neck. It made my top stick to my skin. The closer I got to

Drew the hotter I got. By the time I was by his side, my hair was damp, and my top was drenched.

His gaze came to me, and his face was a picture of my damp attire. "Shit. I almost forgot. You have to imagine there's a wall around your brain. A wall that nothing can penetrate. Nothing gets in or out. You have to do it now." His words came so quick I could only just understand them. I looked into his eyes as a bead of sweat dripped down his temple. "Do it." It was hard to think about anything but him. Shutting my eyes was the only way to stop thinking about him and me in the bed naked. I had to push him completely out of my mind before I could imagine this wall he was on about.

It took a lot of mind power to build this imaginary wall. But once it was complete, the sweat started to slow down. In my mind, I could see the wall that circled all the way around it. It was harder to think of than I thought.

I looked into Drew's eyes. Those few seconds was like I had been daydreaming. A few more beads of sweat had appeared on his face. "What was that about?"

"When two werewolves are attracted to each other, then their auras reflect this. Like I told you before. Since you weren't stopping your aura, that meant I could sense it. Right then I was finding it hard to fight it. We would have been on the bed in seconds if I hadn't told you to block your mind."

"Do you have yours blocked all the time?"

"As often as I can. Obviously, when I sleep, I can't, but as soon as I wake up, my wall goes up. A werewolf's aura, if it goes unchecked can be a dangerous thing. A man could pick up on yours, and he wouldn't be able to stop himself. It could get violent, and then he would lose. That's when you get your problem."

"I'll remember to keep my walls up at all times."

"Good. Otherwise, I might jump on you in the middle of the car park." He pulled an extremely sexy smile. It didn't matter if he had his aura behind a wall, that smile alone had my hormones zooming around for attention. I would happily give him that attention even in the middle of the car park.

I tore my eyes away from his sexy smile to keep my hormones down to a minimum. We both walked out onto the small pathway but didn't venture any further. We both looked around. Apart from the dirt track, we traveled up and a small walking trail off to the left, we were completely surrounded by trees. Despite it being the middle of the night I could make out the green of leaves so clearly. The brown, even though it was still a dull colour, was easier to make out.

A bird chirped and I was able to pinpoint the exact location of it. It was flying in the sky, and I was able to see it in detail. It would have been a small dot before. Now the bird was a larger blob. I could see the wings flapping and the feathers getting caught in the wind.

I looked over to the building which held the reception area and the manager's little office. The side facing us didn't have a window or anything. It was a solid wall, not giving anything away of what was going on behind it. Drew followed my eyes. "Bet you can't guess whether the manager is in his office or not."

"Can you?"

"I've lived with my skills for a while now. It becomes like second nature. I've used them so many times. I want to see how long it takes you?"

"Okay." I stared at the building hard. Listening to my senses, I got rid of taste, touch, and sight since I wouldn't need them for this challenge. With my eyes shut the sounds of the forest around the motel came to life in my ears. Birds chirped louder. Little legs of insects were scurrying across the ground. The wind slipped through the branches giving off a slight whistle. They all dropped into the background as I brought the building and all the noises from within to my ears.

As I listened, I concentrated. But I couldn't hear anything. There was no tapping of his footsteps and no breathing and definitely no bad singing. There was some noise in the form of words, but they were coming from what sounded like a radio. All evidence leant towards him not being inside.

I opened my eyes and looked over at Drew. He hadn't moved from his spot, but he wasn't looking over towards the reception like I was. He was staring off down the dirt track that led into the woods. I peered over that way but couldn't see anything that stuck out. "What's wrong?"

"Sniff the air."

I did so, "There's nothing out of the ordinary."

"Sniff again. Be more thorough." I did what he said. Again turning down my senses and listening to my nose. I took a long sniff of the air. As the different smells came to me, I rifled through them. I eliminated the normal ones like the smell of trees and the rain that would be coming in a few hours. I got rid of the minty smell and Drew's natural scent. I found a sweet smell with a hint of ash that led to Cassie's room.

I was about to give up when I smelt the boring scent that didn't belong. It reminded me of the smell I was hit by when I walked into the reception area. I locked onto it and found its trail. It started at the small building, moving across the gravel and off down the little trail through the woods. I couldn't find the end of it and the only way would be to go have a look. His voice snapped me out of my concentration. "You found it?"

"Yeah. What would he be doing in the woods?"

"There might be some kind of storage shed out there."

"Storage for what?"

"Wood? Maybe tools."

I looked around the reception building. "The storage shed is over there." I pointed so Drew could see what I was on about. He saw the small structure that couldn't really be called a shed. It was more like a large toy box made out of metal. A shovel was leaning up against the side, giving away its purpose.

"Fancy taking a walk?"

"It's probably nothing."

"Probably but I wouldn't mind taking a walk with you in the woods. Plus it is better to be safe than sorry."

I contemplated what he was saying. "What about the other two?"

"I imagine Cassie will go and hunt in a little bit, she said she felt hungry, didn't she? And by the sounds of it, Logan has fallen asleep."

"Really?" I let my ears pick up the rhythmic sound of Logan's gentle snoring. Drew smiled which was filled with intent and desire. If we hung out alone for too long, I didn't know how long I could stop myself from losing control. "Just the two of us it is then."

"I'm glad." As we set off towards the trail, I let my mind think up what it would be like to have Drew in my bed. Unfortunately, they were cut short as we got to the trail. I grabbed hold of the manager's scent, whipping me back into the here and now.

We paused at the mix of dirt and gravel for a little longer, looking into the woods. It was clear as feet had marked out the trail for years. The branches blocked out the moonlight, but that wasn't a problem when you had werewolf essence coursing through your body.

My eyes automatically adjusted to the sudden drop in light. The deeper we went, the clearer things became. In the dirt beneath our feet, I could see small indents made by a pair of large boots. I hadn't noticed what kind of footwear the manager was wearing, but it was the only trail I could see. At least the only one that resembled a shoe. I could see a trail belonging to a dog of some kind. It wasn't very big, but the indents where the claws would be were deep. I bet the animal that left this print would do some damage.

We had only been plodding along for a minute when there was a break in the trees to the left. The trail kept going, but the scent veered off through the trees. There was a small worn away track that had been made from multiple journeys. Instead of following the dirt track we passed through the thin branches. Following our noses.

Maybe there's a little shack down there where he goes to read magazines in peace. Hell, he could have a caravan out here where he lived. I hadn't spotted a car at the motel. It made sense until we found the shed. It was made out of concrete and could easily be mistaken for a bomb shelter.

The walls were made out of large grey blocks instead of small red bricks. The doorway was just a large black hole but thanks to my sight, I could see a grating a little way into the out of place building. It was round like an igloo giving the top a nice domed shape.

As we grew closer, the scent we had been following mixed with something else. It didn't take long for me to place it. I would have gotten the same smell up my nose anytime I walked into a butcher. It was the smell of raw meat and blood. It overpowered a slight hint of mint. I didn't know if it was new or just some coming off of Drew and mixing with the air. It was hardly noticeable, so I put it down to Drew's closeness.

The trees around us seemed to be stretching towards the sky with thin fingers. It looked eerie from this position. What had looked like a nice green forest from the trail now had a dark, creepy feeling to it. That alone had my heart racing. I would never have thought a werewolf could get scared. They always seemed so fearless in the movies.

I stared down into the blackness, but my eyes couldn't pick anything out. There was no manager. There was nothing inside. I walked forwards in confusion. The only thing in this small room was the grating in the wall. A padlock hanging on a bar swung as I pulled it open. I looked again, this time catching the slight change in colour to the stone by my foot. It was the first step of a flight of stairs. My eyesight suddenly changed to night-vision, but this didn't help as the stairs curved sharply a few steps down.

I placed a hand on each side to keep my balance on the thin steps. The walls felt cold under the touch of my fingers. I tuned my hearing to try and pick anything up. The only thing that came up from the abyss was talking. It was a male voice and one that I had heard before. The manager was down here but who was he talking to? I couldn't hear the other side of the conversation. The words that came in response to his words were muffled. So much so I couldn't tell if it was male or female.

I could hear my heart beating faster and faster as I descended down into the bunker. It was almost loud enough to block out Drew's soft footsteps following me. I didn't know what I was thinking going first. In the future, I would have to make sure that I think things through before just walking ahead.

I had no idea how far down we had gone when I spotted a little glow of light. It seemed so bright until my eyes automatically flicked back to normal. The light illuminated the last few steps making me feel better as I got to the floor. My shoes tapped on the concrete. It wasn't very loud, but the sound carried through the room, bouncing off the walls. In the end, two lanterns were hanging from bars that were sticking out of the wall. Beside us in the corner was a weird looking stand. At the top of it, bars formed a bowl. Sitting inside it, burning softly, were a few small logs. The three sources of light lit the room perfectly.

The manager was standing at the end of the room in front of someone who was gagged. Not only that, but she was also chained to the wall. I could feel a sting in the air. We would have to be careful because that sting on my skin meant there was silver down here.

We crept closer making sure our steps made as little noise as possible. I gave Drew a quick glance over my shoulder. He gave me a smile, but by the looks of it, he was just as scared as I was. The setting wasn't exactly comforting, and we had no idea what was going on. The fact Drew seemed scared had me on edge even more. This was getting worse and worse. I wanted to turn around and get back to the motel. That small building was looking like the safest place at the moment. However, we crept even further into the room.

As we neared the end, the sting of silver became so bad I could have sworn someone was jabbing it against my flesh. We got a few metres away from the motel manager when my foot struck a stone sitting on the floor. I froze as it skipped along kicking up noise.

I cursed myself in my head as the manager spun around shocked. I was about to rush forwards and attack when his hand shot out. In his fingers was a long poker. It didn't have a red-hot end but judging from the sting I was feeling all over my body, it was made of silver. Drew stepped forward, so he was next to me but didn't go any further. The poker would do mass amounts of damage if we got stabbed. This damage was evident when I looked past the man and to the woman.

Her long brunette hair covered the top half of her body as her head hung there. Her legs, however, showed the damage the silver had done. The manager must have cut slits in her jeans and then pressed the poker against her skin. There were burn marks on any piece of flesh that was on display. Her legs looked so shaky that if it weren't for the chains, she would be a mess on the floor.

When she raised her head, her sweat soaked hair fell back showing her stomach. Her red top had been cut open, and there were three long burn marks across her skin. This sicko had even used the poker on her young face. It looked awful.

Drew whispered to me as the manager kept eyeing us

cautiously, "If we don't get those chains off of her soon, she won't be able to heal."

Great, now we had to hurry. The manager wasn't looking very stable at this point, and I didn't want to be chained up myself. The poker end seemed to be getting closer as we stood there with our stalemate. I knew it wasn't, but it made me feel uneasy. Half of me wanted to get this over and done with, and the other half just wanted to forget it all. My body was filled with tension as I watched out for the poker. My foot moved a centimeter sending the man into action. Only he didn't attack with the poker. He still kept it pointing at us, but he was backing away. He grabbed a big book that was sitting on a large, thick wooden shelf. He threw it on the floor and flipped it to a certain page. He switched his look from the book then up at us, still holding the poker. He now reached his empty hand out and started chanting. I just stood there. I was caught in between confusion and intrigue. Drew tried to move closer, but the dangerous poker followed his movement.

With no ideas popping into my head all I could do was stare at the silver weapon and hope he didn't attack me. But then an opportunity opened as the young woman had some fight left in her. I just saw her bring her leg up and crack her heel into the manager's ankle. It was only a small hit, but with her werewolf blood it dropped him down to one knee.

That's when Drew moved with a growl and blinding speed. He was so fast I barely had time to register what had happened. One second he was by my side and the next he had the manager up against the wall. The silver poker was sent out of his hand from the force of it. Drew kicked it away from us three as he tightened the hand around the manager's neck. His gasps for air made me smile in delight at his pain. Fingers were squeezed even tighter making his gasps gargle in his throat.

I rushed past them and over to the damaged woman.

When I got a bit closer, I noticed how young she was and my hatred for the manager grew worse. Reaching up without thinking my fingers burned at the touch of the chains. Shaking my hands, I studied the cuffs that held her wrists. They were boring metal. There must be silver underneath against her skin. Since she was still pretty out of it, I grabbed the bottom of her top and ripped it off. Wrapping it around my hands, I grabbed the cuffs and pulled on the chains. It creaked and gave way to my strength as they popped free from her wrists. Seeing the silver sitting inside I kicked them away.

Looking up as the young girl fell forwards onto me. If I hadn't had the werewolf strength, I would have been flattened by the sudden weight. She let out a little moan as I lowered her to the floor.

As I rested her on the concrete, her eyes opened and saw me. Her lips barely moved as a soft voice came out of her mouth. I had to lean closer to hear what she was saying. "Food." Where was I supposed to get food? Then I remembered the smell I had sniffed out earlier. I sieved through the smells in the air and found the smell of blood again. Looking over my shoulder, I saw a metal box sitting against the wall.

Leaving her for a moment, I moved over to it. The hinges creaked as I lifted the lid up. The smell hit me like a wall. I tried to shut it out, but it was already in my nose. It wasn't making me feel sick, but I didn't like it.

I looked over to Drew who was still holding the manager up against the wall. The situation seemed to be under control, so I let the werewolf out of my body. It meant the smell of the meat that sat inside the box wasn't as potent. Unfortunately, my human body didn't like the sight of it all sitting in there. My stomach rebelled against the smell, and I threw up on the floor. My sick splashed against the concrete with a horrible sound. Closing my eyes, I reached in with my hand still covered in her top and threw her a piece of meat.

I didn't bother checking to see if she noticed it. I made a hasty retreat to the steps. The smell was still lingering in the air, but it wasn't too bad over here as the breeze from outside brought in the sweetness of the forest.

I took a seat on the bottom step and took another look around the room. Drew seemed to be questioning the manager, but I couldn't hear what they were talking about. The girl had picked up the piece of metal and was digging into it like it was her last meal. If she finished it, she could get herself another piece of meat. I wasn't going back towards that metal box. In fact, I should have shut the lid to keep the smell from filling up the cellar-like room.

It wasn't long before the girl's meal was finished and she was crawling to the open box for more. Blood was dripping from her chin and onto her chest. Once across the floor, she paused there. I watched as her human body reshaped into a beast. With the full-moon under a week away, she looked like a large wolf. From the size of her jaws, she could bite my head off in one swift move. I almost thought that was going to happen when she barked at me viciously. A paw was moved in my direction, but then she quickly shoved her snout into the meat box.

The burn marks that had been on her skin were now breaks in fur on her body. As I stared at them, I could see the skin of the beast healing. She lifted a large piece of meat out of the box and padded over to the corner. As her teeth started cutting through the meat, she started shifting back into human form. Her top couldn't have gotten any worse, but her jeans were definitely ruined now. All she seemed to care about was eating though.

From here I could see the good her shifting had done to her injuries. Most had already scarred. Only the three deep ones on her stomach were still painful looking. She devoured her second piece of meat and seemed to settle down a little in her corner. This was also around the same time Drew stopped questioning the manager. He let go of his neck allowing the air to change his face colour from blue back to normal.

He gasped in air trying to fill his lungs. Drew stood over him, prepared to attack again if needed. He didn't notice the girl move across the room behind him. I tried to get to my feet, but without the speed of a werewolf, I was no use. I was only a metre away from the steps when Drew caught her hand just in time. Her claws were fully extended, and I'm sure she would have ripped the man's throat out if Drew had let her.

Twisting around he pushed her back against the wall. She snapped her head forward, her canine teeth were extended out like a beast's. Drew held her there easily. Her weakened state meant he could hold her without even trying.

She calmed down once she realised there was no escape from his grip. The manager was still sucking in mouthfuls of air on the floor. I walked closer, keeping an eye on him. In my human state, he could get past me, and I wouldn't be able to stop him. I, however, didn't want to leech off of Drew again.

I could smell the blood coming from the metal box even with my human nose. Drew spoke softly to the girl, ordering her. "Calm down. You just need to calm down." She stared at him trying to figure out whether he was a friend or a foe. She must have believed he was a friend because she stopped struggling against his grip. Soon he let her go, and she just stood there in front of him. I could understand her hatred and need to kill the manager. Drew had mentioned earlier about the bad tempers werewolves had.

Once Drew was happy she wouldn't try anything he turned back around to the manager who was starting to look normal again. My werewolf being the protector that he is chucked the man back into the wall. Drew pushed his hand flat against his chest. I saw his nails beginning to extend and dig into his skin. "What the hell are you doing?"

The manager spat in his face which flared anger up in

his eyes. He pushed his claws deeper making a scream fill the small room. "Last chance. If you don't give me the answer I want, then I'll let her take her revenge." He nodded towards the girl who suddenly seemed happier. The manager didn't seem too bothered by it. I was disturbed by the sadistic smile he pulled. Then his mouth started moving quickly. The words were unrecognisable and sounded more like noises. They were repeated over and over. I was shocked when his whole body started glowing. It was a dark kind of glow. It seemed to suck the light out of the room. The glow got bigger until Drew had to back away, so he wasn't blinded. It was weird to see a dark glow have that kind of effect. I prepared to leech off of Drew if I needed to.

What happened next happened in a blink of an eye. I didn't have any time to react apart from shutting my eyes and throwing my hands up in defense. The manager erupted into black flames. I felt a force hit my body and was glad I didn't feel body parts or blood. When I opened my eyes, there was a black scorch mark on the wall and the floor. I couldn't believe what had happened.

There was nothing left of him. Not even a finger lying on the floor or a smear of blood. He had just vanished into thin air. One second he was there and the next he wasn't. A bunch of chanting and he's gone? Moving forward my foot hit something heavy. Looking down I noticed an old looking book covered in dust. I picked it up, immediately feeling a weird tingle on my fingertips.

I looked at the two pages the book had been opened to. None of it made sense to me. There weren't even words on the page. The symbols were scrawled in black ink, and the pages looked extremely old. I flicked back a few pages and still couldn't find anything I recognized. Shutting it, I let my eyes move over the brown leather cover. It had black embroidery all over it making curved shapes.

At the bottom, it said, DESTRUCTION FOUR. Two

larger words were in the middle of a diamond spelling out LUANA CHRONICLES. With these two and the two at the bottom, I knew exactly what this was. This was a spell book. It must be one filled with destructive spells. Was that what the manager was trying to do? Did he just blow himself up? Things were getting weirder and weirder now I was inside this new world.

First, he has a werewolf chained up in this bunker and now he has a spell book. Can't we go anywhere without supernatural things happening?

I walked over to Drew who looked at the book with a worried look, "We need to tell the others."

"Definitely."

"My name is Elise by the way." We both turned around to the girl now standing in the corner. She had enough jeans left to cover her modesty, but she had to hold the ripped parts of her bra.

"Hey. I'm Beth, this is Drew." I tried to keep my voice from shaking, but it was no use. This situation had shaken me too much to keep it together.

"Thank you for helping me. For that, I'll forget that you're a leecher."

"Had some run-ins with them have you?"

"Hasn't everyone at some point." I wondered how someone so young could have bad stories to tell already. Were my kind really that bad?

Drew smiled at her comment, "Do you have a pack to get back to?"

"I'm not sure. Our alpha was killed and some of the others. I was just told to run and don't look back with the other pups. I lost them in the woods. I'm not too sure if I could find them or not." She started crying, pulling her arms tighter around her own body.

I was about to move and cuddle her but Drew beat me to it, pulling her tiny frame against his like a big brother would do. Drew knew what it was like to lose your pack. "If you don't feel safe looking for them, head north until you reach Hannow Lake. My pack lives up there. Ask for Malcolm and tell him I sent you. He'll look after you and treat you as his own pup."

"Really. That would be great. I don't want to be walking through the woods. Thank you again." She grabbed hold of him tighter, fingers digging into his top. Pulling away slowly she sent me a soft smile. "You've got a good one here."

"Excuse me."

"I can smell his hormone levels. He really likes you."

I smiled, but I was a little annoyed she knew when I could detect a hint of it. "Thanks."

"Thank you. I guess I should be off. Don't want to get in your way."

"You wouldn't be." Drew looked down at her body. Scanning it but it wasn't anything sexual. Despite the lack of clothes, this girl didn't seem to mind. But I didn't blame her with a guy like Drew. "Give me your bracelet."

Elise did so without question. Drew took it and to my surprise held it out for me to put on. My hand rose up, and he slipped the clasp shut around my skin. Elise spoke in her soft voice, sounding a little more steady. "Looks good."

"Thanks." It was the only word I could muster up from my confusion. I pulled a funny face at Drew to try and get some answers.

"It so we can find her after all this is done. Make sure she is okay."

"Oh right. Sounds like a good idea." Looking up into his sweet eyes made me fall for him and his sweet personality even more. I turned to her. "I guess we might see you at a later time then."

"Yep and thank you once again." She smiled and then she was moving. Drew quickly shot out his arm before she could get to the steps. "Take this."

He was half-way through taking his jacket off when she spoke, "It's okay. I'm going to shift into wolf form as soon as I get into the woods."

"Okay." The echo of her feet on the steps was the last thing we heard of her. Then she was gone and out of our lives for the moment. For some reason, I knew we would meet her again. I would have liked to know when and where so I had something in my future I knew about. All these surprises were going to kill me at some point.

Drew grabbed some of the meat for Cassie and maybe for him as well. The walk back through the trees was much slower this time, and I found myself staring around at the beauty. Even in the dark, I could see how amazing this place looked. Didn't give a hint to the horror we just left.

Once back at the motel we head over towards Logan's room. As we neared the door, I didn't need werewolf hearing to know there was someone else in his room. I turned around to Drew, "Can you take that to Cassie's room. The smell is killing me." Amusement filled his eyes as he smiled and walked off. My eyes followed him as he did.

I was about to knock when I heard my name being spoken by Logan's visitor. My curiosity peaked, so I leaned against the door and listened intently. "She's more important than you Logan."

"Why? It doesn't make any sense."

"I need to do more research into the matter, but I have to say that most of it is confidential. I was lucky to get this much."

"Thank you for doing it. I know it's a risk."

"It's not like I haven't done it before."

"True. What about the other thing?"

"I found out all I could. It's all in the file along with a background check on his son."

"Anything interesting?"

"Not really. He's a werewolf. That's about it."

"That's good to hear." Unhappy with the way they were talking about me and Drew I threw the door open suddenly. Moving into the room, I suddenly got a chill that seemed to wrap around my spine. That horrible feeling got worse when I could only see Logan standing in his room. He sat at the bottom of his bed, looking at me like I hadn't just burst into his room. Pretending everything was normal. "How can I help you?" I didn't answer him. Instead, I concentrated on the cold in the room. It wasn't like a breeze from an open window. It seemed to be all around me.

Listening to my leecher skills, I looked for a trail, but it wasn't like that. Instead of something I could follow it just seemed like it was everywhere. I looked back at Logan. He seemed to have a look of recognition in his eyes. "She can sense you, Melvin. You might as well come out."

I waited a few seconds before I noticed a change in the room. The chill seemed to move from all around me and over to a single column of cold. White wisps started dancing in the air until a mannequin-like body was formed before my eyes. Then dips appeared in the head to form eyes. A nose pointed out at me and lips morphed out of the white.

The arms and legs got more defined. No clothes appeared, but the wisps of white didn't need them. Its body wasn't defined enough to cause offence. He looked like a bald male with a pale skin problem.

Then it spoke with a hollow voice that seemed to make the chill worse. Making my hairs stand up on end. "You must be Beth. It's a pleasure to meet you. I would shake your hand, but I'm sure you can see my predicament with that." He moved his arms out emphasizing his ghostly appearance. "It is a pleasure though. I've heard so much about you."

"From Logan?"

"Not exactly." He looked over at Logan who nodded. A confirmation between the two of them. "I work for the government in archives. To be more specific I work in the leecher unit. I hand out assignments and check up on cases. A lot of information comes through archives. At the moment a lot of it has something to do with you."

"Me. Why?"

"That I don't know. They've been marked confidential."

"That's a shame."

"It is indeed. I've been trying to intercept some reports before they get to archives but so far I haven't been successful. As you can imagine the security in the government is quite high."

"Well, don't take a big risk for me. I'm guessing you two know each other from when Logan worked as a government leecher."

"You could say we worked together." Logan was leaning back with his arms out behind him. He seemed very comfortable. I still couldn't shake the chilled feeling in my bones. It was so bad my fingers had started to go numb.

"Does the government mind you looking up on me?"

"I do a lot of work for them. I go to victims' houses to check up on them. They don't look into everything I do."

"Why do you check up on them? Shouldn't they be doing that?"

"They don't care about that kind of thing. Once they save them, they believe they'll be saving them again in the not-too-distant future. I do it off the clock anyway, so they're not losing out on anything."

As he answered my questions more just kept popping into my head. "How come you help Logan?"

"I remember the day I lost my faith in the government. I had popped around this woman's house. She had lost her arm in a werewolf attack. She told me that a man changed right in front of her and just attacked. It was nowhere near a full-moon which led me to believe he did it for fun."

"Did they catch the werewolf?"

"No, it escaped. Later that week I got a report from archives. I looked it over and realised they had used the woman as bait to bring the werewolf out of hiding. She lost her life so they could kill this beast. They should have done the job right in the first place. I searched Logan out and have been working with him ever since." The ghost shifted its weight if it had any.

"Thanks to you I was always one step ahead of them."

"Now it's more like half a step. What are you doing here? You do know they have a factory just down the road where they cut people like your friends open and study them."

"Since when are we ever too far from a government facility doing God knows what. Do you know what they're up to there?"

"When you told me where you were I had a little look. It seems they've been studying supernatural creatures on a DNA level. Seems they have opened up Project Underworld again. You have to be careful. They're putting a lot of effort and manpower into this, and with you running about with her, you're more likely to get caught now."

I had to cut in at that point because it was hard to keep my frustration under check, "What is so special about me?"

"I don't know a lot, but if they've reopened Project Underworld, then it's not good."

I looked over to Logan. "Project Underworld is what exactly?"

Neither of them seemed very happy, but with Melvin, it was harder to tell. "It was shut down a long time ago for many bad reasons."

Logan gave Melvin a quick glance before explaining, "The government started breaking down supernatural DNA. The idea behind the whole thing was too find out how to make them from scratch."

"To what, sell off to the highest bidder?"

"Yeah, but there's a little more to it. If they could find out how to make them, then they could control others. Put a simple thing in their head, and it will control them on a DNA level. No one would be able to do anything without the government's permission. Before all this happened they were in charge, then they lost out when all these creatures came along. Now they are trying to put themselves back on top. There needs to be wiggle room for us to survive but if the government constricts the world so much, there won't be any place for us to hide. The only option would be to join them, be imprisoned or killed. We can't allow that to happen."

"Don't we have enough things on our plate already?" My question was aimed more at Logan than Melvin.

"We do have things to do, but this is important. If they manage to figure this out, we won't be able to help anyone. If they can control people's movements, their motives, then maybe they can block out our ability. We would be human in every way. This is important if you plan on having any kind of life after this."

"I can understand that." I could understand it, but I didn't want to. How did I get into this whole mess? My whole life had been documented and controlled even before I was blacking out.

Melvin's soft voice made me jump, "What other things do you have on your plate? I know about the government looking for you two obviously, and you said something about the debt Jewel owes The Saracen. What else, if there is anything else?"

"With the debt problem we've talked to Drew's father. Griffin."

"The businessman and I are using that phrase kindly."

"Yeah. With Drew being his son and his hatred towards The Saracen, we thought he would be willing to help. From what he says he is."

"Just be careful. Never trust a guy like that fully. I've read about them too often. They make the government look good."

"We'll be careful. Unfortunately, we need his help for now."

"I can look into some people who could be willing to help."

"Wouldn't be a bad idea to have a backup plan. Keep me informed."

"Oh, and here's the file you asked for." He moved his hands around like he had an invisible sphere in his palms. A few seconds and white wisps formed some kind of package in his hands. I expected him to open it, but instead, he just tossed it towards Logan. As the package came into contact with his hands the white dispersed like it reacted to human skin. In his grip now was a file. "I'll keep in touch, okay." Logan just nodded in reply. "It was nice to have finally met you, Beth." I also gave him a nod. Then that was it. He divided into little slithers of white and then he was no longer there.

Once the room was clear the chill disappeared from around my skeleton. I wriggled my fingers to get some feeling back into them. Then it hit me. I had just seen and talked to a ghostly figure. What was he?

Logan was the one with those answers, but before I could ask anything, there was a loud crash like a vase smashing. I guess Logan was too busy reading his file to even notice. I wasn't about to disturb him, but I found myself just leaving the room. He was keeping things from me which was more annoying due to the fact that it involved me. So I decided to go check it out on my own.

Moving along the small path I just walked straight into Cassie's room. I wasn't greeted with smiling faces like I had hoped. Instead, it was more a scene from a murder. Drew was on his knees with Cassie leaning over behind him. Blood covered the floor and Drew's arm. It stood out like it was a neon light in a room of black.

I heard the greedy sucking as Cassie fed on werewolf blood. There was no way I would be any match for a vampire, but she was sucking the life out of my werewolf. My whole body filled with anger and I rushed forward.

But she pulled back as soon as she heard my footsteps, retreating over into the far corner. I dropped to my knees and grabbed hold of Drew. As my fingers touched his arm his other hand grabbed one of my wrists. His voice came out soft like he didn't have much energy, "It's okay. I told her to." I looked over to Cassie. She was crouched down with her knees up against her chest. I couldn't be sure, but I thought I could hear her sobbing.

I checked that Drew was okay. When I touched his cheek, his eyes flicked up at me. Even when he was weak from blood loss, he was still able to pull a smile that sent my hormones into somersaults. "Go check on Cassie. She needs you more than I do. I'm going to shift shape, don't come near me. I might not be in as much control as I would like."

His smile was smaller but still just as cute. Climbing to my feet, I moved away. Watching Drew strip and then turn over onto all fours, he started shifting. His limbs didn't stretch, they shortened. His face transformed into a snout and his eyes burned dark blue and were so beautiful.

His head swung my way, and he bared his teeth reminding me that he was an animal out of control. But to my relief, he started moving his head away from me. Those amazing eyes locked on mine until the whole body moved in the opposite direction.

With his hairy head facing the other way I looked down at his front leg. It had the blood all over it, but the two bite marks were pretty much gone. I watched them close up and heal over. The only marks that were left from Cassie's bite were two little bumps.

Turning my back on the wolf, I knelt down next to the vampire. I could feel my heart pounding so hard. The thought of Cassie hearing this made me want to run away. But I placed my shaking hand on her wrist. I was so afraid she was going to go nuts and rip my arm off just to get some more blood. When she raised her face to mine that thought fled like a bunny in headlights.

Her fangs were extended but barely touched the bottom of her lip. They were dripping with Drew's blood. As her eyes locked on mine, she flexed her jaw, and her teeth slid back into her gums. She looked so sad and distraught. A tear drizzled down her cheek for an inch then turned to dust. Another fell from the other eye, but it too turned to dust. "I'm so sorry. I didn't want to do it." More tears fell, but they didn't last any longer than the others.

Drew's voice made me jump as it came from behind me, "I practically had to force her to. She ate the meat, but it wasn't enough. She needed more blood, so I offered her some of mine. She was very reluctant, but she did it in the end. I wasn't strong enough to pull away when she got a little carried away. She smacked me into the table after which I just let her take my blood."

"That would explain the smash I heard."

"A glass fell off of the table. Is she okay?"

"She's just sad. She'll be fine. I think we all need to get some sleep anyway. I know I do."

"Sleep?"

"My body feels so drained with everything that's gone on."

"Do you want any company?"

"I said I want to get some sleep." I walked over to him and softly punched him in the stomach. Werewolves clearly stayed in shape because it felt like hitting a brick wall. "Either I'll wake up and see you then, or you can wake me up when everyone else is ready. See you soon." It was hard to just walk past him when all I wanted to do was to take him on Cassie's bed. His eyes didn't leave my body until I left the room. It felt good to feel his want in that look. It was nice to know I had that effect on him even when I was human.

I really needed sleep, but all I could think about was having him in my bed. I thought about when we would have some time to ourselves. Every smile he gives me has been filling me with intent and desire. I wanted him to unleash it. I wonder if I could handle a werewolf in bed. There would be only one, very fun way to find out. Just not right now.

I took the short trip to my room and emptied my pockets out onto the bedside cabinet. When I pulled the ring out, it was only for a second, but when my fingertips touched the metal, I swear something tried to call to me. It was a weird feeling, but it went as soon as the ring left my fingers. I tried figuring it out, but my brain was too sleepy to think about anything right now. I slipped my clothes off and climbed under the sheets with nothing but my underwear to keep me warm. The mattress was more comfortable than I thought it would be. It was nice to finally get some time to rest. It did take a while for me to switch my brain off but when I did, I fell peacefully into sleep.

CHAPTER 8

The sleep I had was undisturbed and peaceful. The way I was woken up was everything but that. At first, I started hearing a voice speaking to me, but the words were just noises to me. I tried to look around, but nothing but blackness filled my view. The voice came again a little clearer. This time it felt closer.

It whispered right in my ear making me toss and turn. Whispering away until my name came through as clear as glass. It came again and again until I was tired of hearing it. The voice seemed to sense my frustration because it then shouted right in my ear.

At the sudden volume, I jolted up in my bed, finally awake from that bizarre dream. Taking a few deep breaths to calm my heart I turned onto my side to get some more sleep. That's when I noticed the ring sitting on the bedside cabinet. I remember placing it nearer to the lamp. Now it was sitting right on the edge next to my bed spinning on its side. If it spun any faster, it would take off into the air.

I reached out with a shaking hand, wondering if I was still asleep or not. When my finger touched the silver of the ring, I heard my name again. It was the same haunting voice I had heard in my dream. My hand jolted back at the sound as it suddenly stopped and fell over.

I picked it up, wary of the voice calling my name again. My ears didn't pick up even a whisper, but there seemed to be something different about the ring. It didn't feel the same, but I couldn't find anything wrong with it. I held it between my forefinger and thumb, thinking about sliding it onto my finger. Last time it had tightened and scared me so much. The fact I was thinking about doing it again was even stranger.

Despite my worries, I did it. Just as my fingertip touched the inside of the metal my name came to me again. I wanted to pull my finger away and throw this ring out into the woods. But something about it made me want to slip it on.

So I took a deep breath and shoved it onto my finger. As soon as it touched my knuckle, it constricted around my finger. It pinched my skin and then my vision went black. It felt like there was a large blade slicing my brain into two. Then I saw flashes of light. At first, they were like spotlights. All the colours blinded me, making my eyes ache. Then a single image came through it all.

It was of my friend again. He was on his knees, screaming in pain. He had blood staining his white shirt, and the side of his head was injured. Blood was dripping down onto the floor. He had chains linking his wrists together. This time I saw someone else. In the background, I saw a man sitting on the floor. He was wearing clothes that could be mistaken as rags. He had a damp piece of cardboard lying over his legs. Dirt covered the man's face. His surroundings were different to the dark room where my friend was. Near the back, it spliced into an alleyway. This was where the homeless guy sat.

Just behind him was a red brick wall. It was strange. A shimmer ran across the brickwork like it was fake. Everything was just becoming clear when it started shaking like my brain was experiencing an earthquake. The two parts of the image started splitting. They swapped around and then back again. As the shaking got worse, it was harder to see the details, becoming blurry in seconds. Bits and pieces fell apart and became shattered.

Suddenly a white ball of light appeared in the middle and expanded. It covered my entire vision until all I could see was white. The middle of it shimmered with a black line as a voice came to me. It was Jewel's. It came through clear like she was right there with me. "There isn't much time. You have to find me in the city. I'm on Howard's Street. Please hurry." I thought it was over, but I was wrong. Suddenly someone screamed. "BETH!" The volume of it made me jump. It was a voice I used to hear all the time when I was younger. It wasn't one I had heard in many years, but I could never mistake Frank's voice. To my annoyance, there was no information about where he was and how he had become hurt. I tried to recall the image I had seen, but the white light seemed to have erased it from memory.

The only thing that was left now was the homeless man in his alleyway. Jewel's voice hadn't come last time so why was it now? She must know something about Frank or maybe a way she could find him for me. I needed to help him if he was in pain. And by the sounds of her message, she needed help as well.

I just had to persuade Logan to help me do this. Jewel wasn't his favourite person right now since she fled and got us into this mess. With everything going on he would be even less inclined to help me find my friend as well. And he may have some questions about the ring. I needed to find Frank though. If he was in that much pain, it was my duty as a friend to help him. He might be able to help me understand this ring as well. After all, he was the one who got me it.

Drew's voice came to my ears this time, saying my name in that sweet tone of his. It washed over me like a wind. I held onto it hoping it would bring me back to reality. As it came again, it was closer. I could feel the wind brushing over my body. Each time I heard my voice, it seemed to get louder. It kept coming, and it kept getting louder. Repeating until my eyes shot open.

As soon as I saw Drew's face, I threw my arms around his neck and buried my head into his shoulder. I didn't want him to ask me any questions because I wasn't sure if I would be able to answer them. I just wanted to be held and comforted. Drew's arms brought me just that and nothing less.

Unfortunately, he didn't hold me for long. He pulled back, keeping one hand attached to my arm. I wasn't about to fall off the bed, but the warmth of his touch felt nice. He looked into my eyes with concern. "I'm fine. It was nothing." I dropped my gaze to my finger. The ring was no longer there. I quickly scanned the floor all the way up to the bed. I couldn't spot it anywhere. I wasn't very discreet and Drew saw my obvious actions. "What's going on?"

"I'm just looking for my ring. I must have accidentally knocked it off during a dream."

"A dream? Is that what you're calling it?" I looked at him confused. "When I came in you were having a fit. Then you just laid there like you'd died. For a few seconds, I couldn't hear your heartbeat. What happened?"

I didn't know if I should tell him but I needed to say something, "It was just a bad dream that's all. It's a recurring nightmare about my death. I usually fall off my bed when I have it, so I'm grateful you came in when you did. Thank you."

"It didn't look like just a nightmare." I got up off the bed but Drew stood up and grabbed my wrist softly. He slowly turned me to face him. "What's wrong?"

"Nothing." I blew out a big sigh. "I'm still a little sleepy."

"Okay. Do you want me to give you a minute?"

"Please. I'll knock on your door in a bit. Just need to get my bearings." I pulled the best sleepy smile I could. All he did was eye me suspiciously, then left.

When the soft thud of the door came, I dropped to my knees and started searching for the ring. I ran my hand over the rough carpet but didn't find anything. I held onto the side of the bed and lifted myself onto my knees. As I raised my head, I noticed it on the bed. I quickly slid my hand over the sheet and grabbed it. As I touched it that homeless guy popped into my head, but it was gone in a blink.

Pulling it close I inspected it. Somehow it didn't feel so weird like what I had seen had been erased from it. It went straight into my pocket along with the other things I had put in the bedside cabinet. The last thing I grabbed was the check from Keith. I looked at the number again and still couldn't believe it was all mine. At least it would be as soon as I could get to a bank and cash it into one of the accounts on Keith's list.

I slipped it into my back pocket as I checked around for anything left of mine. Happy I wasn't missing anything I pulled open the door. As I did, a note taped to the wood flapped in the breeze. I couldn't believe Drew left me a note. My heart did little skips at the thought of how sweet he was. Opening it sent my heart beating faster but with fear instead of excitement. It wasn't a note from Drew. It was a list. Two lists in fact. On the left were our names. They went Jewel, Logan, Bethany, Drew than Cassie. Next to each name was a number going from one all the way down to five. That made me number three. At the bottom, it had the time, noon. I looked over at the digital clock over next to the bed. It said noon. The note was confusing. What the hell did it mean?

Holding the note open still I walked up to Drew's door. I was about to knock on it, but then I noticed another note. Quickly ripping it free I opened it and found an identical list.

The door suddenly swung open, the gust kicking the end of my hair up. He gave me a smile, a genuine smile. "Did you find your bearings?"

Before I could think of the words, my eyes caught the bumps on his arm where Cassie had fed on him. A concerned look from him made me reassure him. "Yep, along with this." I held up the notes for him to see. "Any idea of what it means?"

"I have an idea, but I wouldn't like it to be true."

"What's that?"

"You're not going to like it."

"Tell me anyway."

"It could be Kellen. Weren't you told he would be on your trail? What if he's already on it?"

"Maybe. Then what're the numbers about?"

"Since Jewel has the debt, that makes her number one. Logan is the person who's been helping her all along. He's number two."

"Why am I number three?"

"You're the next leecher. Maybe since he's a vampire himself, he sees Cassie as less of a threat. That sorts out the last two numbers." He looked at me. He must have read my look. "I might be wrong though. It's only a thought. What has Logan said about it?"

"I came here first."

"Let's go talk to him then. He's the one in charge isn't he?" There was a slight tone in his words, but I ignored them. He may have a problem with Logan, but unfortunately, he was right about him being in charge. I focused back on Drew has his delicious lips moved, "Let's go."

"Check in on Cassie on the way?"

"Why not." He gave me a big smile and joined me on the path. A muscly arm wrapped around my shoulders. His touch always helped me forget about the problems we had. For a few seconds made me feel like it was just us out for a walk.

I knocked but then just walked in. She couldn't really open the door herself with the sun bearing down upon us.

She threw a smile our way as our feet hit the carpet. Cassie was sitting cross-legged onto of her pillow, she looked like a little girl on holiday. The television was on, but the volume was so low I could barely hear anything. Obviously not a problem for a vampire.

I plopped down next to her. She kept her smile up. "Are you okay?"

"I'm doing better now." She looked over my shoulder, "How's your arm?"

"Just two little scars. Nothing compared to others I have." Curiosity stirred inside of me, but I pushed it aside for now.

"Good. I'm really sorry."

"Hey, it was my decision. It was my idea wasn't it?" Drew moved closer and sat down at the bottom of the bed.

"I know. I shouldn't have lost control though. I told myself I wouldn't get like that ever again."

"And I'm sure you won't. Beth and I will make sure of that."

"Of course we will." I smiled. It seemed to be infectious because she smiled back. "We've found these." I placed my note on the bed as Drew threw his over my shoulder. I heard some paper being played with then another came my way. It was the same as the rest, and I wasn't shocked by it. I must have missed it on Cassie's, but Drew didn't. "They were on ours and your door. There will probably be one on Logan's door as well. We're going there now. Since its noon we can come back to get you when it's a little later. Okay?"

"Thanks. I don't like missing things, but I'm sure you'll fill me in."

"Of course." I gave her knee a little squeeze to reassure her.

"Plus, I'm watching this cool program about dolphins. Always liked them." I smiled as I got off the bed. "Have fun."

"Logan isn't much fun at the moment is he?" She let out a little laugh. It was nice to hear her laugh after last night. This whole thing really needed to get over and done with as soon as possible so we could get on with our lives.

We left her alone to watch her dolphin program. At least she was happy at the moment. I hoped it would be like that for a little longer. No doubt something around the corner would dampen our spirits and give us another thing to worry about.

Like I had thought, there was another note on Logan's door. I didn't even bother looking at it. I knocked on the wood and Logan told us to enter. I figured he was too busy reading his file to come to the door.

I entered and was surprised to see Logan coming out of the bathroom in a towel. Water made his chest glisten, and I had to admit he did look good. Drew's footsteps came from behind me, so I forced my eyes away from his figure. "What's wrong?"

"We've found some notes on our doors. Here." I chucked the one I took from his door onto the bed. It landed next to the file Melvin had delivered. His eyes filled with concern as he read the note. "What do you think?"

"I'm guessing it's Kellen."

"That's what Drew said. He thinks the numbers are what order we're going to be... let's say, visited."

"You mean killed." He smiled. "Might as well face it." He looked back down at the note. "Looks like we'll be needing to split up."

Drew stepped forwards, "Split up? What do you mean?"

"If the list is saying what order we'll get visited in." He tossed a smile at me. "Then we should split. If we put two and four together, Drew and me. Then we stick three and five together, you and Cassie. It means if Kellen does get to me, then he has to go find you two just to keep his order."

It made sense except for one problem, "What if he just decides to kill us any way he likes?"

"It's a possibility, but the little I've read about him shows he likes the hunt. He likes to feel the fear from his victims. The perfect way of doing that is to give them the anticipation of their death. Otherwise, he would have just come into our rooms and killed us without anyone knowing. These notes give us fear of the upcoming events. Just like what I have read."

"How much information have you read about him?" Drew started moving closer to Logan. "Is the source reliable?"

"I read all this stuff when I was working for the government. It's all reliable."

"Then we split up. It's a good idea." Drew turned around to face me. "It keeps you, safer."

"But."

"There's no point arguing. With two groups, it means we can concentrate on two things. We can head over to try and speed my dad up, and you and Cassie can see if you can find any information out about this Kellen guy." Drew turned to Logan. "Do you know anyone that would be willing to help? An old friend from your government days, perhaps." My mind thought of Melvin, but if he had any information, then he would have given it to us already.

"I do." He grabbed a portion of his file off the bed and handed it to me. "There are a few people in there that can help. I've circled their photos. You've got their addresses and anything else you need to know."

"Okay." I was reluctant to do it, but it was two against one. It had to look like I was going to follow the orders I was given. All I wanted to do was chuck the file away and go find Jewel. I wouldn't be able to do that though until Cassie and I got separated from Logan. If Cassie was game, then I was going to do it. I didn't know why but a small part of me felt like I would be abandoning Drew and Logan. It felt wrong. But I needed to find Jewel so I could then find Frank. I couldn't just leave him all alone and in pain. He was my only true friend in my whole life.

"The time at the bottom, if this is the time he put them on the doors, it proves how powerful he is. He's old enough to withstand the sun at noon. Showing off once again."

"How much trouble are we in?" It wasn't the first thing on my mind, but it made it seem like I was still part of the conversation.

"Tons. Drew and I should get going. You and Cassie are taking the car. Drew and I will run back to the city."

"Why are we taking the car?"

"It's got sat nav. Easier for you to find the people in the file. Werewolf stamina will get us back to the city."

"Okay." I looked down at the file cover. I wondered how long it would take to get Jewel back. Would we actually be able to get around to visiting any of these people?

"Can you two leave so I can get dressed please?"

Drew stepped forwards before I could agree. "We also found this." The witch's chronicle was offered to Logan.

"Wow. Where did you get this from?"

"That's a bit of a weird story."

With the file in my hand, I just wanted to get out of there. Have as much time to look for Jewel and get our search for information done. "I'm going to get going. Get as much stuff on Kellen as I can."

"Okay sure. Let me get dressed, and we can discuss the book after."

Drew nodded in agreement. "Sure."

"I'll go tell Cassie what's going on." I gripped the file, wanting to throw it away.

"That's a good idea. See you in a bit." I smiled and left the room. Drew closed the door behind us.

"I'm going to go talk to Cassie. You should wait here for when Logan comes out."

"Do you want me to knock on the door when we leave?"

"How about we say goodbye now." I stepped forward and raised my lips to his. My body was pulled close to his by the tight grip he had on my hips. The kiss was long and passionate. I didn't want it to stop, but I needed to talk to Cassie. It was hard to break away, but I slipped out of his grip slowly.

His smile made his eyes twinkle. "A good goodbye?" I asked.

"The best."

"We'll see." I smiled at him then left him there on the little path with his smile. My breathing was out of control as I walked away from him. If that's how hot and heavy I got from just a kiss, I was looking forward to when we could spend some alone time together.

I had gotten my ragged breathing steady by the time I walked into Cassie's room. The dolphin program was now running through the credits. "Was it a good program?"

"It was good. So what's going on?"

"Because of the notes, we're going to split up. You and I are going to be visiting some people in this file. However...." I sat next to her on the bed and lowered my voice to a whisper. "I was hoping you would help me with something."

"What?"

"You know my ring?"

"Yeah. What's wrong with it?"

"I put it on, and I got a message from Jewel. She's still in the city on Howard's street. I want to go get her."

"What did Logan say?"

"I didn't tell him, but he hasn't wanted to go find her from the start. She can help though. She's a witch, and she's the one who has the debt. We need to find her."

Her eyes narrowed at me, "There's another reason isn't there?"

"It's my best friend from back home. He was in the message I got. He looks hurt, and I need to help him."

"How come you haven't said anything until now?"

"I guess I didn't want to believe what was happening. Plus I have no idea where he is. Jewel might though. That's why I want to find her."

"Then we'll go look for her." She looked down at the clock. "I do need to wait a little longer though."

"What time can you handle?"

"I should be okay in a car in half an hour. The trees around the road should shelter me enough until we get into the city."

"Good. I'm going to go see if I can find some food. I'll be back soon." We both smiled, and I left the room on a mission to get something for my stomach. A quick scan of my surroundings showed no vending machines. The only other place I could think to look would be the manager's office. He wouldn't mind anymore. Hopefully, he has some food stashed away. I would devour it in seconds. Hunger had hit me all of a sudden. Might have something to do with losing the contents of my stomach back in that bunker.

I left the motel and walked into the small building. Looking into the office, I saw that it was a terrible mess. The desk was covered in papers and magazines. The filing cabinets had only one closed drawer. The rest were partially open with files sticking out. There wasn't much of the floor showing and the small part that was had weird stains on it. The manager definitely wasn't a neat person.

A soft humming led me to the small fridge sitting in the corner. I pulled it open and found a sandwich. There was no way I was going to turn my nose up at a sandwich. I didn't even check the contents and just bit straight into the meal. It actually tasted nice, the mustard on the bread made it almost perfect. I took another mouthful just before I heard something from outside. It hadn't been thirty minutes yet so it couldn't be Cassie. I attuned my leecher gift and found the source. It was a vampire. Maybe Cassie had run over here. I dropped the sandwich on the desk and peered into the reception area. A car had parked just outside of the door.

It felt like my heart stopped beating as I stared at the driver. After a few seconds, he got out of his car and looked through the window at me. There was no use hiding in the office, he had already spotted me since my feet had refused to move.

I took a few steps and stood behind the desk. His long hair was slicked back with a grease-like substance, and his brown goatee somehow looked greasy as well. He wore black jeans and a leather jacket over a black t-shirt. He didn't look like he would blend into a crowd very easily. I suppose he was going for a death kind of look that vamps seemed to go for in films. To me, he just looked like a weirdo.

He stood by his car and looked around. I took this chance to sniff out Cassie's scent. I compared the two and felt that hers was the stronger one. I leeched off of her just in case things went sour. The power filled my body giving me a feeling of confidence. I felt different than the last time. I felt full. The hint of thirst that had been there before was there no longer an urge that needed satisfying. It had been sated since Cassie had taken a pint or two of werewolf blood. That fact seemed to make my body stronger. Seemed to make my hearing better and my sight sharper. It felt good. I could understand a fraction of the need vampires had to feed. It felt amazing to have a body this powerful.

As I looked out of the window again, my eyes seemed to hurt at how bright the sun was. Then I wondered how this vampire was walking around in the sun like this. It couldn't be Kellen because Cassie's wouldn't have been the stronger essence.

The man took a step towards the reception door. It made me push my thoughts to the side and focus on the vampire with the greasy hair. Hopefully, he was just here to ask for directions. At a stretch, I could perhaps give him a room. I saw how the manager had done it.

I cleared my mind even more as the vampire walked into the reception area. The ash smell hit my nose hard. It hit a barrier and just sat there, wanting to get in. I ignored it easily and focused on the approaching man. He placed his hands on the reception desk and looked into my eyes, "Where's Stephen?"

"He's gone out. I'm in charge for a bit. How may I help you?"

"You can help me by getting Stephen."

"I said he was out."

"He knows I'm coming today so I very much doubt he went out." Then his eyes narrowed. I saw his nose move like he was sniffing the air. I didn't know if he was suspicious or not. I opened my mouth to say something else, but he launched at me sending my heart up into my throat.

His body flew over the desk in a second, and his hands were grabbing my top. I twisted around and pushed him off of me. He slammed into the wall and fell to the floor with a hard thud. I backed away, trying to think of what to do. He was up on his feet and running in my direction in the next instant. As he neared me, I threw my fist out. It smacked him in the throat sending him into a backflip. His head smashed into the desk, sending wood to the floor. He let out a grunt as he landed but he was up on his feet and attacking again quickly. It was hard to get any thoughts into my head with the constant onslaught of attack.

He threw punches and kicks and somehow my instincts blocked them all. With Cassie's speed, dodging the attacks wasn't a problem. However, I wasn't trained to fight. All the power and speed I had was useless unless I could come up with something. Quickly I was backed up against the wall when I got a break. I dodged his punch making his fist smash into the wood. The second he took to recover was just long enough.

I pummeled my fist into his ribs hearing a loud crack as one of them snapped under the pressure. With him, in pain, I wrapped my arms around his body and picked him up. I felt his fist pound into my back. The adrenaline blocked out most the pain, so I swung him around. He flew into the air towards the wall. Thanks to his punch I hadn't had enough strength. The vampire twisted around and landed on his feet with ease.

He stood there watching me carefully as he moved his hand along the side I had punched. I heard a soft pop, and then he no longer looked in pain. He grinned at me showing his short fangs. He snarled, and then they mimicked the ones I had seen before. Stopping just at the bottom of his chin, ready to feed on my blood. He gave me another snarl allowing spit to dribble out of his mouth. He looked like a rabid dog.

I had no more time to think about what he looked like. His feet shifted against the floor, but I wasn't going to be on the defensive again. I ran forwards using Cassie's speed. We met in the middle with a massive crack. For a split second my mind searched for any broken bones, but there didn't seem to be any. The vampire was stumbling back, so I kept running forwards.

I grabbed onto his jacket and launched myself into him. His back hit the wooden wall, and under the force of it, the thin wood gave way. We both flew out into the sunlight. The feel of it immediately started to burn into my brain. The whole world around me seemed to be on fire. My vision was going a weird colour, and things were beyond blurry.

I couldn't lose concentration though. We were still flying through the air, so I had time to push the pain away. It was hard, but by the time we hit the ground I could feel my grip on the vampire, and that would have to do for now. We grunted as our shoulders hit the gravel. I let go of the jacket and pushed my body as fast as it would go.

I was up on my feet first. I took a handful of his arm and pulled him up to my level and twisted. His feet came up from the ground, his face filled with pain from his arm being bent the wrong way. As I blurred into movement, he seemed to slow down for a split-second. I twisted his arm again hearing a slight pop then I hit him with my spare hand. His body flew with great speed into the reception building.

He hit the corner and the pain of it flared up in his face

had me smiling for a brief moment. I rushed forward, but I wasn't ready for him. He plummeted a fist into my stomach. My momentum sent me past him. I fell over and skidded across the floor. My shoulder hit the storage box I had spotted earlier. Trying to ignore any kind of pain I felt I got back up ready to continue fighting.

My enemy came at me. Not only did I remember the storage box, but I also remembered the spade. I quickly grabbed the wooden handle and swung it upwards. The metal spade smacked into his chin, snapping the garden tool in half and sending him back into the car park. I went to carry on with my attack, but I noticed my brain was feeling better. It was like someone had surrounded it with ice packs. I looked up at the sky and couldn't see the sun. I checked the floor and realised I was in the small area of shade created by the reception building. I didn't want to step out from my protected area, but with the vampire still on the floor, this was my chance.

I quickly walked out holding the broken spade in my hand. The vampire rolled over onto his back. His jaw was broken in at least two places, and he had a few teeth missing. To my delight, one of those missing teeth was a canine. I hoped something like that was similar to a man losing one of his testicles. I would have mocked him for being half of a vampire, but there wasn't time. Before he could mend his wounds and attack me again, I brought the pointy end of the handle down. The wood pierced through his leg easily, moving deep into the ground under him.

He screamed out in pain as blood started squirting out of the wound. It didn't look red like it should have. It came out almost black. As it landed on the ground, it started bubbling. The reaction from the wood looked painful if that was going on inside his body. I placed my foot on his chest and studied his face.

He didn't seem bothered by the sun beating down on

both of us. I, on the other hand, was finding it unbearable. Sweat was covering my whole body. I let the vampire scent leave my body and became human again. The sun no longer boiled my brain, but I didn't have the power or speed of a vampire. I couldn't allow him to notice that. I took my foot off his chest and stood back. I was out of reach but close enough to question him.

I hoped the stick would hold him down long enough. Before beginning my questioning, I glimpsed at his injured leg. More and more blood was pouring out black like tar. "Who do you work for?"

"You're really stupid if you think I'm going to tell you anything." I gave the pinned leg a soft kick which made him scream out. His arms tried to reach down, but he was too weak.

"I'm sure we can come to some kind of arrangement." I took a small step closer to him and tapped the stick with my foot. He let out a small grunt of disapproval. I wanted to move it enough to hurt him but not enough to dislodge it. I didn't want to fight again especially since I had him in such a good position.

Placing my feet on top of it I wiggled it before pushing down firmly. I wasn't expecting to push it further into the ground, but I could at least move it about without worrying. The more I moved it, the more blood squirted out of his leg. Bubbles were seeping out of the wound and popping on the surface.

I casually walked over to the other half of the spade. Running my fingers over the pointy end, I walked back to my pinned vampire. "You can answer my question, or I can ram this through another part of your body." He spat onto the floor as a way of reply. I thought about it for a second and then leeched off of him. I thought I would be safe from the sun like him, but that wasn't the case. As beads of sweat formed on my skin, I quickly rammed the wooden end through his arm. As soon as I could I let the vampire scent out of my body. I welcomed the burning sun on my skin instead of inside my brain.

Once his screaming went silent, I asked my question again. He wasn't willing to hand over any information. I leant down to try and get a better effect of dominance, and that's when I heard it. There was a soft buzzing noise. It was low, so I hadn't heard it through the fighting. Now I was close enough to follow the noise and find a weird object underneath the vampire's t-shirt. I pulled the stretchy material down to find a pendant hanging from a silver chain. As I tugged on it, the vampire winced. A simple tug and he was feeling pain? I pushed his head against the ground making sure my skin went nowhere near his mouth. I didn't need him biting down on my arm and sucking the blood out of me.

Once I felt like my blood was safe, I looked closer. I saw where the chain linked together. It looked like an ordinary chain apart from a small section that didn't move over the skin. I pulled on the chain, and a needle started coming out of his nape. I could hear him moaning in pain, but I was too curious to stop. As soon as the needle came clear of his skin, the vampire started moaning even louder. I retreated back to a safe distance and watched as the effect of the necklace became clear.

His free hand was pounding against his head. He violently wriggled, not being able to roll on the floor in agony because of the stakes. Sweat was pouring down his face. His eyes were rolling into the back of his head. His mouth shot open, and a high-pitched squeal came out. I tried to cover my ears, but it didn't do any good. I couldn't hear anything over the screaming.

Soon his blood wasn't the only thing that was bubbling. The skin on his cheek was becoming thinner and thinner. It was horrible to watch and most likely twice as horrible to feel. I moved forwards and grabbed the stick holding his leg down. I didn't pull it out. Instead, I snapped a small section off. I held it over his chest, prepared to pierce his heart. I shouted over his voice, "Give me my answer and I'll end the pain."

"I work for Jenkins. That's all I know. I get my orders through an email system. Please."

"What were you doing here?"

"Please just end it."

"Answer the question!" His eyes darted to me, filled with his plea to finish him quickly.

"Stephen was holding a werewolf. I was here to make sure things were going okay. That's all. I answered your questions now please." He had answered my questions. I gripped the stick tightly then pushed with all my human might. It went through his t-shirt with ease. The stake slowed down going through skin and muscle. I had to give the top a hard whack to get it through the rib cage. As soon as the wood impaled the heart, the screaming got even louder. Three seconds later it died down. A soft noise came out of his mouth as his skin started to go black. It was like watching a match burn when his body started to flake and get carried away by the wind. It wasn't long before there were three small patches of blood on the floor. One from his leg, one from his arm and one from the puncture wound in his chest. Not even his skeleton survived the process of being killed. His clothes were nothing more than burnt pieces of cloth getting kicked up into the wind.

I left the three pieces of wood where they were and picked up the necklace he had been wearing. The needle was dripping with blood. It was at least two inches long. The silver chain was thin but strong. The pendant was the most interesting part. It was in the rough shape of a triangle. The points were rounded, almost making it into a circle. On the front, there was a circle with three small dots showing the inside of the pendant. There seemed to be a glass vial encased inside, containing some kind of red liquid. Since I had taken the needle out of the vampire's neck, it had stopped humming. I was tempted to stick it into my neck to see what it could do, but it was quickly forgotten as a crazy idea. I didn't want to shove the needle into my neck and judging from what had happened, there was someone else who could benefit from it more.

Letting the necklace dangle from my fingers I went to Cassie's room. I was about to touch the handle when it flung open. "You alright?"

"I'm okay. Just had a run in with a vampire."

"Yeah, I was watching. I would have helped but the sun." A tear started to gather at the bottom of her eye.

"Hey, it's okay. I'm fine. You helped me with your essence. Without it, I wouldn't have survived." I looked over my shoulder at what was left of him. "He was sent here to check up on Stephen, the manager. Someone called Jenkins sent him. Have you heard that name before?"

She thought for a few seconds before answering, "No. Haven't heard Logan mention it either. Did you get anything else out of him?"

"No, I staked him. He was burning in the sun."

"That's a shame."

"Maybe we should search his car for any clues."

"Sounds like a good idea." She leant down and popped her head out of the door. Her eyes rose to the burning sun. "You might have to start without me for a bit. Don't know how long I'd be able to stand this heat."

"I have something that could help with that." I held up the necklace. Confusion was painted all over her face. "I took it from the vampire."

"How will that help?"

"I can't explain it, but he didn't start burning in the sun until I took it off of him. Maybe it stops that vampire's weakness."

"That sounds brilliant, but…." She pointed to the blood covered needle. "That looks painful."

"I know it does. He didn't seem in pain until I started pulling it out though."

"What the hell, it's worth a try. It's not like I've never experienced pain before." I nodded. "Just one second." She took the necklace then disappeared back into her room. She was back before I knew it with the necklace in one hand and a tissue in the other. Three wipes and the blood was gone. Without thinking, she wrapped the chain around her neck, linked the two parts together and then slid the needle into her neck.

There was only a second of pain on her face, and then it was gone. She didn't seem different. She tucked the interesting piece of jewellery into her top and out of view. "Let's give it a try." Without hesitation, she stepped out into the sun without a single hint of fear. I watched her, waiting to see any signs the necklace didn't work. There was none. She peered up into the sky and then turned to me. I couldn't stop my own smile when I saw hers reaching her ears. "I forgot how good the sun feels on your skin."

"A little too hot for me but I can understand your point."

"Let's get to work then."

"Cool. Just got to sort out my room." I walked in there and grabbed the wedge of paper I had found before. But instead of bringing it with us I just binned it. I didn't need reminding of my status as the primary target.

Cassie was waiting by the car, still staring up at the sun in the sky. I could swear I saw a tear of joy or two but couldn't be sure since they had disappeared by the time I got to her. My hand reached out towards the car handle, but I noticed it was locked. Looking back to where I had staked the vampire. His clothes had been blown away by now, and I couldn't see any keys sitting on the floor.

"Everything okay, Beth?"

"It's locked. I can't see the keys anywhere."

"The heat we give off when staked is powerful enough to melt metal. I doubt they survived. But we don't need them." She gently nudged me out of the way and gave the handle a hard yank. The lock broke, and the door opened gently, "You can take this side, I'll search the back seat."

"Cool." I slipped into the seat quickly searching the little compartments of the car only finding a pair of sunglasses. I leant across to the passenger's side as Cassie climbed into the back seat. There was nothing in the door, so I clicked open the glove box. As it fell open, a pistol came tumbling out, hitting the plastic and then the floor with a dull thud. My eyes automatically shut just in case it went off. But all I heard was the startled yelp of Cassie in the backseat. I giggled a little which got a grunt in reply.

Picking it up I was surprised at how heavy it was. Cassie's hand came through from the back, "Can I see that please?"

"Sure." Sliding it into her hand, I watched her handle it like she had been trained to. A click came, and the magazine shot out into her grip. We both looked at the bullets, seeing a silver tip. Clearly, he was expecting to run into a werewolf or two. Looking back in the glove box I saw three more clips. Pulling them out one by one I looked at the top bullet. One of them had the same silver tips like the other. The last two had wooden tipped bullets inside. Vampires and werewolves seemed to be the most popular creatures out there. Or the government hasn't caught many of the others, so their weaknesses aren't as known.

I showed Cassie as she slammed her clip back into the pistol. Nodding in acknowledgment. "We should keep hold of them. The number of unsavoury people we run into."

"Good idea." I quickly gave the inside of the glove box another look and saw something I missed before. There was a simple piece of paper sitting there. I picked it up and unfolded it. Scribbled on the paper was a number. It was eleven digits long, and my first guess was a mobile phone number. I folded it back up after showing it to Cassie. "I don't think there's anything in the front." I reached under the steering column and yanked on the lever there. "I'm going to check the boot."

"I'll join you. There's nothing back here either."

I met her at the rear of the car. The space in the back of the car was dominated by a large black bag. It reminded me of the bags people used to hold ransom money. Cassie leant forwards and unzipped it. As the side fell open, we both gasped. Sitting inside were guns. Lots of guns. I could see two more pistols. Below that were rifles. There were different kinds. Clips of all sizes were bundled together at one end.

Why would one person need all of these guns? Was he expecting to run into a lot of trouble? It didn't make sense to me. If it was just a visit to see how things were going, then why the arsenal in the bag?

We left the bag alone and looked around the rest of the boot. There were the usual things like screen wash and a breakdown kit holding a jack and a tyre iron. There was nothing else that would be of interest.

Cassie pulled the bag out of the boot, "It wouldn't hurt to take this with us."

"Okay. I'll just grab the file I left in the car, and we can get going."

"I'll take this to ours." We went our separate ways until I returned with the file. Cassie had taken her place in the driver's seat, so I slipped into the passenger's. Once I had my belt buckled, she started the engine, and we left the motel behind.

We pulled onto the road and headed back towards the city centre. She pulled the sat nav off of the cradle and handed it to me. "Howard's street, yeah?"

"Yeah." I went through the menus and got our journey logged in. The route popped up with the total miles, the miles left to go and the time we would arrive. Judging from the small map, we wouldn't have to go too far into the city before we got to the right street. I pressed the done button, and it came up with the usual screen. I set it back on the cradle so Cassie could see. I looked down at the file sitting on my lap. It wouldn't hurt to have a look now. Would save time later on.

I flipped the cover over and started looking through the people Logan had picked. They all used to be snitches for the government. Voices on the street that would give them information. The men and women in the photos weren't what I was expecting. They didn't look like the kind of people that would be snitches. I looked at the addresses but didn't recognise any of them. To be honest, I wasn't expecting to. Cassie's voice cut through my concentration, "Are there any of them near Howard's Street?"

"I have no idea."

"Say the addresses. I might be able to figure it out."

"The four people Logan has picked live on Feldon Road, Kingdon Avenue, Drayton Road and Hollybow Lane. Any of them ring a bell?"

"Nope. I think there's a road that has residential houses on it called Willow Street. Any of them live on that road?"

"Logan says to just visit the ones he picked."

"Did he say why?"

"Nope."

"Then it doesn't matter. Just check, you do want to go get Jewel don't you?"

"Okay." I flipped through the pages. "How do you know some of the streets then?"

"I've lived for a long time now. I've been around. Spent a few years in this particular city working as a bike messenger."

"Delivering packages?"

"Yeah. Got to see a lot of the city. It was a while ago though so I can't remember all of my routes."

"At least it might help." Then I flipped the page and found someone who lived on Willow Street. "Here's someone. That was lucky."

"What information does it have?"

"Photo, address, telephone, usual stuff really. Nothing interesting. There's a short description at the….." I paused.

"What's wrong?"

"He used to be a leecher. He retired, twenty-three years ago. Doesn't have anything after that."

"Maybe we should pick someone else if he used to be a leecher."

"He's old though. Look at the photo." I held it up so she could take a quick look. "He shouldn't be a problem."

"Are you sure?"

"He's the closest one to Howard's Street. We can go in, see what he says and then leave."

"That reminds me." She turned the car down into a small road. We came out the other end onto a larger one. We went up a ramp and joined the thicker traffic on some kind of highway. I looked over the edge as we traveled around through the buildings. It was a hell of a view. "Did Logan tell you what we need to ask them?"

"He didn't really say much about it. Just said to visit the ones he picked and get information about Kellen. See if there's anything we can find out that will help."

"Maybe we should pick someone else. Would a retired leecher know about him?"

"If they tried stopping him in the past he might."

"Fair point. And it's near Jewel."

"It is." I sat there in silence as we drove off the motorway and down the slip road. "It would be good to get some information on Kellen." I quickly started flicking through the pages of the file again. I checked the addresses and the other information of the four people Logan had chosen. All of a sudden I was worried about what we were doing. Logan had specifically picked these people, and there had to be a good reason behind it. Maybe we should follow Logan's instructions. We needed the information these people could know. I was about to reach over and grab the sat nav when Cassie spoke. "We're here."

"Howard's Street?"

"Willow Street actually. Howard's Street is just around the corner. I figured we could get some information first. That way Logan can't complain."

I was a little hesitant, but we were already there. "Make's sense." I thought about the message Jewel had given me through the ring. Frank looked like he couldn't take much more. The pain on his face filled my mind. What could put him in that much terror? Who could do that to someone? Was it just to get to me? If it was then I would have to rip their throats out to show it was a bad idea. That sudden thought made me wonder what I was becoming. I never had that kind of thought before all this. Would I be the same person after all this?

I turned my head to talk to Cassie, but she was already out of the car. I quickly moved after her, "What number is it?"

I looked down at the file that I still held in my hands, "It's number thirty-nine." Putting the file in the car before Cassie locked it, I joined her on the path, and we headed towards the house. I hadn't even noticed our surroundings had changed from the tall skyscrapers to terraced housing. It looked so peaceful around here.

It must have been the weekend because both sides of the road were littered with parked cars. Most people would be at work any other day. I rubbed my eyes as I tried to think what day it was. How could I forget something as important as the day? I decided to focus on the now. Dwelling on things like that wasn't going to get us anywhere.

Our feet tapped against the pavement as we arrived at number thirty-nine. My eyes studied the building. I would have thought someone who used to work for the government would have a better house. This one didn't look that great. The three windows that looked down upon us had white net curtains hanging in them. The paint on both the window sills and the door was starting to peel away. The white gave way to the dull colour of wood.

We climbed the large stone steps up to the front door. There was a large golden knocker screwed to the wood, but Cassie used her fist to pronounce our presence. The sound seemed to echo through the wood enhancing the noise. I heard shuffling from inside the house. The occupant seemed to take forever to get to the door. I heard the sound of a lock, and then the handle turned. The door was opened slowly like it weighed a ton.

Once it was wide enough to look through, an old face suddenly appeared. He was the man from the file. He looked at both of us very disapprovingly and spoke like we had kicked our ball into his back garden for the hundredth time. "Who are you?"

Cassie spoke in a very formal manner. "Are you Mr. Chalke?" He confirmed what we already knew with a quick nod. "We would like to talk to you. May we come in?"

He gave us a look up and down, "Sure." His voice sounded just as weak as he looked. He shuffled back from the door to let us in. I took a step through than remembered something. As my second foot touched down on the carpet, I looked back at Cassie. She looked sad as she stared at the wooden door frame. I looked back at Mr. Chalke. "Are you sure we can come in?"

A brief hint of amusement touched his mouth. "I'm sure. Please come in, vampire."

I shouldn't have been surprised really. He was a retired leecher after all. He would have been able to smell her ashy essence. I wasn't looking for it, and I couldn't ignore the slight smell of it in the air.

We followed the man as he shuffled his feet towards a red

chair sitting in the corner of his small living room. There was a fireplace opposite us as we walked in. The mantle above it was covered in photos. They weren't of family members though like I would have expected. They were all of him. The backgrounds and his pose were the only things that changed. They ranged from a safari photo to one taken whilst he was climbing a snow-covered mountain. The view in the last one looked spectacular.

It looked like he had a lot of fun when he was younger. Now his head was covered in thinning grey hair, and he had trouble walking from the front door to his chair. It was hard to believe they were the same two people.

My eyes searched the rest of the room. In the corner opposite his chair was an old television. Next to that was a magazine holder made out of dark brown wood. The only other piece of furniture in the living room was a small table sitting next to Mr. Chalke's chair. He had a mug sitting next to a folded-up newspaper. The contents of his mug didn't look much like tea or coffee. It had the orange tint of whiskey. Everything including the flowered wallpaper made me feel like I was back in time.

"What do you want from me now?"

I was confused by his sudden question. "I'm sorry. What do you mean?"

"You said last week, that it would be the last visit. That I could now live my life the way I want to."

"Are you saying you saw us last week?" He had to be mad. It would suit his look.

"Of course, not you, daft girl. It was a tall leecher and a werewolf. The tall one said that it would be the last visit. Now you two have appeared. What does the government want from me now?"

Cassie looked at me in confusion, "What did they want from you last time, if you don't mind me asking."

"They took a few vials of blood. They said it was for

some kind of project they had started recently. They didn't give me any more information than that and I didn't ask. I just want to live what life I have left."

"Did they say what the project was called?"

"I don't know if it's my memory or if they never said but I don't recall it. Why is this important to you?"

I looked at Cassie, not sure whether I should say anything. I didn't know if we should come clean and explain everything or if we should lie. Either way, we needed to get this over and done with. Jewel needed our help, and she was so close. I was so stuck words were no longer forming in my head.

Luckily Cassie took the lead and was very convincing, "We are part of a different division of the leecher unit. We work with cold cases mostly. We have just come here because your name popped up."

"Oh, which case would that be?"

"I can't remember exactly, we've been working all day. I do remember it was a case involving a very old vampire. Maybe the oldest one we've come across."

"My memory isn't what it used to be but giving me a name might help."

"His name is Kellen, but he used to go by the name, Gerald."

The old man's face dropped, and horror filled his eyes, "I haven't heard that name in many, many years. When I met him, he was known by the second name you said." His whole body slumped down in the chair. The look of horror hadn't disappeared. In fact, he looked even more frightened. A shaky hand grabbed the mug, and he took a big gulp. He placed it back and looked up at us with a grimace. "We had a whole team of leechers after him. He killed five of us so quickly and maliciously. He then started playing games. Toying with us like we were mice."

He took a bigger gulp of his alcoholic drink and continued. "With three of us left he took his time and picked us off one by one. He killed my friend and then left me for dead. I only survived because I leeched off of a vampire that found me. We weren't prepared to face Gerald."

"If you were all leechers then how come he survived? Surely, each one of you would have been a match for him. There would be no way he could fight all of you."

The man let out a big sigh, "Like I said, we weren't prepared. Somewhere through the years, he found a spell. He had a witch enchant him so that no leecher would be able to use their ability on him. It was a very old vampire against eight humans. That's when the government started making weapons for us. Just in case something like that happened again. I don't know if Kellen figured out what they were doing, but he disappeared. He went from being the most well known and most dangerous vampire to being a bedtime story the higher-ups told leechers to scare them. No killings were reported, nothing." Another two gulps and the whiskey was all gone. As he placed the empty mug on the small table, I noticed his hand shaking even more.

He cleared his throat and carried on with his story, "I comfortably say that he is the most powerful vampire out there. There has been no record of him changing anyone. He has kept his power to himself. No one can say for sure if he was turned or if he was one of the first ones. Either way, no one can stop him." A long pause filled the living room. Neither Cassie nor I wanted to break it. The old man seemed deep in thought about something. Maybe something that had been buried deep inside and this story has brought it to the surface.

His droopy eyes rose up from the carpet to stare at us. In those eyes was a dangerous force that I didn't like the look of. I suddenly had a bad feeling about this. I sniffed the air to see if I could find anyone else. There was a scent in the house somewhere, but it was extremely weak. For all, I knew I could be smelling a supernatural creature that lived next door.

I forgot about it and kept Cassie's ash scent near my nose, just in case. The old man's eyes narrowed slightly, "Why are you asking questions about this vampire? You could find out all you need to know from the archives."

"Melvin said it would be best to come visit you since we were in the city." I held my breath, waiting to see if he bought it or not. I would have thought if Cassie needed to breathe, she would have done the same.

The seconds before he spoke felt like minutes, "That makes sense." The tension that had filled his body so quickly seemed to disappear. "I may have something else. Some information about Kellen before all that digitising went on at the office." A wrinkled hand lifted up and pointed towards the small number of books he had on a shelf. "The old one. Light brown cover. Take it. Maybe that will hold something you can use"

"Thank you." Cassie went and grabbed it, slipping it into a pocket for safe keeping.

"Is there anything else you can tell us, Mr. Chalke?" There wasn't a response to my question. Following his locked gaze, I looked out the front window as well. But nothing was standing there. Nothing moved out on the street. "Mr. Chalke?"

He kept looking past us and out the window. When I turned back to him, I saw the horror on his face. It was like he had seen his own death. "What's wrong?"

"He's here."

"Who?"

"You have brought him here to finish the job. All these years I've waited for him to turn up on my doorstep. I actually thought he had forgotten, but he's here. Damn you both!" He shot out of his chair and down the hallway like he was fifty years younger. We followed him into the kitchen at the back of the house. There he seemed to be stuck as his malfunctioning hands couldn't undo the gold chain.

At that moment the door flew outwards making the old

man stubble into the garden. The screws holding the hinges to the wood broke away easily. The door crashed into the grass a few metres away. Dust from the sudden movement blew about near the open doorway. The cloud seemed to linger in the open space like it was waiting to be invited in.

As it drifted down to the ground, it stretched upwards until it was barely visible. It formed into a silhouette then it vanished in an instant, and there he was. The sudden rush of ash hitting my nose took my breath away. I shut mental walls over my senses and watched in horror, not able to move.

A powerful hand shot out and grabbed Mr. Chalke around the throat. A groan came from him as the vampire closed his grip around the windpipe. Not even my fingers could move. I would have felt better if I wasn't even there. I wanted to be back home or at Logan's bar. Anywhere but here staring death in the face.

Two black eyes looked past the body being held off the ground. They looked directly at me. A sadistic smile showed his short vampire teeth. They were barely visible. He must have just fed. Which meant that anything that happened now would just be for fun.

His arm muscles flexed underneath his long trenchcoat. I expected him to pull Mr. Chalke towards him and bite into his neck. Instead, I watched the old man's body being flung like he was as light as a tennis ball. He landed on top of the kitchen table which turned into pieces of wood. The old man had to be dead from that. He could have leeched off of Cassie, but I believed he was too frightened to even think.

With Mr. Chalke out the way, I got my first proper look at this vampire. He was short, only an inch or two taller than me. He had broad shoulders that stretched the material of his jacket. He had black boots on, matching them with his black jeans. I couldn't help but notice how tight they were around his thighs. If he shifted his weight, then I could have seen his leg muscles tensing. They weren't the only things that were tight. His black t-shirt showed his body off through its thin material. His six-pack moved in and out with his breathing. He looked solid like not even a knife would penetrate his skin. He was clearly going for the dark night-stalker look from the movies.

If it wasn't for his evil smile, he could have possibly looked cute. He had a soft face and kind eyes. The black depths of his eyes looked deep enough to go swimming in. His hair was spiked up at the front and slicked down at the back. If he walked into a nightclub, he would have women draped off his arms within seconds. I dare say I would be one of them if the situation were different.

When he spoke, it was deep and controlled. It made me fear him even more, but I couldn't explain to myself why, "So we finally meet number three." If that was a way of intimidating me, it worked. It took all my will to stop my legs from shaking. "You have my thanks. I wasn't expecting to find Mr. Chalke again. I was hoping you would lead me to Jewel." My voice got caught in my throat. I wished Cassie would say something, so I knew she was still there. I could feel her presence behind me, but that wasn't enough. I wanted to hold her hand even though that wouldn't make me any safer. Kellen could kill us both and be out the house in seconds if he wanted.

I could hear my heartbeat going faster than I thought possible. No doubt Kellen was listening to it. Enjoying what he was making it do. Listening to it pump my blood through my veins. "Aren't you two going to converse with me? You're being very rude." He smiled again. It sent chills running through my skin.

Cassie spoke making my heart skip a couple of beats, "What do you want?"

"That's not the question you should be asking. I want to collect my reward for killing Jewel."

"Doesn't The Saracen want the money?"

"I convinced him to see it my way." There was a twinkle in his eye that gave his statement a disturbing feeling.

"So you work for him then? Like a little puppy dog." My heart must have skipped into overdrive at her insult. It felt like it would burst at the pace it was going.

Kellen's face didn't change. He clearly wasn't fazed by the insult. It reminded me of a cat who knew he had his mouse right where he wanted. "I consider myself freelance. The Saracen isn't the only person I work for, and he's by far, not the worst." There was so much we didn't know about this vampire. He knew that fact, and it seemed to make him happy. He casually strode into the house. "So what have we been up to?"

Was he really asking that question? He was acting all friendly. I wasn't about to give away what we're up to, but I couldn't help but speak, "What have you been up to?"

"Visiting some new friends. I left them some notes." He smiled again. It reminded me of the order he had left in those notes. I knew I wasn't first on the list, but I didn't feel any safer because of that fact. His voice came again all calm and slick. "You were very good when you killed that vampire. Have you figured out how the necklace works yet?"

My jaw would have hit the floor if it hadn't been attached. "You were watching me?"

"I was. Very entertaining."

Cassie took a step forwards. I didn't know how she acted so calm. "Do you know about the necklace?"

"There are many things I know. Would you like to know something?" I slowly nodded, not sure about what he would want in return, positive he would want some kind of payment. "I have information about you, not even that ghost Melvin can find out."

"How do you know then?"

"The government's security can't keep me out. They didn't even know I was there. Makes the words restricted and confidential completely pointless. Would you like the information?"

"What will the payment be?"

His smile was wider this time, "All I ask for is one simple taste."

"Taste of what?"

"Of your special blood."

"You're SICK!" I spat it out without thinking. I wasn't about to let him rip into my skin for a taste of my blood. His laugh at my answer made my whole body shiver.

"You do know I could just grab you and take as much as I wanted. There would be nothing you, Cassie or the creatures upstairs could do about it."

"What creatures?" Cassie's voice came from behind me, closer than I thought.

"Can't you smell them? Oh well. Don't worry, you can meet them very soon. They're coming down to introduce themselves." I heard thuds moving around upstairs. I used my leecher gift and sniffed the air. That smell I had noticed earlier was getting stronger. It smelled like fire. I never knew fire had a smell, but that's what I imagined in my head when this scent hit my senses. I couldn't figure out how many there were. From the sounds of it, I would have guessed a hundred but that had to be wrong. The house was so small you couldn't fit a hundred people in the whole place let alone upstairs.

Both Cassie and I turned around to stare down the corridor. I had my back turned to Kellen, but his stare and his arrogance were burning into my back. Either way, I looked, I was in danger. I had to believe Kellen would wait until he had dealt with Jewel. It was a horrible situation, but I had to believe in that.

As the thuds reached the bottom of the stairs, we waited, but nothing appeared immediately. I sucked in Cassie's ashy scent and let her vampire essence fill my body. I quickly switched to my infrared vision. It didn't help. In fact, it made things worse. Nothing was visible. All I could see was a large heat source near the front door. It was worse than my normal sight.

I switched back as a weird squawk filled the air. The noise was like a dagger in each ear. I shook my head, but it didn't do much to help. Then the house fell quiet. I could only hear my breathing in the silence.

The next few seconds felt like hours. A sudden thud made me jump and then they were moving. There were four of them coming down the hallway. Their legs were moving like they were running, but their feet were barely touching the floor. Cassie blurred into movement and shot down the corridor. I let my instinct come to the surface in my mind and waited in the kitchen. The first two attackers jumped over Cassie with ease, grazing the ceiling. It was almost like they floated down to the floor and kept running. A blur of fighting was happening behind them that I couldn't follow.

As they came to the doorway, they had to go in single file. The first one came through, and I moved. I moved as fast as I could, seeing the kitchen around me blur into streaks of colour. I grabbed a chair from the floor and spun around with it at head height. The first man jumped up into the air making me just miss him. The second one hadn't seen it and took the hit to the head, sending blood onto the wall. His body tipped back, spinning around before hitting the ground like a rock. Dropping the wood, I spun to see a fist coming towards me.

I moved to the side feeling the breeze against my face. With his side open, I rammed my fist into his ribs. A soft squeak came out of him instead of a grunt. I ducked under his swinging arm and flicked my leg out. He saw this coming and jumped into the air. His body twisted sideways and his feet came to rest on the floor. These guys were very light almost like they were filled with helium.

He lunged at me, hands ready to grab some hair. I ducked

again and shot my leg out. Once again he jumped, but I was ready this time, grabbing his leg and spinning around, cracking him into the corner of the kitchen counter. His head hit the wood hard enough to crack it all the way back to the wall.

He was up on his feet before I knew it like he hadn't even been hurt. As I was waiting for his attack, a flash of orange came from my left. Then I had arms wrapping around my arms, holding me in place.

Before I could do something about it, I felt two punches to my stomach and one to my cheek, sending an aching pain through my jaw bone. The man let out another squeak before moving in for the kill. My eyes were stapled open with fear. As he neared me, I watched his mouth reach out towards me. The skin turned into a hard material and formed a black beak. The point of it looked sharp enough to rip me to pieces. He was about to grab me when his body shot backwards like a bullet. He hit the counter again, turning most of it into small pieces of material this time. He didn't get back up.

I looked over to the doorway. Kellen was casually leaning up against the doorway with his arms crossed over his chest. His huge smile told me he was enjoying this.

He smiled at me, "Do want help with that one as well? You better be quick before the first one comes back." Comes back? The body had been used as a wrecking ball to destroy the counter, and Kellen thought he was going to come back. I wasn't about to wait and find out if Kellen was right. I stood on a foot and threw my head back. Cracking into the man's nose, I spun around quickly as I was released. I saw a flash of blood covering his mouth. A small part of me wanted to lick it up, but instead, I kicked him between the legs with all my might. His mouth opened but nothing but a gurgle came out as he fell to the floor in pain. These guys might be weird creatures, but they were still male and had male parts I could crush.

I stepped over him to see how Cassie was doing. She

seemed to be on top of things. One of her attackers had been rammed into the small cupboard under the stairs. She was moving fast and was handling the other one with ease. I was too busy watching her when another orange flash came, lighting up the kitchen. I turned around to see what it was when a body crashed into me.

We both traveled back until we hit the wall. My head snapped back and hit the brick hard sending little stars across my eyes. My vision went a little blurry until my body was filled with pain. My shoulder felt like it was being ripped off. It was only for a second and then the body was pulled off me. My hand shot up to feel blood coming out of me like a tap. I looked up at Kellen. He had the man with the beak held in the air with one hand. The weird one was kicking his legs and using an arm to try and hurt Kellen. Each hit was useless. Kellen didn't seem bothered by any of it.

I twisted my head and looked at my wound. That thing's beak had gashed a big hole in my shoulder. The wound was wide, and the inside was torn. I closed my eyes and called on the vampire inside of me. I willed the vampire essence to heal my wound. I had seen it in the movies and hoped it was one of the things they had gotten right.

In seconds my question was answered. I felt an ache starting to replace the searing pain in my shoulder. I looked down as my skin started growing back. The wound started closing up as the blood stopped leaking out of me. Soon there was a clean patch of new skin surrounded by blood. I touched it feeling a slight ache, amazed at what had happened. I rubbed off as much blood as I could and then returned my gaze to Kellen.

"You know, you should be more careful." He still had the man in the air. "You should do your research before you come into someone's house. All retired leechers have creatures protecting them. I found it funny that they never come when the leecher is in trouble. They've been given orders to wait and then try and capture the intruders, after death."

"Why?"

"They get rid of an ex-employee who knows too much, and they find someone who's capable of killing a leecher. In this case, it's not a big deal. He was very old after all. I'm guessing you have never come across this kind of supernatural creature?" I shook my head making the ache in my shoulder flare up for a few seconds. "I had a run-in with a gang of them twenty years ago. Or was it thirty? It's hard to remember. Decades tend to blur into one big period of time after a while." He laughed. It was a soft laugh that was more to himself than anything else. "They're a sub-species of shifters. They take after the mythic creature, the Phoenix. I've been told they smell like fire to you leechers." He stared at me with narrowed eyes before continuing. "You see the phoenix lives its life. When it dies, it bursts into flames and turns to ash. It's from this ash that a new one is born both living a new life and continuing its previous one. Now, these guys don't turn into ash, but they burst into flames before coming back to life. That was the orange flash you kept missing. It really is quite beautiful. They also have a beak that they use to kill or injure their enemies." He raised his free hand up and flicked the hard beak. "Fortunately there is a way of killing them, so they don't come back." He dropped the man, using his power to push him to his knees. He grabbed a handful of hair and pulled the man's head to the side, leaving his neck open. I watched as he slashed his teeth into his flesh like an animal. The beaked man squeaked. It started out as an ear-piercing noise, but as Kellen sucked on his blood, it got quieter until it died down. The man was still alive though. His eyes blinked, full of sadness and pain.

I wanted to look away, but I couldn't do it. My eyes were glued to Kellen with all his power. He pulled his teeth away from the skin, letting blood drip down his chin and onto his t-shirt. It wasn't over. He dug his fingers into the hole he had made and pulled. For him, it was like pulling the head off of a doll. For me, it was like watching a horror show. The amount of blood that was coming out of the holes was gruesome.

He kept pulling, sliding the phoenix shifters spine out of his body with a horrible sound. Finally pulling it free he marveled at his work. My stomach rebelled against the show. It rose, and there was nothing I could do to stop it. I rushed forwards and hit the sink with the contents of my stomach. I hadn't managed to finish that sandwich, so it was all stomach bile. It hit the sink with a sickening noise almost making me throw up again.

Kellen's soft voice came again. "Of course, pulling his head off wasn't necessary. Killing the brain would work as well. I just wanted to prove a point. I'm not a man of mercy, Beth." He chucked the head and the spine onto the draining board next to me. The blood dripped down the dents and into the small drain joining the mess that I threw up. My stomach threatened to rise again, but I swallowed that feeling deep down.

I saw out the corner of my eye that Kellen was now back by the door. "I'll be seeing you soon number three." Then in a blink of an eye, he was gone. I looked down at the sink and regretted it quickly. I threw up for the second time. Turning around once I was done I wiped my mouth with a tea towel.

I looked down at the headless body and then at the other one that had attacked me. I looked around the kitchen. My eyes fell onto the knives magnetically attached to the wall. The biggest one looked like the best option, so I grabbed it and walked across the kitchen. I crouched down and pressed the steel to the side of shifter's head. It felt weird because he looked dead. I knew he would be back soon though so I had to do it. I quickly pushed on the handle. Thanks to Cassie's strength on my arm, it slid through skin, bone and then his brain easily. The top of his head popped off onto the floor like the end of a loaf of bread. There was no movement or signal that confirmed his death. Then again not many people would be able to survive a knife through the head, I hoped.

I left the knife where it was, not wanting anything more to do with it and moved out into the hallway. There was no longer a man sticking out of the cupboard. Cassie was down the other end mid-fight. There was a body between me and her which suddenly burst into bright orange flames.

He was quickly on his knees with his eyes on Cassie. I rushed forwards. With one hand I grabbed the back of his t-shirt, and with the other, I grabbed his hair. I lifted him up off the ground then brought his head down onto the corner of the radiator. It made a metallic bong louder than I thought it would.

I thought that would have done it, but his fingers were twitching. So I pulled the radiator from the wall and brought it down upon his cranium. It burst like a balloon full of guts. The wall had taken most of the blood and brain, but I didn't want to look at my work.

I turned to Cassie, "Destroy his brain. It's the only way!" I yelled. She didn't acknowledge my words; she just put them to practice. The Phoenix man threw a punch. Cassie moved with grace and power. She ducked the attack, spun around and knocked the top half of the banister off. The piece of wood was now a weapon that she had created. As she kept spinning around to face him, she grabbed a handful of his t-shirt. He was lifted with one hand and pierced through the chest with the broken banister. He squawked and wriggled, trying to get free. Cassie gripped the wood in her hand tighter and used it to spear him through the head. He stopped wriggling after that. Cassie turned to me, a little out of breath. "What the hell were they?"

Before answering her, I allowed the vampire essence to leave my body, returning me to my human self. Then I answered Cassie, "Kellen said they were like shifters but not quite. They take after the mythic creature, the Phoenix."

"Is that why they kept coming back alive?" I nodded. "Where is he?"

I looked back into the kitchen and was happy to see it empty. "He's gone."

"Good. Don't think I could deal with him after all this. We need to go get Jewel and get back to Logan and Drew, quickly." She started walking towards the front door.

"Wait. I don't think that's a good idea. At least not the first part."

"You were the one who wanted to come get her. Why the sudden change of heart?"

"Kellen wants Jewel. He followed us here expecting us to lead him straight to her. Why would he stop following us now?"

It dawned on Cassie what I was talking about. "So what do we do? Is there a way we can warn her or something?"

"I think I know what to do." I pulled the ring out of my pocket. "She sent me a message through this. Maybe I can send one back to her."

"You know more than me about what's going on with that ring of yours. It's up to you." There was a look of worry in her eyes.

"I want to try it. I don't know what could happen though."

"Okay. Perhaps you should sit down."

"Good idea." We both walked into the small room at the front of the house. I took a seat in the red chair that used to belong to Mr. Chalke. I breathed in deep and gave Cassie a smile. She gave me one back which calmed my nerves but didn't make them go away completely.

I thought about the last two times I had put the ring on. I hoped Jewel was still connected. This way we're not leading Kellen straight to her. "I'll tell her to go back to The Four Elements bar."

"Good idea. I'm sure Drew's dad has that place under control; we just won't be able to return ourselves. Good thing

I charged my phone up this morning."

"Logan can give us some advice." She nodded in agreement. I forgot about all that stuff and concentrated on the ring. I lifted it to my finger. The silver felt cool against my skin as I slipped it on. As it hit the base of my finger, my mind went black. The next second it was filled with the same image as last time. It seemed to appear unstable though. Each part of the image kept jumping to the front like each one was trying to get my attention over the other.

I locked my eyes on the homeless man in the alleyway. He jumped into the foreground, sending Frank back, dampening his cries of pain a little. I stared the man in the eyes. They seemed to be familiar. When he spoke, it was a voice I had heard before. It was not what I was expecting. It was a feminine voice, and it belonged to Jewel. It was weird to be seeing a man and hearing Jewel's voice. I really needed to get some spells from those books. If Jewel could make herself look like a homeless man, they could come in handy in a sticky situation.

I listened to the words coming out of the man's mouth, "Where are you?"

I focused, not sure if I was speaking out loud or not, "We're close by, but Kellen appeared. We can't meet you because we would lead him straight to you."

"Okay. What are we going to do then?"

"Go back to The Four Elements pub. Logan and Drew will be there. We'll get in contact with them and see what he wants us to do with Kellen on our tail."

"Okay. I guess it's been long enough, I should be able to move now."

"Good. We won't see you at the pub, but we'll see you soon."

"Okay. Be careful, and I'm sorry about running off the way I did. I guess I was more scared than I let on."

"It's fine. You be careful." The man smiled at me like a

friend. I hadn't gotten used to it, and there was no more time. Hopefully, it would be the last time I would need to use the ring. Jewel will hopefully be able to find another way to help me find Frank. That's only if she can help me at all.

As the alleyway slowly moved backwards, Frank came into the foreground. It was nice and slow at first, but then he shot forwards. I jolted back as his face almost smacked into mine. He screamed so loud I could smell his breath on my face. I tried to pull off the ring, but it wouldn't budge. Now it felt like Frank's hand was wrapping around my wrist. He was suddenly staring at me silently, making my blood run cold.

I stared into his eyes that seemed to have carried on screaming for help. His voice came out as a whisper, "Don't leave me." I watched as his eyes started rolling around into the back of his head. I pulled on the ring as hard as I could and shook away from his grip.

As his face faded away, Cassie's came into view. She had her hands on my shoulders. My name kept coming out of her mouth over and over. She only stopped when I placed my hand on her arm and spoke. "I'm fine."

"What happened?"

"I spoke with Jewel. At least, I spoke to someone with Jewel's voice." She looked confused. "It's hard to explain. I told her to go to the pub like we decided."

"I meant at the end."

"Oh. My friend who gave me this ring has been appearing in my head whenever I put it on. He's been becoming more and more real. This time he came right up to my face screaming. He grabbed my wrist just before I came out of it." I raised my arm to emphasize what I was talking about. I looked at the skin and found my breath catching in my throat. Printed on the skin was a dirty handprint. It was exactly where Frank had grabbed me. On one of the fingers was a clear mark where my skin shone through. It must be where he's wearing a ring. A link between the two seemed to be how he was talking to me like that. I felt the cool silver inside of my palm. Amazing what a piece of metal can do with a little magick. I needed to find out who was making this link. If I found out who it was, it could lead me to Frank.

Now thinking about it, I should have asked Jewel if she could help me with the Frank situation. If she could speak to me, maybe she could find out where he was. I contemplated putting the ring back on, but I wasn't too sure how many more times I could see Frank like that. Next time he could grab me and drag me into that slice of hell he was in. There was no telling what kind of magick was being used, or it's possibilities.

Cassie helped me up to my feet. I slipped the ring into my pocket and started rubbing my arm. It took a while, but the dirt finally came off. Once I finished, I looked up at Cassie. "What do we do now?"

"There's a park around here. Maybe we should take a break and sit down. Would be nice to stop moving and enjoy something for a change. Give my brain a rest."

"That actually sounds like a really nice idea. God knows I could do with a proper sit-down."

"We can scan through this book he gave us. See if there's anything we can learn about this Kellen." I nodded in agreement as we left the house, leaving it the way it was. The government would no doubt have someone coming round to clear all this up.

We were back in the car and ready to drive to the park. From now on we would have to be careful. Kellen was a monster. There was no way Cassie and I could win in a fight against him. He would rip us apart. Once again, I found myself wishing for a normal life. I wondered how far I would have to run away to get one. How far would the government and Kellen follow us? Would it just be easier to give in, go to the government and hand myself over? If I did that, what would happen to the others? Would the government make me hunt them down? I couldn't do that to them. Not after all we've been through together.

I forgot about my worries and stared out the window. The whole trip was spent in silence. It wasn't awkward, just silent. Most of the time I spent thinking about Frank. I thought about the things we did when we were younger. He used to help me sneak out of my parents' house when I had been grounded. The number of stupid things we did. Every day of the summer it was him and me getting up to mischief. Even at school, we used to get into trouble together. Now thinking about it, most of the time it was my fault. He would never allow me to take the blame though. He would join me in detention every time.

I shouldn't have started reminiscing about the old days. It made me want to talk to Frank. The only way I could do that now was with the ring. Without noticing I had been tracing the impression of it in my jeans. I stopped it as soon as I realised. I looked around not knowing where we were. A few turns and we pulled up into a little car park.

As I climbed out the smell of burgers and hot dogs filled my nose, and my stomach rumbled in response. Looking up I saw the smoke puffing up from a burger van on the corner. "Perfect. I need some food."

"Didn't you find any at the motel?"

"What I did have was lost in Mr. Chalke's kitchen sink."

"We can go grab a bench in the park and eat. Look over the information we got."

I was too busy looking forward to my meal. "You can look. I'll be too busy eating all their food." I mentally went through what I was going to order, wondering if I would have enough cash. My thoughts were cut short when a black car drove past. I automatically turned my back to it as it crawled by. "Don't worry. It wasn't the government. The couple was too interested in kissing each other than concentrating on the road."

A smile crawled across my face as I thought about Drew and the kiss we shared back at the motel. I could feel the warmth of his lips on mine like I was kissing him again. That was until Cassie interrupted my daydream with a pat on the arm. "I know what you're thinking about."

"Do you now? What would that be?"

Her voice was laced with sarcasm, "I don't know. Maybe a certain werewolf?"

"Nope."

"Liar." I laughed. "You really like him don't you."

I pictured Drew in my mind, and just the sight of his smile had me grinning like an idiot. "I know it hasn't been long, but yeah I do."

"That's good."

"Have you ever felt like that?"

Her eyes seemed to go quiet, "Once. Let's get you some food, and I'll tell you if you want."

We joined the back of the queue for food which was longer than I was hoping, "You don't have to tell me. If it's too painful."

"It's fine. It's probably about time I told someone." As we stood there the smell of food mixed with the essence of supernatural creatures. There were multiple scents in the mix, but the two I recognised was the ash and mint scent of vampires and werewolves. I looked around at the people walking past and the single file that was standing in line for something to eat.

I locked onto some vampires as they walked past. Despite the fact, they would have known what I was if they were bothered, but they just seemed like they wanted to get on with their lives. Walking along minding their own business and I couldn't blame them. It was exactly what I wanted to do.

I looked at the line that was between me and the satisfying taste of meat. The longer I smelt it, the bigger my appetite grew. It even had my mouth watering at the thought of eating a good amount of food. My stomach grumbled again, protesting at the wait it had to endure. If it had gotten any louder, the vendor would have heard it over the sound of the street. Instead, the man in front of us turned around and smiled. "That almost sounded like the word food."

"Give it time, I'm sure it will." I smiled at him as his scent washed over me. He was a werewolf but nowhere near the same as Drew. He was skinny and only an inch or two taller than me. His face was skinny with his cheekbones almost poking through the flesh. His eyes were sunken back, but the bright blue iris made them sparkle. He opened his mouth to speak then stopped. His eyes searched mine. He frowned and asked, "Where do you work?"

"I study at a university not too far from here."

"Shouldn't you be in class or something?"

"I've been having a rough few days."

"I'm sure." He gave me a smile that was completely fake. "Bye." He walked out of the line and carried on until he turned a corner and was out of sight.

I turned to Cassie, "What do you think that was about?"

"He was a werewolf right?"

"Yeah."

"He probably smelt no scent on you. That can only mean one thing."

I lowered my voice, "That I'm a leecher." She nodded. "I need to get that problem sorted. Do you think that there's a spell that would help."

"Maybe." She paused, thinking about a question. I waited for it as she opened her mouth but it didn't come out.

"If you have a question then just ask." I pulled a really big smile, curious about what a vampire would ask an amateur leecher.

"What do werewolves smell like to you?"

"They smell minty."

"Minty?" Cassie giggled.

"Yeah but it's not just the smell. I can usually tell them apart from other people with a feeling."

"A feeling?"

"It's difficult to explain. It's like a hunch. I'm never a hundred percent sure but I'd trust a hunch." A few people left the line with food bringing me closer to satisfaction. "Can I ask you a question?"

"Is it about my past?"

"Not really. We seriously don't have to talk about that if you don't want to."

"Ask your question." She smiled making her seem softer and more like a friend instead of a powerful supernatural creature.

"You seem so human."

She pulled a funny face then lowered her voice to a whisper, "How do you mean?"

I lowered the pitch of my voice to match hers, "With the sunlight thing. The crying back at the motel. I just wasn't expecting tears. Especially ones that turn to ash."

"What did you expect?"

"I don't really know. I didn't ever expect to see a vampire cry in the first place."

A soft chuckle came out her mouth, "Here's the way I look at it. The human body is like a shell. The soul fills the body and makes people human. A vampire is just the shell."

"Vampires don't have souls?" She shook her head. "I suppose that means you're not the undead then."

This time she laughed out loud but then lowered her voice when she got some looks. "Vampires aren't the undead. We're just humans without souls. We still have feelings."

"That's a good way of looking at it. Do you have a way of explaining werewolves then?"

She quickly looked around at the people, then said, "It's like werewolves have schizophrenia. One personality is human whereas the other is a beast. Sometimes they have control over the beast side and other times they don't."

"That's brilliant. It really feels like another person is trying to take control of your body."

Her look seemed to register that this was all new to me still. "I bet that feels really weird."

"It might feel the same with a vampire's need for blood."

"Maybe."

We finally got to the front of the line, and I got my first look at the list of food. I scanned the items I wanted. My eyes met the stare of the pudgy man waiting for my order. I was momentarily distracted by the horrible stains on his t-shirt before speaking, "I'll have a burger, a hot dog, and some chips please."

"Right away. Anything for you sweetie?"

"No thanks," Cassie replied politely.

"Be a couple of minutes."

"Thanks." I turned back to talk to Cassie. "Don't suppose you have a way of explaining witches?" I caught the weird look we were getting from the person behind us in the queue. I gave her a smile and explained, "Media studies."

She pulled a smile back before Cassie replied, "You will have to talk to someone else about them. Jewel has been the only one I've ever met. Unfortunately, not all of them are like her."

"The world would be too peaceful if that was the case."

"Your food is ready, sweetie." I returned the chubby smile the man was flashing whilst tapping my pockets. Feeling the note, the cheque and the key Keith had left me. What I didn't find was my purse or any kind of money. I could have sworn I had it with me and I couldn't even think back to the last time I saw it.

I was about to turn to Cassie and start pleading for some money when my fingers felt something in my jacket pocket. I pulled it out and was relieved to find a ten-pound note. It had slipped my mind since I hadn't worn this thing in a while. I gave him the money, received my change and then my delicious looking food.

We walked off and into the park area. It dipped half-way creating a lower tier of grass. A pond sat over to the right with a small playground for toddlers next to it. On the other side was a larger play area for older kids with a skate park as well. The large oak trees cast shadows over the people. There was a wide path leading right through the middle with unlit lamp post and benches.

We cut across the grass and took the nearest seat. The bench didn't look in the best condition, and it creaked as it took our weight. I almost dropped my hot dog for the third time, but I wasn't about to lose any bit of my food. My stomach wouldn't have been happy about that.

I wriggled my bottom, getting comfortable then took another look at the view. It was beautiful. The sun was still bright like earlier, and it gave the park a summer feeling. I could even hear birds chirping away. From this view, it seemed like the park was flooded with trees. Some were in clumps, and some were dotted around the grass standing alone. From here it was easier to the see the two lines of oak trees that bordered the path.

I people watched as I started and finished my hot dog in just a few bites. Families were sitting around on blankets stuffing their own mouths with picnic food. Joggers sped past wearing tight outfits and listening to music. Dogs ran about chasing after sticks and balls. It would be easy to just forget about everything that had gone wrong and enjoy this moment. I could enjoy the heat from the sun and the soft breeze grazing over my face. How could I be running away from the government and a killer vampire on such a day like this? The problem was, we would have to sort everything out before we could enjoy a day like this properly. I couldn't remember how many times I had wished I had a normal life up to this point but I found myself wishing it again. I knew it wouldn't be the last time either.

I looked down from the view and began eating my burger. It tasted so good I wouldn't be surprised if I ended up going back for a second. The last bite went down into my stomach. It was only now I noticed Cassie had been reading through the journal we had acquired.

I wiped the burger juices from my chin and started on the chips as she read through a few pages. I only spoke when I got half-way through the portion, "Find anything good?"

"I've only gotten through a few pages. So far it's just been about Kellen's past. Things he's done or places he was spotted. You carry on eating. I'll let you know if I find anything important."

"Okay." She wasn't going to have to tell me twice. I carried on with the chips that were still hot. There was a part of me that wished I had put some ketchup on them, but the thought disappeared when another chip went into my mouth. They were going down just fine like this.

It wasn't long before they were gone and Cassie hadn't read much further. I bundled all the rubbish into one big ball and chucked it towards the bin a few metres away. It hit the rim and bounced off onto the grass. I blew out a breath and pushed off of the bench. Now realising how bloated I felt. Plopping the rubbish where it belonged I returned to the bench and sat down, rubbing my belly. It was there on the bench that I brought up everything that we had going on and slotted them into sections. Compartmentalising it all hoping it would make it seem less scary.

CHAPTER 9

First and most problematic was the government. They were everywhere and could get to us at any time. I couldn't even start thinking how we could stop them. How we could manage to get away for good. Logan had managed it a few times by the sounds of it, but this was more than just one person. Would we have to split up and never see each other again? Losing friends I have only just gained in this crazy new world.

Another issue just as problematic was Kellen. We know very little about him, and even if we knew more, he was playing a game. Whether his employer knew what he was up to was a mystery. The notes were another troubling thing. He could keep to the list and kill us in order, or it could be a trick to get our guard down. That way he could carry on with his games. Then there was the moment he helped us. Was it a genuine thing or was he just making sure he was the one to end our lives? He seemed to be half-guardian angel and half-devil.

The Saracen was the third problem. That was hopefully going to be sorted out soon, but there was a part of my brain that still didn't trust Griffin Gaynes. This was a man who practically alienated his son and didn't seem too bothered about it. My gut twisted every time I thought about him aid-ing us.

The last problem I could think of is if one of us gets caught. If it's by the government, then we could probably sort out an escape plan. If The Saracen catches us, then it could be more complicated. Things could get even worse if Kellen took one of us hostage. There would be no telling what would happen. There are so many little things that could go wrong. The problem was I couldn't do anything about them by worrying. I forced myself to push all bad thoughts out of my head. Dwelling on them was pointless.

A soft thud made me jump. I twisted my body to see Cassie standing there chatting to someone on the phone. I didn't interrupt and just listened. "Okay. We'll be there in ten minutes, maybe twenty, I think." She listened to the other person before speaking again, "Yes, I know the plan. Don't worry everything will be fine." I listened to her grunting to some words. Then she hung up and pushed the phone into her pocket. She saw my stare, "Got news from Logan."

"What's happening?"

"We have to meet them at Hoover View Point."

"Where's that?"

"It's a little like a holiday camp place. Not too far from here luckily." She looked off into the distance.

"Is that where this whole thing with The Saracen is happening?"

"Yeah. We better get going if we're going to get there in time. I'll fill you in on the plan on the way."

"Sure." We got back to the car and back on the road. As we passed the vendor again, I thought about grabbing a burger for the road, but I felt full enough as it was.

The short journey only felt like five as my vampire friend explained the plan. She and I would be hiding out in the woods, using it as a vantage point to see what was going on. Logan was making sure the whole place is deserted. That way there won't be people there confusing things. The rest of the plan was going to be given to us when we arrived which I didn't really like.

The car was turned down a dirt track that disappeared between some trees. We past by a sign carved out of a massive log with the name of the place dug into the grain. Either side of us were rows and rows of trees setting the scene for a bad slasher movie. I could see the title dripping with blood. Getting the public in to watch it with the promise of blood and tits. And this movie would be staring us if this meet didn't go as planned.

Soon the trees gave way to two fields, one on each side of the track. The one on the right sloped down to an enormous lake. It sparkled as the sun shone down upon it. In the middle of the body of water was a small island. From this distance, the only thing I could make out was the small shed that sat next to a group of trees. The back edge of the water was lined with more fir trees that carried on to encircle the whole place.

To the left of the road was everything else. Next to the car park at the end of this track was a large information centre. It was completely made out of logs. It had a pointed roof with a flag sticking out of the middle. All the way to the left were cabins for over-nighters. They looked simple from this distance but who knew what they would hold inside. Between them and us were various sport pitches and courts. I could see a group of small children playing a game of cricket. I guess Logan's scheme for emptying the place hadn't started yet. Either that or it hasn't worked very well.

I turned my attention to the information centre as Cassie parked the car. Climbing out we stood on the small path leading around the building. A breeze hit me and filled my nose with the smell of trees and flowers. It smelt like summer and reminded me of the summer holidays I used to go on. It reminded me of the many fights I used to have with my parents on those holidays.

Another breeze hit me knocking my thoughts and filling me with a hint of happiness. Right then I could have grabbed a hamper full of food and sat on a blanket staring up at the clouds. That would have suited me just fine.

I looked away from the soft green grass and spotted Drew standing outside the centre. I didn't know what I was doing until my feet had carried me over to him. As soon as he spotted me a smile erupted across his face. I jumped the last step, and he caught me with no effort in his arms. He felt strong and sturdy as he wrapped them around me. Any tighter and he would crush me, but I didn't care. It felt so nice to have someone hug me like this. To make me feel so protected from the world around me. I didn't want him to let go. Unfortunately, he did as Logan walked out from the centre. He smiled at us. Drew plopped me back on the gravel path.

The first thing I noticed was someone was missing. I looked at Logan, "Where's Jewel?"

He held a finger up to his lips before looking around. "She's around." He nodded over my shoulder. Both Cassie and I looked behind us. I didn't see Jewel anywhere. The only person I saw was a young boy playing with some marbles on a picnic table. I didn't notice it was her until he looked up and smiled. Despite the childish face, the eyes that stared at me were Jewel's. I turned back to Logan who said, "We're in the cabin at the end. I've paid the man behind the desk to leave in about an hour. I've checked, and we'll be the only ones staying so the place should empty out in thirty or so minutes."

"So where exactly are Beth and I going?" Cassie was asking the exact question I wanted to know. The answer wasn't what I was hoping for.

"We brought some camping gear on the way here. You two will be in the forest just behind the second hut. We need to cover every angle on this one. Let's start walking. I'll explain the details inside."

Our feet echoed on the wood as we moved from the grass

to the deck of our cabin. Logan opened the door and ushered me through. The inside of the cabin was just like I expected. There was a small seating area to the right with a little coffee table. To the left was a decorative table with a telephone and a welcome pack. In the wall above the table was a long window that was the only source of light at the minute. That was only because the window in the kitchen at the back of the cabin was covered with thick, striped curtains.

The kitchen was small but seemed to hold everything you would need. In between me and the kitchen was a large oak table. It looked thick enough to use as a weapon and knock someone out. On top of it was a large drawing. As I got closer, I noticed it was the layout of Hoover View Point. It had places marked with a pen, even the spot where Cassie and I would be setting up camp.

There was a long arrow following the dirt track into the camp. I tapped it and gave Logan a curious look. He answered as Drew joined us at the table. "That's where the meet is happening. Drew's father suggested this place because he has some fish-shifters. When he mentioned it, it sounded like a good thing." His eyes darted to mine. "A good idea for help."

As Drew cleared his throat Logan's eyes dropped back to the map. "The plan is for The Saracen to come meet Griffin Gaynes. Then us and Gaynes' men will take care of him. With his death, Gaynes can take over his business. We get Jewel off the books, and it's all sorted."

"I don't know if it will be the end, but at least we'll get Jewel's debt cleared." Drew smiled at me. I felt the flutter of my hormones in my stomach. "How long do we have before we need to be ready?"

"A few hours. Why?"

"I was wondering if I could borrow Bethany for a little bit."

"I suppose so." He gave me a look. I couldn't help my smile at the thought of Drew taking me somewhere so we could be alone. I wondered if he had booked a third cabin for us to use or were we going to be sitting on the grass like a normal couple. Maybe have a picnic.

His smile was just as big as mine, "Great." I was surprised when he came around the table and dragged me out of the cabin. My heart pounded in my chest as we disappeared into the next cabin along. Drew opened the door for me like a pure gentleman. As I walked past him, I made sure I wiggled my butt for his viewing pleasure. I could feel the heat of his gaze. I heard the door shut and then noticed a small bag sitting on the table.

I walked past the rolled up sleeping bags and a tent. I peered down into the white bag and saw what Drew had in mind. I pulled out the contents and turned around to face him. I had a bikini top in one hand and the bottoms in the other. I walked over to him with my eyebrow raised. "Now what do you have in mind?"

"I thought we could take a nice dip in the lake."

"And how do you know this will fit me?"

He pulled his cheeky smile, "Just a hunch. You can put it on in the bedroom and see for yourself."

I looked down at the material in my hands, "Hold on to your socks then." His next smile was full of anticipation and practically took my breath away. I walked off to the bedroom swaying my waist from side to side. Giving him a quick smile before shutting the bedroom door between us.

Once out of my clothes and into my new bikini I made sure my hair looked reasonably good in the mirror. I looked down at the white material, and the large red flowers dotted about on it. I had one on each breast and a larger one planted on my butt. At least that would give Drew something else to look at. I made sure the two knots holding my bikini top to my body were done up tightly before walking out the bedroom, feeling a little conscious of how much skin was on display.

That worry vanished when I opened the door, and Drew's jaw practically hit the floor. "That good, huh?" I threw my hands up and did a little twirl for him. His mouth started moving, but the words seemed to be getting caught in his throat. I casually walked over to him making sure I worked it all the way. When there was only a couple of inches between us, I stopped. I ran my tongue over my lips to tease him with the idea of kissing him. He brought his head down to place a kiss on my lips, but I was feeling playful. I slowly backed away and then slipped around him and to the door. I placed my back to it and held the doorknob in both hands. "Where's your swimsuit?" He smiled and started to undress.

First to go was his top. He draped it over a chair as I scanned his toned chest and abs. My gaze fell down along with his hands as he removed his trousers. Underneath, much to my sadness were long swimming shorts. I was hoping he would just be wearing some underwear, but I guess they would have to do, for now.

He walked over to me with a smile that held a lot more than his cuteness. I could read it like a book, and I knew what he was planning on doing with me. I wasn't going to be easy, I wanted him to give chase for a little bit. Only for a little bit because I could feel the deep urge to have him growing quickly.

I twisted the doorknob behind my back and retreated out into the hot sun with Drew in close chase. The heat felt nice against my bare skin, heating my body up. It was made perfect by the soft, cool breeze coming across the lake that brought all kinds of smells with it. I turned around feeling the grass tickle my feet as we started walking towards the water hand in hand. I looked at the blue coolness that was going to feel so good.

Another thing that would feel good on my body would be Drew. I would have to keep those kind of ideas under control right now. The last thing we need is getting caught in the water doing something and getting kicked out of here. I'm sure Logan wouldn't appreciate that.

The feeling of the grass blades stroking my soles gave way to wood again. It echoed through our steps as we walked along the short jetty that stuck out over the water. As we got to the end Drew stopped and sat down. He dangled his legs off the edge letting his toes just probe the surface of the water. I took the space next to him, hoping I wouldn't get a splinter in my butt.

I looked down at the bright blue water as I allowed my toes to touch the cool liquid. The temperature rose up my legs bringing my body to the perfect coolness. We both sat there watching the families and friends playing games in the lake. As I thought about the silence, I turned to Drew. Maybe he didn't want to talk. Maybe he just wanted to have a sit-down and spend some time just me and him.

Even though it felt nice to relax, it did give my mind time to think about Drew's body. The things I could do to it and all the things he would do to me in return. Sitting there wasn't going to do my hormones any good. I thought about the fun all the children were having, and it gave an idea. I waited until his gaze went off in the other direction and I gave him a strong push. A smile hit my lips when I saw his butt slip off the edge but it was short lived when he twisted around and took hold of my wrist. I had gotten him into the water, but I soon followed with a big splash.

The coolness that had been licking at my toes was nothing compared to the full impact of the water. It swarmed around and through my body, immediately making me take in deep breaths. Drew swam over to me kicking up small waves. "You cold?"

My teeth started chattering as I spoke. "What do you think?"

"I think if your teeth chatter any harder they'll break. Come here." He softly tugged on my hands, gliding me over to him. As his arms wrapped around me and my body touched his, I was amazed. Despite the cold of the water, his body felt like it was on fire still. The heat from him seemed like it was heating up the water around us.

I looked at him and saw more heat in the depths of his eyes. That had nothing to do with temperature, but it did have mine hiking up enough to make a bead of sweat drip down my nape. His arms tightened a little pulling me closer towards him. He placed a light kiss on my forehead then let his lips move down. They softly brushed the tip of my nose then they found my lips. There was nothing gentle about this kiss. It just showed me how much he had been holding back. It showed how much I could really enjoy a kiss.

It felt nothing like I had ever felt before. The water dropped away. There was no longer any sound coming from the children or the birds. All I could feel was his lips and his body. I could have melted away at this moment and lived in it forever. My lips feeling electric from his.

After what seemed like forever we broke away from each other. Our heavy breathing mixed together. His hot breath swept over my face allowing me to taste him on my lips. I wanted another kiss, and I wanted it to last much longer. Pursing my lips, I was ready to lean in. Only his smile went from sexy to cheeky, and then I felt his hands on my waist. The next second I was soaring through the air like a bird. Before I knew what had happened, I was plummeting back towards the lake.

I stretched out and made my body a long thin torpedo. My fingers broke the surface of the water then my body shot under. My hands dug into the muck at the bottom before I twisted around. I could see Drew's legs slowly kicking, keeping himself afloat at the top. I moved my legs and arms, propelling myself forwards. He must not have seen my blurry shape because I caught him by surprise.

I grabbed his feet and yanked down hard. The look of

surprise on his face was priceless and something I would remember for the rest of my life. I shot myself upwards, sucking in air whilst I could. His soaked hair came up from the water followed by his cheeky smile. There were a few metres between us, but I knew he could close that down in seconds. So, when he started coming towards me, I quickly started swimming in the opposite direction. I could hear the splashing his feet made and soon I saw him in the corner of my eye. A few more seconds and he was in front of me, swimming like a majestic mermaid.

I slowed down my own pace allowing him to take a position in front of me. He wasn't even breathing heavy whereas I was trying to fill my lungs with as much air as possible.

He slowly paddled over and just took me in his arms again. "You look sexy all wet."

"I bet I do." I flicked a little water on his face. "You're a good swimmer."

"It's only doggy paddle." We both laughed at his extremely bad joke. I found his eyes again, his stare was filled with more heat than last time. Then it was me moving first. I found his lips. My arms pulled him closer, pressing my lips against his harder. It was just as passionate as the last kiss, and I didn't want it to stop. I kept pulling him closer, not wanting there to be any distance between us. Body to body. His burning skin scorching against mine.

When I opened my eyes his lips slowly moved away from mine, and I noticed we were back near the jetty. Drew must have been kicking his legs as we kissed. I hadn't felt a thing. "Playtime isn't over is it?" I gave him my best innocent look. He wasn't buying it, and I couldn't blame him. Being a werewolf, he would no doubt be able to tell how much I wanted him.

"We can play again in a bit. Thought we could chat." With that, he let go of my body and grabbed the edge of the jetty. I watched him pull himself out of the water with ease.

I had to say, it was a hell of a show watching those muscles tensing and moving. He perched himself on the edge spilling water all over the wood. I did the same but had a harder time making it look as effortless as he did.

At the end of the day, he was a werewolf, and I was just human. Part of me disliked that, but a larger part was happy about it. Whenever I've been around Drew, I've found myself glad that I'm human. I wanted him to be with me the way I am, not as a supernatural creature. I was comfortable in my human body so he should be comfortable with it as well. If he wasn't then I would most definitely miss the kisses we had been sharing recently.

I fidgeted a little so that the wood no longer pricked my thighs. Looking up my eyes moved across the space of water, unable to stop the smile from curling my lips at the beautiful sight. Then I turned to look at my werewolf, and that smile grew even larger. It was then I saw the concerned look on his face. "Is there something you're not telling me?"

"Not exactly."

"What's wrong then? I can see the worry on your face."

"My father." I didn't like the fact we were trusting Griffin so much with this. Especially with the number of problems his own son had with it. "He's not an honest man. I can't even believe he's agreed to help us. Well, I suppose he's actually agreed to help me."

"Drew." He turned to face me. I placed the palm of my hand against his cheek. The feel of his skin tingled against mine. "What are you trying to say?"

"I want you to be careful."

"Of course I'll be careful."

"I mean it, Beth." He moved his hand to my cheek, mirroring my position. I pressed my cheek into his touch, feeling the warmth of it. "Any sign of trouble and I want you to run as fast as you can. You leech off of Cassie or anybody, and you run. I don't want you to look back or stop. You keep going until you're safe. Promise me you'll do that."

"Ok. I promise." I said the words easily. I saw the effect of them immediately. His face no longer held the look of worry and sadness. His smile was real, and his eyes twinkled. It was a shame I didn't mean the words that had made him so happy. If there was any trouble, I was sticking around and making sure my friends were safe. I wouldn't be running off and leaving them, but he didn't need to know that. It was just so sweet that he was this worried about me.

He smiled a great big smile which showed off his white teeth. "That's all I really wanted to say."

"Okay." I lifted my hand off his cheek and onto his shoulder. I was planning on pushing him in for a second time. This time I was going to make sure my arms were out of reach so I could stay on dry land. I was concentrating on this so much I hadn't noticed Drew's hand slipping from my cheek to my back.

He pushed me hard enough for the impact to sting my skin. The temperature of the water reminded my body of how cold it was without Drew near me. I flicked my head back as I surfaced, sending my hair into a large arc. I just stared up at Drew who was wearing a devilish smile. "I suppose you find that funny."

"Didn't you when it was the other way around?"

"I would have if you hadn't of dragged me in as well."

"I would apologise if your expression hadn't been so funny." He chuckled to himself.

He had just pushed me into the freezing cold water but somehow hearing his chuckle sent a flame of heat through my body. It was such a nice sound. I narrowed my eyes at him, "I'll get you back when you least expect it."

"Good luck sneaking up on a werewolf." His smile reached his ears as he stood up. I enjoyed the view, gently kicking my legs to stay on the surface. His chest and his abs were glistening from the water. Those swimming shorts were already quite revealing, but now they clung to his thighs and everywhere else. It left very little to my imagination, and it had my heart pounding in my chest. I enjoyed the view until he bent his legs and sprung into the air. My amazement doubled as he flipped over twice before entering the lake with a perfect dive.

As soon as his head came above water, I started clapping. "I'll give you a nine out of ten. I'm afraid your dive got a five but since the view was so nice, I upped your score."

"How generous of you." Suddenly I was being pulled into his body. Both his arms and his scent surrounded me. His sweet aroma drenched the air and seemed to make the water feel thicker. I allowed everything about him fill up my senses as I stared into his eyes like I was star gazing. They were deep and beautiful. I didn't know if I was getting high on him, but I felt great. I felt light and warm. He definitely was having a good effect on me.

I leant forwards and gave him a kiss. It was just a peck, but somehow it was just as good as the others. We both smiled at each other, and a little giggle came out of my mouth.

His rich voice breezed across my ear in a whisper, "So, do you fancy playing around in the water some more or do you want to go back to the cabin." His eyebrows sprung up, adding a cheeky effect to his grin.

"What did you have in mind?" It wasn't really a question I needed to be answered because I was already making my way to the jetty. He followed me out of the water, and we both walked across the grass, hand in hand. To an onlooker, we looked like we were just out for a stroll. That was until we were behind the closed door to the cabin.

My body was suddenly crushed up against the wooden door, and my lips were being explored by his. I couldn't feel anything. All his kisses and all his touches felt like one big caress that had my skin creating beads of sweat.

His hands were on my hips, pulling my body to his. I had

my arms loosely draped around his neck. When the ache to have him got too much, I pushed off the door. I broke the kiss and pushed on his chest. He was so much stronger than me, but he allowed me to take control. My own breathing matched his as I watched his chest rising and falling rapidly. Knowing I had this effect on him had me wanting him even more.

As he stopped at the dining table, keeping the hand to his chest to tell him to do nothing, the other reached behind me. Fingertips pulled on the knot slowly. I watched his eyes focused on my chest as the material of the two cups became looser until I took it off and dumped it on the floor.

I could not only see the delight in his eyes, but I could also smell his arousal in the air. He wasn't controlling his aura at the moment or maybe he couldn't. I let it move around me and drown me in his desire. My own arousal kicked up causing a few beads of sweat to trickle down my spine and my breathing to catch every few fast heartbeats.

When I took them, my steps were more like leaps and then I was in his arms again. I slipped my hands down between us feeling the hard bumps of his abs. I tugged at the knot on his swimming shorts frantically. I couldn't wait any longer, and I didn't care about being treated like a lady. I didn't want anything between me and satisfaction.

Once the knot was undone, I started lowering myself into a squat. As I moved down, I did the same to his shorts, revealing more and more of him which had my head all fuzzy. As I moved lower, I pressed my lips to his skin. Feeling the heat as I dragged them down.

Feeling his belly button brush my mouth I stopped there. Just shy of feeling his manhood and damn I wanted to feel it so bad. But the burning I saw in his eyes would have melted steel, and I wanted to keep him like that.

As soon as he stepped out of the wet shorts, I leaped upright, pushing him back hard past the table. His back hit a door which he threw open in the next second. And without me noticing he scooped me up into those powerful arms and cradled me in the bedroom. How easily he held me just had me wanting him even more. I had to stop myself from calling out to him, begging him to just take me.

Drew plopped me down onto the bed, and then everything happened so fast. My bottoms were ripped off into two pieces. Then all I could feel was his masculine frame on top of mine. Dwarfing me with his power and strength. I don't remember lifting my legs up, but soon I was pulling him closer with them wrapped around his waist. Pulling that thickness inside me and it felt amazing.

Pleasure burst into my soul making me bite down on his shoulder hard. The pain seemed to spur him on as he growled in response and moved against me harder. My breath was being thrust out of my lungs. I couldn't concentrate on anything, not even the pleasure. Every movement he made sent pulses of electric through every nerve. I had never had sex like this before. My mind was being pounded into mush.

All I could do was try and breathe and just enjoy it all, and it wasn't long before my climax came. It hit so suddenly, shaking my body and curling my toes. My sexy werewolf had my moans turning into screams, and they were loud enough my friends could have heard me.

Breathing in deep when I could my breath got caught in my throat as the last wave of pleasure rippled deep into my soul before I fell silent and Drew slowed to a complete stop. Keeping his full length inside me as I laid there trying to catch my breath. I had never felt anything that good before in my life. It took a few blinks to get my vision completely back to normal. But when it did, I saw Drew's massive grin hovering over me. When he spoke, his breathing showed that he felt just as much pleasure as I had which had me smiling. "I hope I wasn't too rough with you."

"Wow." I paused to keep my breathing steady. "Everything was so good. I couldn't believe how fast it came."

"Well, that's just the first. I can be sensual as well."

I couldn't respond to his words. My mind went all muddled at the thought of more of this. And it wasn't over for a long time. Every single breathless second was filled with pleasure both primal and sensual. After that first orgasm, he decided to take his time. He teased me in all the right places until all I wanted to do was beg. I couldn't have picked out a specific point that was the best because it was all amazing.

CHAPTER 10

─ɘઠ‿ତૺ─

We untangled from our last position, and I rolled off of him. My back hit the sweat drenched sheet cooling down my body. I could have fallen asleep right then I was so exhausted from it all. I was so drained of energy. My breathing took a while to get back to normal which had Drew chuckling.

Once I had enough energy, I rolled off the bed and stood up, my knees still feeling a little weak. I saw Drew's eyes falling down my body then climbing back up to my eyes. At least he didn't just stare at my breasts. Then again, he did just have them inches from his face. I looked around for my bikini bottoms then remembered he had ripped them off during the heat of our actions. So I just stood there naked in front of him, placing my hands on my hips and giving him a cheeky smile. "Since someone ripped my new bikini bottoms, I'm going to have to dress in my normal clothes."

"It would be a shame to cover that body of yours up."

"True but I think I might get done for indecent exposure. Plus, we have to go join the others for tonight's plan."

"There is a bag of clothes in the bathroom. Figured black might be a good colour for later. Plus there's a nice thick jumper in there as well. Would hate for you to be cold."

"Thanks. You're a really sweet guy you know that?"

"I do." Pulling a sexy grin almost had me climbing back into bed with him. But I resisted. "Anyway, I know the plan. I can tell you all the little details if you come join me." The sides of his mouth curved up making him look even more gorgeous.

"I'm going to jump in the shower and then get dressed. I suggest you cover that body up." He didn't say anything. My look traced down his muscles and realised he was ready for another one of our pleasurable sessions. He made one hell of an argument, but we didn't have time, unfortunately. It was a good thing I felt satisfied and was able to resist the urge to jump on him again. Even if it only slightly won over the idea of riding him for the rest of the day.

Turning away from that delicious sight I gave out an inaudible groan. Leaning down I quickly chucked a pillow we had knocked off at his head. Drew caught it easily, so I quickly shot out of the room before he tossed it back.

Safely inside the small bathroom, I quickly jumped in the shower. After drying myself with a thick towel, I slipped on the simple but sexy underwear he had got me as well as the black jeans and black vest top. I tossed the thick jumper over my shoulder and slipped my feet into some trainers. There were no price tags to tell me how much he had spent but everything felt nice and comfortable. It couldn't have just been stuff from a local shop.

I exited the small room and made my way down the stairs. Luckily for my hormones Drew was dressed and yet still looked good enough to eat. He gave me a nice smile as I walked across the space between us. A simple peck on the lips and we were ready to leave.

Drew left the key in the door making me believe he had cleaned up after us. My hand was caught in his, and our fingers intertwined like our bodies had been earlier. Looking up at him our eyes met and I couldn't stop myself from leaning up and pecking those gorgeous lips. Pulling back just an inch

I stopped and gave him another before setting back on my soles.

Then we were walking. We got about half-way to the cabin when a sudden gust of wind kicked up a scent. It didn't tease my senses, it crashed into them. I whipped my head around trying to follow it. Even though it was the usual ash scent I've smelt plenty of times before, this time I knew exactly who it was. The distinctive scent belonged to Kellen. I had no idea how I was able to differentiate between him and other vampires, but every part of me was sure of it.

My eyes darted around the camp trying to pinpoint where the scent was coming from. Drew's voice came, but I wasn't paying much attention. "What's wrong?" I felt his hand on my shoulder, but I ignored it. I had to find this vampire, this terrible and dangerous vampire.

Then I spotted him, but he looked so different. He was just coming out of the information centre wearing a pair of white swimming shorts with a towel tossed over his shoulder. My eyes stared at his bare chest as his muscles almost shone under the sunlight. Making them glisten like he was already wet.

There was a large distance between us, but my leecher nose picked him up like he was standing right in front of me. "What's wrong? Beth!" His sudden change in pitch snapped me out of my stare. "What's wrong? What are you looking at?"

"Kellen." I nodded in his direction.

"Can you see anyone else?"

"I don't know. He seems to be by himself." Then he turned his head. I could feel his stare like a caress. His eyes from this distance still seemed dark and filled with death. Then a cheerful smile appeared, and he just gave us a wave. It was so casual like we didn't matter to him. Like we didn't pose any threat to him.

Then he turned and walked off towards the lake. Judging from his attire, he was actually going for a swim. It just didn't fit his personality. He was a killing machine who liked to play games but right now he was off for a dip in the lake. Something wasn't right about him which made him seem even more dangerous. He was unpredictable. "We need to tell Logan."

"Do you want me to keep an eye on him?" Drew went to move forwards, but I grabbed his arm quickly.

"Probably not the best idea. If he were here to harm us, he would have done without us knowing. I'm betting he'll wait for his boss to arrive."

"Maybe. We should go this way." Drew grabbed my elbow, and we moved down between the cabins to the woods behind. Going out of sight just in case Kellen was watching us.

A sudden crash made both of us jump. I ducked behind a tree whilst Drew turned, ready to fight whatever came our way. But there was no one coming to fight. No danger.

Moving out of my hiding place I noticed an open window to one of the cabins. There was smoke floating out from a cigarette. Drew seemed to wrinkle his nose at the smell of it.

I lowered my voice to a whisper, "Now we're out of sight, let's get going."

Once behind the correct cabin, we got Logan's attention, and he opened the window for us. "What are two doing back there? On second thoughts, I don't want to know."

Drew quickly corrected his naughty thought, "We weren't up to no good. Kellen is here, so we snuck around the back."

"Good thinking. Best get in quickly before Kellen comes to take a look." I held onto Drew's hand as he helped me through the opening. Then he followed me with a lot more grace.

I joined the other two at the table where they had the map still laid out. Drew came over with two glasses of water, offering one to me. I took it gladly, feeling thirsty at the sight of the cool liquid.

Logan cleared his throat and spoke to us all calmly, "There are a few risky areas. We can't expect The Saracen to play things down the straight and narrow. We should assume he has guys hiding in the forest and possibly the lake. Griffin has said he would have fish-shifters in the water and he will no doubt have people amongst the trees. All he knows about us is that we will be here to take care of his rival."

"What about infrared. You told Drew and me that Kellen could have followed us with his. Couldn't another vampire do the same or a werewolf sniff us out?"

"Absolutely, which is why Jewel has done some spells. She's practically made us invisible apart from with the naked eye. And she's done an invisibility spell on the tent so no one will spot it. Now, whilst you two are in the tent you need to keep your wits about you. If anyone creeps in that way, then you need to deal with them silently. We don't want to jump in early otherwise there will be a much bigger fight."

"So what kind of fight are we hoping for?" Drew didn't sound too impressed by the plan so far.

Logan shared a tense stare before looking back down at the map. "Well, once the deal between the two happens. They will let their guard down because Griffin will make a note of letting his men leave on the condition The Saracen will do the same. That's when we take care of him, and your father takes over his business'. He will clear Jewel's debt, and we'll all be free from this problem. Then I will disappear from the government again. Of course, we need to cover the possibility that we're not that lucky. Especially now we know Kellen is here."

Logan picked up a cookie that was sitting on the table and shoved it in his mouth. With crumbs spraying over the map he continued talking, "Now, if things get really bad we retreat to the information centre. If you can't get there, then get to the stash I put in the forest." His finger came down on a little circle. I have hidden a car behind the information centre. We all meet there and get out alive. All five of us." Logan pulled a big black bag from under the table and dropped it on top with a thud. "This bag is for the tent. Inside you have a walkie-talkie and some binoculars to keep an eye on things."

"We took the bag from our car to the new one as well. Extra firepower." Cassie hadn't spoken until now which wasn't like her. "I also grabbed some snacks for you, Beth. Just in case you got hungry again."

Logan looked over to Cassie, "How are you feeling?"

"I'm okay." She seemed surprised by his sudden question.

"Good. I got some pigs blood in the fridge for you just in case. You two better go get comfortable. Drew and I will go through the finer points that his father told us about. Once set up all you need to do is keep an eye on things. If bad things start happening then just get to the information centre as quickly as possible. Now, off you go. It will be getting dark in a few hours. I want to be ready by then. Everyone should be getting here around eight, and the camp will be empty by then." Cassie grabbed the bag by the handles and gave me a nice smile. "Turn the walkie-talkie to channel three as soon as you get into the forest."

"Will do." Cassie gave Logan a salute before walking off towards the kitchen window. Looks like we would be leaving the same way. Before leaving the table, I rose up on tiptoes and planted a soft kiss on Drew's lips. As I backed away, he shot forwards and gave me another. I felt the tip of his tongue caress my bottom lip making my breath catch.

Our eyes locked in a heated stare as we pulled apart. I could just see his cheeks rise up as he smiled. I had to tear myself away from him otherwise there would be a repeat of what happened in the bedroom. I flashed a smile and followed my friend back through the window.

As I dropped down onto the grass, I could see Cassie staring at me and smiling from ear to ear. "What are you smiling at?"

"Don't try and pretend. I can smell it on you both."

"Smell what?" She just gave me a you-know-what kind of look. We moved into the treeline and out of sight. "What are you talking about? Cassie?"

"Did you two have fun? I don't need your answer because I already know." I couldn't help the wide smile that my mouth turned into. "I knew it. You two were drenched in the smell of sex." There was a short pause in our conversation as we passed an open window. Cassie continued her interrogation when we cleared the cabin. "So how was it?"

Another big grin gave her the first clue it was amazing, and then I confirmed it, "It was the best I've ever had. True, I haven't been with many guys, but it was mind-blowing." Hearing myself, I sounded like a school girl talking about my first crush.

"I have heard that werewolves are extremely great in bed. Never had the chance to find out for myself though."

"If you get the chance, do it. You won't regret it."

"Judging from your smile I wouldn't."

"I can't help it if I'm smiling." She just laughed at me. "How much further?"

"We're camping just in here." She ducked under a low branch and moved into a small clearing. Twigs crunched under our feet. The green canopy above only let in a ray or two of the sun. Cassie chucked the bag into the black tent that stood between two massive tree trunks. It was hard to spot already, and by the time it was night it would be damn near impossible.

The two of us stood out at the front of it and looked out towards the lake. Logan had picked the perfect spot. We could see all the way down to the other bank. The cabins didn't block the meet, and we could just make out the entrance of the information centre.

We ducked into the tent and Cassie started pulling out

objects from the bag. Placing the walkie-talkie and the binoculars to her left. Then some snacks were placed on my side. The last to be pulled out was the bag of pig's blood. The contents swashed around like red oil and I didn't like the thought of watching her drink that stuff.

Looking away I opened up a packet of ready salted crisps and munched on them. A click made me turn back towards the body on my left. Cassie was loading up a pistol with a clip full of wooden bullets. "Is that the gun we found at the motel?"

"Yeah. I took a few clips out of the bag whilst you and lover boy were swimming." I gave her a flick in the arm. "You don't like that nickname?" She gave me a wicked smile. "Anyway. I thought it would be a good idea just in case."

"Just in case someone comes looking for us?"

"Exactly." She crumpled up the bag and chucked it out the way at the back of the tent. I carried on eating my crisps as she turned her head and stared at me. Boring a hole into the side of my head.

"What?" I asked, spraying crumbs into her face.

"So, tell me what it was like."

"I already have."

"No, no. I mean what happened. I want details." I looked at her funny. "I might be a vampire but I'm still a girl, and I need gossip just as much as I need blood." She looked at me for a few seconds before we both burst out laughing. For the next half hour, I told her every detail of what happened.

Afterwards, we talked about everything until it got dark. We even talked about Cassie's past conquests with guys. She hadn't had many, and from what she said, they ended badly. She had almost killed one of them during an argument. A reminder never to piss off a vampire.

Everyone had cleared out of here just before the floodlights came on. The place was completely deserted bringing an eerie silence to the place. We didn't see any sign of life until the moon was out, lending the camp a beautiful glow. Cassie told me she heard a car engine. When I didn't hear anything, I thought she was hearing things. Then a set of headlights came driving out of the treeline. It followed the track perfectly and came to rest at the car park.

Three people got out. Cassie offered me the binoculars since she didn't need them. I peered through the two eye holes, and the three men sprang closer. The one wearing the expensive suit was Drew's father. The two standing behind him must be the muscle. I was surprised he only brought two men. If The Saracen was as bad as I had been hearing, two men weren't going to be any enough.

I felt a nudge on my arm. I looked over at Cassie. "Check the tree line on the left side of the lake." I took her advice and moved my sight that way. Scanning along where the water met the trees I couldn't see anyone. I gave her a confused look. "Use my infrared." As I thought about her essence, it came to me like it had been cloaked all this time. Suddenly swimming around but not in a dangerous way. I sucked it in slowly.

Once my body had made the change into becoming a vampire I looked back at the scenery. The three waiting by the car were clearer than when I had used the binoculars. I looked up towards the trees. With a blink, I switched my eyesight to infrared.

Suddenly body shapes flared up in red and orange. There were at least five of them. I searched the rest of the camp, but they were the only ones I could see. Jewel's spell must have worked because I couldn't even see Drew or Logan. Just to make sure they were still there I smelt the air. I knew I wouldn't be able to find Logan because he was a leecher. However, I should have found Drew's minty smell coming from the right. Only I couldn't. The one I got was from one of Griffin's bodyguards. Worry started boiling up, but I pushed it away. Believing that it was all part of the plan. If

Jewel could trust Logan to sort this out, then I could trust him as well.

She pointed over to the right. "That must be The Saracen." I looked and saw the large orange blob traveling down the track. I switched to my normal vision and saw it was a large black jeep. It pulled off onto the grass and stopped. Four people got out and stood there, staring at the others. Switching back to infrared I looked on the other side of the lake. There were more bright colours moving through the trees. The Saracen clearly trusted Griffin Gaynes as much as he trusted The Saracen. Judging by the number of people he brought, he trusted him even less.

I hoped he was just being cautious and not trying to pull anything. Unfortunately, only time would tell. I looked to my left as Cassie spoke, "I can't see Drew anywhere. The trees aren't making it easy. I can hear Logan in the cabin still. But I can't find your boyfriend."

I wasn't going to waste time explaining he was my boyfriend. Instead, I replied calmly. "I can't find him either."

"Can't you sniff him out with your leecher smell or something?"

"I can try, but it didn't work before. He might be too far away."

"Give it a try anyway." I nodded in agreement. I pulled in a deep breath and allowed the smells of the forest and everything that came with it to wash over my sense of smell. Losing my human smell and listening just to the leecher inside myself I sifted through the scents I got. I got the same minty scent before, but I knew it wasn't Drew's. His had a thicker feel to it like I had attuned to his personal essence.

Moving on from the vampires that Griffin had brought with him, one caught my attention. It smelt like being at the seaside. If I closed my eyes, I could pretend I was sitting on a boat in the middle of the ocean.

Still using Cassie's infrared vision, I watched as this new

creature knelt down to the lake and slipped under the surface. His shapeshifted and got much smaller. It must have been the fish-shifter Logan mentioned.

After scanning the rest of the orange blobs, I had a horrible thought. "I can't sense Drew, but I also didn't find Kellen." Dread washed over me. The sudden urge to run all over this place to find my werewolf hit me. My legs started to twitch with the need to move. "Where could they be?"

"I don't know, but we need to stay here. We have to follow the plan."

"What about Drew?"

"Maybe he's gone into the information centre. We don't know what could have happened. Logan might have sent him there to check on things." I quickly looked over to the information centre. There was no one in there. Then I remembered Jewel and that I couldn't sense a witch in this whole place. Speaking to Cassie with hope-filled words, "Maybe he had to take Jewel somewhere."

"Did Logan mention Jewel to you? I had totally forgotten about her."

"Other than the spells he didn't say anything."

I was about to speak again when a voice from outside the tent made me jump, "Beth, can I speak to you for a second." It was a voice I recognised, and it had my heart pounding in my chest. It had the little hairs on my nape standing up on end. "Oh, leave your vampire friend in the tent when you come out. Don't want an unnecessary death now do we. Her ashes would blend well with the forest floor."

I looked over at Cassie who was slowly shaking her head. "I have to. He might know where Drew is."

"He might also be playing with you."

"He wants Jewel."

"I'm waiting, young girl." I heard his hand tapping the tent. "I only want to talk. I give you my word." I gave Cassie a reassuring smile and started moving out of the tent. The darkness leant the forest a sinister kind of look which made him look even more menacing.

Kellen was leaning up against a tree casually with a soft smile. He was dressed from head to toe in black. Tight t-shirt with its long sleeves pulled up to his elbows. His trousers were tight around the top, but they loosened up as they went down to his black boots. "Where do you get your clothes from? You look like a cat burglar."

"Well, my boss did tell me to blend in with the scenery. I thought I might scare you if I just materialised out of the shadows like a monster from a bedtime story." He looked down at himself. "Don't you think I did a good job?" I was about to make a sarcastic comment when he just vanished into the night. It was like the shadows from the forest came forth and swallowed him up. My instincts kicked in and I switched to infrared. His body filled my vision. Standing just an inch from me and I hadn't even heard a single footstep. The split second it took him to decrease the space between us was long enough for him to snap my neck. I wouldn't have stood a chance.

I kept my body still not letting on what I had done. At the bottom of my vision, I saw his hand move up. At first, I thought he was going to scratch an itch on his face, but then it came towards me. I thought about the choices I had and not standing there frozen was my favourite right now.

As it inched closer, I slapped it as hard as I could. His face shone brightly with shock even in infrared. He took a step back. "You wouldn't be leeching off of your friend now would you?" I switched back to normal vision, seeing he had shaken the shadows from his body. Now visible I could see his huge smile. It reminded me of a shark swimming after its prey. I was determined to not be the latter in this situation.

"So what did you want to talk about?"

"Your boyfriend."

"What makes you think he's my boyfriend?"

"If he's not then he's one lucky guy. I can smell him all over you even after your shower."

"Fine." I snapped at him. "What about him?"

Just thought you'd like to know where he is."

"What are you talking about?" He smiled. "Where is he?!" My fists clenched from the anger boiling inside.

"He's somewhere very cold and wet." My head whipped around as I switched to infrared. Eyes scanned the body of water but couldn't see anything other than the fish-shifter. "I wouldn't have put him in the lake now would I?" His sudden closeness made me jump, whipping my head around to find him by my side. I couldn't understand how he could move so silently. "I mean, how would I keep him sunk at the bottom? Plus he can't breathe underwater. He's not a fish-shifter is he? He's just a simple werewolf." I felt his hand on my shoulder. "Now, you have to make a decision. Is it worth running from here to there just to find out if I'm telling the truth or not? You could run over to cabin number one and ask Logan for help but do you really have that much time?" He pretended to look at a watch on his bare wrist. "I don't think so. You can't ask Cassie for help because when you leave, I have a totally different mission for her."

"How come you're so sure that I'll believe you? You just want me to ruin the meeting."

"Meeting? Now how would you know what is happening over there?" I wanted to kick myself for being so stupid. "Don't worry, I already know. The boss told. You didn't think he would keep his top dog out of the loop did you and as soon as I heard it was about a meeting with Drew's father. I put two and two together and came up with you."

How the hell did he know all these things? Unless it was The Saracen, who knew and Kellen was told.

"That's right. You're just his dog aren't you?" I turned away from the camp and stared into his eyes. Judging by the stupid grin still on his face, my barbed comment hadn't even made a dent. He knew how much stronger he was then both Cassie and I put together. He had gone through most of his life being the strongest. He would have a supernatural amount of arrogance. It wasn't an attractive quality. "What do you get out of this?"

"What would you mean by that?"

"If I go running through the middle of the meet and dive into the lake. What do you get out of it? Why would you want the meet to be ruined? Your boss wouldn't be happy about that."

"You're right. He wouldn't. But then, what makes you think you'll even get to the lake. You could be shot down as soon as you're spotted."

"You can't allow that to happen. I'm number three."

"Well, maybe I just want to see you all nice and wet again. Shame you're not wearing your little bikini."

"Drew ripped it right off me before we had sex." I didn't know why those particular words fell out of my mouth, but his reaction had me curious. There was something in his eyes that resembled jealousy. I didn't know if it was fake or real, but there was a flash of it. With Kellen, there was no telling what it actually meant.

The vampire cleared his throat before continuing, "You're running out of time. There's only one way of finding out if I'm telling the truth. How long do you think your werewolf can hold his breath? Plus, you haven't got long before the rest arrive."

"The rest? What are you talking about?"

"That would be telling. You need to concentrate on one thing at a time. Off you run." His hand made a shooing motion like I was a pet annoying him. Then he turned his back to me and started walking away.

"Keep talking. I want to know who else is coming."

"Run along to your little dog." A surge of anger filled my body. Along with it came stupidity. My feet carried me over to him, my hand spun him around, and I shot my fist out right towards his jaw. But he moved so fast I could barely keep track of him. I blinked as pain pulsed through my body as I was pinned up against a tree face first. My arm twisted up behind me, keeping me in place.

Kellen's face peered over my shoulder until it was inches from mine. Despite being a creepy vampire, he did smell really good. A hint of strawberry whiffed up my nose, somehow making him seem more masculine.

The sudden pain from my twisted arm snapped me out of my thought. His mouth moved to speak. I wasn't waiting for his words. I brought my head back to the bridge of his nose. I didn't hear a crack, but I was let go, and I acted as quickly as I could. Turning around my feet pounded into the soil. As I breathed in heavily the ashy scent around the trees moved inside. I knew it wouldn't make me any faster because I already had Cassie's essence inside me.

Kellen's eyes flicked up at me. I brought my arm back and clenched my hand into a fist. I launched it, and my body sped into a blur I had trouble following myself. To mine and Kellen's surprise, my balled-up hand smacked into the side of his jaw. His body was sent down with a thud.

I stepped over him. Not too sure what I should do. He looked up with shock on his face and burning anger in his eyes. As he got back up, I retreated away a few steps. I wanted to look menacing like I knew what I was doing, but I was so scared I could feel my legs shaking.

I watched his eyes, staring straight into the anger that was boiling behind them. He took a step forward making me move another back. Then suddenly, he laughed. I was too shocked to do anything but jump at the sudden noise. The anger had gone, and all I could see was happiness. His hand dropped to his side, "I didn't realise Cassie was that powerful." She wasn't. I had never moved that fast before. I was positive she wasn't unless I hadn't pushed myself hard enough. I was still new to this whole thing. "You've still got your decision to make."

Drew! I turned to the lake. I had no idea what to do. Then I remembered the way I felt in bed with him. It wasn't the pleasure he was giving me but the intimacy I felt. It was like he was the part of me I had been missing all my life.

Before I knew it, my feet took me out of the forest and over the grass between two cabins. The wind pulled at my clothes as I zoomed through the area. As I burst out from the line cabins, I veered myself away from the meet. A very quick glance told me they had almost finished. The Saracen and Griffin Gaynes were shaking hands and muttering some words to each other.

My body cut through the air as I ran faster than I had before. I left a trail of parted grass behind. Not even the guys at the meet noticed we move across the open space to the lake. As I met the water's edge, I launched into the air and pointed into a dive that sent me down to the bottom of the lake.

The splash shook my entire body, creating a downpour of rain. I didn't care if people turned around to see what it was. I had a boyfriend to save. My eyes stung a little when I opened them, but I didn't care. Turning my head from left to right, scanning for my werewolf.

When I didn't spot him, I started kicking my legs, shooting through the water like a torpedo. It wasn't long until I had swum through the lake twice and I still didn't find anything. Kellen had tricked me into doing what he wanted. I couldn't believe I had been stupid again.

I pushed off the ground and surfaced. What I saw could only be described as mayhem and carnage. The number of people had almost tripled, and everyone seemed to be fighting everyone. The only one I could make out was The Saracen lying dead on the ground. His short dreadlocks lay outwards like a halo around his head.

I started swimming towards the destruction with the

need to find Drew. A few seconds later and half of the lake behind me, I felt a nip on my foot then a sudden sharp pain. Numbness starting swarming up my leg. I kicked as hard as I could; trying to get off whatever had its vice grip on my flesh. After the third flick, I felt teeth rip out of my skin. Then all I had was a dull ache where the numb feeling had reached.

I dipped my hand into the water and felt the bite mark that almost took half my foot. Another attack and that's exactly what I could be missing. I looked down at the water. My blood made it hard to see anything, but something was still moving down there. I felt the water stirring around me until another nip came. Twisting my whole body, I made sure it didn't sink those teeth into my body. Feeling it swim past me I changed my vision to show its heat. The dark blue around me showed the bright colours of the creature. It was small but had one hell of a bite on it.

I kicked my feet, keeping me afloat and my hands-free to protect myself. The red blob circled around me a little then darted towards like a shark. I shut my ears off to everything. No gunshots, no birds chirping, not even the sound of the water around me. I waited for it to close the gap. Then without warning, the fish shot forwards like a bullet.

Fortunately for my stomach, I was faster. My hands clamped around it, feeling it's scaly skin trying to wriggle free. Yanking it up out of the water I regretted it as I got a face full of sharp inch long teeth. They gnashed at me. Trying to rip my face off.

Holding the body back I prepared my muscles to crush the fish. Only it stopped wriggling and started growing larger. To my delight the teeth shrunk and became less dangerous. Fins became arms and scales became skin. In seconds I was holding the neck of a human man.

There wasn't enough time to figure out if he was one of Gaynes' men or not. I tightened my grip until I saw the lack of air affecting the colour of his face. Turning a slight shade of blue as he coughed for breath. Watching as he suffocated to death in my hands. Taking his life away.

As he stopped struggling and floated there lifeless, I let go and followed his movement as the water took him away from me. I blinked and forced myself not to think about it. Leechers weren't supposed to feel emotions as strongly as humans, but I still felt guilty.

I turned back towards the mayhem as the volume kicked back up in my ears. There wasn't time to wade in and help, and I didn't particularly want to anyway. All I wanted to do was either find Drew or punish Kellen for messing with me. If I couldn't manage the first, then I was going to make the second one last as long as I could. No doubt a bad idea but I didn't care at this point. My anger was doing most of my thinking.

Leaving the dead shifter in the water, I kicked my way to the nearest bank. With my vampire speed, I arrived in seconds and was quickly moving through the trees with immense pace.

Branches snapped against my body, but I barely noticed. I was more annoyed at the way my wet clothes clung to my body, trying to slow me down. As I came out of the treeline, I got a closer look at the battles before me. Some people were fighting hand-to-hand. Beasts both werewolf and other fought each other. The speed of some people leant to the theory they were vampires or something faster. Men in suits were hiding behind their cars firing off weapons, picking people off in a cowardly way.

I wasn't able to spot Griffin Gaynes anywhere. If his guards did their job, he was either gone or hiding out somewhere. Maybe he had been pushed back into his car for protection.

It was at that thought when a car exploded up into the air bellowing black smoke and orange flames. I watched it spin before coming back down with a smash. If anyone had been inside, then they were definitely dead or burning alive.

I jumped out of my skin as my ankle was snatched. Some vampire I would make. My gaze shot down at the bloody body lying on the floor. The eyes that looked up at me were bloodshot but soft. For some reason, I bent down.

He murmured something before letting out a final breath. I looked down at the gashes on his body. Red liquid was still pouring out of his wounds filling the air with the metallic scent of blood. It made my stomach churn, but then it rumbled. My human side wanted to throw up, but the vampire inside me wanted to lap up that blood. It needed it as much as I needed air.

My hands automatically moved and ripped open his already torn top. Now they were nothing more than rags, revealing the extent of his wounds. It looked glorious and disgusting all at the same time. There was mass mayhem behind me, and still, the vampiric need to feed was winning.

I stood up, lifting the body above my head. His arms dangled either side of my head. His wounds faced me, and I opened my mouth to invite the blood in. I watched with anticipation as the drops slowly gathered at the bottom of one of the slashes. My mouth watered as the drops of blood started pouring down towards my open mouth. I even stuck out my tongue to try and catch as much as I could.

As soon as I tasted it the powerful urge to have more was so overwhelming. It was like that need pulsed and pounded inside my head so I couldn't think of anything else. Like loud music drowning out any other thought or whim.

I brought the body down to my mouth. Extending out my teeth I sunk them into the flesh. Sucking that throbbing blood down my throat. My canines weren't very long which didn't mean I needed to feed. It was just that want of blood. Not to quench thirst but to satisfy a curiosity. The urge for the blood was vibrating through my whole body.

As I kept feeding my world descended into pleasure.

Blood erupted into my mouth with every greedy suck. The sweet liquid trickled down my throat making me feel even stronger. Like I was invincible.

But as it hit my stomach, it seemed to rebel against it. Boiling like a bad chemical reaction. Was it my human side still in there, forcing me to react like this because my mind wanted more of this delicious crimson drink. Only until the pain hit every nerve in my gut, twisting it back and forth.

Pulling my head back I looked at the mess I had made with my teeth. The blood still pouring out of the open wound. I wondered what the hell I was doing. When leechers leech, they turn into that creature fully. So why was my human side getting in the way of it?

As I contemplated a drop of blood hit my chin. My tongue shot out instinctively and took it in, but that's when my stomach chucked up everything I had eaten lately which wasn't much. Chunks and bile hit the floor with that sickening splat. I tossed the body away like an eaten apple. I wanted answers from Logan, but I needed to find Drew first. Nothing could get in the way of that now.

Spitting out the last of the sick and blood I had drunk I started walking over to the information centre. That was the meetup point if things went bad and this was right on the nose in a colossal way. Plus I could use some help finding my werewolf.

As I neared the door, Logan's words of thinking had me pausing as my hand reached out for the handle. Switching to my infrared vision, I scanned the building. Not a single flared of red showed up. At least there weren't any enemies inside waiting for me. Yanking the door open I got a whiff of mint hitting my sense of smell. Hope pumped through my veins with my blood.

My wet shoes squelched on the shiny floor. Looking down I could see how drenched I was in my reflection. Wooden chairs sat in front of a reception desk that seemed to be made out of thick tree logs. Picture frames hung from the walls with photos of mountains and forests.

As I went past the desk and down a small hallway, I switched from my infrared since I still couldn't see anyone. The minty scent was still in the air even if it was faint. Following it, it took me into a little cafe and around the counter towards the kitchen. As soon as I saw the large walk-in freezer, I knew what Kellen's riddle had meant.

My hand moved with blinding speed, pulling the door open with enough force to snap one hinge and bend the other. That essence of mint hit my senses, and my heart started pounding because I knew it was him before the cold mist had settled.

Drew fell forward into my arms. The sudden weight of him knocked me off balance, so I twisted and lowered him to the floor with ease. That's when I saw his smashed up face. Drew's right eye was swollen so much I couldn't see the eyeball through the thin slit. His clothes and skin were ripped open. I had no idea if it had been Kellen or maybe he was just playing games.

My heart did a little dance as I listened to the soft thud of his heart. I tilted his head forward. His vacant eye locked onto mine as his body shivered against mine. A wink appeared which with just the one eye could have been classed as a blink. "Hey, beautiful." His voice was just as weak as his smile.

"What happened?"

"Kellen. He didn't want me interfering with his plans."

"You mean The Saracen's plan?"

"Nope. Kellen doesn't answer to him."

"Does that mean he's off the leash?"

"Not by the sounds of it. He was talking about new orders. He didn't seem very happy about it. He even apologised beforehand. Unless I have a concussion and I imagined that part." He winced a little as he laughed.

"That was nice of him." Layering my words with thick sarcasm.

"That was before he punched me in the face."

"Maybe not that nice then."

"Right. Help me up, please." We took it slow since every single movement seemed to put him in immense pain. "We should head for the car. I think I need to lay down until my healing fixes more of me."

"Good idea." Once he was more steady on his feet, we moved towards a service entrance and out the back of the building. Sitting under some branches of a fir tree was our car. Hobbling over I got him onto the back seat so he could rest, but before I could climb in after him, I was attacked.

A hand grabbed my shoulder, but I was too quick for them. Twisting two of those fingers until they snap. Twisting my body my other hand grabbed the woman's top and I cracked her forehead into the metal frame of the car. Checking her pulse, I was happy I just knocked her out. I was a little shocked at how quick I was to violence. Hoping it was the vampire essence that was changing me instead of my human side changing.

Dumping her body into the nearby dumpster, I ducked my head back into the car and told Drew I would be back in a moment. He mumbled in response, but I didn't know if it was in agreement or not. But it didn't matter because I was gone.

Moving back into the reception area showed me that the fighting had spread into the building. A body stumbled back after a blow to the head. With my instincts bubbling under the surface I dipped my shoulder and threw the man into the wall.

Barging my way past the others fighting I broke out into the fresh air through broken doors. Despite the hike in numbers of dead bodies, the fighting still raged on. The blood seemed to glow on the grass with the moonlight giving it that sharp shine. The urge to drink it boiled in my thoughts. I had to push it deep down and listen to my morals before I could concentrate on anything else. I didn't know how Cassie managed this kind of thing on a daily basis.

Looking over towards the cabins there were a few people and some animals fighting. I worried about Logan but mostly Cassie. I had left her with Kellen all alone, and she was no match for him. I sniffed the air and could tell there was a vampire still up near the tent. I just hoped it was my friend and not an enemy. Sadly I couldn't tell at this distance.

Bursting into a sprint I cleared the grass in no time, dodging through the branches as they whipped against my body. Nearing the tent, I followed the ashy scent. But I knew it wasn't Cassie before I even saw the figure leaning against a tree. Kellen stood there, looking like he hadn't even moved an inch since I ran for the lake. His lips curled into a smile that I didn't return. Instead, I just snapped, "Where's Cassie?"

"She's currently pre-occupied. Would you like something to drink?" His arm reached around behind him. My eyes bulged as he pulled a body off the floor with ease. Blood poured out of him filling the air with the metallic smell of it. By the looks of it, Kellen had already had a few bites from the neck. It wasn't my stomach that urged me to drink but my heart. I might not be hungry for blood, but my body still wanted it. I wasn't about to lose control especially not around Kellen. This display showed that's exactly what he wanted.

I froze my feet on the spot and refused to move, controlling my urge to a calm simmer of want. He pulled a fake surprised look. "You don't want some?" He chucked the body, so it landed at my feet. I gave it a quick glance but looked back up quickly when I saw the blood covering the man's face. Kellen was pulling that arrogant smile again. I just kicked it to the side. "Not hungry? I can see you have indulged in some feeding already."

I didn't want a conversation with this vampire, so I asked

again. "Where's Cassie?"

"She is busy. Not to be disturbed. However, I feel like Logan could do with some help in cabin one." With this information, I didn't want to talk anymore. Speeding off towards the end cabin. Using my infrared showed me two bodies moving around inside. Slowing down I sneaked up to the kitchen window making sure my footsteps were silent.

I couldn't see anyone in the kitchen, but the heat signatures were moving around in the living area. Throwing arms and legs around at an invisible opponent. Must be Logan and he was outnumbered. He had the training to take care of himself, but an extra pair of fists would be even better.

My fingers grabbed the window ledge and prepared my legs to spring me into the cabin. But I froze when I felt a dark presence behind me. Turning slowly I saw Kellen's smug face right there in front of mine, "You're not thinking about smashing through the window are you?"

"Shut up and leave me alone." I could have punched him square in that smug face, but I knew it would be useless.

So I turned back to the cabin but Kellen refused to stop pestering me, "I wouldn't go through the window. At least, not the kitchen one. Why not the one that leads into the bedroom. It would make more sense you know. Sneak in, take them out from behind. Surprise attack." His voice was beginning to grate on my nerves. "Don't want you being killed too early now do we. I need you to stay alive long enough to lead me to Jewel."

Huh? From what Drew had said, he shouldn't be looking for Jewel anymore. "What's your interest in Jewel? Aren't you on your dog leash?"

"That was never my life. However, you are slightly right. Something has changed. Unfortunately for you, the order hasn't. You're still number three. I just have to find number one first to start playing the game." I turned to him giving him the evils. He just gave me a quick smile and then vanished into the shadows of the trees. I could have followed his body heat and make sure he left me alone, but I couldn't be bothered.

I called to those violent instincts inside my brain, and I moved like a vampire. Blurring through the window with a sudden smash. Before the nearest enemy knew what the noise was, I already had his arm twisted at an odd angle.

The man sneered at me before his mouth started moving out into a snout. Growling seeped out of his mouth as he started to morph into a werewolf. The only way to stop him would be to kill him. But his body was changing into something much bigger than mine which had a little bit of fear snapping at the heels of my cool.

Pushing the werewolf back until I cracked the wall of the cabin with the force. My head spun around to see Logan snapping the neck of the other enemy in the room. As I breathed out of relief for my friend, I noticed a bullet sitting on the table where the map was. I recognised it as the wolf bane weapon the government had weaponised.

I didn't know how it would react with the beast I still held for the moment, but it was my only chance. So I snatched it from the wood and shoved it back into the open snout that was trying to rip my face off.

My hand clamped around the animal's jaws, and I heard the glass breaking. The liquid must be trickling down into his throat. There was no reaction to it at first, but as soon as this weapon touched the werewolf's stomach, he roared out in pain.

The sheer volume of it had me stepping back in fear. I wasn't attacked, so I just stood there and watched this thing do its job. It was fine until blood started bubbling up out of the man's human mouth. Becoming a waterfall of death as he bent over and fell onto all fours. As he coughed more of his insides came out. Turning the colour red into a sick shade of orange.

I was happy when the screaming stopped, and the body just slumped forward, laying on the floor lifeless. I and Logan both waited, but the man didn't move again. The wolf's bane must have burnt his insides like acid.

Turning around and seeing Logan's face made my whole body relax. Feeling the adrenaline from the fight slowly disappear. Then my eyes picked something up behind him. I wasn't too sure what it was until it moved again. A shadowy figure slipped across the floor like it wasn't even there.

It crept up behind Logan, so I moved with instinct. My nails grew sharp, and I slashed them across the black figure. They cut through something, but no blood poured out. There was no sign of life being drained.

Instead, the person or thing froze to the spot and slowly dropped to the floor. Disappearing into nothing. "What the hell was that, Logan?"

"I'm guessing it was some kind of spell. A shadow entity maybe."

"Unbelievable."

I took the break in violence to survey the room. Five bodies littered the cabin with a few piles of ash in between. Looks like Logan had quite a fight on his hands. "What are you doing here?"

I looked up at him. "I'm trying to find everyone. Kellen shoved Drew into a walk-in freezer. He's in the car behind the information centre. Cassie has gone missing, and Kellen is still playing games."

"That's not the point. You can't be here. You need to get to the car and wait there."

"No, I'm not defenseless, and I can help. Do you know where Cassie and Jewel are?"

"Not a clue. Get to the car and wait for me, I'll find them."

"No. That's final. Now, where do you think they could be?" I rose my voice over his to make it final.

He gave me a stubborn look in return but eventually blew

out a breath, "Jewel can be anywhere. She's probably hiding. Sniff her out. You find her, and I'll find Cassie. Listen to me this time and get going. We need to get out of here before this war ends."

"Good." Logan walked off to the door, but I wasn't leaving that way. I left the same way I entered, dropping down onto the grass. As I made my way to the corner, I tuned out any unnecessary senses and listened to one that could find my friend. Sifting through the smells that came my way as I brought in a steady breath.

Two ashy scents came to me, so I brought them to the front of my thoughts. One of them seemed to give off a male feel, so I tossed it aside. The second was more feminine, so I kept the end of it at the tip of my sense. Focusing on Jewel. Concentrating so hard I could swear a faint trail showing up in the air. It looked like small droplets of water floating ahead of me.

Ignoring all the action, I let my eyes move through those droplets to where they stopped. There was a small patch of grass over near some trees where none of the mayhem had spilled over to yet. I was hoping I would see Jewel hiding out somewhere, but there was nothing at all.

Using my speed I zoomed off through the trees, taking the long way around to where the trail droplets ended. Slowly making my way out of the safety of the trees I ventured closer. As I neared them, I felt a tingle moving over my skin like a wave. As I took another step, a man suddenly appeared in front of me. My fist clenched ready to attack, but he just smiled at me.

"Beth, it's me, Jewel. I'm hiding." It was a hell of a hideout. No one would see her unless they walked right by. "I just saw Logan run off somewhere. Where is everyone?"

"Drew is waiting in the car after being banged up bad by Kellen. Logan is off finding Cassie, and I'm finding you."

"You've succeeded. What's the plan?"

It was hard to see him as Jewel. "Find everyone and get the hell out of here."

"Simple. I can do a simple finder spell to see where Cassie is."

"That would be really helpful."

"Okay." She breathed in deep but froze there with wide eyes. Looking behind me told me why.

Kellen was walking by only a few metres away. It was weird watching him, knowing he wouldn't be able to see us. His gaze moved over us not registering our presence. He took a few steps then looked down at his watch. I had never noticed him wearing one until now. It was silver and shiny. Looking very expensive and very out of place with the rest of his dark outfit. I couldn't see it clearly, but the face looked like it was glowing red.

After a few seconds of staring, he raised his head, eyes locked in our direction. I stared back at him, studying the look of confusion on his face. He took a step forward. I wanted to do the opposite and move away from him. The only problem was, Jewel was in the way. The effects of her spell would wear off if I ventured out of the invisible bubble.

He took another step then stopped. Kellen looked up and down from his watch and back at us. More confusion spread through his face. Then he started to sniff the air. I only now noticed that I had been holding my breath. Letting it out slowly, so it didn't make even a whisper.

With a few more sniffs his eyes filled with recognition as they locked onto mine. His body relaxed, and he started speaking to the empty space in front of him. If anyone witnessed this, they would believe he had gone insane. "I know you're there. My nose can pick up the sweet scent of your blood."

I was about to take a step forward, feeling the need to protect Jewel from this monster. But she grabbed my hand before I moved too far. Whipping my head around she simply shook hers from side to side. Despite it being a man's face I could see the softness of her in the eyes.

I knew Kellen must be speaking to Jewel. She was, after all, number one on his list. He had to kill her before he could come after the rest of us. That was if he stuck to his own rules. Then again, who knew what things had changed with his switch of allegiance. As he stood there, I felt the anger of what he had done to Drew boil to the surface. However, with Jewel's hand gripping my arm, it kept me frozen to the spot.

"I know you are there. Not only do I have my sense of smell I also have a very special watch I took from an old acquaintance. It's a little flashy for my liking, but it has a very helpful spell on it. It glows red, and the hands point to anyone who owes the wearer a debt. I was worried that with his death the watch would stop working. Only, that doesn't seem to be the case. You see." He held it out for us to see. It was an analogue watch, and it was glowing red just like he said. The hands were pointing in our direction making me believe his story. "So I can follow these hands all day long. So why don't you just come out?" He took a step into our bubble. At first, I wasn't sure if he could see us, then his eyes glinted with excitement. "Hello, Jewel." He nodded at me. "Beth." His voice was full of dominance and that arrogance he wore so well.

"You're not getting anywhere near her." I stepped in front of Jewel prepared to defend her by any means.

"Who's going to stop me? You? I don't care who you've leeched off of, you are weaker than me in every single way."

"Then how come I punched you earlier? I saw the surprise in your eyes."

"That was just luck. I let my guard down. I assure you." His tone lowered a couple of notches. "It won't happen again." When he pounced like a predator on its prey, I moved just as quickly. Catching his fist in my open hand, I threw one of my own. I had trouble tracking my own movement, but he didn't, blocking it easily. Despite the catch, I could still see the worry in his eyes of my power. Was I the first person to put up this kind of fight?

The vampire tossed my fist away and pulled his from my grip. I was ready in a stance for fighting, but his body seemed relaxed. It was tempted to attack whilst I could, but his voice kept me on the spot. "Haven't you figured my game out yet?" He was putting confidence in his voice, but I could see the doubt in his smile. He didn't know how I can move as fast as he can and that made two of us. I was sure Cassie couldn't do it. I'd been fighting with more strength than was possible.

I may not know how it was possible but if I could fight Kellen and keep him at bay maybe I could give Jewel enough time to escape. She would have to make a run for it though. Kellen isn't going to give up even if I could put up some kind of fight against his powers.

The evil vampire cracked a smile, but instead of speaking again he attacked. I disconnected my thoughts and my worries and allowed my instincts to move my limbs. Happy I managed to block three punches, but then I felt the pain of a kick to my thigh. I dropped to one knee in pain. Looking up in enough time to block his fist with both my arms. I held onto the sleeve of his jacket as he tried to pull his hand free of my grip. Allowing it to bring me back up to my feet.

With my feet purchased on the grass, I yanked down on his arm, bringing my knee up towards his face. Only for it to be blocked. Arms wrapped around my waist, so I brought both elbows down onto his back. Kellen grunted but was still able to lift me up high like a trophy. Before he could crash me down into the ground, I buried my thumbs into his eyes. Blood trickled over my hands before he dropped me.

I let my lips turn into a grin as he tried to wipe his vision clear. Turning to Jewel. "You need to run. I'll contact you through the ring when it's safe."

"You shouldn't do that anymore. The magick it holds is too unstable."

"What do you mean?" I looked over my shoulder to see Kellen still trying to get his sight back. It wouldn't be long before his eyes had healed themselves.

"I took a risk using it to contact you before. I latched onto the magick it already holds. If you keep putting it on, whoever it is will track you down."

"The government?"

"Whoever it is, it's not safe."

"What about my friend? Did you feel anything about him?"

"I saw him, but it could just be an illusion. Forget about him and the ring. If you're smart, you will throw the ring away." I didn't know what to say. The one person who I thought could help me was telling me to toss it away. "I'll find you guys."

"Fine." My reply held an edge of anger at her lack of help. It slowly drained as she stepped back and the bubble swallowed her out of my vision.

A twig snapped behind me, but I didn't turn in enough time. I heard a thick crack come from my side as Kellen's fist cracked two of my ribs. The pain of it temporarily made moving impossible. The pain rolled through my entire body making me hiss in pain.

He lifted my face up with a single fingertip. I saw that arrogant smile at his win. "You know that ring? You shouldn't use it. Bad idea. In fact, maybe I should take it." His hand darted towards my pocket. I didn't know how he knew where it was but it was mine and I needed it to save my friend.

My hand towards his, fingers wrapping around his wrist and twisting. His arm shot out at an impossible angle as bone broke. There wasn't even a grunt of pain as he pulled his arm away from me. "That wasn't very nice." As I breathed, I felt the ease of pain in my chest as my ribs started to heal. Kellen snapped and twisted his arm back into its original place. "That will heal in a few seconds. Now, where did Jewel go?"

"I don't know."

"So I'm supposed to believe you don't know where she's gone?" He took a step towards me. Despite being only a few inches taller than me, it felt like he towered over me right now.

"Believe what you want, I don't know. Why don't you follow her with your new fancy watch?"

I saw him flex the wrist I had broken, "Unfortunately it has a limited range."

"That's too bad for you." He pulled a fake smile. I looked over my shoulder at the fighting. There wasn't much going on anymore. Either they had found somewhere else to do it, or most of the people had been killed. I turned back to face him. "So what now?"

"I have a few ideas, but I want to know what you plan on doing?"

"Me?" What the hell was he up to? "What I want to do is stop playing games. Think you could do that for a few seconds."

"Depends."

"Depends on what?"

He crossed his arms over his chest in a completely relaxed state, "Tell me about your friend?" I gave him a confused look. "His name is Frank isn't it?"

"How the hell do you know Frank?" I stepped closer trying to make my tone threatening, but he simply chuckled at it.

"Through an acquaintance."

"Tell me."

"I don't think so."

"Now!" Shooting forwards I found it so easy to lift his body up high above my head. Slamming him into the ground brought out nothing more than a laugh. It sent shivers of anger through every fibre of my body. I grabbed his arm and rammed my knee into the back of his elbow. It snapped easily, and I kept pulling. This time he couldn't stop the pain from creating a groan which made me smile in satisfaction.

I shouldn't have stopped to relish in his pain. The enemy was up on his feet in a second and sent me down with an elbow to my back. I hit the hard ground with a sledgehammer like a thud sending a break back into my healing ribs.

Kellen bent over me so close I could feel his breath on my face. "Forget about the ring and forget about your friend." He straightened his arm, and it made a sickening popping sound. It sounded worse than when I had snapped it in the first place. "Now I have some friends who want to talk to you, so be nice." He looked up and over my head. I sat up and followed his gaze. Three men were walking over in suits. They both looked and smelt like government. All three were human, and I could easily glamour them to kill themselves.

The only problem was if there was going to be some kind of fight I needed to be one hundred percent. I placed my hand on my ribs which emphasised the pain emanating from my injuries. I took a deep breath and slammed the ball of my palm into them. The two broken edges grated against each other until they slipped into the right place. Taking a deep breath brought less pain than before, and I knew my healing ability would start working immediately.

If I could stall for a few minutes, I knew I would be ready for a fight against three humans. Knowing I would have to wait until I was away from Kellen. Thinking about what will happen until I felt a prick in my neck. My hand shot up, and I pulled the little dart out of my skin. One second it looked fine then it suddenly went blurry. I felt Kellen lowering me to the ground. The last thing I saw was his arrogant grin hovering over me. If I weren't about to reach unconsciousness, then I would have loved to kick it right off his face.

CHAPTER 11

When I woke, I wasn't fully with it, grogginess clouding any thought I could muster. Moving slowly I was glad to feel no restraints were holding me down on the uncomfortable bed. Cracking my eyes open I saw a single light in the middle of the ceiling.

A wall sat on one side of me. The other side was a small cell ending in a wall of glass. Sitting on the right was a metal door. A small hatch was open halfway down, and a tray of food had been left there. The smell of it was probably what had woken me up when the drugs had worn off.

I sat up very slowly ignoring the pain moving through my body. When my feet touched the floor, it sent chills up my legs as I stood. Taking an unstable step, I felt a prick on my arm. Peering over my shoulder, I saw a drip attached to a clear back holding some kind of blue liquid. I yanked the needle from my arm quickly not wanting to think about what they had been putting into my body.

Retrieving the food, I retreated back to my bed. Looking down at it didn't make my stomach grumble. I may not need food as much thanks to my leecher body but who knew when my next meal would be. So I ate the chips first which were a little cold, then the pizza which was hard to get down.

Leaving the empty tray on the bed, I just stared at the

hallway on the other side of the glass. Even with the little hatch in the door open, I couldn't hear any noises beyond my confined space. The vampire essence had left my body, and a quick sniff of the air meant there were no supernatural beings down here or the government had a way of blocking this ability.

I was getting bored of just sitting there, so I let my eyes move around the cell. Spotting a camera sitting up in the corner of the room with a little red blinking light flashing at me. I wasn't about to be watched, so I walked over to it, using the toilet and sink to rise up high enough to grab it and rip it from it's placed. Chucking it against the wall with the small amount of strength I could muster.

With that gone and the visual of their prisoner blocked surely someone would be here soon. Then I might be able to get some information about where I was. Only it took some time for someone to arrive. Moving from my feet to the bed and then back up to stand in front of the glass. I stared at my reflection seeing the hospital gown I was wearing and feeling even colder because of it.

Shoes clicked towards where I stood. My eyes watching a shadow bouncing across the wall before a short, skinny woman appeared. Her brunette hair was pulled back into a neat ponytail, and she looked very professional in her black uniform. Looking at the badge sitting on her chest, I knew she was security and was no doubt here to see what had happened to the camera. She stared at me standing there in my gown. Then she turned her head to look up into the corner. Then her gaze fell down to the where the camera was lying. She rolled her eyes before pulling a gun out of its holster. She poked it through the hole in the door, and before I could react, she pulled the trigger without blinking.

Instead of a loud bang, all I heard was a soft release of air. I reached up to my neck and felt the dart sticking out. Stumbling back I was happy to feel the bed breaking my fall as I fell unconscious for a second time.

Waking up again, I felt the grogginess that I almost shook off was now back, clouding my head. The drip wasn't back in my arm, so maybe I wasn't out for long. However, it was long enough for them to replace the camera. A new one stared at me with its mocking red light blinking. I thought about climbing back up there and ripping it down again but getting shot with another dart wasn't my idea of fun.

Sitting up I got a whiff of aftershave. Looking over to the glass wall I saw a man standing there. Unlike the security woman, this person was wearing a nice suit. His stomach domed out making the suit jacket crumple up at the front. His face wasn't any better. A bulbous neck podged out over his shirt collar. A big round nose housed a pair of thick, black glasses. He looked more like a pencil pusher. Filling in forms and doing all the paperwork.

As I got to my feet getting annoyed at the cold floor once again, he stepped over to the door and slid two files onto the little shelf. As he leant on the glass, I noticed he held a third file. I wondered what he was holding back.

Grabbing the files I moved back to the bed, keeping a distance from this mysterious government worker. Opening the top file revealed a photograph of a woman. She was pretty but in a girl next door kind of way. It said her name was Tina Booth. It didn't ring a bell, but I wasn't expecting it to. I turned to the second and last page. It had a bunch of information about her that I didn't care about.

I looked through the second folder and found the same stuff. Only this time it was a picture of a man. He wasn't much to look at except for his eyes. They were a shade of green I had never seen before. His name was Gary Moore. Another name and face I didn't recognise. With no actual information from these folders, I closed them and carried them back to the shelf. I looked at the man expecting an explanation from him. Instead, he looked at me with his cold eyes before handing me the third folder with no expression.

I didn't bother going back to my bed. If it were just as empty as the others, it would be a wasted trip. Opening it made me gasp, and my fingers almost dropped the folder. The picture sitting on top was of me. I was a lot younger, but I recognised that cheeky grin from the pictures around my fake parent's house. There was no doubt about it. I stared down at myself.

Instead of a name beside the picture like the other two, it simply had SUBJECT 128. Too many things ran through my mind that it would have been classed as beyond chaos. I flipped over the page. A picture showed me laying in a cot at ten months old. Scanning through the small paragraph informed me that I hadn't shown any signs of my leeching ability.

The next ten pages showed me growing up to seven years old in stages. All through those years, I hadn't shown any ability of my true being. Not until I was placed in a family setting. According to whoever was studying me, I was just a late bloomer. There was speculation about it being the atmosphere of being in a family, but that was cast aside.

I still didn't know what this was all about apart from the fact I was studied from a young age. What I didn't get is the family situation. What the hell was that and who were the people in the other two files? I closed the folder and looked up at the greasy man. He was staring right at me. "What is all this?" I asked, tossing my file out of the hatch, sending those pages all over the floor.

This guy didn't seem bothered by my little tantrum. "Your past." He had a slimy voice. It slithered over my body making me feel unclean. "Would you like me to enlighten you?" I simply nodded needing to know my true past. "As you can tell from the file I just gave you, we've been watching you from the very start. Then again that was very easy when you were bred right here in this facility."

His words hit my heart like a knife adding to my confused thoughts. "What are you talking about?"

"You were a result of a special program."

"Which was?" I was getting impatient. Why couldn't he just come out and say it? Was it part of government training to be as vague as possible. "What am I?"

"It was a breeding program. You're the daughter of two leechers. We were trying to amplify a leecher's abilities. At first, we were just breeding leechers with humans. No matter what combination of genders we used, the result was always the same. The fetus didn't make it any older than a few days."

"Wait, because I'm a leecher I won't be able to have a child with a human?" He ignored my question. "What about other supernatural beings?"

A smile hit his lips that had me squirming. "The next logical step was to have both parents as leechers. All the babies survived apart from a few here and there like typical births. Most of them grew up to be fine leechers but nothing too extraordinary. Not what we were trying to achieve." He cleared his throat and carried on with the story. I listened intently, waiting for the part where he explained what I was. "Tina Booth and Gary Moore were the last pair to have gone through the process before it was eventually shut down. Tina and Gary are your parents."

"What?" He nodded slowly with a smirk on his face like he was enjoying my shock. "So you're telling me I'm a lab result of some project just to make more powerful leechers?"

"That's correct. At first, you didn't show any signs of inheriting your parents' gifts. So we decided to let you have a normal life. Then you started having blackouts. Weird things would happen to other kids as you got older and we covered it up. It was decided by the men at the top to leave you there. Just keep an eye on you and clear up any messes you created. It was getting harder and harder as the years went on. You were getting better at leeching off of people. By the end, it was getting out of control, and the bodies were stacking up."

"Bodies?" I had flashbacks to the number of times I woke up with blood on me. "How many have I killed?"

This guy kept ignoring my questions which added to the annoyance in me. "That's why you were moved. You were put under surveillance so to speak. We had no idea that you would stumble across Logan. Now thanks to the recent events, we have him locked up. We can finally put an end to his interference."

I had led them straight to the man they've wanted for so long. It's my fault that we were all in this mess. I had dragged Drew and Cassie into it for just being around them. "Where is Logan? Tell me!"

He just simply ignored me and carried on like I hadn't said anything. "Your lot put us through hell recently. Releasing prisoners who were being held for the safety of mankind. Killing retired agents and current ones for that matter. You and your group of misfits have been causing us a lot of pain. Never the less, your friend Logan did us a favour. He started your training which meant we didn't have to capture a wild leecher. That would have been interesting, to say the least." He pushed off the glass and spun on his ridiculously expensive looking shoes with an even more ridiculous looking smile. "Now, do we have any questions?"

"Where is Logan?"

"No comment." His smile was cocky and the most annoying one I've seen from any government grunt before. "Next?"

"Where's Drew?"

"Who?" He stood there with a serious face before a laugh crackled out of his mouth. "Just kidding." I wanted to reach out and slam his head into the door. Sadly he was just out of reach, and I would have my human strength and nothing else. "No comment. Next? Oh, don't bother asking where Cassie is. You'll get the same answer."

"So what can I ask?"

"What do you have on your mind?"

He was really starting to get on my nerves. "Fine. Where are my real parents?"

"Finally, a question I can answer. Dead. Next?"

"Wait, they're dead?"

"Yep."

"Can you tell me anything useful?" I couldn't be bothered to hide the anger in my voice.

He pulled a fake, hurt face, "You don't have to be so mean. I could leave."

"Then why don't you. You're not giving me any information. At least tell me what I'm doing here before you leave to mess with someone else's head."

"You are here for testing. You see, we've been trying to find what makes supernatural creatures so, supernatural."

"I know. You're finding out what makes them tick."

"Precisely." If he was shocked at the fact I knew that, then he wasn't showing it. "Our research came to a dead end. We were trying to find the specific part of the DNA that makes vampires allergic to the sun and wood. What makes werewolves allergic to silver and so on. We never could find anything until we took your blood into account. Because you were left for so long before being trained, you became more powerful than any other leecher ever born."

"Me?" That would explain a few things.

"Yep. Since we took some of your blood, we have managed to make breakthroughs in all kinds of fields that have been locked up in dead ends for months, some of them years."

"Such as necklaces that make vampires impervious to sunlight."

"You've met someone with one?" I nodded. "What happened?"

"I ripped it out of his neck." He didn't need to know that

I gave it to Cassie. If she had been caught by the government, he could already know that.

His reaction said otherwise. "You didn't keep it for yourself? That would have come in handy if you ever leeched from a weak vampire. Grab him and drag him into the sunlight, problem solved."

I didn't want his opinions, I just wanted information. "What other things have you solved?"

"I'm glad you asked because we have something to show you." He looked off to the right and motioned with a wave. There was a buzz, and the door to my cell opened. He stepped sideways across the open doorway with a pair of handcuffs. "Don't try anything. I have a taser, and I would love to use it. Turn around, please." He pulled another greasy smile. It was so tempting to grab his arm and yank on it. To smash his face into the glass until it was nothing more than a bloody mess. I threw the image and the thought away and simply turned around.

I felt the ping of metal as the cuffs locked around my skin. "You can turn back around now." I did so, and he tugged me out of my room. The door shut and locked behind me as I was escorted down the long hallway. Most of the cells along this way were occupied by various people. None of which were my friends.

Coming to the end, a guard punched in a code on a number pad, and the door beside him slid up into the ceiling. The room beyond was completely white with three closed doors. My escort took me into the middle of it then off to the left. The man called down an elevator which I was pushed into. Turning around I looked at the other two doors. Did they lead to more leecher holding cells or were there others here?

My escort shot out a chubby finger and pushed the button for level two. The door slid shut silently, and then the elevator was moving. Nothing was said for the trip, but I could feel his eyes on my body. I shook the feeling off, trying to stop myself from swinging my leg up and kicking him between the legs. That would no doubt show more leg then what's already showing thanks to my gown.

Once the doors opened my escort took me through a labyrinth of hallways making it hard for me to figure out where I was exactly. He swiped a plastic key card and shoved me through the open door. His voice came through the open hole, "Have a fun reunion."

Then it slid shut leaving him and me on opposite sides. With silence falling around me I quickly scanned my surroundings. There wasn't much to look at. I had the door I had been pushed through and another one opposite. It was mechanical like the others I had seen. The dim light from the other side of it did little to illuminate my dark surroundings.

Since I couldn't do anything, I just stood there. When a beep came, it had felt like I had been waiting for ages. The door in front of me lifted up and light flooded into the room blinding me for a few seconds. I blocked my eyes with my arm until they adjusted. With the light not seeming so bright I stepped out into the large room stretched out before me. The floor looked like metal, but it was soft like it had padding. This weird substance covered the whole floor and also the walls by the looks of it.

A door sat directly in front of me on the opposite wall. The right wall had a long black mirror stretching from side to side. I stared at my reflection wondering who was on the other side. My escort could be standing in there with a bunch of scientists waiting to see what I can do. I wasn't in the mood to play guinea pig, but it looked like I didn't have a choice like usual. Unlike the last room I was tested in, this one had no windows. I thought back to the labyrinth of corridors and got lost just thinking about twists and turns. There was no way I could get out. I was stuck playing there games until the scenery changed.

My heart sunk when that door opposite me opened but

then it skipped rapidly when I realised it was my werewolf. My feet took me across the room. I hit him in a tight hug as he dropped to his knees. But I backed away immediately when I heard him hiss in pain.

His face looked worse now than when I saved him from the walk-in freezer. His left eye was so swollen he wouldn't be able to see out of it. The right was almost as bad. Blood was both wet and dry on his face, and the bruising on his chest had me thinking many of his ribs were broken. "What happened to you?"

His voice was weak and croaky, "I haven't been the best-behaved prisoner." A quick smile only reached one corner of his lips. "What's going on?"

"I don't know, it seems like some kind of viewing room. The black glass is most likely where they're watching from."

"I have a bad feeling about this."

"What's wrong?"

"Do you know how long we've been here?" Our conversation was cut short with a loud mechanical noise. Our attention was sent skyward as the ceiling started parting. I saw what must have been the top floor of the facility above ground, looking like some kind of mansion.

As the lights were dimmed a little, I noticed the sparkling stars on the dark canvas. I thought it looked beautiful until I saw the round ball of reflecting light that was the full moon. I looked back down at Drew. "How come you haven't changed yet?"

"I don't know. The beast is still there, but it's like there's an extra layer of protection." It hit me right then and there. The reason why I was in this room with him. It was all to do with my blood.

There wasn't a necklace, but as my eyes scanned his chest, my hands slipped down his arms. One of them hit into the shiny, metal watch clasped around his wrist. I would never have picked this out for Drew in a million years which meant it had come from them.

Lifting it up I stared at the face. It seemed like an ordinary watch until I turned his arm over. I saw small vials of red blood in each clasp. There wasn't much, but the necklace hadn't contained a lot either. If my blood was able to stop a vampire burning in the sun, why wouldn't it stop a werewolf from changing on a full moon?

I looked up to see Drew's face. He was just as shocked as me. "It's my blood, Drew. My blood is inside the watch."

"You're saying I'm not changing because of this watch and your blood?"

"It's a long story but yes." I lifted the clasp up and saw the sharp point sticking into his skin. I left the piece of jewellery alone before I messed it up and had to deal with my werewolf on a full moon.

I left the watch alone and studied his injuries. The bruises were bad and if the watch was affecting his change then maybe it had similar effects on his other abilities. Maybe his healing was moving slower than normal. Since I didn't know enough about the watch, I was about to suggest he shapeshift. It could be powerful enough to keep the caged animal at bay but who knows what would happen if Drew let it out. Or even if he could.

Keeping my eyes on my man but letting my thoughts drift elsewhere. Why would we be brought to this room for just this? It doesn't make any sense. Everything pointed to a show of some kind. Some kind of test. If it was something this simple, couldn't they have just taken these strangers to his cell? It was a lot of effort for something so small.

A touch of Drew's hand made me jump back our reality. Lifting my own to touch fingertips to his cheek. Our eyes locked and suddenly there was a flash of desire flaring up like an inferno, but then he blinked it was locked behind his mental wall.

Instead, his eyes were sweet depths of brown. He smiled

a sweet smile that made all his injuries seem to disappear. His voice came out husky which sent a shiver through my body, "So what do we do now?"

"I haven't got a clue." Looking over his shoulder, I saw my reflection staring back at me in the black glass. My arm shot out and fingers wrapped around the first thing they found. Flinging some kind of wooden block at that one-way window. It bounced off with a plastic-like sound before tumbling onto the floor.

The echoing thuds kept hitting my ears, relentlessly telling me it was stupid to have tried that. I was human, and this room seemed to be used to show off supernatural creatures. Of course, it wouldn't have broken it.

Before I could look down at Drew, I heard metal scraping against metal, and then a prick hit my neck. Before I reached up, I knew it was a dart to knock me out. Arms wrapped around me holding me tight. Then I heard a whisper in my ear, "Pretend to be out." The voice was muffled behind something, but I was sure I recognised it. This situation couldn't get any worse, so I did what I was instructed. Hoping it wasn't a mistake.

Arms slipped under me, and I was carried. Bouncing as this man took some stairs. I cracked an eye just to see the moon glowing in the night sky, lighting up the large building out on the green grass.

Coming up to the same level of the building I could see that it looked like a hospital. But not one that anyone could walk in to get seen. This place looked like it had a specific client list with heavy bank accounts.

My body was half-carried over the grass and through the line of some trees. They had thick, looming trunks. Underneath the thick canopy of leaves sat a brown van in a little clearing. The doors were open, and that's where I was sat down on the metal edge. Looking up as the helmet was pulled off of a guard's head. I couldn't stop the smile as I saw Cassie looking at me with a massive grin.

I jumped up and hugged her tight enough that her uniform dug through the gown I wore. "What the hell are you doing here? What happened to you?"

"I was staked to the floor, but that's a story for another time. Jewel found me."

Just then the other guard removed their helmet and flicked out her long hair. "So glad that you're okay, Jewel."

"You and me both." Drew made some kind of groan, but his head slumped back so he could recover. "His healing ability will cure him in no time of any injuries."

"Yeah, is it just you two?" I looked around hoping to see another guard be revealed as one of my friends.

"Melvin is here with us. It's actually how we figured out your location. Hopefully, he will be showing up soon with Logan."

"Logan was brought here as well?"

"It's a leecher facility for research. Melvin says they have rebooted an operation here about breeding or something."

"That makes sense. Drew must have been brought here for testing. They're using my blood to stop things like vampires burning in sunlight and werewolves turning on a full moon. God knows what else they've managed to do with it."

"Just with your blood?" Cassie finished dumping her guard uniform, standing there in black combats and a black long sleeve top. It was tight which reminded me how good shape she was in. "What makes your blood so special?"

"It's her parents." A voice came from behind them which made me smile. Logan's friendly smile shone past some cuts and bruises on his face. I leapt at him and hugged him like a long-lost father I hadn't seen in years. Making me smile wider he hugged me back just as tight.

"You know about my parents?"

"Melvin has shared some information with me." I looked at the third guard. There was confusion inside until I saw a white wisp traveling across her pupils and I knew that Melvin was in there somewhere. Inside that body. "Now we need to get out of here. The debt is clear, and we deleted our files, so we are clear to start over."

I pulled back from him to see his eyes. "You're only allowed to start over if we're all coming along for it."

"What?"

I turned to Jewel and Cassie. Even giving the body Melvin had possessed a nod. "Do you all agree. This is the only family I've had that truly feels real. Everything in my life has been a lie. It feels like I got reborn into this new life to be given a chance to actually live one. We must all stick together from now on. As a family."

Cassie was the first to speak up, and I could see in her eyes that she truly meant it. "I'm with you like a sister."

"Same here." Jewel came over and hugged me which took me by surprise.

There was a grunt from Drew. I knew he had no real ties to anywhere apart from me, so I took it as a confirmation. Melvin tapped Logan on the shoulder, "I will also be in debt to you so the information will keep coming whenever you need it."

"I appreciate that, friend." They shook hands as I turned back to the leecher. "Looks like I'm stuck with you a lot now."

"You know you wouldn't have it any other way."

"True."

For the first time in my whole life I smiled, and it was one-hundred-percent happiness. I could feel my eyes welling up at the emotions fueling that grin. But then a gust of speed and power snatched this moment from the air like the wind snatches away a child's kite. Snapping the cord and sending it off to never be seen again.

Turning to a snicker, we all stood metres from Jewel. Her face was contorted in pain and lack of oxygen as a smug Kellen had a tight grip on her throat, holding her off the ground in one extended arm.

My blood boiled as he spoke. "Well, isn't this a touching moment. I'm not sorry at all that I have to ruin it." His lips bared and vampire teeth poked out from his gums. A grin appeared that was like staring at a shark about to devour its prey.

CHAPTER 12

My eyes went to Jewel as she gasped for air. Her tanned cheeks were turning a shade of blue. Cassie planted her feet and got ready to fight. This brought a cocky laugh out of Kellen's mouth. "I wouldn't try anything little vampire. I could beat you and keep my very tight grip around your friend's neck."

"Want to bet?" She stepped closer, baring her teeth in aggression.

"Cassie, don't." Logan ordered her sternly, "Stay where you are. He's too strong and too fast."

My ears didn't pick up his comment, taking a step forward myself as I felt the need to protect my friend. The powerful vampire looked at me, and I was happy to see his smug grin diminish a little. That simple act was like a chink in his armour, and it filled me with confidence. Rolling my shoulders, preparing my body for a fight, I found that essence of Kellen's vampirism. It was becoming all too familiar for my liking, but I pushed that disturbing thought aside and sucked it in through my nose.

It was hard at first, but then it whipped up my nose making me gasp. That feeling of having my body go through the change of human to vampire spread out through my body. There was an immense hike in what my body could achieve with this strength and speed. I had never felt anything like this. The word invincible was too small to describe it. Finally, I understood how he could be so cocky all the time.

My nose picked up the smell of blood riding the air, thick and tasty but there was something else with it. I had never smelt it before and yet with my new mindset I knew it was fear, and our group was reeking of it. But to my delight, I could smell a strain of it coming from Kellen. I could see it in his eyes.

I smiled at the thought, and the look on his face told me he knew I could smell it. He blinked and then his smugness was back like a mask. I was a match for him, but I couldn't risk Jewel's life. He was up to something like usual. "What do you want?"

"Isn't it obvious. Even though my old boss is dead. Even though the debt doesn't exist anymore, my list still does. I'm a man of my word, and my word says that Jewel is number one." His fingers tightened squeezing her windpipe taking her closer to her death.

"You know what I can do, don't you? Which means I'm just as fast as you and just as strong."

"Since I know my own speed. I know you won't get close before I snap her neck like a twig." He gave me a wink which made me take another step forward. I hated how I was falling for his baiting behaviour.

"According to your word, you're going to kill her anyway. So why can't I just beat the hell out of you?"

"Because maybe there is a way you can save her."

"What way?" It came out rushed and desperate. It brought a smile to his face. I blew out a frustrated breath. "Just tell us."

"I know about your blood and the properties it holds. I know how valuable it is."

"So?"

He dug something out of his pocket and chucked it over

to me. "All I ask is a small sample of your blood."

I looked at the vial and then back at him, "Why?"

"They have something of value to me that is rightfully mine. I want to make a swap. It's that simple."

"Fine." They already had my blood so it wouldn't make much of a difference to me. I lifted my wrist up to my mouth and let my fangs extend past my lip. Sinking them into my skin my mouth filled with my blood. First I spat it out onto the ground and then let the last dribble drip into the glass.

There were murmurs behind me, but I ignored them. They didn't know what had happened in the facility. Kellen would have something worthless, and we would get Jewel back. It's a win-win situation for us.

I looked up from the vial to see a smile twitch Kellen's lips. Then he moved so fast I didn't see the damage. All I heard was the clear snap of bone. Kellen moved so fast that Jewel hovered there in the air like she was still alive. Dropping like a puppet with cut strings.

I didn't have time to think. As Kellen moved further away from us, I pumped my legs as fast as they would go. My breathing was out of rhythm from the loss of a friend. I had only moved a few steps when I felt an ashy smell fill my nostrils. I didn't want it, but my breathing was too heavy, and I wasn't thinking straight. Kellen was so fast, and no matter how much I tried, our speeds were matched so there wasn't a chance of catching up with him.

Then I noticed his figure getting closer. The world around me was a stream of colour and nothing else. My eyes focused on the movement ahead as I was bearing closer to the runaway vampire. We were moving so fast I couldn't tell if we were still in woods or not. The ground felt nothing more than a feathers touch to my feet.

I smiled as I noticed Kellen slowing down. The big bad vampire was climbing into a flash looking car. I couldn't tell what make or model because before I knew it the metal was right there in front of me.

Just in that split second before impact, my enemy noticed my rapid approach. And in that single moment, his face twisted with shock, worry, and fear which pumped my body with the power to inflict more damage.

Dipping my shoulder, I crash into the car like a missile. The metal dented into Kellen's body. Wanting to keep the car going as I lifted up onto two wheels my hand gripped into the frame. My grip denting into the car as I threw my arm up.

Blowing out a big breath as I pushed. My body stopped moving as the car was sent into a spin. Flying up into the air. Metal smashing through trees, sending branches to the floor. Grinning as the bashed up vehicle came flying down like a wrecking ball, creating a small crater in the dirt.

I was about to rush over to finish him off when a gunshot rang out in the air. It came from back where the hospital was, and it distracted me enough so Kellen could shoot off from the wreck.

I went to follow after him when quick footsteps came from behind me. Turning I saw Cassie come running over like she was moving at the normal speed of a human. It was strange to take everything in so quickly. I smiled as she seemed determined to catch up to me with her slower movement. It really was amazing to leech off of Kellen.

My vampire friend stopped in front of me looking a little out of breath. "What the hell was that?"

"What? The gunshot?"

"No, your speed. I definitely can't move that fast, and I haven't heard of any vampire doing so either."

"Yeah, somehow I was gaining on Kellen. Like I could run faster than him."

"How is that possible?"

"I don't know." But as I said those words, I remembered sucking up more ashy essence has I had been running. I didn't think there was a way of leeching from a single person more than once. So the only option was that I must have leeched from two. With Kellen's and Casie's abilities added together, I could have easily caught up with him. Looks like my body was still spilling out tricks. I wondered what else I was capable of, but then another gunshot rang out.

"We need to go, Beth. They could be in trouble." Without confirmation, I started running. Leaving Cassie behind which I'm sure irritated her, but I had a boyfriend and friends to protect. I couldn't lose another after Jewel's death.

Coming to a skidding stop just as I saw the van in the distance. I could hear Cassie's footsteps, but they were still far off for now. Peering through the branches of a bush I saw my friends. Down on their knees but there were only two men with guns. One of them was Drew's father, Griffin Gaynes. The other I didn't recognise, but he seemed to be the one in charge. Doing all of the talking as they both held the group at gunpoint.

I attuned my hearing and listened from this distance. "It was a simple deal. As long as The Saracen wound up dead and you guys were delivered into their hands, they welcomed me back with open arms. All my old businesses. Old contacts. Back to the position I once had before being shoved out because of obvious reasons." He seemed to wave his gun in Drew's direction who seemed to be laying on the floor now.

"He came back, and we got you. The Saracen had been giving us a few troubles so getting rid of him was a plus. Now, we will escort you three back to the facility." Three of them. That wasn't right. I narrowed my eyes and counted. Drew, Cassie, and Logan. There was another body in a guard's uniform laying on the floor. It was Melvin, but he was so lifeless.

Just then, I got a chill, and I turned to see a white face morphing in front of my face. "Bethany."

"Melvin. Who is that guy?"

"He's in charge of the leecher unit. That guy is the person who has been hunting you and Logan down. And we

393

need to take him out because he will kill them without thinking about it."

"Right. I'll sort it out."

"Wa….." His voice was lost to the wind whipping past my ears. I shot across the grass but as I came within a few metres of this new enemy my body slowed. The world came back to me in my last few steps, and I fell to the floor as the essences were ripped from my body.

Taking a deep breath as I looked up. The barrel of a large gun filled up my vision. "What the hell happened to me?"

"It's called a deadener. Sucks any supernatural traits from anyone. Except for witches. Luckily Kellen already took care of that for us." This guy looked down at the body still sitting on the grass. My eyes went to Jewel and found my anger growing inside me. But I couldn't do anything about it.

With no speed and no strength, I wouldn't be able to move an inch before getting a bullet. It may not be a fatal wound, but I didn't want a bullet lodged anywhere. So I took a long breath and looked back up at the two gun wielders.

"You have me now let my friends go."

A sickening laugh came out of his mouth as he threw his head back. "Let them go? We have Logan who has been a pain in my arse for so long now. Then we have Drew. I have a feeling as long as we held you, prisoner, he wouldn't stop at anything to get you out. Love can be so maddening."

"You could cut your losses and let us all go?" Drew's speech was slow, but his laugh was the one I had come to enjoy.

"If only it were that simple son." Griffin moved over to him as he still laid there.

"Since you've just gotten back into the swing of things Griffin. What do you think we should do with Logan and your son?"

I looked over at my boyfriend's dad hoping that I would see some kind of humanity. Instead, his glare was nothing but darkness. A smirk hit his lips that had me cringing. "We kill them both. Of course."

The man in charge laughed again before cocking back the hammer on his pistol. It was lifted up and aimed directly at Logan's face. At that close distance, I could imagine it blowing it clean off his shoulders.

Instead of a loud bang came a whistle cutting through the wind. It was too fast to follow, but I saw a small rock crack into the man about to shoot Logan. He doubled over in pain but what caught my attention was the machine sitting by his knee. It was smashed, and that's where the rock was embedded.

As my breath slipped in through my nose, I smelt the mint essence of Drew's beast. I went to breathe it in, to become a powerful werewolf but I looked up, and my breath got caught in my throat. A gun was aimed right between my eyes, and I couldn't move or breathe.

My ears picked up a groan which quickly turned into a roar full of raw power. I spun my head to the left and saw skin burst into fur and a wolf launched from the back of the van. A paw knocked Griffin Gaynes out of the way, and lethal claws reached for the other man. The one about to shoot me.

I didn't let out my breath until that gun was sent flying from an open hand as teeth sunk into his arm. Blood burst out of his veins, cascading out of Drew's animal mouth. Drenching the grass as he shook that massive fur covered head from left to right. The scream coming from his victim's mouth was lost to the angry growl vibrating my bones.

Drew was so powerful and amazing. He was dominating this guy and tearing him apart. I couldn't tear my eyes from the massive wolf as he let go of the arm but got a better grip on his head.

The muscles in his neck lifted the body from the floor which was still yelling in pain. He thrashed and yanked until I heard a loud snap. Suddenly he stopped and dropped it down like a piece of spoiled meat. A large paw came up and nudged into the head that had horrific teeth marks. Blood poured out like the heart was still pumping it through his veins.

Then that gigantic wolf's head swung my way. Bright blue eyes burned into mine. Despite how dangerous he looked like this. Despite what I had just witnessed him do to another human being. He simply looked magnificent.

I reached out a hand not even thinking about the wild beast controlling this wolf. Just wanting to run my fingers through that thick coat. Knowing just by seeing that it would feel so soft to the touch.

Fingertips touched and sunk through, losing my hand to those hairs and loving it. The touch tapped against warm skin, and I smiled. Looking into those sparkly eyes and seeing not the beast but Drew.

That connection was burst as a loud gunshot rung out followed closely by a whimper. The wolf shot back from me and turned towards the shooter. Griffin stood there with his gun still aimed at Drew. Only there was no need. My eyes welled up as I witnessed my werewolf dropping to the floor. Blood dribbling out of a bullet hole in his side.

Rage filled every fibre of my body, every thought. There was nothing but that single feeling. Eyes burned at Griffin, and all I wanted to do was kill him. Only I didn't use my leecher gifts. Instead, my hands wrapped around the cool steel of the gun in front of me.

Stealing it from the dead grasp of the man, Drew had maimed and lifted it. Locking this terrible father in my sights and I pulled the trigger. The bang shook my body and made me jump as I watched a hole rip into my targets shoulder. I pulled again, another bullet hit him in the arm.

And I kept pulling that trigger. Firing all the bullets until Griffin was leaning back against the van with blood drenching his shirt. His stare was vacant, but somehow I felt it on me as the gun in my hand clicked over with each shot. Now empty, giving off soft clicks as the tears fell down my cheeks.

Looking as my victim fell to the floor. I knew he was dead, but I wish I could keep shooting him. Filling him up with those holes that leaked out his life. I heard a whisper in my ear, but it didn't stop. Nothing did until I felt the gun being slipped from my grip.

As soon as it was gone, I dropped and filled my hands with fur. Feeling the stickiness of the blood covering it as I laid my head on Drew. I couldn't lose another person in my new life especially someone I felt so deeply for.

I knew leechers had control over their emotions, but I seemed to be losing it. Another side-effect of being special. Leaning my head on fur my tears seeped into it with the blood. My body felt numb and barely felt the shaking as Logan grabbed me. My name was whispered in my ear, or maybe it just sounded like a whisper to me.

I looked up at him. "What?"

"We have to get out of here before guards come looking."

"What about Drew?" My fingers curled into his blood-soaked fur, not wanting to let go or be moved away from him.

"I'll put him in the van." Cassie suddenly appeared in my vision.

"Where have you been?"

"I followed Kellen. I thought he had come back this way, but I must have been mistaken."

"Wait, weren't you the one who threw the rock?"

"Rock?"

Whilst Logan and Cassie talked about something that didn't really matter right now I looked at the wolf lying in front of me. Those blue eyes looked up at me like they were pleading for something.

I leant in close making his ears perk towards me and whispered. "You're not going anywhere. I can't lose you. I need you in my life. By my side. I love you, Drew." My lips pursed against short hairs on his snout which brought out a whimper. It wasn't a painful one, almost like he was saying it back to me which made me cry even more.

Hands grabbed my shoulder, and I was pulled back. This motion had my fingers gripping into that drenched fur which brought out a whimper of pain from my wolf. I immediately let go which had the tears cascading down my cheeks.

Through that blurry vision, I could make out my petite friend picking up the injured wolf with ease. We were both put into the back of our van. Either Logan or Cassie started the engine, and we set off. I heard Logan's voice shouting through into the back. "We have to run. Get away from this place. Where no one knows us. But we do it together. It's a risk but with our files deleted and the head of the leecher unit dead, along with Griffin Gaynes, they won't know who they're looking for."

I sobbed back at him. "As long as we stay together." As I said it, my eyes were locked on Drew who was still just lying there. The fur covered chest was slowly moving up and down with his breathing which filled with a drop of hope that I will still have my werewolf.

I rested my head on the fur, not caring about the blood covering my skin. Closing my eyes, I listened to the beating heart of his life. It was there that I fell asleep. Holding onto the sound of Drew's heart. That beat reassuring me that he was going to be fine. Only then was I able to drift into sleep where I met my man and his killer smile in a dream. The most perfect dream that I could have wished for and that made me happy.

EPILOGUE

The sound of the shopping centre was loud, but I liked it. It was a part of a normal life, being barged into by rude shoppers, having to fight your way through to shops to find queues of people in your way. But I was out on a normal day with my best friend, Cassie and as far as anyone here knew, we were normal women out for a shop.

After what happened at the facility I had taken a few quiet weeks with Drew. We didn't leave the bedroom for most of it. The thought of those days brought a smile to my lips. "You're thinking about Drew again aren't you."

I turned to her as she gave me a massive grin. "I don't know what you're talking about."

"Yeah, right." A guy bumped into Cassie. He swore at her as she nudged him to the floor. "That'll dent his ego a little."

I laughed, "You do have a way with the boys don't you."

She got called a name before he jumped up and jogged after his laughing friends. "I do alright. Just because you and your pup are all lovey-dovey right now, doesn't mean you can mock me."

"That's exactly what it means. That's a plus of being in a relationship."

"Maybe I'll find my own werewolf, and he'll be hunkier than yours in every way."

"Ha ha." I punched her in the arm hard, knowing the pain wouldn't even register. In retaliation, she shoved me gently, but it still sent me into oncoming traffic.

My arms shot in and I tried to make myself as small as possible. Excuses left my lips a million times until Cassie pulled me out of danger. She was laughing her head off. I thought about punching her again, but the same thing would happen.

Cassie moved closer as we carried on walking, lowering her voice, "Have you thought about what happened with Kellen? How fast you were running?"

"What do you mean?"

"When you leeched off of him and me at the same time."

"There's no proof that's what I did."

"That's the only explanation. You need to talk to Logan about it."

"We're not having this conversation again. I've barely thought about it." Cassie dropped the subject and pointed over to a shop. "I'll wait here. Not my kind of clothing."

"Sure. Be back in a minute or ten." She gave me a cute smile before moving off to the people. I took a seat on one of the wooden benches circled around a fountain.

I had told Cassie I hadn't been thinking about what had happened. But I couldn't lie to myself as much as I wanted to. It had been on my mind every day since it happened. Even when I was with Drew, there were moments it would drift back to the front of my mind. What I had done was impossible, and Cassie was right. Leeching off of two creatures was the only explanation. Only it wasn't something I wanted to explore.

Cassie might have been right about talking to Logan though. He's helped me so much. I'm sure he would be willing to help again. Just then his voice came to my ear. "Bethany."

I looked up as the sun shining through the glass ceiling

bounced off of his head. "Hey, Logan. What are you doing here?"

"I wanted to have a chat and Cassie had mentioned you two were having a shopping day."

"Yeah, a piece of normality."

"We all need that from time to time." He sat down. I noticed a folder gripped in his hands. "I have some information I wanted to share with you."

"Yeah? Anything important?"

"That's for you to decide, not me." He slid it over and placed it gently on my lap. "It's about your parents."

My fingers suddenly grip the cardboard tightly. Digging in and dented the edges. "What about them?"

"This folder holds information about them. Not something for me to tell you. But something I wanted you the chance to learn. It's completely up to you. If you're not ready yet, I will hold onto it, until you are."

His hand hovered there, open and ready to receive the folder back. My grip lightened, and I contemplated opening it, but I looked over into Logan's eyes. There I saw the father figure I never had growing up. Someone who truly cared about me and I wasn't even his blood. So I slid the information back into his hand. "Not right now. I have all the family I need."

"Okay then. It'll be there for you when you want it." He gave me a soft smile and pulled me in for a hug. "And you'll always have me here as well."

"Better not go anywhere. Need help keeping Cassie's spending in check."

He laughed out loud which I could hear over the chatter of passing shoppers. "No one can keep that in check. I'm going to head to the bar though. Gotta get things all sorted for when we open next week. You still sure you want a job there instead of going back to university."

"I'm sure. No lecturer can teach me about vampire's

weaknesses or the powers a witch possess. I have you for that."

"Right. And we'll start you're training next week as well. Enjoy a piece of normality whilst you can."

"I will." I got another quick hug, and then he got up and walked off, waving over his shoulder before disappearing into the crowd. As my eyes lost him, they picked up random faces as they moved past me.

Closing them slowly I listened to that ability inside myself. That leeching effect I could call upon. Those scents came to my nose quickly, and there were so many of them. Opening my eyes, I locked onto people and how they smelt. Dismissing ones I didn't know or recognise. Naming the rest, seeing how normal they looked right now.

Even a piece of normality was pinned right in the middle of a supernatural world even if I tried to forget about it for an afternoon. This supernatural world was now my life, my world. And with Cassie, Drew and Logan. I wouldn't have it any other way.

About the Author

I've had a few jobs, working in warehouses and a fast food restaurant. They gave me the chance to work on my writing in my spare time. Currently, working nights allows me to work on my days off with little distractions from friends and family since they're fast asleep.

I live in a little bungalow in Weeting, Norfolk in England. I get to spend a lot of time with my amazing girlfriend and weekends with my son who makes me proud every single time.

I post on my facebook page www.facebook.com/DMB-books about what I get up to. Often ask random questions which influence my writing with names of places and characters. I would love to see pictures of purchased books both paperback and ebook. Would be amazing to hear exactly what you liked about my book, leave reviews and hopefully share with friends.

Leecher Chronicles

Book 2
Sunlit Blood

Chapter 1

The park had been taken into the night with the disappearance of the sun and the rising of the moon. The full moon had been a few days ago now, but it was still bright up on the blanket of black. Stars twinkled around it, surrounding it in sparkles of light. Each time I saw the moon, it reminded me of my werewolf boyfriend. Even though we were having a little disagreement at the moment, it still brought me fond memories of the time we spent together.

I looked down from the sky and looked around at the people walking through the park this time of night. Couples taking long walks after a meal out. Single walkers taking their journeys home from work. Then there were the shifty looking ones who you couldn't tell if they were homeless or were about to hold you at gunpoint and steal your money.

Then I spotted my friends. Cassie was standing by the hot dog cart flirting with the young vendor which wasn't at all surprising. Logan was on a bench along the long path through the middle. A newspaper was open on his lap. However, I knew he wasn't reading any of it. The three of us were here for a reason, and it wasn't to spend a night out in the cold in the park.

We were here to stop a group of werewolves who were mugging and beating on people in the parks around Thornton City. Usually, Logan wouldn't want us getting involved in something like this even if we had moved to the city a few months ago to start over. Only, Logan's ghostly friend Melvin had informed us that the government looked into it and decided to leave them to it.

In the past whenever this had happened, there was a hidden reason, and Logan was curious to find out what it was. We had successfully taken us ourselves off their radar and with Melvin keeping an eye on their search for us, we were able to stay ahead. Logan saw this as a safe risk to take especially if it gave us leverage over the people searching for us.

Keeping my eyes running around the faces that moved past me I wrapped my black denim jacket around me tighter and crossed my arms over my chest. It did little to protect me from the chilly breeze that ran across the vast open space.

Catching Cassie in my sight again I noticed her clothing was less for winter than mine and I remembered that her body didn't need the heat as much since she was a vampire. So I used my own natural ability of leeching and focused on her ashy scent. Breathing in slowly, I felt it in my body. Suckling on it with my nose until I felt the change in my body.

That's where I stopped. I didn't need her full strength or speed. So I left the change small and felt the need for warmth slipping away as my body temp went neutral. Letting my arms rest to my side I smiled as Cassie kept flirting.

Honing my ears, I let my sense of hearing reach out to their conversation. Having her sweet voice coming to my ears like she was standing right next to me. Smiling as she flirted with the cute guy in the red and white striped apron. "Have you ever picked up a girl in the park before?"

His soft chuckle felt nice, half listening to his response and half watching the park for our werewolves. "I haven't. Tend not to get the nicest of people walking through here at this time of night. Until now."

"Oh, you flirt. I'm not usually this forward...." The rest

of her line was cut short as I burst out laughing at her blatant lie. I looked over at them to see if the guy was laughing as well but saw her glaring my way across the grass.

I smiled and sent over a wave as I said, "Forward? I think this is the most laid back I've seen you around a cute guy."

A little smile cracked through her glare as she stared. She didn't reply, but as she turned back to carry on her conversation, I noticed her middle finger sticking up behind her back at me. It made me laugh as she made an excuse and left her number with the vendor before walking off.

She walked over the grass and came to rest her shoulder against the tree I was standing by. "That's not funny."

"Oh come on. Do you pull those kinds of lines out all the time?"

"Only when the guy is cute and innocent looking. They tend to believe anything a woman says."

"Well, I don't think he kept his eyes off of you as you walked away, so it seemed to work."

"I'm sure he will give me a call."

"Well, I can't wait to meet him. I hear wedding bells in the future." She punched me in the shoulder, but I just shrugged it off thanks to the vampiric body I now had. "Any two people around here getting married soon would be you and Drew."

"Not too sure about that."

She looked over at me with a look of concern. "You two still fighting?"

"Yep."

"Over something as silly as a strip club?"

"It's not silly. He could pick any kind of business to open up in the city. God knows his dead father left him enough of them to take over."

"You know he didn't want anything to do with his dad. Hence why he sold all those businesses."

"I know." I blew out a breath feeling a little annoyed that

my best friend was on the werewolf's side. "I think I would prefer him to own a crooked business instead of a strip club."

"You don't mean that. Drew is a great guy, and he adores you. He wouldn't do anything to mess with you because then I would have to shove silver up his arse."

My laugh was so unexpected I almost choked on the breath I sucked in. "Now that would be payback. I know he loves me and wouldn't hurt me. I trust him. I just don't trust the kind of skanks that do that kind of job."

"I think you've been watching too much television. It isn't all like that. Just pop down there one night. See for yourself what it's like. You might enjoy it. They have guys strip there as well."

"Now I know why you're always down there."

"I go there to support a friend and his place. Nothing to do with the half-naked hunks dancing on stage."

"I'm sure." I smiled at her because she could always make me feel better about anything in my life. Just her smile alone had me feeling happier. Like it was infectious.

Just then Logan's voice cut through our light conversation with some news. "They've just entered the park through the east entrance." We both looked over to the iron gates where a group of four guys came walking through. I gave the air a quick sniff and verified they were all werewolves.

Logan's voice caught our vampire hearing again. "Bethany, rank them in power. Weakest to strongest."

"Give me a second." My breath brought in the four minty scents they were giving off. Analysing each one I got different hints of strength and speed but also other hints that I had been noticing lately. I didn't know what they meant yet, but that would come with the training Logan was giving me.

"Second from left, far right, one next to him and the strongest is the far-left werewolf."

"Perfect. How much essence do you need to take in to acquire their speed?"

"Speed is medium."

"What else is medium?"

"Strength. The only time you need to take in the full essence is if you want all their abilities."

"What about their weaknesses?"

"A being's weaknesses come to you as soon as you take in any amount of essence."

"Good. You've learnt a lot since we moved here. You up for a fight?"

"I remember my training if that's what you're asking."

"Okay then. Let's get this thing started. We follow them back to their hideout, and that's where we attack."

"What happens if there are more of them there?" Cassie had a good point, and it had my stomach knotting up a little.

"Then we do recon on the headquarters. Attack when some of them leave. Really we only need the alpha or the leader of the pack."

"Okay then. Let's get following."

Logan folded up his newspaper and dropped it into the bin as he stood. We moved away from the tree and started our walk. Keeping my eyes on the four men, they took a left and followed the smaller path towards the north side of the park. As soon as they left through the gates, they suddenly split up and bolted.

Logan ordered us which ways to go. He went left following two of the werewolves, the two weakest. Cassie was ordered to head straight, and I took a right following the second strongest werewolf.

Before leaving her company, I sucked on Cassie's essence to bring the rest of her abilities into my own body and used her speed to shoot off into the darkness. Flicking my eyesight to night vision as the werewolf shot off into an alleyway.

My ears picked up his footsteps around a few corners until suddenly they stopped. I froze there on the corners, searching for any sign of him. When I couldn't spot a movement, I shut my eyes and used my ears. Tuning out the traffic of the city and the bustle of city dwellers, I cornered off everything but the alleyway.

Moving deeper until I heard the steady breathing of the werewolf. He wasn't out of breath like me which was slightly annoying. If his stamina had been less than my own, it would give me an edge in a fight.

I pin-pointed his position behind a dumpster ahead and slowly walked forwards. Keeping my feet from making any kind of sound even to his werewolf hearing. Moving forward my foot tapped into a small puddle of water sending the echo of ripples across the walls.

A loud thud came, and the dumpster came skidding across the concrete towards me. My first thought was to dodge it out of fear, but then my training kicked in, and I listened to my instincts. As the metal box came within reach, I kicked out my foot.

I knew I was stronger than this beast and even though it ached my leg to do it, I sent the bin back towards my enemy with a new dent in the side. Luckily he hadn't anticipated it, and it thumped into his side, crashing him back into some wooden boxes.

I shot forwards and jumped onto his chest, pinning him down to the floor and punching him square in the nose. It broke under the immense pressure shooting blood out of his nostrils. He slumped back onto the floor and didn't move.

The punched hadn't knocked him out, but the pain would keep him down on the floor for a bit. Standing up I looked down at the werewolf. "Stay down, or you'll get another punch."

He groaned back in response which I took as a yes. Taking a deep breath, I let it calm my body down as the vampire inside of me wanted to lick up that blood trickling from his nose. Cassie might be old enough to withstand the sight of blood, but I hadn't had that much training in this area, so it was still tough for me.

I was tempted to release the vampire essence when I felt another presence in the alleyway. Looking one way and then the other I didn't spot anything but the feeling of being watched was still pressing against my skin.

So I used my leecher ability and sucked the air in around me. With it came that familiar scent of a vampire who had been popping into my life more and more recently. Not due to friendship. It was the complete opposite especially since he had killed my friend Jewel. "Kellen, I know you're there."

"How the hell do you do that?"

"Would it be too mean to say that you smell bad."

"Spell after spell, and you keep catching my essence. You're one of a kind."

"What do you want? Here just to pester me?"

"I wanted to try this new spell out, and it appears it doesn't work as well as the witch made out. Think I might have to kill her."

"Because that's your answer for everything."

"It works."

He slipped out of the shadows that he had pulled around him, and I scowled at him. "Why don't you do everyone a favour and just go sunbathing for the day."

"You'd miss me too much."

Not able to think due to the anger I felt for him I bent over, picked up a piece of wood and launched it at his chest as hard as I could. Annoyingly enough he caught it just in time. "I'm getting closer."

Kellen's lips curled into a grin. "We both know how powerful you are. If you really wanted to kill me, then all you have to do is suck on my essence and combine it with the one inside you already and throw again." He tossed the wood back to me like we were playing catch.

I caught it in my palm and tightened my grip. Following his own idea, I pulled on his essence and let it mix in with

Cassie's. My body pumped up with power, but then I felt something strange in my core.

A small ping of pain before it shot out like a flare and burned my insides. I breathed out letting every sniff of essence escape including Cassie's. My hand went to my chest which was warm from the burning inside. "What the hell just happened?"

"Luckily the witch wasn't lying about that part. You might be able to sense when I am near, but you will never use my essence against me again."

"You did that on purpose."

"I used your hate for me against you. We both know now that you can be stronger and faster than me. But I'm still devious enough to stay ahead of this fight. Don't forget that."

"Just get out of here."

"Fine with me. I proved my point. Don't you forget it either." Then he blurred off into existence. I was tempted to shout after him about how much I hated him, but it wouldn't be any good. Even with his heightened hearing, with his speed, he would be out of earshot in no time.

So I turned back to the werewolf on the floor only he was no longer there. I blew out a frustrated breath and found I hated Kellen even more than normal. I turned to head back to the park, but as I did, I came face to face with the guy I had punched. His nose had fixed itself and in his hand was a sharp piece of wood.

I may not be a vampire anymore, but that weapon would still kill me easily. He attacked, and all my training went out the window through fear of dying. I knew all I had to do was suck on his minty essence and move out of the way. It may still hit me, but with a werewolf's healing factor it wouldn't be fatal.

Only I just couldn't do it. My body was tense with horror, and I was stuck to the spot. The tip of the wood pierced through the air coming towards my chest until I heard it sink into flesh and muscle.

But it wasn't my flesh. There was no pain. An arm was stretched across my chest, and I looked up to see Kellen looking down at me. There was no hint of pain on his face. It was more like the wood burning his blood was just a tickle in his arm when I knew it must have been painful.

Within a blink of my eyes, he turned, ripped the wood from his arm and rammed it into the man's neck. And he didn't stop there. Teeth came sliding out of his gums and he sunk them into this guy's skin. Sucking on his blood and drinking it down like he had been on a deserted island for months and his body was a glass of water.

When he ripped those teeth from his neck, I saw the massive wound and the mess he had made. Standing there shocked at what had happened in a few seconds, Kellen lifted up the body and dumped it down into the dumpster.

I swallowed past the lump in my throat and cleared it with a cough. "Why did you do that? Why did you save me?"

The hateful man turned sucking on his arm. He spat out blood and tiny shards of wood from his mouth. "That's a simple answer. You're on my list. Only I get to kill you."

That small ball of gratitude was smashed to pieces by his answer. "Next time just let me die. I'd love to deny you the pleasure."

With his canines still extended out past his lip, it made his grin even more menacing. The blood on his chin made him look disgusting. "Until next time, Bethany."

"Fu….." I was going to swear at him, but he was gone before the first word could come past my lips. My eyes looked off into the distance where he had disappeared, wondering if I would ever get rid of this vampire shadow I had acquired. It had been six months since he had killed Jewel and as far as I know, he hadn't attempted to fulfil his list. Logan was second, and I would like to think he would tell me if Kellen had tried to kill him. Then again, Logan wouldn't be able to leech off of his attacker so if it had been attempted, Logan would be killed.

Anger burned inside me at the knowledge that if he wanted, we would all be killed before we knew what happened. So what was Kellen waiting for? The reason the list was created in the first place had been settled, but this particular vampire was a man of his word. If he said that it would happen, then it will. The question was when and how and they were questions we would never get the answers to until it was too late.

Pulling my new phone out I dialled Logan's number to find out where he was. He picked up on the second ring sounding a little out of breath. "Hey, you okay?"

"Yeah. The werewolf is dead though. I'll explain later why."

"As long as you're fine. Cassie and I are at a warehouse on the industrial estate. I'll send you the address. Use the map app and come join us."

"Be there as soon as I can." As I hung up the phone, a message came through with the address. Using the map on my phone, I got directions and made my way over. The first half of the journey took ten minutes but then I came across a vampire who's essence helped me do the rest in no time.

Coming up to the warehouse it looked abandoned. The perfect place for a pack to hide out. Only one of the windows hadn't been shattered or cracked and where the big shutter door used to be was just a large hole.

I could hear Logan's voice carrying out with the wind as I entered. The large area was filled with pillars that looked like they were holding up the roof, the state of which was filled with holes and looked like a strong breeze would bring it crashing down.

Walking over to my two friends, I noticed one of the werewolves from the park chained to a chair. I didn't think they were silver, but they looked thick enough to stop him from escaping.

Logan was interrogating him with questions, so I just stood by Cassie and didn't interrupt. Half paying attention to the werewolf's responses and half on alert for any of his friends.

Lying on the floor were a few bodies that must have been the rest of the group from the park. Judging by Logan's line of enquiry he was asking about their connection with the government. The beast in the chair wasn't having any of it. Never answering a question with anything but insults.

So I let my mind drift off with my leecher ability. It was a training activity Logan would have me do. Suck in a load of different essences around me and sort through them as quickly as possible.

So I reached out my radar and brought in all of them. Putting them all into a messy ball, I pulled on the ends like undoing a knot. Sorting Cassie's first since she was the most familiar. Then the werewolf within this building and then moving further afield. Sorting out the strands of scents with how far away they were from me, creating a web of blips in my head.

I had been getting quicker at this over the months, and now I could do it without even trying. It came so naturally to me sometimes through our training Logan had seemed a little annoyed at me. Especially when we found out that my radar reached further than his did.

I came to the last strand but found something strange. It felt the weakest, so I would have put it the furthest away, but when I concentrated on it, the blip was coming within the building. Pulling it to the forefront of my thoughts I analysed it.

The smell wasn't like anything I had gotten before. It wasn't so much a smell but a feeling of drifting through clouds. Locking down its location, I told Cassie what I was up to and walked away towards the offices at the back of the warehouse.

Moving through a doorway and down the hall, I came to a door which held the essence behind it. Only it didn't match the rest of the building. It was almost brand new with a few scratches from use. It had a built-in number pad which I didn't have the code to.

What I did have was an ability that gave me options. I let my mind move out to where the other three were. Sucking in Cassie's ashy scent, I felt her strength fill my body. My arms tensed with their new power and I threw punch after punch. Balled up fists pounded against the metal, denting each time around that number pad.

Until I slammed my fist into it and the lock snapped within the wall, and the door swung open crashing into the wall behind. Revealed to me was a small room with a single metal chair sitting right in the middle.

Sitting within it, tied with ropes was an elderly woman. She held her head down over her lap, long white hair draped over her knees. I rushed forwards and dropped to my knees. Gently lifting her head up, bright green eyes blinked a few times like she was just waking up. They focused and then something in her look made me feel like she was seeing an old friend.

Her mouth opened but I cut her off first, "Don't speak. Try to save some energy."

She moved her mouth again against my suggestion. "It is you. I have seen you every time I call upon my inner eye." The aged woman took a deep breath and carried on speaking with a shiver in her words. "My kind has a purpose in this world, and that's to help certain people realise they are meant for bigger things. Each of us has one of these people. And I have finally found you after years of searching. There really are no coincidences."

"I'm sorry. You're not making any sense. Save your energy, and I'll get you out of here as fast as I can."

Her grip suddenly wrapped around my wrist with the

strength of someone on steroids. "You have to stop her re-turn. She cannot walk the ground with the living again. Only you are able to stop her. You are stronger than you think. Train your abilities. Fight her back to hell when she comes to take over this world."

"You have the wrong person."

"Bethany Warren. Daughter of Tina Booth and Gary Moore. Subject of a government experiment. The only suc-cessful one at that. You only recently found out what you truly are. I have years of visions showing me all kinds of information about you. Including your future and what you will accomplish. As long as you realise your potential and put yourself in a dangerous situation to save the world."

"Look, you can talk about all this once we are out of this place."

"I won't be leaving with you. This is my message to you. Therefore I have concluded my job as a mindwalker. I can drift off peacefully after a hundred years on the planet." With that, her skin started wrinkling even more than it already was. Her eyes drifted off like she spotted something off into the distance. Hair fell out until only a few strands clung to her wrinkled head.

That grip that had felt so strong slipped from my skin, and her body slumped forwards. I didn't need to check her pulse to know that I had just witnessed someone dying right in front of me.

Slowly climbing back up to my feet I looked at her look-ing just how I had found her. My anger boiled up in my body, filling with the heat of revenge. What were they doing with this old woman tied to a chair like this? How could they be so savage?

This anger moved my feet with purpose. It got worse as I made my way out into the main building. Blowing out breath after breath to try and calm myself down but it was no good. I stomped straight up to the werewolf where he sat. Cassie's strength still coursed through my muscles and I swung my fist into this guy's jaw.

There was a loud snap of bone under the immense pressure as he went flying across the floor with the chair still attached to him. Logan's yell was more like a whisper to my ears, "What the hell was that?"

"They had an old woman tied to a chair back there. She died after saying some nonsense to me. Died in a dingy old warehouse. No one should die like that, especially someone like that."

I took a step towards the downed werewolf, but Logan's grip on my arm stopped me. I had to blow out a breath of anger to stop myself from hitting him instinctively. "Stop. He deserves it, I agree with you, but this isn't how it's done."

My eyes searched his, knowing he was right and despite not wanting to listen to his reasoning, I still did. I let out the ashy scent from my body and returned to being human. The anger was still there, rolling around like a tornado of rage but at least in this body, I couldn't do much damage. Especially to a werewolf.

"Who was this old woman?" Cassie joined the little circle.

"I don't know. She was spouting some kind of nonsense about me. Saying she saw my future."

All of a sudden Logan seemed interested in the conversation. "Did this woman call herself a mindwalker?"

"Yeah, she did. What are they?"

"I'm not entirely sure. There is a lot of information floating around about them but who's to say what is truth and what is just rumour. What did she say exactly?"

"It was all rubbish about stopping someone coming back to life. Keeping her in hell or something like that."

"Anything else?"

"Try and remember exactly what she said."

I thought back to the old woman in the chair. Trying to think of anything that might have sounded crazy but could hold a hint of truth but I got interrupted by a loud howl. Our head whipped around to find the werewolf I had punched on all fours covered in hair and howling up towards the ceiling.

Logan rushed over with superhuman speed and cracked his boot into the wolf's head. It flopped over onto its side with shallow breathing. He had been quick to act, but it had been too late. Off in the distance howls rode the chilly breeze. So many of them in response to the first.

Loud shrills of power riding the air were getting closer as more werewolves came running to aid their pack member. Trouble was coming, and we were stuck in the middle of it.